FIVE PLAYS

JOHN O'HARA

Random House   New York

First Printing

© Copyright, 1953, 1961, by John O'Hara

All rights reserved under International and Pan-American Copyright Conventions. Published in New York by Random House, Inc., and simultaneously in Toronto, Canada, by Random House of Canada, Limited.

Library of Congress Catalog Card Number: 61-14888

Manufactured in the United States of America

To
Robert Charles Benchley (1889-1945)
The Best of Company

CONTENTS

FOREWORD

EVERY ONCE in a while I write a play. In the past nine years I have written these five plays, not one of which has had a Broadway production. It would seem, therefore, that for me the writing of plays is an unprofitable pastime, and it is if you hold the view that profit is best measured in terms of money. But if I exclude journalism, my work in Hollywood, and some of my early potboilers in *The New Yorker*, I have never written principally to make money. I have made a lot of money for myself and for a great many other people, but I could have made a lot more. I could have tinkered here and there with my novels so that they would be acceptable at the *Ladies Home Journal*, and I could have tricked up hundreds of short stories for *Collier's* and *Cosmopolitan*. I could also have been a writer-producer; I was offered that job long ago when I could have used the money. But money isn't everything, and with the present and future taxes the way they are, it damn near isn't anything. So there is no sense to writing for money. There is a lot of sense to writing what you want to write, and in my case that includes an occasional play.

My Broadway "credit" consists entirely of my work as librettist for *Pal Joey*. I did write that. But the profit motive was not uppermost in my mind. If it had been I might have cut my throat on the opening night in Philadelphia, December, 1940, when the story editor of one of the major film companies loudly declared: "George Abbott better take his loss on this one, and stay out of New York.

A middle-aged broad and a young pimp?" And the New York reviews a week later were not all ecstatically box-office. The first reception of *Pal Joey* was similar to the greeting I got for *Appointment in Samarra*, my first novel. It is simply not true that the show and the novel got off to rave notices. I always have to wait awhile, and while I am waiting, I work. I just remembered, by the way, that Harold Ross, who bought the first Pal Joey story and urged me to write a hundred of them, later said to Wolcott Gibbs, "How the hell is O'Hara going to make a musical comedy out of *that* character?" Well, I did, and it was fun at the time, and every once in a while I write a play.

As the reader may know, *The Farmers Hotel* has appeared as a short novel, with some success. There are those few who like it better than anything I have ever written before or since. It started as a play, I offered it to Rodgers and Hammerstein as a possible play-with-music, but Joshua Logan did not like it and Rodgers and Hammerstein went along with Logan. Several years later the Actors Studio did a semi-private performance of it, and Cheryl Crawford produced it at Fishkill, New York. The Fishkill opening night was sold out to the Rotary Club and my heart sank as I watched them enter the theater, in their white dinner jackets and summer frocks, and a few somewhat the worse for the martini cocktail. But they were a good audience. They laughed, and they cried, and there were some calls for the author. After the performance, however, Miss Crawford had some suggestions that made me think she wanted to turn my play into *Seven Keys to Baldpate*. Then a friend of mine, a prominent playwright who has also done some directing, got interested in the play and we had several sessions, but he wanted to rewrite the play and I did not want to reveal to him that *The Farmers Hotel*, novel and play, is an allegory, very tightly written, and to tinker with the play would be to shatter the allegory.

I moved to Princeton, New Jersey, in 1949 and for a

time I made myself available to the community and the university, rendering all sorts of services, from chaperoning house parties to speaking at banquets. During that period I was asked by the Community Players, an amateur group, to provide an original play. That was *The Searching Sun*. The Broadway crowd came down, made their wisecracks, and departed. The local people made a little money, had their little tiffs and a few laughs, and that was that.

I wrote *The Champagne Pool* to occupy my mind during the days just before and after the publication of a novel, *Ourselves to Know*. As a mind-occupier it served its purpose; for seventeen days I put off reading the reviews of the novel, which was a book on which I had worked very hard in evolving some new constructional techniques. I change techniques with every novel I write, but *Ourselves to Know* was the hardest to do and I knew the technique would be apparent. I needn't have worried quite so much. The reviews of the book were largely favorable, and few critics commented on the constructional devices. This play has wandered about among the Broadway managers, who are at least amused at the portrait of the Broadway manager ("I know exactly who you had in mind") and full of suggestions, or one suggestion, as to who should play the director. But they don't like the third act.

The play called *Veronique* is The Village Revisited. I lived all over Greenwich Village in those days and the only book I ever read that really got that atmosphere was a novel by Ward Greene, the title of which I am too lazy to look up. The principal difference between the Village now and the Village then is that in our day the men and women were always sneaking off to do some work, and a lot of them did good work. Today the Villagers are non-talented bums, most of them from Washington Heights and only down for the night. Or they are college boys and girls gaping at other college boys and girls. We had our bums, heaven knows, our fairies and lesbians and sponges and a comparatively few who were on the junk; but there was respect for accomplishment and there were good wishes for those who were trying to accomplish. The nice thing about living in an atmosphere of universal penury was that everyone was glad when Joe Blow got a $500 advance on his novel or Nancy Ginyan got a job in a Broadway play. True, if Joe and Nancy went on to more popular success they usually moved out of the Village, but that was all right, too; there were others to take their places. There is no need to exaggerate when writing about the Village of those days; just about anything you say happened, including the terminal truths of murder, suicide, and death from poison alcohol, as well as love and affection and kindness. And, in between, laughter.

I am fond of Irving Berlin and I wanted to do a musical play with his music in it, so I wrote *The Way It Was*, which is about a time that he knew. When I finished the libretto I sent it to him in Palm Beach and after several long telephone conversations he arranged to meet me in New York. He was enthusiastic, and he chatted about mutual acquaintances from the Philadelphia Main Line. The meeting took place in his dingy office on Broadway, where he had his famous key-changing piano. He sent out to Lindy's for sandwiches and coffee and we had a very pleasant couple of hours. Then he told me he had already written the title song for *The Way It Was*, and he handed a couple of sheets of music to a pianist, and began to sing. He had not sung three notes before I pricked up my ears. He finished the song and looked at me for my reaction. I said, "Irving, do you mind if he plays the melody, and I'll sing the words?"

"No, go right ahead. Go right ahead," he said.

So the pianist began to play, and I sang the lyric. But it was not the lyric he had created for *The Way It Was*. It was the lyric for *Butterfly*, as he had written it forty years ago. I knew it word-perfect.

"You son of a bitch," said Irving. "I was warned about

you. That song was never a hit. How did you know the lyric?"

Well, I know a lot of song lyrics, and everybody knows Berlin lyrics. But he was embarrassed, a bit ashamed, I think, to be caught trying to pull a fast one. I honestly didn't mind; *Butterfly*, or *The Way It Was*, it's a pretty tune; but I knew I had lost Irving Berlin, and in a few days he went back to Palm Beach to finish work on S. N. Behrman's musical play based on the Story of Addison Mizner. He said in parting that there were some changes that had to be made in *The Way It Was* before he could work on it, and that he knew I would not make the changes. That gave us both a good out.

(As a matter of fact "Butterfly" is a damn good tune. I commend it to the attention of Gisele MacKenzie, Rosemary Clooney, and Doris Day.)

Some, or maybe all, of these plays would have reached Broadway if I had been willing to take writing lessons from directors, but I know of no director whose writing talent I respect. Nor do I know of any director whose contribution to a production will guarantee a hit. Since he cannot guarantee a hit, why not do it your way and succeed or fail on your own? I am tired of hearing about creative directors, creative editors, creative producers, creative hucksters and creative artists' representatives. I worked with one creative director who stole as much of one of these plays as he could, and put it in another play. I worked with another creative producer-director who had just finished his fourth consecutive flop. The director has always been the top guy in Hollywood, for reasons too numerous to go into here; but nowadays on Broadway it is impossible to get a name actor or actress without some director's permission—and participation. No flop is ever blamed on the director, but every hit adds to the director's prestige. He "got a wonderful performance out of her" or he "finally got a play out of that script." Why do you suppose every Hollywood and Broadway ham, facing a receding hairline and a sagging chin, announces that he is retiring from acting to become a director? Why do so many written-out writers end up as directors? And *creative* directors, at that. Create something, boys, and I'll direct it for you. But don't create something that Ibsen has already written.

JOHN O'HARA

Princeton, New Jersey 1961

THE
FARMERS
HOTEL

ACT ONE

The scene is the interior of an old but now renovated farmers' hotel, the village of Rockbottom, in Eastern Pennsylvania. Specifically it is the interior of two rooms on the main floor, the lobby and the bar. At about center is a dividing wall in which are swinging doors. At Right in the upstage wall is a double door, the main entrance to the hotel from the porch, which is presumed to be four or five feet above sidewalk level. To the left of the main entrance is the desk, curved, old-fashioned, with a registry, inkstand, tap-bell, pigeonhole mailbox, old-time gas cigar lamp, etc. This desk is continued through from the lobby to the bar, the bar and the desk being one piece. In the lobby are a few comfortable chairs and a pot-bellied stove. In the bar are a few tables and bentwood chairs, and behind the bar are the usual bottles and glasses and an old-fashioned National Cash Register.

The time historically is the present. It is late November and getting dark outside.

At rise we discover IRA STUDEBAKER, *the owner and proprietor of the Farmers Hotel, with a dustcloth in his hand, and busily polishing here, dusting there, trying light switches, straightening the registry, etc. At the moment he is alone, and permitting himself a pleased smile whenever a light switch actually works, standing back to admire this and that. He is a likable man well past middle years but not an old man. He is wearing a vest but not a coat, and a gold watch chain is strung across the upper part of his vest. He is a man who would be likely to wear a vest on the hot-*

3

test day of summer. He wears high-laced black vici kid shoes and, at the moment, a black bow tie. He is far from stylish, yet he is rather neat and certainly clean. Between little acts of polishing and cleaning he pauses to examine his work, rubbing his hand down his vest as he does so, a gesture that he frequently employs when wondering what to do next. He is whistling—no tune—in a preoccupied way and his general manner is that of a person who is putting the finishing touches to his work.

In one of his pauses he suddenly goes to the desk and taps the bell, which is one of those tall, authoritative ones seldom seen nowadays. He taps it three times, spacing out the taps and smiling at the bell. As the sound of the third tap is dying down, a man in a white linen jacket enters from the dining room, which is offstage Right. (In entering he passes the stairway in the lobby, detailed description of which is to be made by the Author for the Set Designer.) The newcomer is CHARLES MOULTRIE MANNERING, *a tall, thin Negro, with handsome features like a Confederate cavalry officer in an old family portrait. He limps slightly, not in the seriously handicapped way. He carries a feather duster.*

CHARLES   Yes sir, Mr. Studebaker.

IRA   Oh, I didn't mean to bother you, Charles.

CHARLES   That's all right. I wasn't doing anything. Just sitting back there in the kitchen. This duster, it aint even for show. Just didn't think to put in back in the closet.

IRA   Well, everything seems all right to me. All in readiness.

CHARLES   Appears to be.

IRA   The only thing I didn't test was the bell.

CHARLES   It came loud and clear all the way back to the kitchen. That is, if it was three times you rung it. Three times was what I heard.

IRA   Three times is what I rang. But not too loud, I hope. I wouldn't want it to ring too loud.

CHARLES   I wouldn't let that worry you if I was you. I always like to hear the bell ringing in a hotel. You know: 'Bing! Front, boy.' I always like that.

IRA   Yes. That's right.

CHARLES   In a hotel, that bell means business. It means they're getting action. You can't *have* it too loud. If I owned a hotel I'd like that bell going from morning till night.

IRA   I never thought of that before, but it's a fact.

CHARLES   Personally, I even like to hear the bell ringing when I'm passing a fire house in the city.

IRA   You *do?*

CHARLES   It means they'll be rolling, the fire trucks. It don't always mean a serious fire. Sometimes a false alarm. Sometimes— Mr. Studebaker, did you ever happen to take a look in the newspaper, where they have a list of yesterday's fires?

IRA   (*Thinking back*)   Mmm-mm . . .

CHARLES   You take a look some day. Most of the time it says, Loss, trifling. Loss, trifling. You take a look at one of them big hook and ladders on their way back from a fire. Those firemen, hanging on there, waving and smiling. I always get a wave out of them.

IRA   Yesss . . .

CHARLES   Those firemen, they're glad to be *doing* something, according to the way I figure. According to the way I figure, they'd ruther be at a fire than sitting around the fire house doing nothing.

IRA   Oh, they keep busy. I understand they do a lot of work repairing toys, broken children's toys, for the poor children at Christmas. Repairing, painting . . .

CHARLES   Mr. Studebaker, if you signed up to be a fireman, would you want to spend most of your time repairing children's toys?

IRA   No, I guess I wouldn't.

CHARLES   No sir, you wouldn't. Not judging by the work you put in on this place. No sir. On the other hand, if you took a job in a toy factory—

IRA   I wouldn't want to spend my time fighting fires!

CHARLES   Exactly. I studied you pretty closely these last few weeks. No, I like the sound of a bell because it mostly means something. Speaking of which, I have a little suggestion.

IRA   Every time you made a suggestion it was valuable.

CHARLES   (*Agreeing, without humility*)   Thank you, sir. This is my suggestion, on that bell. We ought to arrange some system. Signals.

IRA   Right.

CHARLES   One ring, maybe that stands for 'Front, boy!'

IRA   Mm-hmm.

CHARLES   Two—I don't know what the two should stand for.

IRA   Two could mean, somebody is checking out.

CHARLES   Okay.

IRA   Three?

CHARLES   We don't need a three.

IRA   We don't?

CHARLES   The one for somebody checking in, the two for somebody checking out. Three is too many anyway. Try it.

IRA   (*Tapping three times*)   Yes, it is too many. Unnecessary.

CHARLES   Unnecessary. Three sounds like a fire house.

IRA   Yep. Well, we've got that settled. Shall we fling open the doors and welcome the public?

CHARLES　Fling open the doors? You want me to fling open the doors in this weather? I'll fling 'em open, if that's what you want, but we ought to close them promptly.

IRA　(*Going to door and looking out*)　Well, I'll be! Look at that snow? When did that start?

CHARLES　Shortly after two o'clock this afternoon, it started lightly.

IRA　Well, I'll be. It just shows you what concentration. I've been so busy around here I never gave a thought to how it was outside. Never even looked out the window once, all afternoon.

CHARLES　I said to myself around ha' past three, I said if this keeps up we'll start out busy. The transient trade. We ought to do a big supper business. I said so to Mrs. Fenstermacher.

IRA　I don't know. We're pretty far from any main road, Charles.

CHARLES　Yes, you said that all along. But when you get a heavy fall of snow, like this one here, people get lost from not being able to read the signs. Some fellow gets a flat tire and he don't want to fix it himself. He'd rather walk a mile or two and get somebody to fix it for him. And if he sees a nice cheerful hotel he's gonna come in and ask us is that garage the only one in Rockbottom, and where can he get in touch with the man that runs it? Takes off his overcoat and has a toddy. Nice warm stove. Two or three more toddies. We serve supper here? Do we have rooms? Why should he walk all the way back to that car in all that snow? Spend the night here in this nice warm hotel, with all these surroundings. Where's the telephone? Calls up. Ed—or maybe he calls his wife, Betty. Ed, or Betty, my car broke down in a place called Rockbottom. Snowing like hell here, so I'm gonna spend the night at the Farmers Hotel. Call you in the morning. Then he hangs up, orders another toddy, says where can he wash up, and settles down and relaxes.

IRA   You think that's the way it'll work out?

CHARLES   If there's a man in that predicament. I aint saying that's the only way, but I guarantee you, we'll have rooms occupied tonight. I bet we do a good supper business. That's what I told Mrs. Fenstermacher.

IRA   Well, I guess she's prepared for it.

CHARLES   Prepared, all right, but skeptical. She said that's the way it'd of been when there was horses and carriages. But automobile people, they want to hurry to one of them modern hotels in Allentown or Bethlehem. But I said yes, but maybe they'll hurry themselves into a ditch. And any port in a storm. So she said to me, Charles, you been right about so many things, maybe you'll be right about this.

IRA   I hope you are, not that I want to get any business out of people's misfortune.

CHARLES   I look at it the other way. What a lucky thing for those people we're *in* business, a nice clean warm hotel, comfortable. Honest people running it. In the olden days, you heard about merrie England. A traveler that stopped at the first inn he came across, he run a pretty good chance of getting his throat cut and nothing more ever heard of him. That was a common practice. If it was me I'd be mighty pleased to have a little mishap and discover a place like this.

IRA   That's true.

CHARLES   Sure.

IRA   You speaking of England reminded me of something. (*He goes to front door and extracts a large brass key and holds it out to* CHARLES) Throw this as far as you can. Your arm's better than mine.

CHARLES   Well, I'm no Satchel Paige, but— You mean outside?

IRA   Right. I remember reading somewhere, they had this old custom in England, I think it was England, where they threw away the key the day they opened a new hotel.

CHARLES   I remember. (*They move to the door*) Which direction you like to have me throw it?

IRA   Suit yourself.

CHARLES   Let's see now. Doctor Graeff's house there. If I throw it over his roof. That's a pretty good throw.

IRA   Better than I could do.

(CHARLES *goes out, winds up and throws, while* IRA *stands in the doorway watching.* CHARLES *comes back in the doorway*)

IRA   Let's get inside, Charles. That's a very thin jacket you're wearing.

(*They close the door and amble slowly to the bar, thinking their thoughts*)

CHARLES   (*As they amble*)   Oh, I'm use to being out in all kinds of weather. Tropical hurricanes. I been in them. And arctic blizzards. Well, subarctic. I never was in any those expeditions where they ended up eating the dogs. Mr. Studebaker. That little ceremony, throwing the key?

IRA   Yes?

CHARLES   That means we're open for business.

IRA   The Farmers Hotel, Rockbottom, P A, is now officially open for business.

CHARLES   Then I tell you what I'd like to do. I'd like to buy the first drink under the new management.

IRA   I'll buy the drink, Charles.

CHARLES   That's giving. I'd like to *buy* the first drink. I'll buy you a drink and me a drink with this little dollar bill, then you can have it framed and hung up there over the cash register.

IRA   I kinda like that. Do you want to ring it up?

CHARLES   No, sir. I want you to ring it up. I'll sign my

name on it, and what's the date, and you can have it framed.

IRA (*Going behind the bar*)   Well, what'll it be?

CHARLES   A shot of bourbon, please. Water for a chaser. Have something yourself.

IRA   Thanks, I will. Take a bourbon myself. (*Pours them*)

CHARLES (*Raising his glass*)   Success to the Farmers Hotel!

IRA (*Returning the toast*)   And may you share in the success.

CHARLES (*Putting down his drink*)   I'll just write my name on the dollar bill, then I better start swinging the old snow shovel. (*He signs the bill*)

IRA   You got a pair of arctics?

CHARLES   Oh, yes. I come fully prepared. I know this Pennsylvania weather. Got the shovel and the arctics in that closet under the stairs.

(*They move to the lobby where* CHARLES *takes out the arctics and snow shovel and sits down to put on the arctics.* IRA *stands watching him, with a cigar in hand*)

IRA   Bundle up good and warm now, Charles.

CHARLES   Yes sir.

IRA   And don't try to do too much. You know, they say shovelling snow is one of the hardest things on a man's heart.

CHARLES   For some men. The ones that don't do any physical work but one day of the year, the day it snows. There we are. Now which coat will I put on? My old mackinaw. For shovelling snow you don't want anything long.

IRA   Right.

CHARLES   My old sealskin cap.

IRA   Haven't seen one of those in years.

CHARLES   Given to me by an employer I was coachman

for. Very well-to-do gentleman in Dutchess County, York State.

IRA Well, take it easy, now, Charles.

CHARLES I'll start around by the side entrance and work my way to the front door.

(*He goes through the bar to door at Left, followed by* IRA, *and exits.* IRA *is lighting his cigar as a man in an old-fashioned well-made ulster enters the lobby by the double doors. He is* J. HENRY GRAEFF, M.D.)

DR. GRAEFF (*Calling out*) Hey, there! Ira? Anybody home in this crazy place?

IRA (*Starting toward lobby*) Who's that?

DR. GRAEFF Me. Henry Graeff.

IRA (*In the lobby*) Why, good evening, Henry.

DR. GRAEFF I think I got something belongs to you, Ira. Very mystifying. Does this belong to you? (*Holds out brass key*)

IRA Well, yes, I suppose it does.

HENRY You know damn well it does, Ira. The only other place this key'd fit is the old Moravian Church over at Flour Mill.

IRA That so?

HENRY That's so, and you know it.

IRA Have something to take the chill off.

HENRY Later, maybe, after office hours. Right now I want to clear up this mystery, or you clear it up for me. I was sitting in my back office, trying to bring my records up to date for the young fellow that does my bookkeeping. I have this young fellow come down from Allentown and does the real bookkeeping, but I'm supposed to keep track of visits and office patients. Well sir, I was sitting there when all of a sudden, *clang!* I heard something hit my car. I couldn't imagine what it was, but I didn't like the sound of it. I only have the one car, and I don't want anything to happen to it, especially in this weather.

So I went out and took a look around and I happened to notice there was a hole in the snow on the hood, then down the side of the hood was this line through the snow, and there lying there on the running board was this key. I looked at it for a minute and I knew right away where it came from, but how did it get there. Now then, how *did* it get there?

IRA   Well, I hope it didn't do your car any harm.

HENRY   Don't worry about the car. Worry about me. I'm a practical man. I don't believe keys just drop down on my sedan.

IRA   I can easily explain it. I threw it there.

HENRY   You threw it there. Well, I suppose you think *that* makes everything clear.

IRA   There's an old English custom they used to do when they opened up a new inn. They'd throw the key away, signifying that the inn would be always open.

HENRY   *I* see. Well, a lot of people thought you were crazy when you took over this place. And now I know you're crazy. What else are you thinking of throwing away?

IRA   Nothing. Nothing else.

HENRY   Just money, and brass keys, eh? That's all, eh, Ira?

IRA   'T's all.

HENRY   Ira, you don't think I ought to have you locked up for your own good? I could go to old Judge Laubenstein and get a court order and have you put away some place where they put harmless cases like you. They'd treat you kindly. You could pretend it was a hotel, and you were running it. They'd humor you.

IRA   Well, there's only one thing wrong with that idea, Henry.

HENRY   What's that, Ira?

IRA   Well, if you went into court to get an order to have

The Farmers Hotel   13

me put in the crazy-house, old Judge Laubenstein, he's a pretty wise old fellow. I think Judge Laubenstein might take a good look at you and tell them to lead *you* away. All I'm doing here, I'm trying to have a little fun running a country hotel in my old home town, but you go into court—I don't know, Henry. The judge'd be liable to think to himself: this man's going around treating sick people. He's dangerous. No, Henry, I'd stay out of court if I were you.

HENRY Suit yourself, Ira. I only made the offer in a kindly spirit. But if you're thinking of throwing any more things, be careful you don't hit Elsie Zumbach's property. You know Elsie doesn't think you're harmless. She thinks you want to open up a whore house, that's what she thinks this place'll turn out to be. Of course maybe Elsie's right. Still too early to tell.

IRA If that's what it's going to be, I think I can guess who'd be the first customer.

HENRY Hmm. I'll be back after office hours. Here, give me back the key. If you want to get rid of it I'll drop it in Schaeffer's Dam.

IRA Thanks, Henry. And say, don't say anything about this to Charles, my colored fellow.

HENRY Oh, I won't say anything to Charles. I'm counting on him to shovel the snow in front of my place, and I don't want him to think we're all crazy around here. (HENRY, *during the preceding speech, is standing with the door open a little*)

IRA Listen, come in or go out, but don't stand there with that door open.

HENRY I think you're getting a customer.

IRA Well, close the door, or you'll be getting a patient.

HENRY Yep. Looks like a customer.

IRA Close the God damn door!

(HENRY, *smiling, goes, closing the door behind him, but*

it is immediately reopened by a tall man in a polo coat and fox-hunting habit)

FOXHUNTER (*Moderately amused*)   Wait till I get inside, won't you?

IRA   Excuse me, I was barking at my friend.

FOXHUNTER   I know. Have you got a telephone booth here?

IRA   Yes, there's the booth over there, but I'm not sure it's connected. Just had it put in yesterday and I haven't tried it yet.

FOXHUNTER   I'll give it a try for you. Will you give me a dollar in silver, please?

IRA (*Taking out a snap purse*)   Surely. Twenty-five, fifty, you'll need some nickels and dimes. Sixty, seventy, eighty, eighty-five, ninety, ninety-five, one dollar. To Philadelphia is thirty-five cents.

FOXHUNTER (*Suspiciously*)   What makes you think I'm calling Philadelphia?
(*A handsome woman, also in hunting habit, enters on this speech and goes directly to the stove*)

IRA   Well, just a guess. I'd say you look more like Philadelphia people.
(*The man and woman exchange quick glances*)

FOXHUNTER   Have a couple of brandies, please.

LADY   And where is the ladies' room?

IRA   Just up those stairs and to the right. To the left, I mean.
(*She exits*)

IRA (*To the foxhunter*)   You wish the imported or the domestic?

FOXHUNTER   The imported.

IRA   Do you wish it like a highball, or in one of those small brandy glasses? (*He holds up thumb and forefinger*)

FOXHUNTER (*Reproducing the gesture*) In one of those small brandy glasses, and you can bring me mine here in the booth, if you don't mind.

IRA Another thing about that telephone. It's a different system here. You don't put the money in till the operator tells you to. In other words, not like city phones where you deposit the coin first. Here you wait till the operator speaks to you first and then you give her the number you want and she'll tell you how much to deposit. You know what I mean?

FOXHUNTER I think I can manage that.

IRA Just don't put the money in first, otherwise you lose whatever you put in. That's the system they have around this part of the country. I understand they're changing it, but it won't be put through for quite a while.

FOXHUNTER It may be put through before I put through this call.
(*He closes booth door.* IRA *goes to bar, and with noticeable unfamiliarity finds the brandy ponies, the imported brandy, and pours two drinks, and takes one back to the lobby and taps on door of booth and hands the drink to the* FOXHUNTER, *who takes it and quickly closes the door.* IRA *returns to his place behind the bar, awaiting the reappearance of the* LADY, *which occurs almost immediately. She gives a passing glance at the booth, but proceeds to the bar*)

IRA Your husband's still talking.

LADY I see he is.

IRA Your brandy. You want something by way of a chaser? A glass of water?

LADY A glass of water, fine. And while you're about it, would you mind filling this flask please?

IRA With brandy?

LADY (*Handing him a silver pint flask*)   Mm-hmm. The imported.

IRA   A pleasure. Now let me see, a funnel. Funnel, funnel, funnel. Here we are. Uh-uh. This spout won't fit into the mouth of your flask. But I'm pretty sure Mrs. Fenstermacher will have a smaller one.

LADY Oh, I wouldn't be too sure.

IRA   Do you know Mrs.— Oh, you're kidding me.

LADY A little.

IRA   Mrs. Fenstermacher does the cooking. I don't want to call her the cook. She wouldn't like that much. More of a sort of partner. I'll be right back.
      (*He comes out from behind the bar and crosses to the dining room door at Right and exits. The* LADY *pours another brandy, and the* FOXHUNTER *enters the bar*)

FOXHUNTER   Caught in the act.

LADY God. Don't *say* that.

FOXHUNTER   What? Oh, I see what you mean.

LADY Any luck?

FOXHUNTER   No, not exactly. She's expected back in a half to three quarters of an hour. (*He puts his polo coat on a chair*)

LADY Who did you talk to, the butler?

FOXHUNTER   Yes, I guess so. It sounded like a butler.

LADY Did he sound English, or Irish?

FOXHUNTER   Good Lord, I don't know. He could have been English, or, he could have been Irish. It was a servant.

LADY Oh, you ascertained that?

FOXHUNTER   Sure I ascertained it. What difference does it make whether he was English or Irish?

LADY If he was English it was the butler. I don't trust him. If it was the Irishman, he's the chauffeur and a friend of mine. Patrick would lie for me. Walter, the

Englishman, he might tell a lie, but in such a way that you'd know he was lying.

FOXHUNTER   Well, we can try her again in a few minutes. Give us a kiss.

(She puts down her glass and kisses him warmly but not passionately. They stop embracing before IRA *re-enters the bar)*

IRA   One of these ought to do the job.

LADY   I helped myself to another brandy while you were in the kitchen.

IRA   That's all right. Mister, you ready for another?

FOXHUNTER   I think I'd like something to eat. How about it, do you serve sandwiches?

LADY   Sure. Mrs. Fenstermacher.

FOXHUNTER   What?

LADY   Mrs. Fenstermacher does the cooking here.

IRA   That's correct, and you can take my word for it, anything prepared by Mrs. Fenstermacher, you'll never forget it. That's why if I might make a suggestion to you folks.

FOXHUNTER   What's the suggestion?

IRA   My suggestion, unless you're going to somebody's for a regular dinner and you only want a little something to fill in, I suggest you eat one of Mrs. Fenstermacher's dinners. I guarantee you you'll never regret it.

(The LADY *puts her coat on a chair)*

LADY   I'm afraid we won't have time.

IRA   Well, *that's* too bad. Mrs. Fenstermacher's famous around here, but if you don't have time, you don't have time. What could I get you in the way of a sandwich? At least take a steak sandwich.

LADY   I'll go for a steak sandwich, cut thin, though.

FOXHUNTER   Make that two.

IRA   French fries come with it and a nice tomato salad. How does that sound?

FOXHUNTER   I'll skip the potatoes and salad.

LADY   I think I'll skip the potatoes, but I will have the salad, French dressing. And I'm going to switch to a cocktail.

FOXHUNTER   You are?

LADY   I'm going to have a Side Car.

FOXHUNTER   A Side Car?

LADY   Has brandy in it.

IRA   For that I'll have to get Charles. I've *drunk* every kind of cocktail, but mix them is different. Charles is the man to mix you a cocktail. I'd only spoil it.

FOXHUNTER   Well, will you get him, please? I guess I'll have a Side Car too.
(IRA *goes out to fetch* CHARLES *and the man and woman are left alone. They seat themselves at one of the bar tables. Their manner is that of being strongly in love and beginning to like the Farmers Hotel. He touches her cheek and she touches his*)

LADY   You're beginning to need a shave.

FOXHUNTER   No wonder. Do you know what time I shaved this morning?

LADY   No. What time did you?

FOXHUNTER   About six o'clock.

LADY   I was up at six, too. This must be Charles.

CHARLES   (*Entering bar, removing coat, etc.*)   Good evening, ma'am. Sir. Not a very good day for hunting.

LADY   Good evening. No, it wasn't. Do you know about hunting?

CHARLES   A fair amount, a fair amount. I had one of my employers years ago, he had a private pack. My understanding, he gave it up in '29, due to circumstances. I was always raised around horses till I went in the Army in May '17.

FOXHUNTER   Were you in the cavalry?

CHARLES   No sir, I wasn't. I had a kind of a strange career in the Army. I went overseas as a trombone player. I played trombone with Lieutenant Jim Europe's band, the 369th Infantry Band. I got a Purple Heart, and I got a dishonorable discharge, but I can vote or get a passport just the same as anybody.

FOXHUNTER   That is quite a career.

CHARLES   (*Going behind the bar*)   Mr. Studebaker says you wish a Side Car.

FOXHUNTER   Mr. Studebaker?

CHARLES   Gentleman you been talking to. Owns this place. You like to know how I can vote and all, even with the dishonorable?

FOXHUNTER   By all means.

CHARLES   (*Starting the cocktails*)   Well, with Lieutenant Jim Europe I was stationed in Paris. The summer of '18 I happen to get a parcel of socks and chocolate, steel shaving mirror was inside, a deck of playing cards. That parcel was from a lady that I once worked for her husband. The note enclosed said if I ever ran into their son I was to write and tell them all about it. Well, of course I knew the son very well as a boy, and he I knew was in the Fifth Marines. So I just happened to get a furlough from the band and through a staff officer I knew, a major, I asked this major if I could be his chauffeur, because I knew this major used a general's Cadillac when he went up front, up behind the front lines on liaison. He was doing liaison with the French. That's how it happened, how I got my Purple Heart. The medal, it didn't come till much later, ten years later, but the wound I got on the 13th day of September, 1918, at St.-Mihiel, sitting in the driver's seat of a Cadillac automobile. I got it in the leg and like to bled to death, but at that I was better off than my major. He got his whole head decapitated by the same shrapnel hit me. Took off his whole head. I never did get to see the young man I went looking for. Never seen him to this day. I always meant to write to his mother, but by the time I got through my own troubles the war was over and everybody was back home, everybody that was gonna get there.

FOXHUNTER   Quite a story.

CHARLES   Taste these. I make a pretty good Side Car.

LADY (*Tasting*)   Fine. Perfect.

CHARLES   They'll never get to tell all the stories happened in *that* war. That was some war. The Second was bigger and more global, but the First was more like an old-fashioned *war*. An officer could be sitting having his aperitif at a sidewalk cafe, late in the afternoon. Mud on his boots. Why didn't he get the mud taken off his boots? Because he was going right back to his airdrome in fifteen minutes and they'd only get muddy again. I saw that happen. That was a flying officer, of course.

FOXHUNTER   You told us about the Purple Heart. What about the dishonorable?

CHARLES   That. Well, I went back to Lieutenant Jim Europe's band after I got fixed up, and I guess I began to think I was John J. Pershing himself. Not making excuses for myself, but by the time I got back a lot of the boys were pretty uppity, so I got just as uppity as any of them. I decided it was time for me to light out for home. The war was over and I wanted to see my family. So I just went down to Brest and borrowed a pack and came home with a Pioneer outfit. I was all the way to New York Harbor before they caught up with me, one advantage of being a Negro in the midst of two thousand other Negroes. Then there was a lot of red tape, court martial and all that, and depriving me of my citizenship. But a former employer of mine took an interest in my case and he got me a Presidential pardon, signed Woodrow Wilson. I never even set foot in Leavenworth.

FOXHUNTER Probably because you'd been wounded, don't you think?

CHARLES Exactly. There's men I know, knew in the band, they never did come back. When it came time to come home in '19 they said to themselves: "Why should I go home? I never had it so good at home." Some of them married and settled down with the French natives, and now I guess they got grandchildren, for all I know.

LADY Don't you ever hear from them?

CHARLES I don't want to hear from them. I sowed a few wild oats in Paris. I was a young fellow, and wartime. But I had a family, my wife and in those days the one son. I wanted to get home with my family and make a future.

LADY And that's what you did?

CHARLES Yes, ma'am, that's what I did. Here's a little dividend before I mix you another.

LADY Do we want another?

FOXHUNTER You know we do.

LADY (*Lightly*) Yes, I guess we do.

FOXHUNTER We're going to have to gulp it down, because here's our food.

(IRA *enters, carrying a tray, and presently is assisted in serving by* CHARLES. *The* FOXHUNTER *and the* LADY *become silent as the food is placed before them and* CHARLES, *unbeknownst to them, signals* IRA *to go out to the lobby with him*)

CHARLES (*In the lobby*) I think they want to be by themselves.

IRA Did they give you the hint?

CHARLES No, but I can tell.

IRA   Leave it to you, Charles.

CHARLES   (*Going to swinging door*)   If you want anything just call out. I'll be in here.

FOXHUNTER   We're fine, thanks.

LADY   Charles is being tactful.

FOXHUNTER   Why should he be tactful?

LADY   They're both being tactful. They suspect illicit romance.

FOXHUNTER   I don't believe that for a minute.

LADY   Well, maybe not Mr. Studebaker, but Charles does.

FOXHUNTER   Well, what if they do?

LADY   Oh, I'm not worried. It's rather fun. At least now, this minute. It may not be later, but it is now. I wish we could stay here, all night.

FOXHUNTER   Well, we can forget about that right this minute.

LADY   Oh, I know, but it would be nice.

FOXHUNTER   (*Abruptly*)   Say, have you any money?

LADY   Not a cent.

FOXHUNTER   It just occurred to me. I don't think I have enough to pay this bill. I know I haven't.

LADY   We can always cash a cheque. I'm sure Mr. Studebaker trusts us.

FOXHUNTER   Not if he suspects illicit love.

LADY   Illicit romance.

FOXHUNTER   (*Calling out*)   Charles!

CHARLES   (*Appearing not too quickly*)   Yes sir.

FOXHUNTER   Would you ask Mr. Studebaker to come here, please.

CHARLES   (*Exiting*)   Yes sir.

FOXHUNTER   (*To* LADY)   Now you just keep quiet. I'll handle this whole thing.

IRA   (*Appearing*)   Yes sir? What can I do for you? I can recommend all our pies, all home made right here in our own kitchen, if you care for pie.

FOXHUNTER   Nothing more to eat, thanks, but I have a favor to ask you.

IRA   That's what we're here for.

FOXHUNTER   Wait till you hear what it is, first. You might not be too eager.

IRA   You mean you want to cash a cheque?

FOXHUNTER   That's right.

IRA   How much?

FOXHUNTER   Fifty dollars?

IRA   Fifty is all right. Do you have your own cheque, or do you want a blank?

FOXHUNTER   No, no cheque, and no identification. But I'll tell you what I'll do. (*Undoing his wrist watch*) You can take my word for it, this watch is worth a damned sight more than fifty dollars, or ten times fifty dollars.

IRA   (*Smiling*)   If I didn't think you were honest what good would your watch do me? If you weren't honest the watch could belong to some other person, so if you weren't good for the cheque, all I'd get was stolen goods.

FOXHUNTER   I must have an honest face.

LADY   I never thought so.

FOXHUNTER   No, you never thought so, but apparently Mr. Studebaker does. Mr. Studebaker, my name is Pomfret, and I live in New York. The H. P. on the back of this watch, that of course doesn't prove anything, but those are my initials. Howard Pomfret. That's the closest I have to identification. I left my wallet in my other clothes, back at—where I changed. Quite a few miles from here.

LADY   Isn't there a label inside your—

POMFRET   Yes, that's right. Here's my name on this label.

IRA   Mr. Pomfrey, you're the one that's doing all the talking about identification, not me. I didn't ask you for identification. I may be new in this business, but I was in another business for over thirty years and I didn't go broke, and most of my business had to be done on credit. I'll get you a blank cheque and a pen. If you want to make it for a hundred, that's all right too. (*He keeps talking while getting the blank cheque from the desk*) If I didn't know how to size a person up I could have easily gone broke the first year I was in business.

POMFRET   I have something else to tell you, quite candidly.

IRA   What's that?

POMFRET   Well, if you're doing this for good will—you know I may never get back this way again.

IRA   Why, I don't *expect* to see you again, you *or* the lady.

POMFRET   You don't? Why not?

LADY   Yes, why?

IRA   Well, am I right? You folks don't expect to come here again.

LADY   Unfortunately, that's true, but how did you know?

IRA   Give a person credit for some intuitions.

LADY   You mean we're not married.

IRA   (*Wishing this were over*)   At first I thought you were.

LADY   What made you change your mind? We didn't have that married look?

IRA   I guess that's it. You two people, you're not *kids.*

LADY   Say no more, Mr. Studebaker. Our guilt is written on our faces.

IRA   I didn't say anything about guilt.

POMFRET   (*To her*)   I think you may be embarrassing Mr. Studebaker.

IRA   (*Quickly*)   Or I didn't say I was embarrassed, either. (*He takes the cheque, which* POMFRET *has been filling out, stuffs it in his vest pocket, and from his wallet takes five ten-dollar bills and hands them to* POMFRET)

POMFRET Thank you very much, Mr. Studebaker. We were just about out of everything, money, and gas. Our tank is down to E for Empty.

IRA (*Frowning*) How far do you have to go? You don't have to tell me where you're going, but how far in miles?

POMFRET How far would you say, Sweetie?

LADY Lordy, I don't know. We took so many wrong turns, and I've never been in this part of the state before.

IRA Judging by your clothes you must be from somewhere near the Main Line.

LADY In that general direction. A little to the west.

IRA I was in business in Philadelphia before I bought here. I never lived on the Main Line, but we used to go out there on drives. I always had to live in the city because of my business.

LADY And what was your business, may I ask?

IRA Wholesale fruit and produce I was in.

LADY Then you may have had business dealings with some of my family. You had to see people that owned orchards, didn't you?

IRA Personally very seldom, unless they had a big orchard. The ones with the big orchards, sometimes it was good business if we arranged to buy a whole crop in advance. If you have some relation that owned one of the big orchards, maybe I knew him. But only in a business way, not socially. Half of my life I got up at four o'clock in the morning, that's the way our business works.

LADY (*Getting bored*) Fascinating. I know I'd love to hear about it some time, but I suppose I never will.

IRA (*Catching on*) No, I don't guess you ever will.

LADY (*Immediately repentant*) I'm sorry, Mr. Studebaker. I didn't mean to be rude.

IRA Well—that's all right. I guess you're worried.

LADY I am.

POMFRET To get back to our original discussion, or one of our original discussions.

IRA (*Ignoring him*) Worrying won't get you home, ma'am. Let Mr. Pomfrey and I do the worrying.

POMFRET That's it, and I am doing some of the worrying.

IRA (*To him*) I know you are. (*He sits down*) The first thing is the gazzoline. Across the road over there, maybe you noticed a gazzoline pump, but a pump locked up is as good as no pump at all. I know this friend of mine that owns the grodge [garage]. Dewey Kemp. I'll try to get in touch with him.
(*He goes out to the phone booth, during which* LADY *puts watch back on* POMFRET'S *wrist and kisses his hand.* IRA *returns*)

IRA (*Shaking his head*) Dewey Kemp, the fellow that owns the grodge, sometimes when he's working on one of his inventions he won't answer the phone. Dewey's an inventor, working on some patent and hates to be interrupted. And tonight I guess he figures it's a good night to lock up and go home, work on the patent.

POMFRET A garage ought to be like a hotel. If *you* weren't open we'd most likely be stuck in the snow.

IRA Don't compare me with Dewey Kemp, that's the Original Mister Independent, and you got to admire him for it.

POMFRET *You* admire him, then.

IRA Well, you're pretty independent yourself, Mr. Pomfrey, and I admire that.

POMFRET Mr. Studebaker, if you'll take another look at that cheque you so kindly cashed, look at the signature. My name is Pomfret. Pomfret. Howard Pom-fret, not Pom-free. It's not a hard name.

LADY Howard, let's you and I stop being surly with this really nice man. He's trying to help us, and without his help we may be in a very, very, *very* nasty little *jam*. Will you get that through your arrogant skull?

POMFRET   All right, you handle it.

LADY   All right, I will. Mr. Studebaker, it's absolutely necessary that we get back to my house before at the latest eleven or eleven-thirty tonight.

IRA   That you can easily do, as far as distance is concerned. It depends on the condition of the roads, the snow.

LADY   Fine. Now how do we go?

IRA   (*Rubbing his belly*)   Well, the way I'd go would be take that road that intersects us here at the corner, and head for Wheelwright. Mind now, it's a country road and maybe it's all drifted over, but we can find out if it's passable, and if it is, that's your road. At Wheelwright you'll hit 335, and if you stay on 335 that'll end you up in Norristown.

LADY   It's as simple as that? I wonder where we went wrong.

POMFRET   I could answer that question, but it wouldn't have anything to do with highways.

LADY   (*Not annoyed, but continuing*)   And if the road isn't clear to Wheelwright, then which way?

IRA   Then you'll have to go east on the Dieglersville road, but not all the way in to Dieglersville. You turn right about a half a mile before Dieglersville and that puts you on the road marked Doylestown. You stay on that road till you meet 335.

LADY   Oh. Three-thirty-*five!*

IRA   That's correct.

LADY   Will you write it down, please? Both ways?

IRA   (*Getting some paper*)   I'll write the directions down and draw you a rough map. I'll just put down the principal places to look out for, because once you're on 335 you're headed home. (*Takes out matching pen and pencil set*) These were a present from my drivers and helpers when I sold out to my partner. I always like to show them off. I kind of expected a *little* something from the people in the *office*, and they gave me a cigar humidor I have up in my room. But from the drivers and helpers, they used to give me a lot of trouble. They went out on strike on me three times and cost me a lot of money. But the day before I was retiring, leaving for good, they all came in my office and presented me with this pen and pencil set. *They* didn't have to do anything for me and there for a minute I couldn't think of anything to say. And they couldn't either. Then O'Leary, the big Irish fellow that was supposed to make the presentation speech, he and I started talking all at once.

LADY   What did O'Leary say? I'd like to hear.

IRA *(Modestly)*   Oh, I don't know. It was so flattering.

LADY   I'll bet it was no more than you deserved, Mr. Studebaker.

IRA *(With a delighted grin)*   That's about what O'Leary said, ma'am. That's just about what O'Leary said. Well, now, this isn't getting you to Norristown. I'll go find out about the roads. Would you care for a little libation?

LADY   I don't think so, thanks.

IRA   Mr. Pomfret?

POMFRET   Not at the moment, thanks.

(IRA *exits to lobby, and puts on overcoat, muffler, arctics and gunning cap with earlaps*)

IRA *(To the two)*   Taking a little walk down to where Dewey Kemp lives, I might find him home.

POMFRET   I'll go with you.

IRA   No, no, you stay here and keep the lady company. *(He exits)*

LADY *(After a pause)*   How old would you say he was?

POMFRET   Oh, I don't know. He said he was in the grocery business—how long? I'd say he was around fifty-eight. He's kind of a nice old bird.

LADY You know something? He's about the same age as Alex.

POMFRET Your Alex? Alex Paul?

LADY I'll bet there isn't more than a year or two's difference in their ages. In other words, I'm married to a man about the same age as Mr. Studebaker. *I'm* getting *on*.

POMFRET Oh, hell, you married young and you married a guy a hell of a lot older than you.

LADY The fact remains. You see, the difference between this man and Alex, Alex is always in country clothes, and when did you ever see Alex when he wasn't sunburned?

POMFRET Never, I guess.

LADY And Alex, no lines in his face, or practically none. Good food, the outdoor life, no worries.

POMFRET No worries?

LADY Not so far. The only thing that'll bother him is if people say I just nipped off with you.

POMFRET But you're not just nipping off with me, Martha.

MARTHA If we get away with this little excursion I think I can handle it so he'll give me the divorce.

POMFRET And Esther.

MARTHA And Esther. I'd live with you openly, but he'd take Esther away from me, and I don't even want him to share her. I don't want him to have anything to do with bringing her up. I've fought it all her life and I don't want to see her spoiled now, and this'd be just the time, too, just the time he could spoil her. You don't know what that much money can do.

POMFRET (*Somewhat bitterly*) No, but I'd be willing to learn.

MARTHA   I saw it happen. A girl I know tried to bring up not one but two daughters with that kind of money. What happened? She and her husband parted company and he *didn't* get custody, but he began it very subtly, loads of little presents, then bigger presents, trips abroad, 21, El Morocco. Well, *one* of those girls is only a year older than Esther, but she's pregnant and getting a divorce. The older sister, twenty-three years old, she's already divorced and living with an actor that has a wife and a couple of children. That's what the father did with his God damn money. And they began as wonderful kids, lovely.

POMFRET   And what about the mother?

MARTHA   A drunk, a falling-down, hopeless alcoholic.

POMFRET   Is she married again?

MARTHA   Heavens no. All puffed out, lost every *vestige* of her looks, plays around with a bunch of pansies in New York.

POMFRET   Who is it? Do I know her?

MARTHA   Kitty George. I guess you've probably met her.

POMFRET   I saw her last week at a dinner party. I hardly recognized her.

MARTHA   It could happen to me.

POMFRET   Not to you, Martha.

MARTHA   It might. It could. Nobody ever thought it could happen to Kitty, either. But it did, it did. So far we're not actually in trouble, serious trouble. If we get through to Eleanor she'll cover up for me. I'll tell her to call Alex and say I had one too many this afternoon, taking a little nap at her house, maybe spending the night. Alex will believe anything Eleanor says. As a matter of fact, Eleanor is his favorite cousin.

POMFRET   I didn't realize that.

MARTHA   They're all related.

POMFRET   Won't he want to go over to Eleanor's and take you home?

MARTHA   He'll want to, but she'll take care of that.

POMFRET   (*To* CHARLES, *entering bar*)   Charles, I think I'd like a Scotch and plain water, please.

MARTHA   (*Rising*)   While I use the telephone.
(*He hands her coins and she goes to booth*)

CHARLES   (*Serving drink and looking at dishes*)   Nothing wrong with the meat, I hope.

POMFRET   No, we just weren't as hungry as we thought.

CHARLES   Because Mrs. Fenstermacher, she don't like to see anything left on the plate. You want me to warm up the rest of Madam's sandwich?

POMFRET   I don't think so, thanks. You can take it away.

CHARLES   Hmm. Well, I'll just tell Mrs. Fenstermacher you had those sweet cocktails, took your appetites away.

POMFRET   More or less the truth.

CHARLES   Yes sir, more or less.

POMFRET   Hmm?

CHARLES   I imagine, worrying about getting home, that would take some of your appetite away.

POMFRET   Oh, yes.

CHARLES   Did you take notice to where Mr. Studebaker went?

POMFRET   I *know* where he went. He went to try and rouse up the man that owns the garage.

CHARLES   Mr. Kemp? I could have told him that. Mr. Kemp drove up to Allentown this morning. He wanted to get some tools or something for his invention. He's an inventor, working on some invention.

POMFRET   How the hell can he afford to run a garage that way?

CHARLES   Afford to? Mister—

POMFRET   Pomfret's the name. P. o. m. f. r. e. t.

CHARLES   Oh, the same as the prep school.

POMFRET   That's right.

CHARLES   I had one of my employers sent his son there. He didn't do very well. You? (*Implying "You related?"*)

POMFRET   No connection.

CHARLES   It's a good school. But you asked me how could Mr. Dewey Kemp afford to run his garage that way?

POMFRET   Yes.

CHARLES   Around these parts whenever you see a man living in one of these little villages like Rockbottom, or Wheelwright, or Flour Mill, or Asa, or Sanctuary, any of these little hamlets, you can be doggone sure the man made his little pile. He's living retired. If he's in business, he's living semi-retired, don't have to worry about if the business makes money. Just something to keep him occupied. You take Mr. Studebaker, a very well-to-do man.

POMFRET   I understand.

CHARLES   All this around here is farming country. Mostly the men that live in the villages, they're retired farmers.

POMFRET   I see.

MARTHA   (*Returning*)   Charles, I think I'll have a Scotch and soda, please.

POMFRET   What's the story?

MARTHA   (*With a fast look at* CHARLES)   Well, good, and bad.

(CHARLES *serves her drink and tactfully goes to lobby*)

POMFRET   Let's hear the bad first.

MARTHA   Alex called Eleanor two or three hours ago and she was out. She called him back to find out what he wanted and he said he was worried about me. He said I hadn't come in from hunting, and there was something on the radio about a blizzard. It's not snowing badly down there, but it's snowing. Well, Eleanor stalled. She said she was expecting me, which she wasn't of course, dear Eleanor. And she said she heard me tell somebody I was going to their house for a cocktail, so he wasn't to worry about me. She made a little joke of it. She told Alex I might have had two cocktails, but anyway. He believed her, but just as a precautionary measure he was going to call the police and have them keep their eye out for the station wagon.

POMFRET Oh, God. The cops.

MARTHA The cops. The good part is: she's calling Alex now and telling him I'm at her house, taking a bath and then a nap. Nothing to worry about. She's telling him that she's going to try to persuade me to spend the night.

POMFRET Pretty shakey. And what did you tell Eleanor about us?

MARTHA She guessed. She's known for months that I'm in love with you. (*She laughs a little*)

POMFRET What's funny?

MARTHA Eleanor. She has a good dirty mind. She said we couldn't have had much fun if we were both in riding breeches.

POMFRET Little does—

MARTHA (*Putting her hand over his lips*) Never mind, now. This would have been a wonderful place. I'd like to spend a weekend here, wouldn't you?

POMFRET Yes. Just about this time of year. Have the maid come in and close the window and serve us breakfast.

MARTHA Not in bed, though. I don't like breakfast in bed.

POMFRET No, but a cup of coffee in bed.

MARTHA That'd be all right. Then breakfast in our dressing gowns.

POMFRET Then we'd decide what to do that day. Go for a walk and see the sights.

MARTHA   I don't imagine that'd take very long, here.

POMFRET   I wouldn't want it to. Just a short stroll, then back to the hay.

MARTHA   Aren't you exaggerating your prowess? We just got up, and after the night before . . .

POMFRET   You may be right. I need a little more rest. We could both rest. Maybe no stroll. Just back to bed after breakfast and rest till lunch.

MARTHA   Lunch in our room?

POMFRET   Sure. Spend the whole weekend in our room.

MARTHA   Have you ever done that?

POMFRET   Yes, in Atlantic City.

MARTHA   You didn't have to answer so quickly. You might have pretended to give it a moment's thought.

POMFRET   After a moment's thought, yes, in Atlantic City, I think it was, or Coney Island, it might have been. Or maybe it was the Ritz Hotel in Paris.

MARTHA   It was Atlantic City, and you know it. And it wasn't your wife. Who was it?

POMFRET   Not my wife, and not anybody you know, and in *fact*, and this is the God's honest truth, all I remember is the girl's name was Betty.

MARTHA   That's all you remember?

POMFRET   Of a statistical nature. One other statistic. I gave her a hundred dollars.

MARTHA   Oh, she was a whore.

POMFRET   No, she wasn't a whore. She was kind of a girl around New York. A photographers' model, well paid. I gave her the money because she cancelled a couple of jobs.

MARTHA   (*Sarcastically*)   Did you take her picture?

POMFRET   (*Laughing*)   No, but frankly, I thought of it. She was quite a dish.

MARTHA Yes, and she was probably used to posing for that kind of a picture, too.

POMFRET Listen, girl, it was so long ago. I don't want to remember her. I'm with you. You're my last love, my final love.

MARTHA I am? Why?

POMFRET Because you have a thin nose and sad eyes, and you're the picture of health.

MARTHA My eyes are sad? Am I supposed to like that?

POMFRET The way I mean it you are. Your eyes were the first thing I ever noticed about you.

MARTHA I don't believe *that*. I remember the dress I was wearing, and in that dress nobody noticed my eyes.

POMFRET I did, though. You were sitting down and you had your hands folded in your lap, and you were listening to Joe Lyle. Like this. (*He pantomimes*)

MARTHA And you thought I had sad eyes.

POMFRET I've thought so ever since. Wisdom, tenderness and sympathy, and love. I didn't know who you were or anything about you, but I knew there was love there.

MARTHA There is for you. There isn't for anyone else, but there is for you.

POMFRET I know. I say that because we haven't got time to kid around with each other.

MARTHA No, but thank God we do have the time we have got.

POMFRET You're worried, and I'm worried for you, and yet I've never been happier in my life.
(IRA, *stomping, enters*)

MARTHA Get your breath first, Mr. Studebaker.

IRA (*Puffing*) Certainly wish you folks could stay here for the night.

MARTHA   But *you* know . . . (*Taps her ring finger and shakes her head*)

IRA   (*Taking a drink of water*)   Well, I don't know about that. I guess if we looked back in the history of this old hotel, I wouldn't be surprised if we found one or two couples without benefit of clergy. (*Sitting with them*) Be that as it may. Here's my annual report to you folks. Went over to Dewey Kemp's grodge. Nothing. He's got a light going in his office, but not a sign of life. Next I took a walk down the other end of town where Dewey lives. First I banged on the door, front door. Then around the kitchen door. Even tried the cellar door. Scraped some snow off the cellar door and stomped my feet in case he might be working down-cellar. No answer. So—we don't get any gazzoline from Mr. Dewey Kemp. However, on my way back I remembered. My tank is full. I filled her up the day before yesterday and didn't use the car since, so I could easily spare you ten-fifteen gallons. Ten gallons'll surely take you to Norristown. My goodness, ten gallons oughta take you to—Baltimore, easy, in case you took a notion to drive to Baltimore. So what we can do, we can siphon out ten fifteen gallons out of my car and you're all set.

POMFRET   (*To* MARTHA)   Is there a siphon in your station wagon? A rubber hose?

MARTHA   I doubt it.

IRA   Oh, we can always find something around here. I'll bet Charles'll have a siphon. *Charles!* Oh, Char-rulls! (*As* CHARLES *enters*) The other thing, I spoke to one of the neighbors down the way. From what he tells me, you can't go a hundred feet without chains. Between here and Dieglersville you have a steep hill, up one side and down the other and a pretty narrow road, so you better put your chains on. As to the Wheelwright road, just forget about that. Nobody'll be coming or going that way for a couple days.

POMFRET (*To* MARTHA) Chains?

MARTHA No chains. I keep meaning to buy them.

IRA Well, what's that you have out there, what make?

POMFRET Buick station wagon.

IRA I think my chains'll fit it. Mine's an Oldsmobile sedan, about the same year. Forty-nine?

MARTHA Forty-nine, that's right.

POMFRET I'd have thought you'd own a Studebaker.

IRA On account of the name. Oh, I guess we must be related. They're of course Indiana people, South Bend, Indiana, is where they ended up at, but I guess there must of been some connection farther back. I don't remember whether my father said we were related or not. I know we used to have a Studebaker wagon and a Studebaker manure spreader when I lived on my parents' farm.

POMFRET Well—if Charles will give me a hand I'll steal some gas from your car and we can put on the chains. You know, there's no use my even trying to thank you, Mr. Studebaker.

MARTHA Try, though.

POMFRET No, I won't even try. But *you* can.

IRA Nobody has to thank me. I used to read those ads in the magazines, you know for the Statler hotels? Like how they have the railroad people hold a train for somebody? Or for instance the man that was making a speech at some other hotel and forgot his false teeth, but the Statler people sent one of their bellboys with the man's plate. You know those ads. They make good reading. Well, that's real hotel service, and we want to do as good.

POMFRET Except that we'll never be back.

MARTHA We might be. Some day. (*They are all silent for a moment, then* POMFRET *and* CHARLES *go out. The silence continues, not awkwardly*)

MARTHA (*Quietly but suddenly*) I'm a married woman with a young daughter. My husband is quite a few years older than I am and very rich.

IRA (*Letting her talk*) Mm-hmm.

MARTHA My husband is essentially a good man, kind. But if he knew where I am now he wouldn't want me to see my daughter ever again. My daughter is sweet, quite pretty, and we get along fine. But if her father were to bring her up, without me, I don't think it'd be good for her.

IRA Did you want to say anything more?

MARTHA No, I was just letting you know a little more about—me. Why?

IRA Well, just thinking. Your husband must be a good man. You can't even make yourself say anything against him. So you told me something about him, and about your daughter, and some more about yourself.

MARTHA I s'pose so. Have you children, Mr. Studebaker?

IRA No children. We lost the one, and then my wife had to have her tubes out. Does Mr. Pomfret have children?

MARTHA Two girls and a boy. The oldest girl's the same age as my daughter, then a girl sixteen and a boy eleven or twelve. They're all with their mother. He's been divorced about three years.

IRA On account of you.

MARTHA No, I didn't know him then.

IRA It's a hell of a situation.

MARTHA Up at Yale.

IRA What?

MARTHA Nothing. Tell me about this hotel, how you happened to buy it. I think we're on safer ground there.

IRA Yes. Well, I buried Irma on the tenth day of January, this year. She'd been very poorly for a number of years. When she had her tubes out that was a long time ago, and modern science didn't know as much about cancer as they do now. Had her tubes out, then later the one breast removed, and I'll tell you— What would you like me to call you?

MARTHA   Well, my name is Mrs. Alexander Paul, my first name is Martha. Mrs. Paul or Martha, whichever comes easiest to you.

IRA   I like the name Martha. Well, Martha, so Irma lingered on, but it was a merciful thing for her the day she died. I'd like to have a dollar for every time I was tempted to give her an overdose of some dope and end her suffering. But she always knew what I was thinking. She said to me more than once: "Ira," she'd say, with that sweet smile of hers on her face, "Ira, I know what you're thinking, but don't do it. I could do it myself, or we could do it together, but I'm happy being with you," she'd say. "If we took our own lives, we're not sure of the hereafter, but here we're together and we're sure of that." Then I'd be the one that would break down and cry like a baby, and all the time she was the one in pain. I buried her on the tenth day of January.

MARTHA   Mm-hmm.

IRA   One thing the doctors did know, they knew when she was gonna die. They told me how long she had, and I began making plans to sell out to my partner. I told him, I said I didn't want to be in Philadelphia once she died. The memories. But then what did I do? I brought Irma back here to Rockbottom, to the family plot. Both of us were from here, born here, courted here, married in that church across the way. Except for the one year I was at Normal and another year I was with the Reading we spent all our lives either here or in Philadelphia. We only ever lived in but three houses all our married life, married in '17. Well, after I buried Irma there were one or two things had to be taken care of and I took a room over at the hotel in Dieglersville. This old place was an old place when I left here as a young fellow starting out, but I don't know, I liked it, so I decided to look into the matter. Well, the bank was only too willing to let me take it off their hands and put my own money into it. My partner thought I was crazy with grief. He told me to take a rest and all, and when I told him I was going through with the deal he said if I went broke he'd always offer me a job with the old business. I don't know, maybe I'll be back selling bananas in a year or two, but a man's gotta keep himself occupied. And here I can remember Irma before she ever had any suffering, I remember her more as a young girl.

MARTHA   Mm-hmm.

IRA   I did two smart things, no matter what else I did. I signed up Marie Fenstermacher to do the cooking and act as sort of a housekeeper, and I hired Charles, Charles Mannering. Charles Moultrie Mannering. Mrs. Fenstermacher's uncle owned this place once and I always knew her. Charles I hired through asking around among my customers, hotel and club men in Philadelphia. He was with one of the society clubs in the city. I can just sit and listen to Charles by the hour. I put over a hundred and twenty thousand of my own money in this place, the way you see it now. I tried to keep it as much like the old-time farmers' hotel they used to have around here. You ought to take a look around if you had the time and see how this place is built. No nails in the timbering, not a nail, all pegs. Joists, some of them eighteen inches thick.

MARTHA *(Politely)*   Really?

IRA   Oh, my. Ira Studebaker, you certainly are a windbag. This is the longest I talked to any person since Irma passed away. How about a nice cup of coffee? You're going to want a cup of coffee before you go, and Mr. Pomfret will too. I wish I had a Thermos bottle to send you away with, but I don't think there's one anywhere around.

MARTHA   I'd love a cup of coffee.

(*He goes out and she stands up and strolls about purposelessly, lighting a cigarette, and in a good mood. She returns to her chair. She is just seated when the lobby outer door opens and a* LITTLE MAN *enters, rather tentatively as to entrance, but not vocally. He looks about, sees no one, and calls out*)

LITTLE MAN   Tillers of the soil! I say there, tillers of the soil! My good host! (*He proceeds to the bar and sees* MARTHA. *Delightedly*)   Well, now, say. *Tillers of the soil*. My prat. Are we just in time for the stirrup cup, old dear? Did we have good hunt-ting? Tally-ho.

MARTHA   Tally-ho yourself.

LITTLE MAN   (*Removing his pork-pie hat; he also is wearing a chocolate-brown wrap-around polo coat, soaking suede shoes*)   My name is Jerry Mayo.

MARTHA   It *is?*

MAYO   Oh, now, that's no way to be, Con-soo-ello. It *is* Consuelo, isn't it? It's gotta be Consuelo.

MARTHA   Not even close.

MAYO   This isn't an act, is it? You're the genuine, huntin' shootin', aren't you?

MARTHA   Huntin', not shootin'.

MAYO   You really wear those, uh, ascots and stuff.

MARTHA   (*Hand to throat*)   It's called a stock.

MAYO   Well, it's very becoming, on you. But you could put on an old cement bag and you'd do something for it. God was good to you.

MARTHA   Thank *you*, Mr. Mayo.

MAYO   Ahh, she remembers the name.

MARTHA   I once owned a horse from the County Mayo.

MAYO   A cousin of mine, no doubt. Tell me, what's the pitch here? Is this a private club or what? The sign says Hotel, but you got me wondering.

MARTHA   It's a brand new hotel. Or at least just reopened, today.

MAYO   Oh, I catch. And they invited the gentry for the premeer.

MARTHA   No, we arrived by accident.

MAYO (*Lighting a cigarette*)   I take it, then, you are not—alone?

MARTHA   Are you trying to move in, Mr. Mayo?

MAYO   Don't think I wouldn't like to. Maybe I'm not much bigger than a jockey, but I understand some of them do all right with you people.

MARTHA   Not that I ever heard of.

MAYO   Well, I didn't either, but I always like to believe the worst of everybody.

MARTHA (*With a hoity-toity accent*)   How perfectly appalling.

MAYO   You're a hip girl, Connie, I can see that, and I could bat the repartee with you all night, but where are the peasants that run this flea-bag? I got a couple of freezing broads out in the car. Two more minutes and they won't thaw out till spring, and we got work to do.

MARTHA   Well, bring them *in*. There'll be hot coffee any minute.

MAYO (*Goes to the main door and calls out:*)   Hey! Pickwicks! In!

(*Presently two girls appear, shivering; dressed alike in dyed muskrat coats, open-toed platform shoes, Truman-type caps. One of the girls is at least five years older than the other, and in spite of the identical clothes and make-up and height, they do not look alike. They are carrying small bags from a minor airline*)

MAYO   Connie, it gives me pleasure to present the Pickwick Sisters. This is Conchita, lovely Conchita, and this
is Paulette, pretty pret-ty Paulette. Pickwicks, this is
Connie. No last name.

PAULETTE   (*The older*)   Acquaintance.

CONCHITA   I'm sure.

MARTHA   (*Taking pity on them*)   Will you sit down? The
proprietor's getting some hot coffee.
(*The girls sit stiffly, without opening their coats, hands
folded in their laps. They stare at* MARTHA)

MARTHA   Are you lost, too?
(*They look at* MAYO)

MAYO   You had to be lost to get to this place. The early
settlers must of got lost. Which way you headed, pard-
ner?

MARTHA   . . . Norristown.

MAYO   I never heard of it. Is it far?

MARTHA   Fifty miles, more or less. (*To the girls*) How far
off do you think you are?

MAYO   I got news for you. These dreamboats, they're lost
on Twelth Avenya, and they were born on Eleventh.

PAULETTE   Oh, is that so?

CONCHITA   Is that so?

MAYO   (*To* MARTHA)   Answering your question, Reading,
P A is where we were headed, and where we gotta be
by eleven. Ah, here's our smiling host wit' the mocha-
java-coffee. Could you do that again, Sport? Three more
coffees and three ham on rye.
(IRA *serves* MARTHA *before taking a good look at the
newcomers, and what he sees he does not like*)

IRA   What can I do for you?

MAYO   First wit' the scoff.

IRA   Scarf? What scarf?

MAYO (*To* MARTHA)   He doesn't dig me. Not scarf arund the neck, Dad. Scoff, what you eat. Three mocha-java-coffee, and three ham on rye, and get the lead out.

IRA (*With great restraint*)   With mustard?

MAYO   With mustard to be sure. Mustard, cream and sugar, salt and pepper, a couple slices of dill pickle. The works. Go on now, Dad. We aint got all night.
(IRA *departs*)

MAYO (*To* MARTHA)   Where's the facilities? The little boys' I see, but I don't see the little girls'.

MARTHA   Up the stairs in the lobby.

MAYO   All right, Picksies, you heard the lady. Out there, up the steps. Or do you want me to unbutton you.

PAULETTE   You.

CONCHITA   You.
(*They go out. They walk past* POMFRET *as he comes in the lobby door and proceeds to the bar*)

POMFRET (*Completely ignoring* MAYO)   God.

MARTHA   All set?

POMFRET   I can't start the God damn thing. We siphoned off about ten gallons of gas, then the God damn thing wouldn't turn over. It's not the battery, and it isn't frozen. Charles thinks it may be the distributor. Who's this?

MAYO   Mayo's the name. Jerry Mayo.

MARTHA   Mr. Mayo's been entertaining me in your absence.

POMFRET   He has? How?

MAYO   Just a fellow castaway on life's shores, to meet and then pass on.

POMFRET   All right. Pass on.

MARTHA (*Quickly*)   Mr. Mayo is travelling with two young ladies, on their way to Reading. I gather they're in the theatrical business.

POMFRET Do you own that sedan across the street?

MAYO In twenty-four more payments, yes. (*Rising*) Look, I don't want to spoil your supper. I'm not sticking around where I'm not wanted.

MARTHA Oh, sit down.

POMFRET I can live without him.

MAYO Who writes your dialog, for God's sake?

MARTHA Oh, stop it, both of you. Grow up.

MAYO Who writes *your* dialog, Connie?

MARTHA (*As the* PICKWICKS *march in*) This is Mr. Pomfret, Miss Conchita Pickwick, and Miss Paulette Pickwick.
(POMFRET *rises reluctantly, quickly sits down again*)

MARTHA (*Trying to get peace*) I was just saying, I made a guess that you're in the theatrical business.
(*The girls look at* MAYO)

MAYO Well, yes. We are of the theater, one could say. Not Noel Coward, but we do take an occasional ad in Billboard.
(IRA *appears with the additional coffee and sandwiches*)

IRA Everything okay, Mr. Pomfret?

POMFRET Got the gas in the car, but now it won't turn over.

IRA Couldn't get the chains on?

POMFRET Couldn't start the engine. I wonder if I could have a cup of coffee, please.

CONCHITA Take mine.

PAULETTE Take mine.

MAYO Brother, you're *in*.

POMFRET Am I, brother?

MAYO I got news for you. I never saw them offer anybody anything to eat since I knew them. You *gotta* be in.

CONCHITA Half of my sandwich?

PAULETTE   The lady wish half of my sandwich?

MARTHA   We've had dinner, thanks. But thanks ever so much.

IRA (*To* POMFRET)   I'll get your coffee for you.

MAYO (*To* IRA)   Say, I must be losing my manners. Conchita Pickwick, and Paulette Pickwick, this is Mr. Farmers. Mr. Farmers runs the Farmers Hotel.

MARTHA   Mr. Studebaker.

IRA   Glad to meet you.

PAULETTE   Acquaintance.

CONCHITA   I'm sure.

IRA   I'll get the coffee. (DR. GRAEFF *enters*) Folks, this is Dr. Graeff, J. Henry Graeff. Henry, you introduce yourself while I get this gentleman his coffee. (IRA *goes out*)

GRAEFF   Good evening, good evening.

MAYO   Heavenly days, it's Doctor Gamble.

GRAEFF   Now your name is?

MARTHA   Mrs. Paul. And this is Miss Pickwick, another Miss Pickwick, Mr. Mayo, and Mr. Pomfret. Dr. Graeff?

GRAEFF   I see. Well, some weather.

MAYO (*In a stage whisper to* MARTHA)   I wonder who writes his dialog. (*Then louder*) Taint a fit night out for man nor beast.

POMFRET   That's W. C. Fields.

MAYO   Ooh. Oooh. He's *quick*.

GRAEFF   Anybody care for a little something stronger than coffee?

MAYO (*As they hesitate*)   Well—there was this guy went into a saloon with his horse, and he said to the bartender, "Give my horse a bucketful of whiskey." So the bartender gave the horse a bucket of whiskey and the horse drank it. "Fill her up again," the guy said, and the bartender gave the horse another bucket of whiskey.

"How much?" the guy said, and the bartender said, "That'll be twenty dollars, but how about you having a drink on the house?" "Me?" the guy said. "Not me, I'm driving."

(*The* PICKWICKS *titter,* GRAEFF *laughs,* MARTHA *smiles, but* POMFRET *does not*)

MAYO (*Condescendingly to* POMFRET) The guy said: "Not me, I'm driving."

POMFRET I got it. I got it three years ago, the first time I heard the story.

MAYO I got news for you. Three years is brand new for one of my stories, the ones I give away free.

POMFRET (*Rising*) Going back and see how Charles is coming along.

MARTHA Do you want me to go with you?

POMFRET (*With affection*) Lord, no.

GRAEFF Well, business looks pretty good for the first night. Of course every night isn't a snow storm.

MAYO It ought to be good for the doctoring business. I guess the peasants'll be cracking their skulls all over the ice tomorrow. Say, speaking of tomorrow, we got work to do tonight. Doc, where is Reading?

GRAEFF Reading?

MAYO The place that Bobby Clark sings about. Robert the roué from Reading, P A. Where is it? And how do you get there?

GRAEFF Tonight if you want to go there you'll have to go by dog sled.

MAYO Uh-huh. Now you laid *your* egg. I'll feed you another straight line. You're sittin' there, I'm sittin' here, and I say to you, Doc, how do we get to Reading. Only, this time how about giving me a straight answer?

GRAEFF Well . . .

(*He is interrupted by pounding on the side door at Left. He gets up and opens the door, turning the key to do so,*

*and admitting a husky man in truck-driver's uniform
and mackinaw. The truck driver looks contemptuously
at the company and then goes to the bar and waits*)

TRUCKER   Well, don't I get no service?

GRAEFF   I'm not the bartender, but I guess I can wait on
you. What can I get you?

TRUCKER   Straight rye, water on the side.
(*The doctor puts a bottle and glasses on the bar*)

TRUCKER   Who owns that God damn station wagon?

MARTHA   I do.

TRUCKER   You'll have to move it out of the way.

MARTHA   That's what they're trying to do, but you needn't
be so tough about it.

TRUCKER   *Who's* trying to move it? I didn't see nobody.

MARTHA   Well, take another look, because there are *two*
people trying to get it started. Something about the
distributor.

TRUCKER   It don't take two people to fix a distributor.

MARTHA   Why don't *you* try it then.

PAULETTE   Yes, why don't *you* try it?

CONCHITA   Yes.

TRUCKER (*To the Pickwicks*)   Who the hell asked you for
advice?

MARTHA   If you can start my car we'll be only too glad to
get out of the way. As a matter of fact I don't think we
are in the way.

TRUCKER   Go on out and take a look at my truck. It
makes three of your God damn station wagon. Grampa,
gimme another shot.

GRAEFF   Help yourself.

TRUCKER (*To himself*)   I got a load of milk . . . (*He
interrupts himself to toss off the drink*)

MAYO   You're gonna have another load in a minute, and
it won't be milk.

TRUCKER   Oh, a wise guy.
   (*He saunters over to the table*)

PAULETTE   Don't you touch him!

CONCHITA   Don't you dare touch him!
   (TRUCKER *grins and flips* MAYO's *tie*)

MARTHA   Oh, stop it, you big bully. Go on, get out of
   here.

TRUCKER   (*Grinning but angry*)   Oh, I see you got a necktie on too.

MARTHA   You touch me and I'll brain you with this
   ketchup bottle.

GRAEFF   Cut it out now. If you create a disturbance in
   here I'll send for the state police. Now get on about
   your business and leave these people alone.
   (TRUCKER *returns to the bar and the others watch him
   tensely, silently, until* MARTHA *speaks*)

MARTHA   Why can't you be nice and see if you can start
   my car?

TRUCKER   You wanted to hit me with the ketchup bottle.

MARTHA   I'm sorry about that, but please go and see if
   you can't do something about the station wagon? You
   want to go just as much as we do.
   (TRUCKER *considers this, and while he is doing so a highway patrolman enters from side door, removing his
   gauntlets*)

TROOPER   Good evening, Doc. All these people stuck?

GRAEFF   Hello, Corporal. Yes, they seem to be.

TROOPER   (*To* TRUCKER)   Is that your Diesel out there?

TRUCKER   Yeah.

TROOPER   Well, get moving. You're blocking the highway.

TRUCKER   I can't get by that station wagon.

MARTHA   It's my station wagon, Officer. He's going to help
   get it started.

TROOPER   What's the matter with it?

MARTHA   It won't start.

TROOPER   I gathered that. Is the battery dead?

MARTHA   I don't know.

TROOPER   You're not gonna find out sitting here. Let's take a look at it.

MARTHA   My husband and the bartender are working on it.

(IRA *enters*)

IRA   Good evening, Corporal.

TROOPER   Hello, Mr. Studebaker. I see you're busy already.

IRA   How about a nice cup of coffee or anything.

TROOPER   Thanks, but I haven't got time. I want to get this fellow out of the way and the station wagon.

IRA   They're working on the station wagon. They took off the distributor and they're working on it in my garage, where the light's better.

TROOPER   (*To* TRUCKER) Why don't you go and help them? And lay off that booze or I'll run you in.

TRUCKER   I was just trying to get warm.

TROOPER   Yeah. Get warm and fall asleep and plough into somebody. Go on, beat it.

(TRUCKER *goes out main door*)

TROOPER   Which way you headed, lady?

MARTHA   Well, Norristown.

TROOPER   Go by Dieglersville. The Wheelwright road's blocked. What about you? (*To* MAYO) Do you own the Chevvy with the New York plates?

MAYO   Yes sir. We're on our way to Reading.

TROOPER   Give up. You're lucky to be in a hotel.

MAYO   Why?

TROOPER   You won't make Reading tonight. No roads passable.

MAYO   But we gotta be there by eleven o'clock.

TROOPER Didn't you hear what I said? You can't even get there by eleven o'clock in the morning. You can't even get to Flour Mill, three miles to the west of here.

MAYO But we got a Legion date.

TROOPER I can't help that. Listen, I wish you'd all stay here, including you, lady. The truck, he might get through, but it's gonna get worse before it gets better. Don't you have a radio, Mr. Studebaker?

IRA Mrs. Fenstermacher has a little one in the kitchen she listens to.

TROOPER (*Drawing on gauntlets*) You folks don't know when you're lucky. I wish I could hole up here for the night. Goodnight all. (*He exits*)

IRA Well, I'll be glad to have you all. That's what we're here for. Plenty of room, plenty to eat and drink, and it's nice and warm, with the furnace going and the stove. (*No one speaks*) We even have a doctor, in case we have any sickness.

MAYO Yeah. I got a pain in the bankroll. Can he fix that? (CONCHITA PICKWICK *starts to cry and* MARTHA *gets up and puts a hand on her shoulder and the others try to comfort her*)

MARTHA AND THE OTHERS There now. Now, now. It's not so bad. We're all together. Don't cry, honey.

CURTAIN

ACT TWO

SCENE ONE

*The scene is the same as Act One. The action is continuous.
At rise the people are in the same positions as at end of
Act One, except that* IRA STUDEBAKER *is alone in the lobby,
in a pensive mood, rubbing his hands up and down his
vest, frowning. He is concerned about his duties as boni-
face, his responsibilities to these people. He comes to a
decision, goes to the swinging door and beckons to* MARTHA
PAUL.

IRA   Uh—Mrs. Paul, could I see you a minute please?

MARTHA   (*Rising*)   Of course. Excuse me. (*Joining* IRA
  in lobby)

IRA   I want to get your advice on something.

MARTHA   Yes? I'm going to have to ask yours, too, but you
  go ahead.

IRA   No, you go ahead. Ladies first.

MARTHA   Well, I want to know first of all, how does that
  state policeman get around if the roads are blocked?

IRA   Why, he has a jeep with snow tires.

MARTHA   I see. You don't think my station wagon . . . ?

IRA   I'm afraid not.

MARTHA   But he seemed to think the big truck can get through to Dieglerville.

IRA   Dieglersville, Yes.

MARTHA   Then how'd it be if we followed the truck? The truck would make a path for us and we could follow it.

IRA   Well, of course you gotta take into consideration, the truck is much wider than your station wagon, a wider tread.

MARTHA   You know how important it is for me to get home tonight.

IRA   Yes. I know you can't help worrying, but I have this feeling something will turn up. I just have a feeling.

MARTHA   I wish I had. What were you going to ask me?

IRA   Well, I was wondering—to take people's minds off their troubles. I was thinking I'd set up a buffet here, everybody could help themselves to something to eat, or we could serve it at the tables in the bar.

MARTHA   Mm-hmm.

IRA   First I thought of the dining room.

MARTHA   It does seem the logical place.

IRA   It does. But if we have it in the bar, we're closer to the liquor, and the only way to get people's minds off their troubles is get a few snorts in them. They won't eat much anyway.

MARTHA   A party.

IRA   On the house, naturally. Everything on the house.

MARTHA   As far as that goes I'd just as soon give the party —if you'll take my cheque.

IRA   No, now this was my idea.

MARTHA   All right.

IRA   You'll earn your supper.

MARTHA   How?

IRA   Well, I was hoping you'd act as the hostess. I'm no good at those kind of things, but you I imagine, you

often give those big dinner parties. You know how to
run things, make people feel at home.

MARTHA   But what about Mrs. Fenster—Fenster—

IRA   Mrs. Fenstermacher? Oh, she's worse than I am. She
said when I hired her, Don't count on me to do anything
but the kitchen and housekeeping. I don't want to have
to talk to people, she said. Very shy.

MARTHA   Well, she *will* have to talk to *me*.

IRA   You're different. She meant drummers. She still calls
salesmen drummers. She don't hold a very high opinion
of salesmen. (*He goes to dining room door and calls
out:*) Maria? Mrs. Fenstermacher?
(MRS. FENSTERMACHER *appears, a woman in her late
fifties, wearing a big apron. She is stout, dignified*)

MARIA   Uh-huh?

IRA   Maria, this is Mrs. Paul. Mrs. Paul, this is Mrs.
Fenstermacher.

MARTHA   How do you do, Mrs. Fenstermacher?

MARIA   Pleased to meet you. (*She tries not to be rude
about* MARTHA's *attire, but cannot keep her eyes off the
breeches and boots*)

IRA   Mrs. Paul and a friend of hers got lost and they're
miles from home. Also we got in the bar two young ladies
and a man that also got lost and they're on their way
to Reading, only the roads are out to Reading.

MARIA   That's how many?

MARTHA   Two of us, and three of them.

IRA   They may have to spend the night.

MARIA   Well, we're in that business. The rooms are ready.
We can take care of them all.

IRA   Before that I was thinking— You explain it, Mrs.
Paul.

MARTHA   Mr. Studebaker thought we might have a buffet,
here or in the bar.

MARIA   For how many?

MARTHA   Yes, we didn't decide that, Mr. Studebaker.

IRA   Everybody.

MARIA   How many is everybody?

MARTHA   Yes, I think for instance we ought to invite the truck driver.

IRA   Everybody. Henry Graeff, the truck driver, Charles.

MARIA   Charles ate. He put nearly a whole roast chicken away.

IRA   Well, maybe he can put away another one.

MARTHA   No, not if this is to be buffet.

MARIA   She's right. No roast chicken for buffet. I have a ham and I can give you cold roast beef from yesterday. (*To* MARTHA) Was there something the matter with my steak?

MARTHA   It was a beautiful steak, Mrs. Fenstermacher, but I wasn't hungry.

IRA   She's worried about getting home.

MARIA (*Subtly*)   I would be, too.

MARTHA (*Trying to overlook the crack*)   Well, now. Five of us already mentioned. Doctor Graeff is six. The truck driver is seven. Charles is eight, and you two makes ten.

MARIA   Henry Graeff is lucky if he eats a piece of bread and butter. He never eats.

IRA   I'll make up for him.

MARIA   *You* eat too *much*, that's the difference. I had my supper.

MARTHA   But at least you'll sit with us. Mr. Studebaker wants this to be a party.

MARIA   Mm. Well, I have enough to feed you. I'll put on the sweet and sour relishes, some somer-sausage, bologna, liverwurst, I have this ham and the cold roast beef. Potato salad, I may run a little short there. I have a dozen pies on the window sill cooling. Oh, they're cool by this time. I can mix a bowl of endive salad. Will you want soup? I have a bean soup on the range and soup's good on a cold night.

IRA   Her soup's a meal in itself.

MARIA   It's a good thick soup, and with home-made bread, fresh butter. And I have a couple dozen hard-boiled eggs I could easily devil them. It won't be a regular meal, but it'll be filling if you eat it all.

MARTHA   (*Enthusiastically*)   It sounds wonderful.

MARIA   A good thick brown gravy for the cold roast beef.

IRA   We can put it in here and eat in the bar.

MARIA   I don't understand why you want to eat in the bar. You put all that money in the dining room. (*To* MARTHA) He put all that money in the dining room furniture and now he doesn't want to use it.

MARTHA   I think the idea is it'd be more informal in the bar.

MARIA   Yes, and the liquor's closer. Was that Henry Graeff's idea?

IRA   No, it was mine.

MARIA   It sounds more like Henry Graeff.

IRA   Well now, I'll start setting up the table. I'll get a couple planks and horses, get that little fellow to help me. (*To* MARIA) This one little fellow, he looks like one of those barkers on the Midway during the Allentown Fair.

MARIA   When was I ever at the Midway at the Allentown Fair?

MARTHA   What can I do to help you, Mrs. Fenstermacher?

MARIA   Thanks, but I'll be better off by myself.

IRA   She don't like to have anybody in her kitchen.

MARIA   I'll need help later, but not now.

(*She exits and* IRA *and* MARTHA *enter the bar*)

IRA   Folks, we're going to have a party.

MAYO   Yummy! Can I come?

IRA   Everybody can come. Mrs. Paul . . . ?

MARTHA   Well, Mr. Studebaker would like us to, as he put it, get our minds off our troubles. Most of us are anxious to be on our way to some place or other, but since that seems to be impossible, at least for the moment, Mr. Studebaker, the gracious and hospitable proprietor of The Farmers Hotel, is, uh, well, throwing a party. We're going to have a perfectly elegant buffet, and drinks are on the house.

IRA   Everything's on the house.

MAYO (*To* PICKWICKS)   Eat up, Pixies, it'll probly be your last good meal for a month.

MARTHA   Mr. Mayo, you're delegated to help Mr. Studebaker set up the table.

MAYO   All right if he shows me how.

PAULETTE   What can *we* do?

CONCHITA   Yes?

MARTHA   At the moment, just make yourselves pretty.

MAYO   That'll be a day's work.

PAULETTE   Oh, you.

CONCHITA   You.

PAULETTE   Can we wait? I mean serve?

MAYO   Buffet. Cafeteria style, girls.

IRA   You can help, ladies. After we set up the table you can bring in the dishes and silverware.

MAYO   I'd keep an eye on that silverware, Dad.

THE PICKWICKS   Oh, you.

GRAEFF   Am I elected bartender?

IRA   You're elected, temporarily.

GRAEFF   Well, who wants what?

MARTHA   Do you know how to make a Side Car? That's what I'd like.

GRAEFF   I think I'll have one myself. Anybody else?

PAULETTE   One for me, please?

CONCHITA   I'll have one, please.

MAYO   Without even asking what it is?

PAULETTE   I know what a Side Car is. It has brandy in it.

CONCHITA   See?

IRA   There you are. Well, come on, young fellow.
    (*They exit through dining room door*)

PAULETTE   (*To* MARTHA, *as they sit down*)   Were you in
    some horse show?

MARTHA   Today? No. I was fox-hunting. Mr. Pomfret and
    I. Are you interested in horses?

PAULETTE   I stard out to be an equestrienne.

MARTHA   You did?

PAULETTE   I was born with the John show.

MARTHA   I don't think I know what that is.

PAULETTE   The John Robinson Circus. My mother and
    father were the Palermos, bareback riders. Perhaps you
    heard of them?

MARTHA   I don't *think* so.

PAULETTE   I thought you would because they were a
    famous act. I was intended to be with them, but I
    think Ringlings bought out the John show. Yes, I'm
    pretty sure.

CONCHITA   (*Moving in*)   Did you ever hear of LaRue and
    LaRue?

MARTHA   Let me think. LaRue and LaRue.

CONCHITA   (*Helpfully*)   Dancers.

MARTHA   (*Faking*)   I think I *did*.

CONCHITA   A standard on the Sun time. They were my
    father and mother. Fatally injured in a train wreck out-
    side of Fresno, California.

GRAEFF   (*Serving drinks, humorously*)   If you'd care to hear about my background. I was born across the street and I've never been any place else. How's that for a dull life?

PAULETTE   One of my parents was almost fatally injured in a train wreck near Lebanon, P A. My father.

GRAEFF   That's not far from Reading.

CONCHITA   Lucky for me I was staying with my aunt in Glendale, California, or I'da been killed.

MARTHA   Heavens.

PAULETTE   My father lost the use of his right arm and we sued the railroad for over a hundred thousand dollars.

CONCHITA   You never told me that, Polly.

PAULETTE   But it happened.

MARTHA   Did you win?

PAULETTE   Win what?

MARTHA   The hundred thousand dollars.

PAULETTE   (*Humorously*)   If we'da won that do you think I'd be here? No, all my father got was they paid the doctor bill and I think around six hundred dollars is all.

MARTHA   It doesn't seem fair.

PAULETTE   My mother always said the lawyer we got, she was sure he was in the pay of the railroad company.

MARTHA   Was it the Reading Railway, do you remember?

PAULETTE   I think it was. I'm pretty sure it was, why?

MARTHA   Then I'm embarrassed, because—some of my family have stock in the Reading.

PAULETTE   (*Quickly*)   Then I take it back. I didn't mean to hurt your feelings.

MARTHA   Thank you, Paulette. The only trouble is, your mother was probably right.

(HOWARD, JOE ROGG *the truck driver, and* CHARLES *enter the lobby, look at their hands and exit to the washroom*)

GRAEFF (*To* PAULETTE)   Did your father have to retire?

PAULETTE   Retire?

GRAEFF   After he lost the use of his right arm.

PAULETTE   Well, he had to retire from the act.

GRAEFF   Then what did he do?

PAULETTE   Well, let me think a minute. For a while he played piano for the DeZito Brothers, the carnival show.

GRAEFF (*Making a gesture of playing the piano, especially broadly playing the treble part, none of which* PAULETTE *can see but which is seen by* MARTHA)   Indeed? That's interesting.

PAULETTE   Then after that he was in a ticket booth selling tickets.
(GRAEFF *goes through a routine of selling tickets off a roll, making change, etc.*)

GRAEFF   Mm-hmm. Mm-hmm.

PAULETTE   Pop was a kind of an all-around man when it came to circuses and carnivals.

GRAEFF   He must have been. (MAYO *and* IRA *set up the table in the bar*) And you, young lady, (*To* CONCHITA) did you ever get any money from the railroad company?

CONCHITA   If we did I never saw it. I was raised by my grandmother till I was fourteen, then I ran away. I never thought about that. Maybe I ought to find out.
(HOWARD *enters bar, goes to* MARTHA *and kisses her*)

HOWARD   What goes on?

MARTHA   A party. Mr. Studebaker's having a party for the snowbound.

IRA   Just a little get-together, take our minds off our troubles. The highway patrol says you can't get through.

HOWARD   Maybe not, but we're going to make a try. The station wagon's okay. The truck driver fixed it, and we've got the chains on, gassed up, ready to roll.

MARTHA   The policeman said we can't make it.

IRA   The only way you can make it is if the big truck will break the snow for you.

(ROGG *enters, takes his place at the bar*)

MARTHA   You talk to him, we (*Meaning herself and the* PICKWICKS) can help with the dishes and things.

(*They go out and* HOWARD *stands beside* JOE ROGG)

HOWARD   I have another favor to ask you.

JOE ROGG   Why sure, you old son of a bitch.

HOWARD   First I'll soften you up with a drink. What will you have?

JOE   Nuts, I'll buy you a drink.

GRAEFF   It doesn't make any difference. The drinks are all on the house.

CHARLES (*Getting behind the bar*)   Everything on the house.

JOE   Rye, water chaser.

HOWARD   Scotch and water.

MAYO   Oh, a beer, I guess.

GRAEFF   I'll take a couple of ounces of rye, Charles.

JOE   Be careful, Doc, it might throw you.

GRAEFF   I'll throw it right back.

JOE (*To* HOWARD)   What's the favor you want?

HOWARD   Well, how long before you're leaving?

JOE   What are you, hintin' for me to go?

HOWARD   Not at all, when you go, I go.

JOE   My pal!

HOWARD   Exactly. You see, Joe, here's the situation, apparently the road is blocked, at least blocked as far as the station wagon's concerned. But you, with that big Diesel, you can probably get through, and I can follow you with the station wagon, in your tracks, so to speak.

JOE (*Thinking*)   Yeah. Uh-huh. What's the favor?

HOWARD   Just that we get started fairly soon.

JOE   Yeah? How soon is fairly soon? This old bastard's givin' out with the free booze and all—

HOWARD   Oh, I didn't mean right away. But say in—an hour?

JOE   All right, maybe an hour, maybe not that long. Maybe I'll want to go before an hour, see what I mean?

HOWARD   Fine. Fine. Just so we're on our way in an hour. I'll make it worth your while.

JOE   How? You mean money?

HOWARD   I mean money.

JOE   I got plenty of money. You don't believe that, do you, you big son of a bitch?

HOWARD   Sure I believe it.

JOE   (*Extracting money from a shirt pocket*)   If you don't believe it, here, take a look. Ten, twenty, thirty, forty, fifty, sixty, seventy, eighty, ninety, *one* hundred. A hundred and twenty, hundred and forty, hundred sixty, hundred and eighty, *two* hundred. Two-fifty, three hundred. *Three*-fifty, four hundred. Four-fifty, five hundred. *Six* hundred. *Seven* hundred. *Eight* hundred. And not counting some small change in my pants pocket. Over eight hundred bucks.

MAYO   That's quite a bundle.

JOE   You're God damn right it is, little fellow.

IRA   That's a lot of cash to carry around.

HOWARD   That's what I was thinking.

JOE   Somebody take it off me, you mean?

HOWARD   Well, as What's His Name said, it's quite a bundle, and if somebody saw you with it they might want to *try*. In fact, I'm tempted myself.

JOE   Aah, you old son of a bitch, you're too honest. I can tell by lookin' at you.

HOWARD   Well, thanks. That's not an opinion generally shared, but I'm glad *you* think I have an honest face.

JOE   You wouldn't have to stick me up or like that. Here, you want a hundred dollars? Here.

HOWARD   Be careful, I might take you up on that.

JOE   What's a hundred dollars to you? I can tell a millionaire when I see one, and not only the horseback-riding outfit. I knew a joker in the army, and all of us wearing fatigues, but I could tell him for a millionaire, just by looking at him. (*Puts his hand on* IRA's *shoulder*) This fellow, he got a little, but no millionaire. The Doc, there, Christ he never saw a million, and the little fellow there, I bet he never had five hundred bucks at one time in his whole life. Am I right?

GRAEFF   As far as I'm concerned you are.

IRA   Mm-hmm.

JOE   But what about you, you old son of a bitch? You're not saying if I was right or wrong.

HOWARD   I guess my father may have had a million at one time or other.

JOE   That's what I'm saying. Your old man had it, and you blew it, you blew it on dames and booze.

HOWARD   I got rid of a fair sum, but not a million.

JOE   Maybe Charlie there, Charlie, you a millionaire?

CHARLES   All in gilt-edged securities.

JOE   You're all right, Charlie. And a pretty good mechanic, too.

CHARLES   Well, maybe. Only don't go around offering us millionaires those C-notes.

JOE   Don't you worry, I ain't offering C-notes to anybody that's liable to take them.

HOWARD   What if I'd crossed you? I could have crossed you, you know.

JOE   But I knew you wouldn't. (*Puts money back in*

pocket) You guys wonder how a guy pushing a truck, how he happens to go around with over eight hundred bucks in his pocket.

HOWARD   Why, I thought you fellows made that much every week.

JOE   Aah, you old son of a bitch. We do all right, but no eight hundred a week. No, the way I got this dough. I bet.

HOWARD   You bet. The horses?

JOE   The horses? The horses is for chumps. Nobody ever beat the horses. I bet on football games. I got twenty or thirty bets going every Saturday. The garage where I work out of, and one where I frequent over in Jersey, the guys that push trucks, they bet with me.

MAYO   You make book?

JOE   I make bets. I don't make no God damn book. I bet with guys and they know me. You might say I run a private betting establishment.

HOWARD   Isn't that dangerous?

JOE   On account of the law?

HOWARD   I wasn't thinking so much of the law.

JOE   You mean I'm muscling in? You're right. I am muscling in. I'm muscling in on the syndicate.

HOWARD   That's what I meant by dangerous.

JOE   Yeah, but I'm pretty tough too.

HOWARD   Do you always know who's going to win?

JOE   Pretty near always.

HOWARD   How's Harvard going to do this Saturday?

JOE   Harvard I can count on. Harvard always loses.

MARTHA (*Entering bar*)   Gentlemen, dinner is served.

JOE (*Putting his arm around* HOWARD *and nodding toward* MARTHA)   You son of a bitch, you can pick them.

HOWARD   Well—*this* time.

(*He kisses* MARTHA, *and the people begin the business of picking places to sit, helping themselves to plates and to food, with* MARIA *behind the tables, also* CHARLES *and* IRA. *After a certain amount of milling about* MARTHA *takes charge*)

IRA   Mrs. Paul, will you take care of the seating arrangements?

MARTHA   Well, let's see. The table has room for twelve, and without Charles we're nine. Nine means two men will have to sit side by side, somewhere. We'll start at the head of the table. Mr. Studebaker. Then me, I'm putting myself on your right. Mr. Mayo next to me. Howard, you next to Mr. Mayo, then Mrs. Fenstermacher at that end. On her right, the doctor. Next to the doctor Conchita, then Mister Rogg, and on his right Paulette.

IRA   Perfect. Perfect.

MARTHA   Not quite perfect, but—

GRAEFF   Works out fine, I think.

(*They take their seats and after a small awkward pause,* MARTHA *speaks to* IRA *to get the conversational ball rolling*)

MARTHA   Well, I think this is very pleasant. I'm not only a guest at your first dinner, but I've even had the honor of helping with your party.

IRA   Helping. Without you there wouldn't be any party.

(*Attention now goes to* ROGG *and the* PICKWICKS)

PAULETTE   Are you from this place?

JOE   No, where you from?

PAULETTE   New York.

JOE   New York City?

PAULETTE   That's right.

JOE   Is this here kid your sister? She don't look like you.

PAULETTE   We're supposed to look a lot alike. We do an act together in show business.

JOE   Yeah? What does he do? The little fellow.

MAYO   (*Overhearing*)   I'm a weight lifter.

JOE   You a weight lifter?

MAYO   Military press. Snatch and grab. Sure.

JOE   How much can you lift?

MAYO   I was only kidding. I couldn't even lift the tab for the supper.

JOE   Well then what do you do? Is he your pimp?

PAULETTE   Lay off, now. Be nice.

JOE   Hell, if he can kid I can kid too.

(*The moment of uneasiness passes, but not forever, and with some reservations about the future the others eat and sip as the* CURTAIN *is lowered for the end of the scene*)

SCENE TWO

As the CURTAIN *rises on this scene which in time follows the preceding by an hour or so, the women are removing the last of the dishes, the men are seated, sprawling in some cases, full of food and with enough to drink to make them feel good, but no one is drunk, although* JOE ROGG *is not unaware of* CONCHITA's *walk as she carries out some dishes.*

MAYO   Just right. Just right. I don't even want another cuppa coffee.

IRA (*Going to bar*)   Cigars? Who'll have a cigar?

CHARLES (*Rising from a chair*)   I'll get em. (*To* IRA) The
—uh? (*Implying the expensive cigars*)
(IRA *nods.* CHARLES *gets cigars and starts to pass them*)

CHARLES   Won't find a cigar as good as this within fifty
miles, gentlemen.

GRAEFF   I can vouch for that. Ira, you know all the children I delivered in this community—I don't mind getting up at four o'clock a.m. and so forth and so on, but
the next day, usually it's the next day, the proud poppa
always forces some El Ropo on me. Or used to till I
began telling them I didn't smoke.

ROGG (*To* MAYO)   Don't let it throw you there, little
fellow.

MAYO (*Trying to be pleasant*)   Don't worry about me. I
smoked cigars when I was ten years old. O P B's we used
to call them. Other People's Butts. Man'd throw away
a cigar and us kids grab it before it hit the sidewalk,
stick a toothpick in it.

ROGG   They sure did stunt your growth.

MAYO   Maybe. Something did. I got a brother over six
feet tall.

ROGG   Yeah, but how do you know he's your brother?

GRAEFF (*Covering up*)   There are satisfactory explanations
for those uh, differences in size.

ROGG   If I was married and my wife—

HOWARD   How big was *your* father?

ROGG   My father? I guess you'd call him about medium
height.

HOWARD   How big was your mother?

ROGG   Small. Only about— Come on, you old son of a
bitch. You're trying to trick me. Huh? Trying to trick
me?

HOWARD   Right.

GRAEFF   As I say, there are satisfactory explanations for these discrepancies.

CHARLES   (*Wisely*) Mm-hmm. They can always be explained, especially where I come from originally.

IRA   (*Puffing at his cigar*) Charles, how about a little music?

CHARLES   Sure, why not? What on?

IRA   The horn. Your trombone.

GRAEFF   Do you play the trombone, Charles?

IRA   Name something he doesn't do.

CHARLES   I play a little trombone.

GRAEFF   Slide, or valve? I used to play valve in the Rock-bottom Boys Band, forty, forty-two-or-three years ago.

CHARLES   Yes sir, I played a little slide when I was with Lieutenant Jim Europe's band. That was in World War One.

(MARTHA *enters, going to* HOWARD'S *side*)

MARTHA   Electric dish washer. As big as the Waldorf's, I'll bet.

HOWARD   We're going to have some music.

MARTHA   We can't stay too long, you know.

CHARLES   (*Bringing trombone from behind bar*) A few scales. My embouchure is a little out of practice.

ROGG   Let's have a crap game.

HOWARD   Let's have the music.

IRA   No gambling, please. I like a friendly poker game, but anybody comes in and sees a dice game, it wouldn't look right.

ROGG   Roll anybody high dice for a hundred bucks.

HOWARD   Now you heard what Mr. Studebaker said.

(ROGG *starts to sulk as* CHARLES *plays "Getting Sentimental Over You"*)

ROGG   (*At the end of the solo*) Play "Tiger Rag."

MAYO   Oh, God no.

ROGG   Who the hell asked you?
 (CHARLES *plays "Tiger Rag" and all through it* ROGG *shouts "Hold that tiger" and bangs on the table*)

CHARLES   Mr. Studebaker? Any requests?

IRA   Well—there's one I always liked. A hymn. "Nearer My God to Thee."

ROGG   Jesus Christ!

MAYO   Yeah, that's the general idea.

HOWARD (*To* MAYO)   Don't needle him, he's liable to pop you.
 (CHARLES *plays the hymn while* ROGG *sings "Nero My Dog Has Fleas"*)

CHARLES   The ladies have any preference? Mrs. Fenstermacher?

MARIA   Well—how about "There Are Smiles"?
 (MARTHA *and* MAYO *sing two-part harmony to the song*)

PAULETTE   Can you play—"A Pretty Girl Is Like a Melody"?

CHARLES   Any special key, ma'am?

MARTHA   I have an idea. Why don't the Pickwick Sisters sing a duet? Don't you usually sing together?

MAYO   They sing together *when* they sign together.

PAULETTE   Get *him.*

ROGG   That's right. The dames sing.

PAULETTE (*To* CONCHITA)   Will we?

CONCHITA   Sure, I don't care. I be glad to oblige.

PAULETTE (*To* MAYO)   We do a number from the act? What about a piano?

MAYO   I got one in the car. (*To the others*) Paulette's a girl that one time she lost two bass drums. (*This is a sarcastic reference to her failure to notice a covered piano in the bar*)

PAULETTE   I never lost no bass drum, let alone two.

CONCHITA　No, you shouldn't say that, Jerry.

(HOWARD *and* GRAEFF *push the piano to center, taking off the cover as the* PICKWICKS *smooth their tight dresses and assume the professional manner.* JERRY *plays a phrase or two*)

JERRY　A little number entitled, little song entitled Father Lost His Choon Gum on the Bedpost Overnight.

PICKWICKS　Yak yak yak yak yak yak yak.

JERRY　A little song, a little song entitled Father Cut Your Toenails You're Tearing All the Sheets. (*To* MARTHA) A class act, you know what I mean?

PICKWICKS　Yak yak yak yak yak yak yak.

(MARTHA *sits close to* HOWARD, *they unconsciously take hands*)

JERRY　(*As though to a large audience*)　What this number did for Crosby—it'll never do for us.

(*Goes into* "Mississippi Mud," *with the girls. Throughout the song* ROGG *bangs on the table, never on the beat. The three finish the song and* MARTHA *goes to them and shakes their hands*)

THE COMPANY　Encore! Encore?

JERRY　No encores, thanks, but I got a sneaking suspicion, something tells me we give Mrs. Paul a hand, how about it folks?

(*Applause*)

MARTHA　I'd love to sing. Uh—do you know—"I Only Have Eyes For You"?

JERRY　Sure—and maybe we'll get better acoustics this time, you know what I mean. (*A reference to* ROGG's *banging on the table*)

(MARTHA *sings, and at the end* JERRY *says:*)

JERRY　How about the boys? Wuddia say, lads?

GRAEFF　Sure, I'll sing if the others will, but not by myself.

JERRY　There's safety (*Pronounced say-fitty*) in numbers, eh Doc?

GRAEFF   Right. Ira? Mr. Pomfret. Uh—you. (*Meaning* ROGG)

ROGG   No singing for me.

POMFRET   Sure.

IRA   All right. "By the Old Mill Stream"?

JERRY   (*As though to a large audience*)   Ladies and gentlemen, we are now in for our annual dry spell. "By the Old Mill Stream."
(*They sing, not well*)

JERRY   How about our friend the milkman. Got any songs, dances or witty sayings?

ROGG   No singin' or like that, but I can do a couple tricks. Got a bottle of beer?

JERRY   Now where would we find a bottle of beer in a saloon? What a question.

HOWARD   (*Cautioning him*)   Watch it, Mayo.

CHARLES   Here y'are. Shall I open it?

ROGG   No, no. That's the *trick*. (*He puts the bottle to his mouth and removes the cap with his teeth, and there is polite applause*)

ROGG   Show you another trick. (*He lifts a bentwood chair by the left rear leg and holds it at arm's length, shoulder high*)

CONCHITA   I bet *I* could do *that*.

ROGG   Yeah? What'll you bet? A little kiss?

CONCHITA   I'll bet you fifty cents.

ROGG   Who wants fifty cents? I got plenty of money. Come on, bet the kiss.

CONCHITA   What if I win?

ROGG   Then I'll give *you* fifty cents.

CONCHITA   Aw-right. (*She tries, but is unable to lift the chair*)

CONCHITA   Okay. You win.

ROGG   I'll collect later.

CONCHITA   Collect now.

ROGG   Not me, not in front of everybody. I'll collect any
time I want to. You didn't say nothin' when I was to
collect.

MARTHA   But neither did you. She's ready to pay off. She
didn't bet a necking party.

ROGG   Did anybody ask you for your advice? Keep your
nose out of it.

MARTHA   I volunteered my advice. Conchita, give the man
his kiss and that will be that.
   (CONCHITA *goes slowly to* ROGG, *and when she is very
   close he grabs her and kisses her and mauls her. She
   struggles,* POMFRET *gets up and shoves* ROGG *hard,
   separating him from the girl.* ROGG *throws a punch at*
   POMFRET *but misses*)

ROGG   (*Laughing*)   You wanta fight?

POMFRET   Just leave her alone.

MAYO   He's been a God damn nuisance all evening.

MARTHA   He has indeed.

GRAEFF   Ever since he came, I knew there'd be trouble.

POMFRET   Well, then, Mister, I guess it's time for you to
go.

ROGG   Who's makin' me go? You? You and who else?

CHARLES   Me, maybe.

ROGG   You? You, for God's sake.

CHARLES   Me. And this. (*He holds out his hand, in which
   lies a .38 automatic*) This ain't no water pistol.
   (ROGG *stands still, all the others hold their positions
   for a matter of seconds*)

ROGG   (*Pointing to the pistol*)   If yizz didn't have that . . .
   (*He goes to the lobby, picking up his cap and jacket,
   and goes out*)

PAULETTE   Good riddance. Good riddance to bad rubbage.

MARTHA (*To* CONCHITA)   Are you all right? Did he hurt you?

(*It is notable that* MARTHA *is the only person who goes to* CONCHITA. *The mauling has embarrassed the other women,* MARIA *and* PAULETTE)

CONCHITA   No, I guess not. I was scared more than anything.

IRA   Half a mind to call the state police.

POMFRET   I wish you wouldn't. Not that I give a damn what happens to him, but you know he's breaking that path for us, whether he wants to or not, and we've got to be under way.

MARTHA   Yes.

(*The conversation here is stiff, the gay mood has departed forever with the violent action*)

MAYO   Would you of shot him?

CHARLES   Oh, I'da shot him. I'm a firm believer in don't point a gun if you aren't prepared to shoot. I'da shot him.

MARTHA   Thank the Lord you didn't have to.

CHARLES   I thank the Lord *I* didn't have to, ma'am, but that aint saying he won't *never* get shot. *Or* cut up. *Or* hit over the head. Something. People like him don't live long.

MARTHA   Well—darling?

POMFRET   Right.

IRA   I wish you folks didn't have to go, but I guess you have to.

POMFRET   Charles, you want to come out with me while I make sure the car will start?

CHARLES   Right.

(*They exit*)

MARTHA (*To* PICKWICKS *and* MAYO)   I hope we'll run across you somewhere again.

MAYO You probly won't.

MARTHA I'm not so sure. I go to night clubs, in New York.

MAYO Lady, we don't work many night clubs. Especially ones you'd go to.

PAULETTE You don't have to tell her everything you know.

MAYO Why not? She's a hip dame. Give her credit. She don't think we travel all the way from New York to Reading P A just to do that lousy Mississippi Mud routine—do you?

MARTHA (*Smiling*) Well . . .

MAYO We only do that bit when we think maybe there's cops in the house.

MARTHA I see.

MAYO Yeah. The Pickwicks work better with their clothes off.

MARTHA Now, Mr. Mayo, I think you're embarrassing the girls.

CONCHITA Yeah, you don't have to tell everything you know.

MAYO She don't mind, do you?

MARTHA No, I don't mind. I've seen strip teases, if that's what you mean.

MAYO That's what I mean.

MARIA Excuse me. (*Exits*)

PAULETTE See what you did, Mr. Big Mouth? (*Starts to leave*)

MAYO Where *you* going?

PAULETTE To square it with her. Maybe we might have to spend the night here. Come on, Conchita.

MAYO (*As they follow* MARIA) You're not kidding her, but go ahead.

MARTHA Not that it's any of my business.

MAYO   But what?

MARTHA   But which one is your girl?

MAYO   Well—Paulette and I, we been shacked up for five years.

MARTHA   Oh, you're married to Paulette.

MAYO   I only said shacked up. No, she never got a divorce from her husband. Maybe just as well, or we *would* have been married.

MARTHA   What's wrong with that?

MAYO   Come on, you got eyes.

MARTHA   You're in love with Conchita.

MAYO   Right. In love with Conchita, shacked up with Paulette.

MARTHA   That's *really* a problem.

MAYO   Yeah, it ain't only the rich that have problems like that.
(*The men return*)

POMFRET   Okay. Runs like a watch. Turned over right away. All set, whenever you're ready.

IRA   Charles, do we have a Thermos bottle around?

CHARLES   No sir.

IRA   I was thinking of giving these good people a Thermos bottle full of coffee.

POMFRET   Oh, thanks very much, but there'll be places on the way.

IRA   I suppose so. I'd just feel better if you had a bottle of coffee to warm you up.

CHARLES   I could give them like a Mason jar or something on that order.

POMFRET   No thanks, we'll be fine, thank you. Mr. Studebaker, this has been one of the pleasantest days of my life.

MARTHA   It certainly has. Really, I don't know how to thank you.

IRA   Well, maybe I can look forward to your next visit? How about that?

MARTHA   If things work out as we hope—you'll see us.

POMFRET   You certainly will. Goodbye, Doctor.

GRAEFF   Goodbye and good luck, both of you. (*Shaking hands*)

POMFRET   Mr. Mayo.

MAYO   Mr. Pomfret. (*Shaking hands*)

MARTHA   I'll go in and say goodbye to the others. Goodbye, Charles, and many, many thanks. (*She shakes hands with* CHARLES) And Mr. Mayo, the same good luck to you. You know?

MAYO   Likewise, ma'am.

   (*They shake hands,* MARTHA *exits.* POMFRET *exits through lobby door, followed by* CHARLES, *with* IRA *and* GRAEFF *going as far as the door with them and watching until* MARTHA *comes out of the kitchen. On an impulse she kisses* IRA, *then goes out to car*)

IRA   Well, Henry.

GRAEFF   What's that, Ira?

IRA   Did you ever have a kiss from a lady with riding pants on?

GRAEFF   No, I can safely say I never have.

IRA   Come to think of it, did you ever have a kiss from a lady?

GRAEFF   At my age I'm not gonna start telling professional secrets.

IRA   Well, there they go. (IRA *and* GRAEFF *wave, then they turn slowly and go to the bar*) Care for a cigar, Henry?

GRAEFF   Don't mind if I do, Ira.

IRA   (*To* MAYO, *who has waited in the bar*) Mr. Mayo, care for a cigar?

MAYO   No thanks. Uh, Mr. Studebaker. What are your rates here?

IRA   Why, three dollars single, five double.

MAYO   Eight bucks. Do you give professional courtesy?

IRA   Professional courtesy?

MAYO   Some hotels give a reduction for theatrical people.

IRA   Oh. Well, if that's the custom I guess we will too.

CHARLES   (*Who has re-entered and is behind the bar*) Twenty percent. That brings it to four, plus two-forty, six-forty. Six-forty for the single and double.

MAYO   It looks like we're gonna be here for the night. You been friendly and I don't like to chisel off you, but we're not gonna get to Reading P A tonight, so we don't get paid. I better call those people. (*He goes to phone booth*)

GRAEFF   Why don't you give them a break, Ira?

IRA   I will. In the morning I'll just tell them no bill.

CHARLES   Sure are getting off to a fine start. (*Chuckling*) So far I'm the only one spent a dollar here tonight, and I *work* here.

IRA   Well—even a bank you know, the first day in business they usually used to give away carnations.

CHARLES   We'da done better if *we* gave away carnations. I was wrong. That truck driver, he bought a couple drinks. With the profit on him we oughta be able to put in a couple solid gold bathtubs.

IRA   Charles, I think you're what they call a cynic.

GRAEFF   Somebody better have a business head around here.

(*The* PICKWICKS *re-enter*)

PAULETTE   Where's . . . ?

IRA   Phone booth.

(MAYO *comes out of the booth*)

MAYO   Aaahhhahahahaha, there's good nooze t'night. You know what?

PICKWICKS   What?

MAYO   They postponed the smoker till tomorrow night. We work, kids, we work.

IRA   Well, that *is* good news.

GRAEFF   Congratulations.

CHARLES   Yep. I bet Mr. Studebaker's gonna buy a drink on that.

IRA   I sure will. Young ladies.

MAYO   No. Thanks very much, but no. I want them to get a good night's sleep. Pickwicks, I arrange to have a double room for you two, a single for me. Now say good-night and go up and retire.

CONCHITA   I *am* sorta tired.

PAULETTE   Yeah. The only thing is.

MAYO   What?

PAULETTE   What are we gonna do all day tomorrow if we go to bed now?

MAYO   Hmm. I know what. Tomorrow you come out on the porch with me. There's a big round thing up in the sky. It hurts your eyes when you look at it.

CONCHITA   (*Brightly*)   The sun!

MAYO   That's right.

PAULETTE   He's just bein' sarcastic. Come on, Conchita.

CHARLES   I'll show you to your room. First you wanta sign the register? Put them in Five, Mr. Studebaker.

IRA   Five is all right, Charles. Wherever you say.

PAULETTE   Goodnight, all.

CONCHITA   Goodnight, all.

GRAEFF   Goodnight.

IRA   Have a good rest.
   (*They exit*)

GRAEFF   Think I'll be on my way, Ira.

IRA   You don't have to go, Henry.

GRAEFF   I'll have a busy day tomorrow. If she ices up that'll mean a lot of broken bones, so I might as well get some rest. Goodnight, Ira. Mayo.

MAYO   Goodnight, Doc.

IRA   See you tomorrow, Henry.

GRAEFF   See you tomorrow. (*He yawns and so does* MAYO)

MAYO   All this fresh air today got me sleepy too. Unless you want company.

IRA   No, as soon as Charles and I put a few things away I'm going to bed too. Thanks just the same.

MAYO   Well, goodnight, Mr. Studebaker.

IRA   Goodnight, Son.

(MAYO *does a take on* "Son," *smiles and leaves.* IRA *makes a stab at putting things away—glasses, etc.—then switches out lights in bar and goes to lobby and switches out lights and sits in chair near stove, where he is joined by* CHARLES)

IRA   In the morning you have to show me how to disconnect that beer pump.

CHARLES   (*Seating himself*)   Yes sir.

IRA   I know quite a little about refrigeration. When I was in the wholesale produce business, refrigeration, we had to know about that.

CHARLES   Yes sir.

IRA   I noticed those matches. You know those kitchen matches? I left them on the table in the bar. Do you think that's safe?

CHARLES   Well, I tell you. I don't know how long it's gonna take the rats to find out we're back in business, but wherever you got a large quantity of food you're gonna have rats trying to get at it. And I heard of many's a fire started by rats gnawing at matches. I recommend we don't leave matches around.

IRA I think you're right. I kept out a bottle of whiskey, in case either of us wanted a night cap. You care for a night cap?

CHARLES No, thanks. I'll sleep sound without it.

IRA Mrs. Fenstermacher go out the kitchen door?

CHARLES No. Sleeping here tonight, in the room next to the young ladies.

IRA I *see.*

CHARLES Uh-huh. That's it.

IRA But she didn't have a nightgown or any of those things.

CHARLES I guess she can always manage. She has her comb and brush she keeps here, and I guess she don't need any toothbrush, just a glass to keep them in for the night.

IRA Never enjoy a cigar unless I'm sitting down relaxed.

CHARLES That trouble-maker we had here tonight. I bet he drives seventy-eighty miles an hour with a cigar in his mouth. Sitting down, but not relaxed.

IRA By the way, Charles, I didn't know you owned a revolver.

CHARLES Yes, I had this one about fifteen years or more. Pistol.

IRA Pistol.

CHARLES I had a per*mit* for it, when I lived in New York. I was a sort of a special. Special policeman.

IRA You were?

CHARLES Well, what I really was, I worked for a fellow. You know what the numbers is.

IRA I see.

CHARLES Yeah. So this fellow fixed it for me to get a pistol per*mit* upstate, Rockland County I think it was.

Then my wife found out what I was doing and she made me quit.

IRA   Yes, they find out everything.

CHARLES   They find out too much for their own good. That's why I'm a divorced man. I think we're getting a visitor.

IRA   Probably Doctor Graeff, couldn't get to sleep.

CHARLES   No, it aint any Doctor Graeff. It's the corporal from the state police.

(TROOPER *enters, removing gauntlets and opening his outer coat*)

IRA   Well, Corporal, back for a cup of coffee, I hope.

CORPORAL   No, no coffee—well, all right.

CHARLES   There's some hot on the stove. (*Exits*)

CORPORAL   Some information is what I want. Those two people you had in here earlier, the ones in the riding uniforms. Do you know their names?

IRA   Yes, I know their names.

(TROOPER *undoes throat latch of his coat, takes out cigarettes, slowly taps one*)

CORPORAL   They're dead.

IRA   Dead? Dead? You mean killed?

CORPORAL   I mean killed.

IRA   How?

CORPORAL   They got run into by that milk truck, the one that was outside here I told him to stop obstructing the traffic.

(CHARLES *brings coffee*)

IRA   Did you hear what he said?

CHARLES   Uh-huh. The milk truck left here before they did, and I understand there's only one-way traffic from here to Dieglersville. How did he run into them?

CORPORAL   He left here and the tracks show he turned in at Hummel's farm. Stopped there.

CHARLES   I see. Then when the station wagon come along he come out and hit them.

CORPORAL   That's what happened.

IRA   Hit them from behind.

CORPORAL   Hit them from behind, with that Diesel. The woman went through the windshield, the man broke his neck. We got the ambulance from the clinic. The doctor pronounced them dead. He didn't have to. I knew.

IRA   What about the truck driver?

CORPORAL   I don't know yet. She was pretty, but not now she isn't. I'm on duty, but could you give me just one shot of liquor?

IRA   Charles?

CHARLES   Yes sir. (*Gets bottle and glass*)

CORPORAL   Let me tell you the whole thing. The station wagon caught fire and somebody saw it and called up, and we got it on the two-way.

IRA   The two-way radio.

CORPORAL   We weren't a mile away from Hummel's. We got there and there was the station wagon on fire, and the Diesel. You could read a paper. My buddy got him out, I got her out. I should have left her in. (*Holding up a gauntlet*) This ain't ketchup, you know. Well— you know their names. (*Taking out pen and notebook*) What was his name?

IRA   (*Stalling*) His name?

CORPORAL   *Yes. His name.*

IRA   Corporal, there's a situation here where . . .

CORPORAL   Where what? All I want's their names. We'll trace the station wagon all right, but they didn't have any identification. I don't have all night, Mr. Studebaker.

IRA   They weren't married.

CORPORAL   All *right.*

IRA   She has a husband and a young daughter.

CORPORAL   Now look, you can't cover this up. They're dead. There's some things, ordinarily I might overlook something, but here you got two people dead and we got a criminal offense, leaving the scene of an accident, the driver of the Diesel. I'll appreciate your cooperation.

IRA   Howard Pomfret. That's P. o. m. f. r. e. t. New York City. Her name is Mrs. Paul, Martha Paul, P. a. u. l. Some place outside of Philadelphia.

CORPORAL   Paul. Paul, eh? There was a report earlier, a station wagon, somebody named Paul. Montgomery County.

CHARLES   Corporal, what about the fellow driving the truck?

CORPORAL   Somewhere around. He wasn't anywhere near when we got there, but he can't go far.

CHARLES   As Joe Louis said, he can run, but he can't hide. This fellow can't even run very fast in the blizzard.

CORPORAL   He won't be hard to follow in this snow.

CHARLES   What happens when you catch him?

CORPORAL   We'll hold him.

CHARLES   (*To* IRA)   They'll hold him.

CORPORAL   Well, thanks. I got what I came for.

CHARLES   Can I take a drink out to your buddy?

CORPORAL   No thanks, he never touches it.

IRA   Where did they take Pomfret and Mrs. Paul?

CORPORAL   Schillinger's Undertaking Parlor. Schillinger's a deputy coroner over in Dieglersville. Well, goodnight, men. (*He exits*)

CHARLES   (*After a moment*)   You thinking the same thing I am?

IRA   It was deliberate.

CHARLES   He waited for them. He banged into them on purpose.

IRA Maybe he didn't mean to kill them.

CHARLES You think too much good of people.

IRA I try.

CHARLES I almost wisht I'da shot him when I had the chance.

IRA I'm glad you didn't.

CHARLES So am I, I guess.

IRA Cold blood. *You* couldn't do that.

CHARLES No, I guess not. Well, he won't get away with it.

IRA Not if I can help it.

CHARLES What can you do?

IRA I don't know. But something.

CHARLES He didn't like me, either.

IRA His trouble, he didn't like anybody. Charles, you go to bed. You worked hard today.

CHARLES Work? I didn't hardly lift a finger to what I'm accustomed to.

IRA Go on, now, I know you're sleepy.

CHARLES Well, you *say* the word sleepy and I get a bit drowsy. What about you, Mr. Studebaker?

IRA Oh, I'll just stay here till the fire goes out.

CHARLES You want me to bank it for you?

IRA No thanks, I'll just wait till it goes out of its own accord.

CHARLES You want the loan of my pistol?

IRA If he comes around I'll call you.

CHARLES Okay. Well, goodnight.

IRA Goodnight, Charles.

(IRA *stretches out in the rocking-chair, staring at the stove, and as he begins to nod the* CURTAIN *slowly descends*)

CURTAIN

THE
SEARCHING
SUN

"What Is Our Life? . . ."

What is our life? A play of passion.
And what our mirth but music of division?
Our mothers' wombs the tiring-houses be
Where we are drest for this short comedy.
Heaven the judicious sharp spectator is
Who sits and marks what here we do amiss.
The graves that hide us from the searching sun
Are like drawn curtains when the play is done.
Thus march we, playing, to our latest rest,
And then we die, in earnest, not in jest.

—Sir Walter Raleigh

ACT ONE

SCENE ONE

The scene is the all-purpose living-dining-room of the THOMAS DESMOND MC GARRYS *in a house on the south shore of Long Island, about* 100 *miles out from New York City. It is their year-round residence, and this is the lived-in room. The furniture is for comfort and while in excellent taste does not reveal the hand of an interior decorator; in fact it is more masculine-country style than otherwise. At Down Right is a door which opens onto the unseen kitchen, and near that door is a dinner table with chairs. At Left is a door which leads to an unseen bedroom. Upstage, the length of the room is a picture window at center, to the right of which is a French window which offers entrance on a porch-terrace, and to the left a nonpractical French window. The time is June,* 1951.

At rise we discover at Left THOMAS DESMOND MC GARRY, M.D., *seated in a wheel chair at an angle. In front of him is a bridge table on which is a luncheon tray, and as he sips his coffee he looks up every now and then and out toward Right, obviously watching some offstage goings on.* MC GARRY *finishes his coffee, rings a small silver bell, and begins the business of filling and lighting his pipe. He is dressed in faded khaki pants, dark blue polo shirt, well-*

*cared-for fringed loafers. Hanging from the back of the
chair is a sturdy blackthorn with a black leather thong. He
is a well-built man in his middle forties, somewhat over-
weight.*

*A handsome elderly colored woman answers the bell.
She is* CLAIBORNE CASEY, *cook-housekeeper, wearing light
blue dress and white apron and white shoes.*

CLAIBORNE   Can I get you some Floating Island?

MC GARRY *(Severely but friendly)*   I told you, Claiborne.
No desserts till the Fourth of July. *(He pats his belly)*

CLAIBORNE   What you oughta do, you oughta let me stop
putting butter on your butter dish. They was three there
when I served you. I don't see any now.

MC GARRY   Well, let me try cutting down the desserts
first.

CLAIBORNE   And sockrin. For lunch why don't you use
sockrin in your coffee instead of sugar? *(She starts taking up the luncheon tray)*

MC GARRY   It took me a long time to put on all this
weight, so let me take it off gradually. *(Pointing with
the bit of his pipe)* They all unloaded next door?

CLAIBORNE   Well, I wasn't watching too carefully—

MC GARRY   No, I'll bet you weren't.

CLAIBORNE   —But I think they got the one car unloaded,
the one the mother and daughter come in. The station
wagon they're still unloading. There's a lot more stuff
in there, of course. They got about fourteen pieces more
of luggage, all the very finest valises and hatboxes, shoe-
boxes, golf bags. Two shotgun cases. Who wants shot-
guns this time of the year? They got that little boat on
the roof of the station wagon, that aint unloaded yet.

The lady, I wouldn't call her much help. The husband and the daughter, they're doing all the work, but
the wife she just stands there on the terrace looking out
at the ocean.

MC GARRY   I noticed that.

CLAIBORNE   I noticed it, too. I know who they got coming to work for them—Rose Franklin used to be with Mrs. Barnard last summer. You know Rose Franklin.

MC GARRY   Sure.

CLAIBORNE   Well, all I got to say, Mrs. Stranger-Next-Door, if she thinks Rose *Franklin's* gonna wait on her hand and foot, she got another think coming.

MC GARRY   The new neighbor's an actress, she probably has a lady's maid.

CLAIBORNE   She better, if she thinks Rose Franklin's gonna wait on her hand and foot. That's why Rose Franklin wouldn't go back to Mrs. Barnard this summer. "I don't have to go around picking up after anybody or nobody," Rose said. But I don't see no lady's maid. Only the three of them: the mister and missus and the daughter. That's all came in the two cars.

MC GARRY   (*Bored, takes a* Newsweek *out of chair pocket*) Mm-hmm. (*He starts to read,* CLAIBORNE *starts to leave with the luncheon things*)

CLAIBORNE   Well, the mister aint losing any time getting acquainted.

MC GARRY   Hmm?

CLAIBORNE   You're getting a visitor, the Mister. Shall I let him in?
(*Through the windows up Right a tall, rather handsome man can be seen approaching the practical French window. He knocks and* MC GARRY *calls* "Come in")

STRANGER   (*Entering*)   Good afternoon. Is this Doctor McGarry?

MC GARRY   Yes, come right in.

STRANGER   My name is Douglas. I'm your new neighbor, brand new, as a matter of fact.

MC GARRY   (*Politely extending his hand*)   Welcome to Midhampton.

DOUGLAS Thanks a lot. I hate to bother you, but I've had a dreadfully serious accident. May be fatal. Are you taking new patients, Doctor McGarry?

MC GARRY Well, not exactly. What's the trouble?
(DOUGLAS *extends his left hand and* MC GARRY *examines it*)

MC GARRY Oh, yes.

DOUGLAS We just drove down from New York and the confounded lighter in my car wouldn't work. Tried to light a cigarette while on the move. Whole book of matches blew up in my hand.

MC GARRY A damned nuisance, and painful.

DOUGLAS Well, I don't like to baby myself, but I'm a bit worried about infection. I infect at the drop of a microbe, you know, and we actors—I'm an actor—we're all such hypochondriacs. Do you think I'll lose my hand? Will you have to cut it off here and now?

MC GARRY Oh, I think we can save the hand. Have a seat.
(DOUGLAS *sits down and* MC GARRY *takes another look at the hand*)

MC GARRY The best protection you have is right here, the skin, the blister. I'm glad you didn't open it up. A lot of people make that mistake. I'll put a little something on it for you and give you a prescription. Are you going to be using the hand?

DOUGLAS Well, yes. A lot of unloading and unpacking.

MC GARRY I don't like to put a dressing on, but in that case I will. (*He rings the silver bell and* CLAIBORNE *enters*)

MC GARRY Claiborne, in the bottom row of the medicine chest you'll find a small tube without a label, about two and a half inches long. The tube looks like soft tin. Bring it to me please, and the box of large Band-aids and a cotton finger.

CLAIBORNE The burn stuff?

MC GARRY Right. (*She exits*) Cigarette, Mr. Douglas?
(*Pushes a silver box toward* DOUGLAS, *who takes one,
and* MC GARRY *holds a lighter for him*)

MC GARRY Lighters have their uses, all right.

DOUGLAS I must have fifty, truly, fifty cigarette lighters,
but did I have one today? Oh, no. Oh, dear me, no.
Isn't that always the way?

MC GARRY Mm-hmm. How did you know there was a
doctor next door?

DOUGLAS Well, now wasn't that clever of me?

MC GARRY Yes, it was. My name is on the little sign in
the driveway, but no M.D., or D.R. How *did* you know?

DOUGLAS The license plate on your car, Doctor. I've been
over here long enough to've noticed that. 2 M D 366.

MC GARRY 2 M D 388, but that's very good. But how
come our car's in the driveway? My wife—no, she didn't
take it today, that's right. A friend stopped for her. Well,
here we are. (*He starts attending the burn as* CLAIBORNE
*stands by. He works quickly and efficiently, talking the
while*) I'll give you a prescription for a tube of this
stuff. It's very expensive, but you can use it sparingly.
In fact, you *should* use it sparingly, and it's not a bad
thing to have around. There we are.

DOUGLAS Very neat. I don't suppose I'll get much sympathy, but it is a sort of conversation piece, and I'll make
up some wild tale to go with the dressing.

MC GARRY Would you like a cup of coffee, a drink?

DOUGLAS Do you know what I would like? If you have it?
I'd like a Coke. I haven't wet my whistle since we left
New York, over three hours ago. It doesn't seem quite
fair to my wife and my stepdaughter, but they didn't
burn their finger, did they?

MC GARRY Claiborne, could we have two Cokes, please?
(*She exits*) I understand you've taken the Worthington
place till September.

DOUGLAS   Yes, in fact till October, although I don't expect I'll be here much in October.

MC GARRY   Rehearsing?

DOUGLAS   Yes, but how did you know?

MC GARRY   Only a guess.

DOUGLAS   There's been nothing in the papers about it, not that it's a deep-dyed secret, but I do expect to go into rehearsal about the fifteenth of September, a play for Gilbert Miller, written by a totally unknown young Frenchman. Are you interested in the theater?

MC GARRY   I used to be. I saw you in *Young Mrs. Blackwell*, 1934. One of the last plays I saw.

DOUGLAS   Oh, you did? That was a good play. I was all wrong about it, you know. I thought it was a sure hit for New York. (*The Cokes are served and* CLAIBORNE *leaves*) Cheers!

MC GARRY   Cheers.

DOUGLAS   We ran well over a year in London, and here we did less than fifty performances. Was it the Depression, do you s'pose?

MC GARRY   It may have been. No, I think it was just too English. Sometimes, you know, we'll take fifteen English plays, one right after the other, all so bloody English that I don't believe half the audience understands them, but then the sixteenth will come along, and we just won't have it, no part of it.

DOUGLAS   Perhaps you're right. Satiation, I s'pose. They get tired of our God damn faces. Not to mention our accents. Did you ever act, or write for the theater?

MC GARRY   No. Just went.

DOUGLAS   Interesting thing about doctors, all over the world. It's very seldom doctors don't like the theater. But you said a moment ago, *Young Mrs. Blackwell* was one of the *last* plays you saw. Don't you ever go up to New York?

MC GARRY   Never. I've been in this vehicle since 1934.
No, since 1935. I didn't have one of these in '34. I was
in the hospital for almost a year. Then I bought this
place. I was in an airplane accident in '34 and my legs
were pretty badly bunged up.

DOUGLAS   Say, that was hard luck. That must have been
very soon after you became a doctor.

MC GARRY   Two years after.

DOUGLAS   And you live here the year 'round. I must say I
think I'd rather like that, if I could afford it.

MC GARRY   It's not bad. I came here because I wanted to
be on the ocean, just to look out on it. I didn't want
to see my friends, and I wanted to forget all about being
a doctor.

DOUGLAS   Then you gave up your practice?

MC GARRY   During the war this was two rooms. I took
office patients, more or less to ease the pressure on the
local man. One of the two local men joined the Navy
and the other was working himself to death, so I hung
out my shingle temporarily, but I gave it up in '47. Very
dull work, office work, when you started out to be a surgeon.

DOUGLAS   But don't you get bored?

MC GARRY   No, not very. I listen to the ball games on the
radio. I wrote three quarters of a book a few years ago,
till I found that somebody else had written a much better book on the same subject. I'm class secretary, so I
have a voluminous correspondence. Very conscientious
about it, too. I'm a member of Ducks Unlimited, and
I give them extensive reports on the duck situation. Two
years ago I took up painting and I'm having a one-genius
show at the library fairly soon. I'm a member of the
Village Historical Society, in fact I'm secretary of that
too. You'd be surprised how much history took place
around here. I was . . . I was an airplane spotter during the war. Got a little confusing with my duck-watch-

ing, but no serious damage done. And I have quite a
social life. We usually have people here for Sunday lunch
all year round and Saturday night we have a poker game
and Tuesday night a bridge game. I don't say it's a useful life, but the days pass quickly, one into another.
And finally, a man can always get drunk. A man can
get drunk, and the little chores pile up, and you have
to work extra hard for two or three days while you make
up for lost time. Of course it isn't what I started out to
do, or to be, but I don't know what I was meant to do,
or to be. At least I'm less sure than I used to be.

DOUGLAS   I should say you have a very full life.

MC GARRY   Full of what, Mr. Douglas?

DOUGLAS   Well, I do' know. I take it you always wanted
to be a doctor, and I s'pose I always wanted to be an
actor and I still am one. But it's all I know how to be.
It might be interesting to have some accident that would
put a quick, final stop to my acting career. Suppose, for
instance, those matches instead of putting a baby blister
on my thumb, what if I'd blinded myself, or burnt my
face beyond repair—some accident that would take me
off the stage forever. I wonder what I'd do to occupy my
time. You, you seem to have adjusted yourself to your
new way of life. Just from these few minutes I'd say
you'd done very well adjusting yourself. You've made
yourself a sort of schedule to keep yourself occupied.

MC GARRY   Mr. Douglas, are you trying to comfort me?

DOUGLAS   Well, maybe I am. I beg your pardon. I don't
mean to be patronizing. But when I came in here I
didn't get an impression of an unhappy invalid in an
invalid's chair. Then you told me these things about
yourself and—well, I think you've done yourself proud.
You must have had one hell of a bad time in the beginning, and what I'm really trying to say is that if
something put an end to my career, I don't think I'd
be able to adjust as well as you have.

MC GARRY   Thank you.

DOUGLAS (*Suddenly nervous*)   I—uh—I must go now, thank you very much, Doctor. What about your fee? Will you send me a bill, or shall I pay you now or what?

MC GARRY   Well, I've more or less regained my amateur standing. I haven't collected a fee since I took the M.D. off my sign. Tell you what you do. The fire company will be around asking for contributions next month, and when they do, you donate an extra five dollars to them. I'm a member of the fire company too.
(*As* DOUGLAS *rises to leave* MARY MC GARRY *enters from the kitchen*)

MC GARRY   Oh, I'd like you to meet my wife. Mary, this is Mr. Douglas, our new neighbor.

DOUGLAS   How do you do.

MARY   How do you do. I see you've arrived. What can we do to help you get settled?

DOUGLAS   Well, thanks a lot, Mrs. McGarry. The doctor's already been helping. Wounded myself with some exploding matches.

MARY   Oh. Hard luck . . . Wouldn't you and Mrs. Douglas and your daughter like to take pot luck with us tonight, about seven-fifteen? I happen to know that your cook won't arrive till tomorrow. I saw her in the village and she asked me to tell Mrs. Douglas.

DOUGLAS   Really? Well, I'm sure we'd be delighted.

MARY   Fine. And tell Mrs. Douglas I'll drop in a little later this afternoon to see if there's anything I can do. Lists, you know. The names of the market people, drug store, so forth. I'll make up a list and bring it over later. For instance, you ought to apply for a post office box first thing tomorrow—but I'll take it all up with Mrs. Douglas. (*She waves a fairly good-sized stack of mail as she speaks, then places it on* MC GARRY'S *bridge table*)

DOUGLAS   You're both very kind.

MARY   And meanwhile we'll definitely expect all three of you at seven-fifteen?

DOUGLAS   You're sure it's no trouble? It is, of course.

MARY   It's not only pot luck, it's pot roast, but Claiborne does it very well.

DOUGLAS   Goo'bye.

(*He exits.* MARY *sits down and lights a cigarette. She is a woman in her mid-forties, of the type that can still play good golf and tennis. A smartly tweedy dressed woman and obviously a social cut or two above her husband*)

MARY   He seemed pleasant enough. Have you seen her?

MC GARRY   (*Thumbing through the mail*)   I didn't get a very good look at her.

MARY   And they have a young daughter.

MC GARRY   Stepdaughter.

MARY   (*Keenly*)   Didn't you like him?

MC GARRY   He's all right, I guess. Those bastards always make me talk too much.

MARY   What bastards?

MC GARRY   The English. God knows they talk enough themselves, but I always feel that I was the one that did the talking, and too much of it. I told him the story of my life while I was putting a Band-aid on his thumb.

MARY   And he didn't tell you his?

MC GARRY   No, by God, he certainly did not. He was far from frank. On the top shelf there, see if you can reach it, there's a British *Who's Who*, around 1940 or '42. (MARY *goes to the bookshelves at Left and stands on a chair*)

MC GARRY   The last book on the right.

MARY   (*Extracting it*)   Here we are. *Who's Who*. 1942. Not *Who's Who in America*. I don't think I've ever looked at this before.

MC GARRY It belonged to your father. That time he gave me an encyclopedia and a big batch of reference books?

MARY When you were writing your own book.

MC GARRY (*Nodding and thumbing through the book*) Douglas, Douglas, Douglas. Here we are. Douglas, Archie. Actor, born 29 April 1902.

MARY Hmm. Doesn't look that.

MC GARRY He's kept slender running away from women.

MARY He doesn't seem that type to me, but I've never seen him before.

MC GARRY Not even in the movies?

MARY Now how often do I go to the movies?

MC GARRY I imagine there are quite a few women that only go to the movies to see Archie Douglas. (*Quoting*) First appeared in amateur productions London 1920. What'd he do in the war? Served in Navy 1918-19. He must have been just a kid. Of course they do take them in younger than we do. Films. Zum zum zum zum zum zum. Plays. Zum zum zum zum. *Young Mrs. Blackwell.* That's the one I saw him in. It was a flop. At least over here. He was pretty good in it, but it was a lousy play. Clubs. Garrick, that's a theatrical club in London, and The Players, New York. Yes, I remember a story about his being blackballed at the Racquet Club.

MARY Now how did you know that?

MC GARRY Your brother told me. I gather he was put up for the Racquet and he went around to meet the committee and he was wearing some tie that looked like a Racquet Club tie, and they gave him the heave-ho.

MARY I don't believe it.

MC GARRY It's your brother's story, not mine. Recreations:—

MARY Do they put that in?

MC GARRY Recreations: tennis, photography, shooting. *Shooting?*

MARY   Aren't you skipping a lot? What about her?

MC GARRY   Married Anna Root, 1931. Address: care of Music Corporation of America. That's a theatrical agency.

MARY   Musical Corporation. Is he a musician too?

MC GARRY   Not that I know of. Now let's have a look at her. Root. R,R,R,R, Root. Root, Anna. Actress. Born, Vienna, doesn't say when. Daughter of Herman and Anna Reuther. Married Ernst Schmidt. Marriage dissolved. It doesn't say when for *any* of these things. Child dancer in Vienna, Paris, Berlin, London. Plays: Zum zum zum zum. None I ever heard of. Films. Zum zum zum. Doesn't give any address for her. But she's good. She has a big European reputation.

MARY   What about recreations?

MC GARRY   (*Pretending to read*)   Recreations: Nocturnal. Also matinees Wednesday and Saturday.

MARY   Now really.

MC GARRY   Well, I'd say she was very discreet, at least when it comes to giving out the facts about herself. Did you notice something I noticed?

MARY   I notice she didn't mention having a daughter.

MC GARRY   That's right. And also she didn't mention Douglas. *He* mentions *her*, but *she* doesn't mention *him*.

MARY   Well, I guess if he mentions her they must be married, all right.

MC GARRY   Yes, we won't have to ride them out of town on a rail.

MARY   Probably what that means, her not mentioning Douglas, she probably was married three or four times and just didn't like to boast.

MC GARRY   Just as long as they're married. Can't have any of that stuff going on around here.

MARY   You may joke about it, but you'd be the first to object.

MC GARRY   I probably would.

MARY   Any fascinating mail?

MC GARRY   Why, I always have fascinating mail. You know that. (*He picks up the letters, looks at them one by one. She goes to him, stands behind him and rubs his shoulders, a gesture of tenderness as much as a relaxing massage*)

MARY   How are you feeling?

MC GARRY   How am I feeling? Why, the same as usual. I always feel the same. You know that.

MARY   (*Smiling*)   I know nothing of the kind. I don't know anyone that changes as much as you do, from day to day, from hour to hour. When I left here you were in very good spirits. But when I come back two hours later . . .

MC GARRY   I haven't noticed any change in myself. Will you stop being Daddy's Little Helper, the *Ladies' Home Journal* wife?

MARY   (*Strolling to the windows*)   If those people bother you, we won't have to see them. We can have them over tonight, and I can make the neighborly gestures, but we won't ever have to see them again all summer. I can handle them.

MC GARRY   I wish you wouldn't get ideas about me, and protecting me from people. I'm perfectly capable of handling my own affairs. As a matter of fact, I'm getting fat and stale *and*, as a matter of fact, bored. With myself. I can't jump around and play tennis or drive the car, but I have plenty of strength to do other things that don't involve my using my legs. I'm no cripple. (*He laughs*) Well, of course that's exactly what I am, but that's all I am. I'm *only* a cripple. I've got to find some new thing to do, with my hands, or with my brains, it doesn't matter which, just so it's something.

MARY   What did you and Mr. Douglas talk about?

MC GARRY That had nothing to do with what I'm saying now.

MARY Didn't it?

MC GARRY No. So get over this analytical thing. Don't start seeing changes in me that haven't happened, and don't start attributing these nonexistent changes to, to Douglas and his menage.

MARY Did he have a bad burn?

MC GARRY Pretty bad, for that kind of a burn. Second degree anyway. I wouldn't say he was the bravest little soldier in the world. He was trying to make light of it, you know. Pretending to joke about it. But the very fact that he put on such an act— I've seen people stabbed in Harlem that took it better than he did.

MARY Well, he's an actor. I suppose they have to make a big thing of everything.

MC GARRY Exactly.

MARY He's the first patient you've had since—

MC GARRY Since you. Last summer when I set your finger. And don't think I don't see your line of thinking.

MARY I'm sure I—

MC GARRY Oh, come on, Mary. I can read your mind. You come back from the village and you think I'm upset about something, which I'm not. But you think I am. And you find this fellow here, and you decide he upset me.

MARY Have it your own way.
(*During these speeches she has had her back turned, is looking out the window. A change of attitude indicates that she has finished with the subject and is interested in something else*)

MARY She's going for a walk.

MC GARRY Who is?

MARY Mrs.—Next Door. Douglas. Uh-uh. (*Jumps back*

behind a drape) She just looked up. I wonder if she saw me.

MC GARRY   What if she did? You have a perfect right to—

MARY   I wouldn't want her to think I was staring at her.

MC GARRY   You can look out your own *window*. Remember, we were here first.

MARY   She kicked off her shoes and now she's striding up the beach. Striding, that's the only word for it. She's going to have stiff legs tomorrow, walking in that sand barefoot.

MC GARRY   How are her legs? Has she got ballet dancer legs?

MARY   Well, I can't really tell when she's barefoot. Not bad.

MC GARRY   She started out as a dancer, I think.

MARY   She was a child dancer. It said so in that book. She has a dog.

MC GARRY   Oh, Lord. What kind of a dog?

MARY   Chesapeake.

MC GARRY   Oh, God. Big, and noisy.

MARY   But they're friendly.

MC GARRY   They're too damn friendly. I think I'll get a water pistol and fill it full of ammonia.

MARY   You can't do that.

MC GARRY   Oh, can't I just? You tell Claiborne, not a scrap of food for that damn dog. Or maybe some nice chop bones. That'll fix him. And the first night he howls, believe me, Mr. and Mrs. Douglas get a nice sharp letter in the morning.

MARY   My word. She's standing in front of the Holdens' house and just staring. Lucky for her they're not home. They'd stare right back at her, stare for stare.

MC GARRY   Take a look across the way. What are Douglas and the girl doing?

MARY   Well, they seem to have all the luggage out of the two cars, all piled up on the terrace. They have a little outboard motorboat on the roof of the station-wagon.

MC GARRY   Uh-huh.

MARY   He and the girl seem to be talking about it. They're probably discussing whether to take it off the roof. Don't take it off, you fools. Leave it there, then you won't have to lift it on again when you take it over to the bay. Uh-huh. Uh-huh. Wasn't I smart? That's exactly what they decided. He said something to the girl, then she pointed toward the bay, and he nodded, and now they're leaving the car and going up to the terrace. Now he's putting his arm around her. Around her waist. And she's putting her arm around his waist, and they're walking in step. She's his *step*daughter, isn't she?

MC GARRY   Right.

MARY   She's quite pretty. She has quite a good figure. (*She pauses*)

MC GARRY   What?

MARY   I can't make up my mind.

MC GARRY   About what?

MARY   It may be entirely innocent, but (*Turning to* MC GARRY) it's suddenly very exciting to me. (*Vaguely*) He didn't make a pass, only put his arm around her, and she hers around him. That's all they did. Tom.

(*She bends down and kisses him and despite the awkwardness of his position, he takes her in his arms as the curtain slowly descends*)

SCENE TWO

The same as Scene One.

Evening. (Curtain lowered to indicate passage of intervening time)

Seated at the dinner table, at Right, are TOM MC GARRY *(in his wheel chair),* ZITA SCHMIDT *(the twenty-year-old daughter of* ANNA*),* ARCHIE DOUGLAS, MARY MC GARRY, *and* ANNA ROOT DOUGLAS, *in that order clockwise.*

DOUGLAS No, no, no, no, no. Not another scrap. Not even a dab of the top or anything else. There are two things that would bring me to this country. If the managers only knew it, I'd be happy to play in New York without salary, provided the managers agreed to pay me in lemon meringue pie, and cheese cake. Do you know Lindy's, Mrs. McGarry?

MARY I don't think I do. What are they?

DOUGLAS *They* are a *restaurant*. A Mr. Lindy.

MC GARRY Leo Lindy. I know about him. It's a hangout for song writers and theatrical people.

MARY Oh, like Sardi's.

DOUGLAS Like—and so unlike. At Lindy's every gentleman must somehow contrive to eat while smoking a very large cigar. Apparently it's against the rules for the male patrons to eat without a Corona-Corona in his kisser. That's Lindyese for face. Every gentleman is required to have a heater in his kisser. Heater is Lindyese for cigar, and kisser is Lindyese for face. (*He speaks quickly, with a certain amount of nervousness, and it should be made apparent that he has been doing most*

*of the talking through dinner and, by their manner, his
wife and stepdaughter have been contributing little
conversationally. As a social occasion, the dinner has not
been a success*) Well, the reason I know so much about
Lindy's is I discovered it on my first trip to this country
and on my first visit to Lindy's I ate some of his famous
cheese cake. Since that lucky day I have eaten—con-
servative estimate—fourteen tons of the stuff, and I
hope to live to eat fourteen tons more. As to lemon
meringue, I've almost never had a bad piece of that.

MC GARRY   You've been lucky.

DOUGLAS   I know I have. My favorite, I think, up to now,
is at a little delicatessen in Sixth Avenue. Up to now. My
new favorite, far and away the best I ever ate, was this,
tonight. And I know why. It's because the crust is
better. I think I could eat mucilage on this crust. So
light and flaky.

MARY   There's half the pie still left. You can take it home
with you when you leave.

DOUGLAS   May I? I'll take you up on that, you know, and
I'll probably eat it all before I go to bed. But I can't
go on making a spectacle of myself at table. And I'm
holding everybody up. (*They all rise, except* MC GARRY,
who spins his chair around toward Left) You, Doctor,
you have an iron will. You never touch desserts, you
say? With these lemon meringues right within reach?

MC GARRY   I haven't had a dessert of any kind since the
day before yesterday.

DOUGLAS   Oh, some sort of diet.

MC GARRY   Some sort.

DOUGLAS   Then it must have been torture to sit there and
watch me put away two enormous wedges of that pie.

MC GARRY   Torture's a strong word for it. By the way,
how's your thumb coming along?

DOUGLAS   Oh, it's nothing really.

MC GARRY   I can give you a pill to put you to sleep if the pain's too severe.

(DOUGLAS *gives him a quick look to see if sarcasm is intended; he cannot decide*)

DOUGLAS   I don't think I'll need it, Doctor.

ZITA (*To* MARY)   Couldn't I help with the dishes, Mrs. McGarry?

MARY   Oh, no thanks, Zita. Claiborne doesn't really like to be helped, and besides in a little while you'll hear the Queen Mary, that's our electric dishwasher.

MC GARRY (*To* DOUGLAS)   Cigar, Douglas?

DOUGLAS   You having one?

MC GARRY   No. Pipe and cigarettes are all I smoke, but I've got some pretty good heaters. Not Corona-Corona, but cigar smokers seem to like them.

DOUGLAS   Are we all staying together? In here?

MC GARRY   I thought you and I could go sit on the terrace and leave the ladies to their own devices.

DOUGLAS   Then I'd love a cigar. Anna abhors them.

ANNA   I do indeed. And I don't think men really like the filthy things. They think it gives them an appearance of masculinity, yet the most flagrant homosexual I have ever known was never without a cigar.

MC GARRY   What about pipes, Mrs. Douglas?

ANNA   So long as the tobacco is burning a pipe I do not mind. Some pipe tobaccos can be rather fragrant. But a cigar is vile, vile in its odor, vile in appearance. I do not care for cigars.

MC GARRY   Yes, I knew a female doctor that smoked cigars. It gave her the appearance of masculinity, not that she needed it.

ANNA   I was speaking of a male homosexual, but of course my theory holds true in both cases.

DOUGLAS   Nevertheless I'm going to have my cigar, no

matter how it affects my reputation. Do you want me to give you a push, Doctor?

MC GARRY   I can manage, thanks. (*He wheels himself through the French window, followed by* DOUGLAS. *They sit on the terrace in full view of the women, but their conversation is unheard*)

MARY   I didn't ask you this before. Do you prefer to be called Miss Root, or Mrs. Douglas?

ANNA   On such occasions, Mrs. Douglas. (*Implying on occasions such as this*) Professionally I am always known as Miss Root. It really makes no difference. Whatever comes to your mind. But in the theater or the films, always Miss Root.

MARY   I see. I was just thinking: there isn't any couple known as Mr. and Mrs., is there?

ANNA   I should think not. What a risk! To create a reputation as Mr. and Mrs., and then the husband goes off with some little chippie and the wife must still be known as Mrs. So-and-So. I should think not.

MC GARRY   (*Calling out*)   Mr. and Mrs. Sidney Drew.

MARY   What did you say, dear?

MC GARRY   Mr. and Mrs. Sidney Drew, a famous acting couple.

ANNA   I never heard of them.

MARY   We never heard of them, and you're not supposed to be eavesdropping.

MC GARRY   So sorry.

MARY   What can I offer you in the way of a liqueur? We have quite a selection as you see. (*There is a portable bar at Left*) Brandy, Cointreau, creme de menthe, Benedictine.

ANNA   This much Cointreau, please. (*She holds up her fingers*)

MARY   Zita?

ZITA   Well—Benedictine, but let me help.

MARY (*To* ZITA, *then going to doorway*) Would you tell Claiborne we're ready for the coffee? Mr. Douglas? Coffee?

DOUGLAS Please. No sugar.

MARY Tom. Are you having coffee?

MC GARRY Small. Black. And don't forget us when the booze is being passed around. (*Inaudible question to* DOUGLAS)

DOUGLAS Brandy for both. I'll get it.
(*He comes in off the terrace and waits for the pouring of the brandy, takes it out, comes in again for the coffee and exits with same. During these actions* ANNA *takes a small gold cigarette case from her bag and lights a cigarette, and coolly inspects the room and its contents. Unobtrusively she reaches out her hand and touches the British Who's Who, which has been left lying on an end table. She pushes it around and looks at the spine, reading the title. She glares at* MARY, *unnoticed by* MARY *or anyone else.* MARY *is covering* ANNA's *by-play by being busy with the drinks. At length* MARY *sits down, having poured herself a brandy. The only talk necessary during this phase is the necessary here-you-are and thank-you, so that dialog does not take away from* ANNA's *discovery of the Who's Who*)

ANNA (*Rising*) May I? (*Implying use the bathroom*)

MARY Through the bedroom.
(ANNA *exits up Left.* MARY *devotes herself to* ZITA)

MARY Are you planning a theatrical career, Zita?

ZITA I'm afraid not. Papa—he's not really my father, you know. My stepfather.

MARY I knew that.

ZITA My actual father is dead. I never saw him.

MARY Then you never missed him.

ZITA Oh, on the contrary I missed him more. I've always been curious about him and his family, my family. My uncles and aunts. I must have cousins still alive in Austria and Germany. I've never seen any of them or heard from them. Mama was divorced and went to England and my real father stayed in Vienna. Then when Hitler came to power we could never go back. Mama was very outspoken against Hitler and it would have been worth her life—mine, too—if she'd taken me to Vienna. Then we heard my father was dead.

MARY   Killed fighting Hitler?

ZITA   (*Uncomfortably*)   I don't exactly know for sure. Mama doesn't like to speak about him. Now that I've grown up I realize what I didn't realize as a child—that the divorce was very bitter, acrimonious. I used to think Mama didn't talk about my real father out of courtesy to Archie. But as I grew up, little things here and there. I understand that my real father, Mr. Schmidt, kept Mama's money and everything else. I wish I could go over there and find out about myself, my family. But my papers—jeepers! What a mess they're in. I don't dare leave the country. Born in Vienna, brought up in England till I was fourteen, and Mama married to an Englishman, and the Englishman is changing to American citizenship. I don't even dare go to Bermuda. The girls at school wanted me to go to Bermuda this spring, but Papa's lawyer strongly advised against it.

MARY   What are you?

ZITA   Technically, English, a British subject, because I was legally adopted by Papa. But I want to be an American. I've been living here and going to school here for six years. All my friends are here, except for one or two girls I still write to in England, but mostly they write to thank me for CARE packages. I haven't seen them during those all-important adolescent years, and the friendships are childhood friendships. The real friendships are girls at school, here.

MARY   Where do you go?

ZITA Sarah Lawrence. Before that, the Brearley.

MARY And not going on the stage? You have the looks.

ZITA You should hear Mama on that subject. They practically made me do dramatics at the Brearley, naturally, with Mama and Papa, but Mama went to see me just once and said: Powers Model! That's all she said. Powers Model! In other words, nothing inside. And, I guess she's right. I certainly haven't got the ambition to work as hard as she did to get where she is. Ballet, singing, piano, elocution lessons. Apparently *her* mother was just the opposite. She always wanted Mama to be an actress and trained her for it all her life. She didn't have any real childhood. Of course that's the way they do over there. In the Russian ballet, you know, they used to take children when they were six years old and that's all they ever learned.

MARY What would you *like* to be?

ZITA I ask myself that question every day. At the Brearley I wanted to be Emily Dickinson.

MARY In my day it was Edna St. Vincent Millay.

ZITA Did you go to the Brearley too?

MARY No, I'm afraid I went to Spence, but my literary friends adored Edna St. Vincent Millay.

ZITA Oh, she was good. I like some of her things.

MARY I did at the time, but I was never very intellectual. I'm just perfectly suited to my present job.

ZITA Oh, you have a job?

MARY Oh, yes. I run the children's department at the Village library. Monday, Wednesday, and Friday. I order the books, and I read them too. And I must say I enjoy them. That's as far as my brain developed.

ZITA Children's books are much better than they used to be.

MARY Yes, that probably explains why some of them are

rather deep for me. But then after you decided not to be Emily Dickinson, what?

ZITA   Well, I wrote some short stories. I sent a few of them to *The New Yorker* and one of them didn't come back with a rejection slip. I actually got a little note. They said it was too special, but "please try us soon again." I showed the note to my English teacher and she told me not to let it go to my head.

MARY   That wasn't very nice of her.

ZITA   Oh, she was joking. She said she'd sent stuff to *The New Yorker* for over ten years before she got anything but a rejection slip. She *has* sold some things there, and the *Kenyon Review*.

MARY   Did you keep on with your writing?

ZITA   My writing! How important that sounds! No, I haven't really done any writing lately. I got terribly interested in skiing and consequently I almost flunked out of college, and it's not easy to flunk out of Sarah Lawrence. You have to put your mind to it. Skiing, and I'm very fond of outboard racing. I have a boat, I brought it down here. I understand they do a lot of it on the bay.

MARY   From morning to night, it seems to me. Bizzt. Bizzt. Bizzt-bizzt-bizzt.

ZITA   I have a friend that raced in the Albany to New York race. Finished, too, and that's quite an achievement.

MARY   Is he a skiier, too?

ZITA   Yes. The same one.

MARY   Where is he?

ZITA   At Williams. His home is in Rye.

MARY   Well, that's not too far away. There's a nice crowd of girls your age here. When your friend comes down I'll have them in to meet you. Do you sail?

ZITA   A little, but the sailboat crowd call outboards stink-pots. Horrible name.

MARY   (*Smiling*)   They still do? I know we used to.

ZITA   I have a feeling I'm not going to be very popular here.

MARY   Don't worry about it. In any case, you're out-numbered in this neck of the woods, and sail has the right of way. You must take me for a ride some time.

ZITA   I'd love to.

MARY   And some day when you're feeling like a quiet sail you come along and crew for me. I have a small boat that I go out in about three times a summer.

ANNA   (*She returns*)   The water colors in the bedroom, they are the doctor's, not yours?

MARY   Yes, he did them. Did you like them?

ANNA   Two of them very interesting. The head, it's your cook, of course?

MARY   Yes, but that isn't one of his water colors.

ANNA   I realize that.

MARY   As a matter of fact it was his first picture.

ANNA   It's very strong, very interesting. Then to look at the water colors, so different. I knew the oil was a man's, that's why I asked you to make sure, because the water colors could have been painted by a man or a woman.

ZITA   Excuse me. (*She goes to bathroom*)

ANNA   Doctors begin with a great advantage because they have studied anatomy.

MARY   It is an advantage, yes. At least when you're paint-ing people.

ANNA   Oh, a tremendous advantage, Mrs. McGarry. Have you ever painted?

MARY   Never.

ANNA   Then you have no idea. To know the bones, bone structure. Oh, I found that out when I was painting.

MARY   You painted too?

ANNA   Not well. I was dissatisfied and gave it up when I saw how long it would take to learn properly. For example, anatomy.

MARY   I imagine you're very thorough. From what Zita said.

ANNA   What did Zita say, may I ask?

MARY   Well, just how thoroughly you studied for the theater.

ANNA   I was very thoroughly trained, yes. But training is not all. For the theater one needs—basic. In here. Unfortunately Zita didn't have it. Did she tell you I said that?

MARY   Something to that effect.

ANNA   The child feels the lack in herself, and when she asked me, I told her so. I thought it would be cruel to have her go on, training for years and years. It would have been very cruel.

MARY   Unless, of course, she got pleasure out of the training.

ANNA   The training is drudgery, believe me, Mrs. McGarry.

MARY   Well, you know more about that than I do. Of course there's this to consider: for example, Zita might have had fun uh—dabbling in the theater. You didn't have any fun dabbling in painting, but Zita might have a different attitude. My husband's attitude toward painting. He was never more than the rankest amateur.

ANNA   But as I said before, he knew anatomy.

MARY   Well, I don't see how his knowledge of anatomy helped him with the water colors, the one of the boat on the sand, for instance. The still life of the bottle and the apple and pear on the checkered tablecloth. I know more about the anatomy of a boat than he does, but I could never have painted that picture.

ANNA But you're not interested in painting.

MARY Exactly. And my husband is.

ANNA Oh, I see what you're driving at. The defense of the amateur.

MARY That may be it. I may have been defending the amateur without being conscious of it.

ANNA Actually what fascinated me about your husband's painting was what it told me about him. When he paints a human being, your Negro cook, for instance, he is on sure ground and the picture is strong and masculine. The still lifes and one of the seascapes, they might have been painted by an altogether different person. Not even a person of the same sex.

MARY Well, I have no reason to doubt his masculinity.

ANNA Naturally.

MARY Well, it isn't always taken for granted, you know. He did have that accident.

ANNA Tell me about it, if it isn't too painful.

MARY It wasn't a bit painful—to me. I didn't even know him when it happened. I knew him two minutes later. I fished him out of the water. He was flying an airplane over Long Island Sound and something happened to the motor and he crashed. I was sailing in a race and when I saw him crash I went to where he was and got him out of the plane.

ANNA He owes his life to you.

MARY Literally, yes. Although I just happened to be the first there. There were a dozen other people in the race, any one of whom would have rescued him. In fact, some others did. What I did was keep him afloat till another boat arrived. He was unconscious, and the condition his legs were in, he wouldn't have been able to swim even if he hadn't lost consciousness. Both legs and one arm were broken—multiple fractures—and most of his ribs. The motor was pushed back on him.

ANNA   How did you get him out?

MARY   I opened the door and pulled him out. It was shallow water. I might have left him in the plane but it caught fire.

ANNA   You were very brave.

MARY   Yes, I got a medal for it. I got a medal and a husband.

ANNA   When was this?

MARY   The accident was in 1934. We were married the next year, 1935.

ANNA   And he was an invalid. I think that was even braver than rescuing him from the plane.

MARY   No, that took no bravery. I was in love with him.

ANNA   And obviously still are, Mrs. McGarry.

MARY   I hope it's obvious, but whether it is or not it's true.

ANNA   And you have no children?

MARY   No children.
         (*During this conversation* ZITA *returns from the bathroom and wanders casually out to the terrace, returns, takes brandy bottle to terrace and remains talking with the men*)

ANNA   I would not be capable of rescuing a stranger from a burning airplane.

MARY   You don't know till the time comes.

ANNA   And I don't think I could have married an invalid.

MARY   You don't know that, either. Women have fallen in love with Tom since we've been married.

ANNA   Oh, please don't misunderstand me. Dr. McGarry is charming, utterly attractive. It's just how one is made up, don't you know. I can readily imagine Zita doing these things. Zita is very much like you in certain ways, don't you agree?

MARY I'm complimented. She's a lovely girl.

ANNA I mean it as a compliment, but also to illustrate the differences between myself and my daughter. To begin with, of course, I would not be in a boat on the Long Island Sound. Zita spends half her life in boats, the other half on skis. Do you ski, Mrs. McGarry?

MARY Before I was married. My family had a house up the Hudson and I suppose I skiied before most girls did, American girls.

ANNA I skiied when I was so high, but not because it was the fashion. In Austria. It was a means of getting to school. I hated it. I *loved* skating.

MARY Well, of course that's more like dancing, the ballet.

ANNA Precisely. I have skated at Radio City but then they spoil it by taking my picture and asking for autographs. This is all right for the Powers models, but I went there to relax.

MARY That sort of thing must happen to you all the time, but I suppose you must expect it.

ANNA Expect it, perhaps. Welcome it, no. God knows, we have had enough of it!

MARY Well, the penalty of fame, I suppose.

ANNA Mrs. McGarry, we know what I am talking about. Not fame. I am talking about the other kind, the kind you will not find in here. (*She flips open the cover and a few leaves of the British* Who's Who)

MARY Oh, the divorces and things like that.

ANNA The scandals! Let's come out with it, Mrs. McGarry. I can take it. We are to be next-door neighbors for—one, two, three, at least three months. I want you to feel free to speak of the McKenzie girl. Naturally I hope we find other things to talk about, hundreds of other things, but please do not feel that we must all pretend that the McKenzie affair never happened. When I was a girl in Austria I had an uncle who did away with himself, committed suicide. We never spoke of Uncle Karl, but it would have been better if we had. So much secretiveness, you know? If someone outside our family accidentally said the word suicide he would be embarrassed and we would be embarrassed. We pretended Uncle Karl never lived, and we pretended nobody ever committed suicide. It was constantly a strain on ourselves and on our friends. So—please don't pretend that the McKenzie thing didn't happen.

MARY   Truly, Mrs. Douglas, I haven't the faintest idea what you're talking about.

ANNA   Mrs. McGarry, why would you have out the British *Who's Who*? To look us up, surely.

MARY   Yes, that's true.

ANNA   I see over there a pile of newspapers. I recognize them. They are all the New York papers, the morning papers, the evening papers.

MARY   Yes, my husband reads them every day, all of them.

ANNA   Then you know about the McKenzie affair, so why pretend not to know?

MARY   Oh, now I see. Well, whatever the McKenzie affair is, I don't know about it because I read practically nothing in the papers. I skim over the first page and I look inside to see if any of my friends have died, or their children are getting married, and that's about all. If the newspapers depended on me they'd go out of business. But now you've aroused my curiosity. Is it all right for me to ask what *was* the McKenzie affair?

ANNA   Two years ago in London a young Scottish woman threw herself in the Thames. She left letters, farewell letters to one person. My husband.

MARY   (*Nods*) I remember seeing *something* about it. But of course not knowing any of the people involved, and not being interested in theatrical people, it didn't leave much of an impression. Besides, anyone can leave letters, can't they?

ANNA   Anyone can leave letters.

MARY   And actors, prominent actors, young girls are always falling in love with them. That's always been true.

ANNA   You don't remember this case very well, or you're being utterly polite.

MARY   I honestly don't remember it well at all. A prominent English actor—I didn't even remember your husband's name. And a girl drowning herself.

ANNA   Believe me, it gives me no great pleasure to talk about it, but your friends here in Midhampton, I'm sure many of them will remember it, so better you should hear it from me.

MARY   Yes, I suppose so.

ANNA   The girl was a would-be actress, young and pretty but empty. She had a small part in a play with my husband, what is called a walk-on, which means what it sounds. She played a nurse. She walked on, and walked off. But she was determined. She was thorough. Every day for a year before she got the part she would literally haunt the Ivy. That is a restaurant in London, one of the favorite places for actors and actresses. She would literally haunt the place till she wangled an introduction to Archie. Strange to say, I met her too. She hated me, but I am used to that. Then strange to say she was given this tiny part, this walk-on, and she and Archie were thrown together, during rehearsals, during the run of the play. That was not enough. She telephoned us night and day.

MARY   I should think you could have put a stop to that.

ANNA   She had no pride. She would ring me up and tell me I was standing in the way of a great love.

MARY   Oh, I've heard of those. It happens to doctors' wives.

ANNA   But surely not to you, Mrs. McGarry.

MARY   (*Overlooking the gaffe*) No, not to me. Other doctors' wives. But I don't mean to interrupt.

ANNA   Not at all, but to continue. I said nothing to Archie about the telephone calls. The girl would have been discharged. But that was my big mistake. She should have been stopped early.

MARY   Maybe she wouldn't have stopped. Maybe having her discharged would have made matters worse.

ANNA   How could matters have been made worse? She threw herself into the Thames.

MARY   (*Nods, remembering more of the case*) Now I begin to remember more. Your husband—something about—

ANNA   Yes. She wrote him a note, asking him to meet her at a certain place on the Embankment, not far from our house in Chelsea. He foolishly went there and was recognized by the police. She was already dead. It was all so neat. So carefully planned. And planned so because she hated me.

MARY   Don't you think she wanted to incriminate your husband, because he wouldn't have anything to do with her?

ANNA   It was to destroy me. To make me think there had been an affair, a romance.

MARY   I don't quite see that, Mrs. Douglas. How do you mean?

ANNA   She could not incriminate him, Mrs. McGarry. He was nowhere near her when she threw herself in the Thames, but she planned it to have him dragged into the scandal.

MARY   Yes, I see that much.

ANNA   Hoping I would think there had been an affair, the rest of my life thinking there had been an affair.

MARY   Well, of course you knew the girl. I would have said merely that she was the victim of unrequited love, and wanted to incriminate your husband.

ANNA   No, it was not so simple. It was aimed at me.

MARY   I see. (*Although she does not "see"*) She must have been a very—

ANNA   All mixed up. Utterly.

MARY   Mm-hmm.

ANNA   (*Studying* MARY)   . . . And then underneath it all, underneath all that I have told you. Do you see the deepest motive?

MARY   No.

ANNA   There was a deeper motive. Some time I will tell you. But at least now you know, if your friends ask what kind of person I am, this new neighbor, you will know why they are asking. My husband and I *were* the people you read about in the scandal sheets.

MARY   Oh, well, one consolation. With things the way they are in the world today, people's memories are very short.

ANNA   In *our* world they are very *long*.
    (DOUGLAS *comes in off the terrace, trying with a quick look to guess at the turn the conversation has taken*)

DOUGLAS   (*To* ANNA)   What do you think, old girl? We've all had a tiring day, at least we three, and I imagine Dr. and Mrs. McGarry retire early.

ANNA   I am ready.

MC GARRY   (*Wheeling in from terrace*)   No, I'll be up for at least two hours.

MARY   The Yankees are playing the Red Sox tonight. Sometimes you'll see the light on here till midnight.

I'll be in bed, but if you feel like coming over for a nightcap, Dr. McGarry'll still be up.

DOUGLAS   I thought everyone was for the Giants or the Dodgers. Zita, which is it you're for?

ZITA   Oh, this year the Giants, although they don't seem to be doing very well. They've lost four straight.

MC GARRY   Don't give up on any team that has Stanky. You can have Durocher, but Stanky's my man.

ANNA (*To* MARY)   Do you understand this talk, Mrs. McGarry?

MARY   Yes, I'm afraid I do. If you've lived with it for sixteen years.

DOUGLAS (*To* ANNA)   Yes, and now that I'm being naturalized, I think I'll take it up, and *you'll* hear baseball too.

ANNA   I never paid the slightest attention to cricket.

DOUGLAS   True, you didn't. Well, are we off?

ANNA   Goodnight, and thank you so much, Mrs. McGarry. Doctor McGarry.

ZITA   Goodnight, and thank you ever so much.

DOUGLAS   Mrs. McGarry. Doctor.

MARY   If there's anything you need tonight . . .

MC GARRY   Yes, I won't be going to bed before eleven-fifteen. I'll listen to the ball game and the eleven o'clock news. And I'll speak to the telephone company (*To* DOUGLAS) You can probably have a connection by Friday at the latest. Meanwhile use ours any time.

DOUGLAS   Thank you again, for everything. Goodnight. We go out this way? (*Meaning the French window and over the dune*)

MC GARRY   Oh, sure. It's much more convenient.
    (*They leave*)

MARY   Would you like a drink?

MC GARRY   No thanks. Reducing.

MARY Well, I'm not reducing, and I can stand a drink I can tell you.

MC GARRY Mrs. Douglas?

MARY Why didn't you warn me about their scandal?

MC GARRY Oh, the Scotch girl and Douglas? I don't know. Why didn't I? Did you make a *faux pas?*

MARY No, but she wouldn't believe I didn't know anything about it. She told me the whole story. Or *a* whole story. A whole story out of whole cloth, it seemed to me. What *was* the story?

MC GARRY Oh, he was sleeping with some Scotch girl and she knocked herself off. Drowned herself. She left a lot of letters and it got into the papers. Things have been tough for him ever since.

MARY I wouldn't be surprised if things had been tough for him before that.

MC GARRY Well, he may have asked for it . . . The young girl is nice.

MARY She's sweet. She seems to have a crush on a boy at Williams. We can have a small beach party for her when more of the school crowd start arriving.

MC GARRY Yes, I think the more she sees of people her own age, the better for all concerned.

MARY What's behind that remark? Just a few minutes with Mrs. Douglas and I see double meanings in everything.

MC GARRY Just that Zita thinks Douglas is God, and you saw them making passes at each other this afternoon. (*He snaps on the radio. He looks at his wrist watch as the radio warms up. A radio voice:* "This is WINS, New York." MC GARRY *fills his pipe and is lighting it, she is sipping her drink, studying him.* MC GARRY: "Right on the nose." *A radio voice:* "Hy there, everybody, this is Mel Allen." MC GARRY: "Right on the nose." MARY *goes to him and kisses his nose as the cur-*

tain descends, with MC GARRY *smoking his pipe, beginning to get intent on the ball game, and* MARY *seats herself on a hassock and stares straight ahead, which in this case is in the direction of the* DOUGLAS *house*)

CURTAIN

ACT TWO

SCENE ONE

Evening, a month later, the scene is the terrace of the
DOUGLAS *house. Porch furniture. The situation is now re-*
versed: upstage is the windowed wall of the house but
exterior, as distinguished from the previous scenes, which
were interior and, from the audience point of view, facing
out on the ocean. Now the audience is, as it were, looking
inward from the ocean.

At rise ARCHIE, *in black tie, is helping himself to a*
drink from a portable bar. Before seating himself he waves
his hand, facing offstage toward Right.

ARCHIE   Hello, there.

(*A woman's voice,* MARY MC GARRY'S, *calls from offstage,*
but her words cannot be understood. He holds his hand
to his ear)

ARCHIE   Can't hear you.

MARY'S VOICE   Never mind. See you in a little while.

ARCHIE   Come over any time. Don't wait till eight o'clock.

MARY'S VOICE   We may do that.

ARCHIE   Righto.

(*He sits in a camp chair and stretches his legs as* ANNA
enters from the house, sneaks a look toward the MC-

GARRY *house but makes no effort to speak to* MARY. *She is carrying paper cocktail napkins and as she speaks is busying herself with little preparations for her coming guests. She is beautifully dressed in a summer evening something*)

ANNA   You fool. I don't want them to come over now. I have too many things to do.

ARCHIE   Well, she might help you. She's good at that sort of thing.

ANNA   I see I can expect no help from you.

ARCHIE   What the devil do you want me to do? I'll be only too happy to spread the caviar or put the toothpicks in the sausages. Just tell me what and I'll do it.

ANNA   Spread out those chairs. I don't want everybody sitting in one little circle.

(*He rearranges chairs*)

ARCHIE   There we are. *Two* little circles! How many people are coming? (*Resumes his seat*)

ANNA   I am not certain. Those two next door.

ARCHIE   Naturally.

ANNA   Yes, quite. Naturally. We could not dream of having people in without inviting Dr. and Mrs. McGarry.

ARCHIE   You make it sound as though they'd been spending all their waking hours in this house. He's only been here once, and it seems to me that every time *she's* been here she's been very useful, very helpful.

ANNA   Nevertheless we would not dream of having people in without them, would we?

ARCHIE   I don't see why not.

ANNA   All he does all day long is sit in that dreadful chair and stare over here. At night too. He knows when we turn out our lights—he knows when we get up in the morning. He knows when I am in my bath.

ARCHIE   How can he? The bathroom's on the other side of the house.

ANNA   They will not fit in with these people tonight.

ARCHIE   Then why did you ask them? They have their friends, just as we have ours.

ANNA   Because they would sit there and stare at us and our guests.

ARCHIE   I don't believe it for a minute, not a second.

ANNA   You are determined to come to their defense without knowing any of the facts. If I tell you I can *feel* them staring at me you will refuse to understand that.

ARCHIE   No, but I'll refuse to believe it.

ANNA   And so I'd rather have them here, in this house, than to feel that they are spying on me. Well, perhaps they will go home early when they see how much out of place they are.

ARCHIE   (*Humorously*)   But if they go home early—according to you—they'll just sit and stare at us. You surely don't want that.

ANNA   I fail to see anything comical. Remember, please, this party has a purpose. Henry Countryman has not signed anyone for that play. Alfred and Lynn turned it down. Freddie and Florence turned it down. Rex and Lilli turned it down, but all for good reasons.

ARCHIE   Yes, because it's a bad play, more than likely.

ANNA   It is a good play. This—what's his name—the author.

ARCHIE   Antonio Bellini.

ANNA   Bellini. You watch. I read his last play.

ARCHIE   *Ponte Vecchio.*

ANNA   (*Sarcastically*)   Thank you so much. *Ponte Vecchio.* Utterly beautiful.

ARCHIE   Utterly beautiful, but unproduced.

ANNA   Unproduced? It was produced in Hartford, Connecticut. Harvard, Massachusetts. It was produced all over the map—

ARCHIE   But not in New York.

ANNA   It was not written for New York. It was not that kind of play.

ARCHIE   Look, old girl, you don't really know what kind of play this new one is.

ANNA   (*After a pause*)   For the tenth time, I have talked to people who have read it. I believe what they tell me. It is a great play, a great play. But even if it was a lousy play—I want Henry Countryman to put us in it. I will rely on Henry Countryman's judgment, thank you.

ARCHIE   So will I.

ANNA   Even if it's a flop. I'd rather be in a Henry Countryman flop than a Joe Doakes success.

ARCHIE   No you wouldn't.

ANNA   There you are wrong. There is where you fail to see what this is all about. If we are together as a team in a Henry Countryman play, we are—established as a team. Henry Countryman *means* something. The first-string critics, publicity, other managers pleading with us, *begging* us to read manuscripts. Just because Henry Countryman has put us in a play.

ARCHIE   Oh, Lordy, I'm not underestimating Henry Countryman. After all, I did work for him twenty years ago. But I still favor the direct approach.

ANNA   Oh, sure. Of course. You want to go to him and say, Henry old boy, I hear you have a play by this feller Bellini. Anna and I'd like awfully to do it. . . . Where did the English get such a reputation for diplomacy?

ARCHIE   I sometimes wonder.

ANNA   I continually wonder.

ARCHIE   But if you're determined to be subtle about it, why not just have Henry and his wife here, not a whole houseful of people.

ANNA   That would be fine. That would be utterly clever. We invite Henry and his wife to dinner, to drive all the way from East Hampton, or what-you-call-it, to have dinner with you and me? In the first place, they would not come.

ARCHIE   I don't see why not.

ANNA   But *I* see why not. Henry would be suspicious. He would know we had a reason for asking him. He would know the reason, too. He would say to himself: Anna Root or Archie Douglas knows I have the Bellini play, and one of them wants to be in it.

ARCHIE   Very bright of him. Go on.

ANNA   And he would not come. But I know Henry and his wife. They adore parties. So I invited people they know, people they see on Long Island, and by so doing I see to it that Henry and his wife hear about the party, and they know they are not being trapped. It sounds like just a party. A good party, let us hope, but only a party. Then when they get here and they see us together, you and me, Henry thinks: why not Anna and Archie for the Bellini play? Nobody tells him the idea. He thinks the idea is his own.

ARCHIE   I daresay you're right. But what if he doesn't get the idea?

ANNA   Then we don't get the Bellini play. It's the chance we take. A case of champagne, two pounds of caviar, an extra waitress—all wasted. We have spent five hundred dollars foolishly.

ARCHIE   Five hundred dollars?

ANNA   More than five hundred dollars. How much do you think this dress cost?

ARCHIE   Well, at least you can wear it again.

ANNA   *Not* to any party where the Countrymans will be.

ARCHIE   Oh, what the hell, Anna. Henry knows I haven't been able to get a job. He knows it better than anyone else.

ANNA   I am fully aware of that. But if Henry gets the idea

that we would make a good team, like Alfred and Lynn,
or Rex and Lilli . . . People will say he's a genius.

ARCHIE   And he'll agree, old Henry.

ANNA   They will say: No one else would take a chance on
Archie, but Henry Countryman did.
(*He stares at her, deeply hurt*)

ANNA   Well, it's true, isn't it?

ARCHIE   It's true. And what do you get out of this?

ANNA   Couples always work. Good acting couples always
have good parts offered to them.

ARCHIE   You've never lacked for good parts.

ANNA   We live together, we might as well act together.
(ZITA *enters from the house, very pretty in evening dress*)

ZITA   Sorry I'm late. Can I help?

ANNA   There's nothing for you to do now.

ZITA   Hello, Archie.

ARCHIE   Hello, Zita. I didn't realize you were coming to
the party.

ZITA   Only briefly.

ANNA   She's going to a dinner party with some of Next
Doors' friends. What's their name again?

ARCHIE   McGarry.

ANNA   I didn't mean them. I meant your hostess. What's
her name?

ZITA   Mrs. Eltringham.

ANNA   Am I expected to remember names like—what is
it again?

ZITA   Eltringham. They're the nicest people here, with the
exception of the McGarrys.

ANNA   In my humble opinion they're nicer. They don't
live next door.

ZITA   Mother, what have you got against Dr. and Mrs.
McGarry? You're always making little cracks.

ANNA   I don't like feeling I am living in a goldfish bowl, *their* goldfish bowl.

ZITA   Oh, you've said that before. They have a lot more important things to do than watch us.

ANNA   Then, these more important things, I wish they would do them.

ZITA   Oh—pish tush.

ANNA   (*Slapping* ZITA's *face*)   I will have more respect. (ZITA *exits, not crying, not even coldly angry*)

ARCHIE   I hope the McGarrys aren't looking now.

ANNA   Is that the worst they ever see? A mother punishing her disrespectful daughter?

ARCHIE   I don't know, Anna. It depends on how good their eyes are. (*Rising*) Do you want a drink?

ANNA   I am perfectly calm.
(ARCHIE *is pouring himself a drink when the first of their guests arrives. He is a well dressed forty-fiftyish man,* HAROLD KANE, *an American artist, monetarily successful and within limits socially acceptable. He has his hand way out, goes straight to* ANNA, *takes her hand and kisses it*)

HAROLD   Dear Anna. Was there anyone you wanted me to bring? I tried to get you on the telephone, but Central simply refused to divulge your number. Hello, Archie. Tell me the truth, Anna. If I was supposed to bring someone I can be anywhere on the Island in ten minutes.

ARCHIE   Was that your car I heard?

HAROLD   My spanking new Jaguar.

ANNA   A new one? You have a new one, Harold? You mean not the yellow one?

HAROLD   That one's a total wreck. A young friend of mine borrowed it and was taken in drink.

ARCHIE   Was he killed?

HAROLD   Thrown clear. Not a scratch on him, the lucky little beast.

ARCHIE   Why do you buy these fast cars? You don't drive fast.

HAROLD   Oh, why do I do a lot of things? I wish I knew. Or maybe I'm better off not knowing. Anna, *that's* new. (*Referring to the dress*)

ANNA   Spanking new. Do you like it?

HAROLD   It's a mess, darling. (*To* ARCHIE) I'll bet you wouldn't dare say that about it.

ANNA   Archie hasn't said anything about it.

HAROLD   It's sheer heaven, darling, and you know it. Come to think of it, it *is quite* sheer. Am I getting witty at this age?

ARCHIE   You're always witty.

HAROLD   I am, aren't I? . . . I wish I were British, then I could say aint I. That's the only thing I envy the British, that and some of their uniforms. Years ago I always wanted to wear a mess jacket, but then Fred Waring's orchestra started wearing them. Then I wanted to wear trews, but the college boys took them up, so I guess I'm just as well off. Aint I?

ARCHIE   What will you have to drink?

HAROLD   A Martooni, please.

ARCHIE   I beg your pardon?

HAROLD   (*To* ANNA)   He probably still calls them Marts.

ARCHIE   I'll fool you. I call it Gin and French.

HAROLD   Well I don't want a Gin and French. I want a Martooni, freezing cold, and without further delay, please. (*To* ANNA) All this array of beverages, you must be expecting a lot of people or a group of strangers. Why a group of strangers? Because you don't know what they'll want to drink. So which is it?

ANNA   A mixed group, not large, but large for this house.

HAROLD   Tell me who they are. I may want to go home right this minute.

ANNA   (*Looking at a small card*)   Well, there's you, and you were supposed to bring Pat Ardsley. I left word with your servant.

HAROLD   I know you did, but Pat and I are not speaking. She owes me over seven hundred dollars.

ARCHIE   Pat Ardsley? She has more money than a maharajah.

HAROLD   I know that or I wouldn't tell on her. But she still owes me over seven hundred dollars. She lost to me at Canasta and then refused to pay. She said if *I'd* lost it I wouldn't have paid *her*, which is a dirty lie.

ARCHIE   Is it?

HAROLD   It is, because I never conceivably would have lost to her. At anything. I wouldn't play her if I thought there was a chance of my losing. I practically live off women like her when I'm not working.

ARCHIE   I can understand that.

HAROLD   Oh, I didn't mean anything mean, Archie. Who else, Anna?

ANNA   Mabel and Henry Countryman.

HAROLD   Theatrical folk? What for? Don't you see enough of them in the wintertime? Or—ahh—you're plotting something. Have they got a play you want to do?

ANNA   That's it. You guessed correctly.

HAROLD   Well, Henry ought to be in a good humor if that's really why you asked him. He just made the National after all these years.

ANNA   What is the National?

ARCHIE   It's a golf club.

HAROLD   Oh, you know that, do you? Well, don't count on Henry to put *you* up if that's why you're having him.

ARCHIE   I'm not a golfer.

HAROLD   Neither is Henry, really. And Mabel . . . They're seeing a lot of each other these days, Henry and Mabel. They're very politically minded, vote and everything. I don't know who they're for, but I could find out if it'd be any help to you. Why *are* you having them? To get a part in a play, or because Archie wants to join the National?

ANNA   Do you want to hear the rest of the list?

HAROLD   Continue.

ANNA   Robertson and Alicia Thomas.

HAROLD   Oh, no! Not with the Countrymans.

ANNA   Why not, please?

HAROLD   Well, don't you think it's mixing them up a little too obviously? Theatrical Countrymans, and the Old Guard Robertson Thomases. How did *you* ever get to know *them?*

ANNA   I've known them for years, so has Archie.

HAROLD   But not in *this* country.

ANNA   We've visited them many times, in Hobe Sound and Westbury.

HAROLD   Oh, all right, don't lay it on. You know them, and they're coming. But I wish you'd consult me when you're planning these little do's. I happen to know that in his quiet gentlemanly way it was Robertson Thomas that's been keeping Henry Countryman out of the National.   .

ANNA   Hmm. But does Henry Countryman know it?

HAROLD   No, poor thing. I don't imagine he does.

ANNA   Then we have nothing to worry about.

ARCHIE   Nobody ever died of blackball poisoning.

HAROLD   Now how would you know that, Archie?

ARCHIE   I was blackballed myself, from a New York club.

HAROLD   So you were. Yes, I'd forgotten.

ARCHIE   Oh, yes, I'll bet you had. I'll bet you even know who blackballed me.

HAROLD   I do. Who else, Anna? Are there more?

ANNA   The people next door.

HAROLD   Oh, come, come! Those? In that shack? Who are they? The garage-keeper or some such? The others I can put up with, but deliver me from these village characters, or worse yet, some hearty Wall Street commuter from Cos Cob Conn.

ARCHIE   They're very nice.

HAROLD   I didn't hear Anna say they were.

ANNA   They're nothing like your description. He is a doctor, an invalid, and she's—his wife. And that's all.

HAROLD   I may just quietly slit my veins, and don't you let Docky put a tourniquet on me.

ARCHIE   Have no fear. I'll let you bleed to death.

HAROLD (*As* PAT ARDSLEY *appears from Left*)   Oh, hello, Hateful. I'm not speaking to you. Here's the person that won't pay her gambling debts. How'd you *get* here? I was supposed to call for you but I refused.

PAT (*A striking if somewhat used woman in her forties*) Hello, Anna dear. Dear Archie.

ANNA   He's telling the truth. He was supposed to call for you.

PAT   I came with the Thomases. They're here, coming around the other way.
(*As the* THOMASES *appear: he is a rather distinguished man, sixty-five or so; she is somewhat younger, chic, but no chicken. They appear from Right*)

ROBBIE THOMAS   Good evening, Anna, Archie.

ALICIA THOMAS (ARCHIE *kissing her cheek*)   Hello, dears. Now who was right? Did we come up the right way, or did Pat? She absolutely refused to come the same way we did.

PAT   I got here first. Isn't that the answer?

ROBBIE THOMAS   Hello, Harold.

ALICIA   Oh, here's Harold. Hello, Harold.

HAROLD (*Kisses* ALICIA's *cheek*)   I was wondering if anyone was going to speak to me.

PAT   I often wonder why they do.

HAROLD (*To* ALICIA)   You know about this one, don't you? Doesn't pay her gambling debts.

ROBBIE (*Not terribly amused*)   Oh, now . . . Now.

PAT   He's going around saying the most awful things about me . . . Any time anybody plays *you* for over a hundred dollars they're only playing for fun. If you lost they'd never get their money, so why pay *you*? Would you pay him, Robbie?

ROBBIE (*Embarrassed*)   Oh oh, leave me out of this. (ARCHIE, *throughout, is quietly asking for drink orders, gets them, goes to bar and is helped by* HAROLD, *whose wit is no match for the cold hardness of* PAT. *Here the* COUNTRYMANS *arrive from Right. He is a well-fed man in his late fifties. She is thin, dark, less pretty than the other women but just as beautifully dressed. In this company she is on equal terms with* ANNA, *not with* PAT *and* ALICIA. HENRY *almost speaks first to the* THOMASES *but remembers in time to speak to his hostess and host*)

HENRY (*Kisses* ANNA's *cheek*)   Dear girl.

ANNA   Dear Henry.

HENRY   Old boy.

ARCHIE   Henry.

ANNA   Everybody knows everybody else. Good.

HAROLD   So far, but there are more coming. (*He serves drinks to the* THOMASES)

PAT   Hello, Henry. Hello, Mabel.

MABEL COUNTRYMAN   Good evening, Pat.

HENRY   Pat, nice to see you.

ANNA (*To* ALICIA) Did you have any trouble finding the place?

ALICIA Oh, heavens no. I've been coming here all my life. I used to sail on the bay, in races. When I was a lot younger, naturally. Do you sail? This is a wonderful place for it.

ANNA No, but Zita does. She adores it.
(*They are interrupted by the arrival of* MARY MC GARRY, *carrying* TOM's *chair, now folded*)

ANNA Oh, I should have sent Archie to get that.

ALICIA (*Warmly*) Mary, how nice!

MARY Hello, 'Licia. Hello, Robbie. (*She shakes hands with the* THOMASES) Hello, Pat. (*She shakes hands with* PAT)

ANNA I don't believe you know Mrs. Countryman? Mr. Countryman? Mrs. McGarry. And this is Harold Kane. You seem to know everyone else.

MARY Oh, yes. Old friends.

ANNA And what about Dr. McGarry?

MARY He's coming up the side steps. He'll make it all right. It just takes him a little longer than most. The wheel chair would sink down in the sand, so I brought it. (*She starts to unfold it, with some help from* ROBBIE, *and during this operation* TOM *arrives, supporting himself with crutches. His progress is slow but he stands long enough to say good evening to* ANNA, *then sits in the chair*)

ALICIA Tom, how nice to see you after all these years.

ROBBIE Hello, Tom. Good to see you.

TOM 'Licia. Robbie. Hello, Pat.

PAT Hello, Tom.

ANNA Mabel, this is Dr. McGarry, Mrs. Countryman. And Mr. Countryman, Dr. McGarry. And Mr. Kane. (ANNA *and the* COUNTRYMANS *and* HAROLD *are subtly impressed by the* MC GARRYS' *friendliness with the* THOMASES *and* PAT)

MARY (*To* ANNA)   This is awfully nice. We haven't seen the Thomases for two years, it must be.

ALICIA   And whose fault is that? Every summer we try, you—

TOM   It's my fault, but it really is a nuisance, getting this vehicle in and out of cars. Not to mention getting *me* in and out of cars.

ALICIA (*Goodnaturedly*)   Well, we could come to you, if you'd invite us.

ROBBIE   Exactly.

ALICIA   Mary and I used to sail together. I started to tell you?

ANNA   Oh, yes. Just before Mrs. McGarry arrived. Mrs. Thomas was telling me.

ARCHIE (*To* MARY)   What can I get you to drink?

MARY   Oh—a Martini?

ARCHIE   Right. Tom? (*He does not speak to* MARY *by her first name*)

TOM   Scotch whiskey please. Tall, plain water.
(*Two groups begin to form: in one are* TOM, HENRY COUNTRYMAN, PAT ARDSLEY, *and* ARCHIE. *In the other are* MARY, MABEL COUNTRYMAN, HAROLD, ROBBIE, ALICIA, *and* ANNA)

TOM   Are you down for the weekend, Mr. Countryman?

HENRY   No, we have a little place near Water Mill.

TOM   Oh, did you buy?

HENRY   Yes, we bought the Stanley Rockwell place. Do you know it?

TOM   Yes. It's a beautiful place. Were you badly damaged in the '44 hurricane?

HENRY   We didn't own the place then, but I understand it stood up pretty well. Were you here then?

TOM   Oh, yes. Yes indeed. Very much so. I had to sit it out, right in that house next door. Right in one of these chairs. It was quite an experience for my wife *and* me.

HENRY   It must have been.

TOM   In fact I thought about writing a play about it and sending it to you.

HENRY   I wish you had. Maybe you still can.

TOM   No, I found out that I wasn't cut out to be a writer.

HENRY   You don't know till you've tried.

TOM   I've tried.

ARCHIE   It's an interesting situation, I must say, Tom. You had to stay in your chair, and Mary stayed with you?

TOM   Yes, and could have gone inland. But she stayed. As a matter of fact, we sat through the '38 one too.

ARCHIE   I say, how often do you get them here?

TOM   Well, there was the '38 one. That was worse in some respects than the '44, but not here. A few miles down the beach.

ARCHIE   Thirty-eight, then '44. Six years. Did you have one last year?

TOM   No. Not here.

ARCHIE   Will there be one this year?

TOM   I'll let you know in September.

ARCHIE   Please do, in advance, if possible.

PAT   Yes, let us all know, there's a dear friendly soul. I could close up my house, Mr. and Mrs. Countryman could close theirs, the Douglases theirs.

TOM   And Mary and I could just sit here while the wind blows us into the bay.

PAT   But you're used to it. I was down for the '38 one and I never want to witness another, thank you.

ARCHIE   I should think they'd be very exciting. Dramatic. I've never been in a really bad one, on land. That was a rather good blow in when was it, Henry? When we crossed in the Mauretania?

HENRY   The winter of '30-'31, I think it was.

ARCHIE   Lifeboats torn away, people with broken arms and legs. Do you remember how the piano skittered across the grand salon and smashed to bits?

HENRY   I do indeed. I'd bet over a thousand dollars in the ship's pool, and I lost, needless to say.

ARCHIE   Yes, I remember that. You'd bid over a thousand dollars, but I can't honestly say I felt awfully sorry for you. Two hits in New York and one in London, that year.

HENRY   But that was '30-'31.

TOM   But you've had your share of hits since then. What are your plans for next season, Mr. Countryman?

HENRY   Nothing definitely set. I have one play by an unknown, or practically unknown, but so many things can happen between now and the fall.

TOM   That was a good year in '30-'31, as Archie says. I saw both of them. *The Wondrous Heart,* and *Our World Is Young.* What was the name of that girl that played the nurse in *Our World Is Young?* Nancy—Nancy—Nancy Peary, wasn't that it?

HENRY   Nancy Peary is right. Quit the theater to marry an army officer in India. I saw her in London two years ago. Did you know her?

TOM   No, just fell in love with her for about two weeks.

HENRY   But you *are* interested in the theater.

TOM   I used to go a lot, and I still read plays when they're published, and I keep up with theatrical news. The only stars I ever met are Anna and Archie. I knew a few chorus girls, but we won't speak about that.

PAT   Speak about it, go on, Tom. You know you'd love to.

TOM   I'll tell you about two of them. One of them stood

me up at the clock at the Biltmore and me trying to show off in front of some friends of mine. And the other wanted to drive to Connecticut and get married the first night I took her out.

HENRY   That's quite a range.

PAT   And what about in between?

TOM   They're the ones we *don't* talk about. No, till Archie and Anna moved here I never really knew any important theatrical people. And I guess I'll never see them unless they go on television.

HENRY   (*Politely*)   What about you, Archie? What *are* your plans?

ARCHIE   Well, I've read one or two things but I haven't come across anything I really liked. Maybe it's time I jolly well did something and stopped being so choosy or they'll be forgetting me, but don't you think I'm right in waiting?

HENRY   That's always my advice. If the part isn't for you, don't take it. A chap we both know took a play a couple of years ago just as a stop-gap, a fill-in, and it was a flop. But—while he was in the flop someone else got a part that our friend was ideally suited to.

ARCHIE   Hilary?

HENRY   Right. Hilary Todd. Could have had— I won't tell you the play, but the manager wanted Hilary Todd, but Hilary was working, so he missed out. Oh, wait for the right part, by all means. (*To* TOM) You still read plays, you say, Doctor?

TOM   Most of those that are published in book form.

HENRY   Do you ever read books on how to write plays?

TOM   No, I can't say I do.

HENRY   How about books of criticism?

TOM   No, not them either. I'm satisfied with my own opinions. I read the plays, and I read what the critics say about them the next day, but not criticism in book form.

HENRY   Good.

TOM   Good? Why?

HENRY   Well, I have a play that I'd like to have an opinion on. And I'd like it to be a fresh opinion, non-pro-
fessional. I don't want an actor's opinion, or another
playwright's, or another manager's. If I sent this play
over to you could you find time to read it? You'd be
doing me an enormous favor.

TOM   Hell, you'd be doing me the favor.

HENRY   No, not if you'd sit down and talk to me about it
after you finished reading it.

TOM   (*Humorously*)   You can be sure I'll sit down.

HENRY   (*Embarrassed*)   Well—*you* know.

TOM   Sure. Why I'd be delighted.

HENRY   (*Calling to* MABEL *in the other group*)   Dear? I've
found the man to read the play.

MABEL   Yes, dear?

HENRY   Dr. McGarry's kindly consented to read the play.
(*Attention—particularly lighting attention—is now fo-
cussed on the other group*)

MABEL   Wonderful! But are you sure you didn't bludgeon
him into it?

MARY   Not Tom. He loves to read plays. Is this a play
that Mr. Countryman's written, or someone else?

MABEL   (*Controlling her hauteur*)   Not one that he's
written. (*To* ANNA:)   I'd hate to read a play that Henry
would write, wouldn't you, Anna? (*Back to* MARY:)   No,
Mrs. McGarry, this is a play that was written by—a
foreigner, a European. Henry's terribly keen about it,
but at the same time has certain misgivings about it . . .
I hate to be so vague, I wish I could tell you the name
of the author, and the characters and plot and *all* about
it, but *Anna* understands this kind of vagueness.

ANNA   Utterly.

MABEL   I am free to say this much: I think it's a fine play, but I agree with Henry: we've been wanting a fresh, outside opinion on it, from somebody that's outside the theater, you know? Henry's had his eye out for someone like that, oh, for months. How lucky for him that he met your husband. I wonder why—that is (*Confused*)—

MARY   Why he picked my husband? I'll bet I know why. Tom used to be very fond of the theater, and I imagine when he met Mr. Countryman he lost no time, uh, revealing himself as a—someone who loved the theater.

MABEL   But as an amateur. I know Henry doesn't want it read by a professional. Anna understands that.

HAROLD   So do I. It's simply this: The theater's full of people that don't trust each other—and rightly so. I know thousands, literally thousands of the creatures, and I wouldn't trust a single one of them. That goes for you, dear Anna, and you, Mabel, and Henry, and Archie, and all of you. Completely untrustworthy—

ROBBIE   Now . . . Now.

ANNA   But he's right, Robbie, and Mabel is right, and Henry. It has nothing to do with our morals—

HAROLD   It has, too.

ANNA   Not the kind of morals you are thinking of, Harold.

ROBBIE   Principles. Ethics? That right?

ANNA   Yes. It's just that there is so much competition in the theater that our, uh, ethics have not had a chance to develop.

ALICIA   I think that's very well put. It fits in with everything you and Archie have told us about theatrical people.

ROBBIE   Yuss. Yuss. That's true. But still I think Harold was a bit rough on them.

MARY   Well—will I be allowed to read the play?

MABEL   Frankly, I doubt it, Mrs. McGarry. If I know

Henry's methods, he'll extract a promise from your husband not to show it to anyone. In fact especially you,
because Henry will want only your husband's opinion,
uninfluenced by anyone else's.

ALICIA   Well, if that's the case, Mabel, don't ever show
a play to Robbie. I'd find a way to read it. And Mary
will too, no matter what Henry says, or Tom.

MARY   No, there you're wrong, 'Licia. To be absolutely
frank about it, I don't want to read the play. I don't
read much but children's books, but plays! That jumping from the middle of the page to where somebody says
something. You know: Mary: (*Gesture*) then you have
to go from where it says Mary, to where what she says
begins. The dialog. Then: Tom: (*Gesture*) and what
Tom says. Then Mary, then Tom. Something like watching a tennis match, only worse on the eyes.

MABEL   (*Superiorly, with a smile*)   Hmm.

ANNA   One gets used to it.

MABEL   Are you reading one now, Anna?

ANNA   I've read one or two things but I haven't come
across anything I really liked for next season. If we
found the right play Archie and I might do one together.

ALICIA   How exciting, Anna! You've never done one together.

ROBBIE   That *would* be great. You two.

ANNA   Do you think so, Robbie? I'm so glad you like the
idea. (*To* MARY:) Archie and I never have acted in the
same play . . . But (*A general statement*)—we don't
want to do one of the old standbys, not for our first co-
starring, and we haven't seen anything we like. It would
have to be modern and new, new like us as a team.
Everything new. (*She starts to act:*) Oh, what fun it
could be! Archie Douglas and Anna Root in the new
play by John Jones—

HAROLD   Not *James* Jones, surely.

ANNA (*Ignoring him*)—lovely new costumes, new sets.

ALICIA It would be lovely, Anna. Lovely.

ROBBIE No question. No question.

ALICIA So gay. Wouldn't you love to see it, Mary?

MARY (*Seriously, well consideredly*) I think it'd be wonderful.

ANNA But first!—Find the play.

ROSE (*The cook*) Dinner is served, ma'am.

ANNA Thank you, Rose. Shall we go in?
(ARCHIE *gets behind* TOM's *chair and starts to push, and the others, except* HAROLD, *follow in various kinds of silences:* MABEL *and* HENRY *not quite suspicious;* ROBBIE *and* ALICIA *genuinely in a good mood,* MARY *for the first time seeing that* ANNA *needs to do this play,* PAT *disinterested.* HAROLD *lingers until he and* ANNA *alone remain on the terrace*)

HAROLD You are as subtle as a ton of brick.

ANNA Then help me, you bastard. Be funny. This is no joke to Archie and me.

HAROLD (*Seriously*) I know, darling.

CURTAIN

SCENE TWO

The DOUGLAS *terrace. A very few hours later. The ladies and gentlemen are seated in a crescent-shaped group, as though looking out on the ocean.*

They are seated as follows, from Stage Right to Stage

Left: TOM MC GARRY, MARY MC GARRY, PAT ARDSLEY,
ROBBIE THOMAS, MABEL COUNTRYMAN, ARCHIE DOUGLAS,
HAROLD KANE, HENRY COUNTRYMAN, ALICIA THOMAS,
ANNA ROOT.

ALICIA   Oh, come on, Robbie. Tell it.

ROBBIE   (*Leaning rather far back, with cigar*)   But why
me? Countryman, Henry, you saw money spent.

HENRY   I saw it spent, but those maharajahs. Not our
fellows. Not Americans.

ROBBIE   That's true. You are still an American. Well, sir.

ALICIA   (*To all the others*)   This is real money. Not
maharajah money.

ROBBIE   (*Pontificating, looking way out*)   Well, sir. There
was the time in Pum Beach. Liciar and I were in San
Jean de Luz—

ALICIA   Juan les Pins.

ROBBIE   (*Really going over her interruption*)   Staying at
friends' of ours. This cablegram. Man I didn't *really*
know, I *really* didn't know him very well. 'It is So and
So's Buthday,' he said. 'You and Alicia are absolutely
indispensable.' So by the Lord Harry he arranged for
Aliciar and me to take ship from Naples. Naples, wasn't
it, Alicia?

ALICIA   Naples.

ROBBIE   New York. And a train from New York to Pum
Beach.

ALICIA   But that wasn't the—

ROBBIE   Oh. I see. The wedding?

ALICIA   That. But the coming-out party in Philadelphia.

PAT   Not my coming-out party.

ALICIA   No, not yours, dear. This was some years later.

ROBBIE   When they took the Bellevue. Oh, that. They
gave us a car from Locust Valley. Oh, I remember that
one all right. Yes, yes, Alicia. We were living quite a

ways from Locust Valley, but they sent us our instructions, we were to be at Locust Valley at such-and-such a time and board the car. I must say nothing bored me more than the ideer of driving over to Locust Valley and boarding a car, so I said to Alicia, remember? Have the damned thing stopped somewhere along the way and we'll get on there. But not Locust Valley. The airplane party for the circumcision in Cleveland, but I don't like to fly. I refuse to fly.

ALICIA (*The understanding wife*) Yes. Well, Anna, dear. We must be off.

ANNA Please don't.

ROBBIE I do' wanna go p'ticularly. I just as soon have another brandy.

ALICIA We enjoyed every second. Robbie and I haven't had such a good time—

ROBBIE I don't see any reason to leave now, just when the party's going so well. Archie, aren't you a golfer? Tom? . . . Oh, I beg your pardon. But you and I ought to play. (*Implying age and handicap*)

TOM Not till they invent some motor for this.

PAT (*Rising*) Thank you, Anna. I've had a really lovely time, I really have.

HAROLD (*Rising*) Pat's going home with me. We made it up.

HENRY I think we ought to be going, too.

MABEL I know we simply must. Are you all going to the Powells' tomorrow?

ANNA We're not.

MARY No.

PAT I am, but only for a minute.

ALICIA I thought we might go there.

ROBBIE Is that Dirty Powell, old Dirty? Is he down this year?

ALICIA   Dirty Powell died ten years ago. This is Walter Powell, we went there the Sunday before last.

ROBBIE   (*Rising and struggling to keep his feet*)   If that's the fellow, I for one am never going again. Goodnight, Countryman. Goodnight, Melba. Anna, give me a kiss, you attractive thing. Archie, old boy. Mary, you don't give out kisses. Goodnight, Tom. Goodnight, Kane. Is there anyone I didn't say goodnight to?

MABEL   Goodnight, Mr. Thomas.

ROBBIE   Goodnight, Melba.

MABEL   (*Audibly*)   Mabel.

ROBBIE   I begya poddon. Did I call you Mabel? Melba, dear girl. Countryman. Can we give anyone a lift?

HENRY   If you change your mind about the Powells' we may see you there.

ROBBIE   Quite.
(ALICIA *takes him by the arm and they and* HAROLD *and* PAT *and the* COUNTRYMANS *depart, leaving the* MC-GARRYS *with* ANNA *and* ARCHIE)

TOM   That's my cue.

ARCHIE   (*Eagerly*)   No, stay a while. Let me get you something.

TOM   Have you got a radio? I don't want—

ARCHIE   Oh, for the baseball? No, we haven't. New York are playing Cincinnati, or Cincinnati are playing Chicago, which is it?

TOM   I'm a little tight. If you'll give me a hand? Mary, all set?

MARY   I think I'll stay a minute and have a cigarette with Anna.

TOM   You will? . . . Okay. In that case, Archie. I could use a little help down the stairs. Mary can bring my coach later.

ARCHIE   I'll bring the coach, too. Ladies? In a little while.
(*The men exit*)

ANNA (*After they have departed*)   Nothing has happened
right this night. The plans of this night I had so fixed,
arranged. Countryman owns a play, written by an Italian
young man. I believe this play to be excellent, great. I
know the play. You go back: Miller, Odets, Coward,
the great young men who are fixed right away. I know
this play. The other young men, going so far back to
Coward, Odets. This is all new. I looked at this play.
Mary McGarry, I spent five hundred dollars in bribery
to read a copy of the play, Binelli's play. Countryman
owns the play and I paid five hundred dollars to bribe
to see a copy of it, but Countryman asks, he asks *your
husband* to read it. Mary, this play is life and death to
us, Archie and I. Archie and me. Cognac, Mary?

MARY   I'll get it. (*She does so, two glasses*)

ANNA   The girl in London killed herself because of Archie.
Consequently no one like Countryman will give Archie
a job. Yes! But they won't give me as good a job! Every
job I am offered is less and less. I should not like to tell
you to whom I was asked to take second billing. A
young nothing, big in front, here. "Miss Root, this girl
is a draw, a moving-picture reputation." And don't forget, this was not in my house. They don't come to my
house any more. I go to their offices. "Miss Root, this
girl is a draw, a motion-picture reputation." Out like
this. Acting is all I am, my life. My body, my mind.
I know every play, where to turn, what the author
means, plays I could not act in. What could I do in
Journey's End? But I know two parts in it. Me Hamlet?
But I know *Hamlet*. All-most-every line of *Hamlet*.
Me Juliet? But I know Juliet, in three languages. I
know singing. Have you got a phonograph? No? Then
you do not have my records. I was in Sixth Avenue
three months ago and paid five dollars for a record I

sang. Dancing? Well—no. No. But I know how *Swan Lake should* be done. In there, inside this little house, find a gold cigarette case with my name, A n n a, in diamonds. A *prince* gave it to me. He's dead, too. Robbie told us about how he saw money spent. Oh-ho! A private car? I had a private train one time, and then did not take it. For one year, just for the fun of it, but for one year I did not touch money, not my fingers on money, one penny of money. Crazy stuff. One time my friend—not the gentleman who gave me the cigarette case. Another friend. I said: I am an actress, I want to remain famous. Very well, said he. So in London he paid a man to tell the press that I was looking at plays in New York, and in New York a press man said I was looking at plays in London. A season is very short, but no one knows—hardly anyone—that for one year I was not in any play anywhere. I was in—a Mediterranean country. Then I fell in love with Archie, and then Archie fell in love with a little Scottish girl. In love with her! If she had been in love with him, but no. He was in love with her. I guess Henry knows it, Henry Countryman. And Mabel, I daresay she knows it. If they know it, Archie and I will never do that play. Henry and Mabel will know I was slipping that long ago. Yes, slipping. If Archie could fall in love with the little Scottish girl, then I was slipping. And nobody fell in love with me. Nobody fell in love with me.

MARY (*After a pause*)   You're still one of the most famous actresses in the world, Anna. Even I know that.

ANNA (*Patting* MARY's *head*)   Sure. And Bernhardt. Bernhardt, with one leg, and dead. She's famous, but what is she doing next season?

ARCHIE (*From Right, returning*)   What's who doing next season? Yep yep. Mary, New York are ahead, five to two in the top of the eighth. Or maybe it's the bottom of the eighth. In any event, New York are ahead. And Brooklyn were rained out this afternoon.

MARY   I knew that.

ARCHIE   Can't seem to tell you anything, eh? Well, old girl, I think it went over very well, don't you? Mary, didn't you think it was a good party?

ANNA   Hardly the question to ask one of our guests.

ARCHIE   (*Pouring a drink*)   But Tom thought it was a good party.

MARY   He had a very good time.

ARCHIE   He had. He had. But not you? Was it not a good party? Were there little nuances that escaped me? Some little bitternesses created? Now I'll tell you what was good about it. First off, it was a nice surprise all round that the McGarrys were old friends of Robbie and Alicia's, and you knew Pat. I think in parties it's always a good starter when you invite people, say separate people, and they turn out to know one another independently of the host and hostess. It makes for a warmth, an unexpected warmth. Then of course let me see now: well, Harold and Pat. An antagonism there, but not a genuine one. An old bag like Pat—I beg your pardon, Mary, but—

MARY   I know Pat.

ARCHIE   And Harold. Let's face it, Harold's not going round bothering women in the dead of night, let's put it that way. Suffice?

ANNA   Suffice, if it means what I think it does.

ARCHIE   It does. So a little tiff between Pat and Harold, that isn't going to spoil anyone's dinner, and notice they did go home together.

ANNA   That rather spoils my dinner, an attractive woman like Pat.

MARY   Yes, I'm inclined to agree with you.

ARCHIE   Well—Pat and Harold, the Thomases old friends of the McGarrys—oh, yes, and the Countrymans. I think Henry and Mabel had a good time, don't you?

MARY   I don't honestly know. I know Robbie Thomas did, though.

ARCHIE   Robbie did get rather tiddly, didn't he?

MARY   He was feeling no pain. He's nice, though. And it's only when he feels relaxed, among friends, that he ever shows that side of him. But you know that as well as I do.

ANNA   Yessss. Robbie had a good time.

MARY   If it's the eighth inning I'd better go home. Tom'll want his glass of milk pretty soon. Anna, thank you, thank you ever so much. And goodnight, Archie. Goodnight.

(*She exits, and* ARCHIE *seats himself, legs outstretched, drink in hand and hand almost on the floor*)

ARCHIE   Well?

ANNA   Need you ask?

ARCHIE   I wasn't sure. We don't get the play.

ANNA   We don't get the play.

ARCHIE   You're quite sure of that. Was anything said?

ANNA   No, at least if you mean did Henry say to me, Anna, you and Archie do not get the play. No, that was not said.

ARCHIE   Are you feeling a chill? Shall I get you something?

ANNA   No, thank you.

ARCHIE   So—we don't get the play. It isn't the last chance, you know.

ANNA   (*Languidly*)   No?

ARCHIE   No, it isn't. There may be some little fellow tap-tap-tapping away this very second, over at the Martha's Vineyard, you know, writing the ideal play for us.

ANNA   The Martha's Vineyard. What's that?

ARCHIE   Kit and Guthrie.

ANNA   Oh, yes. Some little man tapping away, for us?

ARCHIE   You're right. It's a slim chance. How much money've we got?

ANNA   In this country? You mean my money and your money together?

ARCHIE   Yes.

ANNA   At the scale we are living, enough for a year.

ARCHIE   Well, that's not so bad. I can—

ANNA   Excuse me. I left out Zita. Four thousand dollars for Zita, minimum. That's without Christmas, and other expenses not in her allowance.

ARCHIE   *Six* thousand dollars, more than likely.

ANNA   More than likely.

ARCHIE   I never knew we were that well off—till we no longer had it.

ANNA   I'll take care of Zita. I have a ring that will see her through.

ARCHIE   I know you have. A ring, a couple of rings, a necklace, two or three bracelets. But I won't permit it.

ANNA   (*Sardonic laugh*)   Then without your permission, kind sir.

ARCHIE   I think I'll motor up to New York tomorrow and see about a job on the television.

ANNA   Do you?

ARCHIE   Are you doubting my word?

ANNA   Are they waiting for you? Tomorrow is Sunday, those executive accounts—

ARCHIE   Account executives.

ANNA   —are playing golf. Greenwich, Connecticut. And where will you stay? The St. Regis?

ARCHIE   I thought I might.

ANNA   Lunch at 21? Sign the chit, thirty-five dollars. Telephone me here you are terribly tied up Monday night, can't get back? El Morocco, sign the chit, one hundred dollars. Car with chauffeur Monday night, forty dollars. A few neckties and things, fifty dollars. A present for me, one hundred dollars? Stay here, Archie. We wasted five hundred dollars tonight.

ARCHIE   This party cost five hundred dollars?

ANNA   With my dress, more than that. I told you it would. (*She laughs bitterly*)

ARCHIE   What's rocking you with laughter?

ANNA   When I bought this dress I was extravagant because I couldn't wear it again in front of Mabel Countryman. Mabel didn't even ask us to dinner next week— but she did ask Robbie and Alicia.

ARCHIE (*Very bitterly*)   What shall I do? Give up smoking? I offered to go up to New York to look for a job.

ANNA   What shall you do? I don't know what you shall do. Stand outside the Colony restaurant and be rude to the autograph morons. Take out the American citizen papers and have two new dinner jackets from London. Make jokes about Ronnie Colman selling beer.

ARCHIE   I have nothing against Ronnie.

ANNA   Wait till he reads that interview, he'll have something against you.

ARCHIE   I won't be pushed around by those bubble-gum morons at the Colony restaurant. And as to the dinner jackets, they're deductible from the income tax.

ANNA   Yes, but what income?

ARCHIE (*After a pause*)   My dear girl, you're not coming out with it, are you? You're not coming out with the fundamental complaint, are you?

ANNA   No. I can't even act any more. Harold Kane told me that.

ARCHIE (*Continuing*)   You won't permit yourself to complain against the Scottish girl. Is it because you think you're behaving as a lady ought to behave? Well, quit it. You never are and you never could be a lady.

ANNA   I *said* I can't even act any more.

ARCHIE   And—you never could.

ANNA (*Very deliberately*)   On-stage, or off-stage? Which performance do you object to, Archie? On-stage, or off-stage? (*She looks at him contemptuously, rises, walks as though to the portable bar, but passes behind his chair and enters the house, leaving him alone and somewhat amazed*)

ARCHIE (*Helping himself to a drink*)   Oh, well.
(*As he pours the drink* ZITA *appears from Left, carrying her shoes, which she puts on one of the porch tables. She goes to* ARCHIE *and places a hand on each shoulder*)

ZITA   Don't start hitting it up again, please, Archie.

ARCHIE (*Smiling, glass in mid-air*)   The jeunesse dorée, for God's sake.

ZITA   Please.

ARCHIE (*Cockney*)   Go 'ome and tell your mother she wants ya.

ZITA (*Indicating* ANNA *with a head-shake*)   This is the worst you've ever had, you two.

ARCHIE (*Wrist watch*)   Why are you home so early? Most daddies ask why you're home so late, but I want to know why you're home so early.

ZITA   It's not early.

ARCHIE   It's early for you and your crowd, a Saturday-night dance. Do you want something? (*He is not tight, but is shaken by the scene with* ANNA)

ZITA   Ginger ale. I'll get it.

ARCHIE   Sit down. Here. (*He wipes beach chair with his handkerchief*) Expensive hankie, not yet paid for by yours truly. Why are you home so early?

ZITA   It was a lousy party, really.

ARCHIE   At your age the only reason a party can be lousy is you had a spat with your boy friend—or he wasn't there.

ZITA   He wasn't there.

ARCHIE   Is that a remark full of meaning, Zita? Am I still your one and only true boy friend?

ZITA   Yes.

ARCHIE   Well—the sad news is—I can't afford you. Were you eavesdropping for that part of it?

ZITA   No, or I guess not.

ARCHIE   I can't afford you. You cost too much.

ZITA   I don't know what you mean, but it doesn't make sense to *me*. I don't cost you anything. The few kisses we have. They don't cost you anything. Once in a while a kiss. A hand-hold, but never a genuine embrace, our hearts entwined.

ARCHIE   Are you tight?

ZITA   I sound like it. No, I'm just so damn tired. I've been up since six o'clock this morning, don't forget that. I played ten sets of tennis and I swam three—no, four times. I'm sleepy more than anything else, that's why the brain isn't working too well, but I love you, and this'd be the perfect time for us to be able to go in and turn out the lights and—the works. What were you and Mum fighting about besides money?

ARCHIE   Just money, and my inability to make any. How much did you hear?

ZITA   Just the very end, where you told her she wasn't an actress. I must say she put you in your place.

ARCHIE   Where is my place?

ZITA   Oh, stop dramatizing. You got in a scandal and you can't get a job on account of it. If Mum's annoyed she has every reason to be. I'm sorry. I wouldn't talk this way if I weren't tired, but I *am* tired. And what good does it do me to come home tired, no

father, and a mother that hates me? A famous actor, handsome, but just a few kisses. I can tell you one more thing, I'm sicker of my life than you are of yours.

ARCHIE   I didn't say anything about being sick of my life.

ZITA   But you are, or you ought to be. But you're forty-eight years old, or near it. I was snubbed tonight. Oh, I was really put in *my* place.

ARCHIE   By whom?

ZITA   By whom indeed. If you want to know the truth, I came home in a taxi.

ARCHIE   Because you thought you were snubbed?

ZITA   This very attractive boy, or at least I thought he was very attractive—yes, he *was* attractive. He sat across from me at dinner, and I knew he was the one I liked best at the party, and liked me best too. Then we went to the dance and we danced together till somebody cut in. Up to then he'd been very nice. *Reasonable,* you know, but when he cut back again, this time he was a sex-boat. I said to him, "Wait a minute, Big Wheel. This is still me, the same girl you were dancing with a minute ago." "I want to talk to you," he said, so I went out on the porch with him. "No," he said. "The car." So I like a damn fool got in the car with him. And then it started. I've been in cars with boys before, but this boy wasn't tight or anything, and he'd been sweet and reasonable, before we were cut in on. Then I guess somebody said something to him and he got a different perspective. They must have said something about me, to make him change in two minutes. No—they didn't only say something about me. They said something about you and me, and Mum. I guess it reflects what they're all saying about us, Archie. You and me, and Mum.

ARCHIE   Saying what, Zita?

ZITA   Do I have to draw a diagram? They know you're not my father. They know what happened in London.

You remember the boy I used to go skiing with, from Rye? His mother finally put a stop to us when she found out who he was going around with. But this boy tonight, I thought he was really nice. Attractive. And reasonable. I came home in a taxi, and I don't think I'll ever go to any of those dances again. I'm sure I won't. God, just a few kisses, you and I. Just a few *kisses*, Archie. (*She rises and starts to go in, still walking slowly speaks:*) I start the evening with a slap in the face, and I end it with a kick in the teeth. I never hurt anybody!

(*She goes off, inside the house, at Right, and* ARCHIE *sits in his chair with head in hands, momentarily looking at the floor. He raises his head slowly as* ANNA, *in negligee covered by quilted bathrobe, enters from Left and sits in a beach chair not too near but not far away from his. Her face is expressionless as the curtain slowly descends, and they both are staring straight ahead*)

ACT THREE

Same as Act One.

About two weeks later, afternoon. TOM *is in his wheel chair, listening to the radio.*

RADIO VOICE Now it's really raining here, ladies and gentlemen, it's really coming down. Oh, if you thought what we had before was a rainstorm, this makes it look like a light sprinkle. It's really coming down—

TOM (*Sourly*) It always does. I never saw it go up.

RADIO Now the ground crew are going out again to try and cover the field with the tarpaulins. Let's see how long it takes them this time. The last time was just a little over three minutes. But it's really no use, friends. That field is soaked already, and I don't think there'll be any more baseball here today. Here in our broadcasting booth we can hardly see beyond third base, it's raining so hard.

TOM It's really coming down, eh?

RADIO Well, that's gonna be all for today. I just got a signal from Plate Umpire Charley Berry. The game is called, baseball fans. And of course you all know, it isn't a legal game. Game called in the bottom half of the third inning. In case some of you baseball fans just tuned in, for you late-comers, this game was held up for forty-eight minutes in the second inning, then they tried to play some more baseball but the game was held up again in the top half of the third inning and again in the bottom half. And now in the bottom half of this game between the New York Yankees and the Cleveland Indians—no score, by the way—they've decided to call it no contest. It's really been raining here at the Yankee Stadium, as you New York fans know. It's not an official game. Called in the second half of the third inning. This is the only afternoon game in the major leagues, by the way, so—

TOM   (*Snaps off the radio*) So Dr. Thomas Desmond McGarry will settle down with a good book.

CLAIBORNE   (*Entering from kitchen*) Game called on account of rain, Doctor.

TOM   Thanks, Claiborne. I know. What's a good book I can read?

CLAIBORNE   Well, I got those eight *Saturday Evening Posts* with that continued story down in my room. I can get you that. You know, the ones you asked me to save. I'm finished with it. The spy story?

TOM   All right, fine.

CLAIBORNE   Some iced tea?

TOM   Mm—later, thanks.

CLAIBORNE   When the gentleman comes from Water Mill?

TOM   Oh, Mr. Countryman. I don't know when he'll be here. He didn't set any definite time.

(CLAIBORNE *exits and* TOM *dials a number on the telephone—three digits*)

TOM   Speak to Mrs. McGarry, please. Isn't this the Library? Isn't this three-oh-seven? Sorry. (*Dials again*) Uh-oh, you're the party I just spoke to, aren't you? Sorry. (*Dials once*) Operator, I've been dialling three-oh-seven, but I'm not getting the Library. Will you try it for me, please? Hello, is this three-oh-seven? May I speak to Mrs. McGarry, please? (*He recognizes her voice and she his*) I've been dialling three-oh-seven and getting three-oh-eight or something. Listen, did Countryman set any definite time? My recollection is that he didn't . . . Good . . . Good . . . Oh, the God damn baseball game was rained out and I have nothing to do till he gets here. No, don't come home. It's going to rain here any minute and that'll mean a lot of business for the Library. I'll see you later. (*He hangs up, looks out the window, toward Right and says aloud:*) Oh, God. (*He sits, trying to look unconcerned until pretending to be surprised by* ANNA's *voice*)

ANNA   Are you busy? May I come in?

TOM   Oh, hello, Mrs. Douglas. Come in. I haven't seen you since your lovely party. I've *seen* you, but . . .

ANNA   May I sit down?

TOM   Why of course. Have a cigarette.

ANNA   (*Holding up case*)   I have my own, thank you, but I don't want to smoke. The fact of the matter is, I'm not feeling well.

TOM   (*In a feeble attempt to be light*)   Then you ought to see a doctor.

ANNA   You are very bitter, aren't you, Doctor?

TOM   No, I don't think so.

ANNA   How is your painting?

TOM   I finished one picture since I saw you, two weeks ago.

ANNA   You work fast?

TOM   I did this one in two days. If I don't finish them right away I never do.

ANNA   Impatient. You give up.

TOM   I lose interest. I'm not going to do any more till after my big exhibition.

ANNA   We received the invitation, thank you very much.

TOM   I was against the idea of sending out invitations, but if anybody pays good money for any of the pictures, the proceeds go to charity, and I'm in favor of charity. Or I suppose I am.

ANNA   I think you are. That's why I came over here. Doctor, what am I going to do?

TOM   (*Professionally stalling*)   That's a large question.

ANNA   When we first came here—I shall be quite frank— at first I somehow resented your sitting here in your house and being able to watch everything that happened in our household. You could watch our comings and goings from the moment we arrived here. That is a monstrous thing, I told myself, for a man to sit like God, or the devil, watching every move I make. I resented you very much, Dr. McGarry.

TOM   I should think you would, if that's the way you felt.

ANNA   It's a strange thing for an actress to say, hating to be stared at.

TOM   Not at all. Cornell, Garbo, Fontanne—they all insist on privacy when they're not on stage, don't they?

ANNA   I lowered the blinds on your side of the house, I used that side of our house as little as possible. I could feel you watching me.

TOM   (*Pleasantly*)   I won't deny that I did watch you, but I didn't make a deliberate effort to spy on you. I sit where I always sit, I didn't move my chair to a better vantage point. In the mornings I sit out on the terrace to get the sun, then I have lunch, and in the afternoon I listen to my radio. As a matter of fact on good days, when the sun's out and I have the radio out on the terrace, I'm facing the other direction, to get the afternoon sun. So I couldn't watch you unless I had eyes in the back of my head. Still, I understand what you mean. The houses are quite close together.

ANNA   But this feeling changed. Recently I began to hope you were watching me. Like God . . . (*He nods, professionally, but says nothing*) In fact, in the morning I would look across, the first thing in the morning, to see if you were in your usual place. And at night, the last thing, I would look to see if you had gone to bed.

TOM   I'm not a psychiatrist, but what do you suppose made you change? The knowledge that I was harmless, or something deeper?

ANNA   I think you know what made me change.

TOM   I might have a theory, but what's yours?

ANNA   I think I began to change when Archie went away, two days after my party. When he didn't come back and didn't come back I suddenly realized I had no one to turn to. I quarrelled with Zita and made her hate me. You know I've been alone in that house for twelve days and nights.

TOM   I didn't realize that. I noticed Archie wasn't around, but I didn't know Zita had gone.

ANNA   They went away together.

TOM   Are they together now? Don't answer that if you don't want to.

ANNA   I *can't* answer it. At least, I don't know.

TOM   All this has been going on under my very eyes. You see how little I observed.

ANNA   That tells me something.

TOM   What's that?

ANNA   It tells me that Mary hasn't noticed either.

TOM   She hasn't said anything. But she's been very busy, getting my pictures framed, and her regular work at the Library. The days pass quickly here, Mrs. Douglas. The seasons, and the years. The summer people arrive and go away, and we're alone, then it's baseball season again and pretty soon the summer people are back—you'd be amazed. I'm telling you this because I didn't realize it *was* two weeks since your party. And you've been alone ten days, was it?

ANNA   Twelve days, and twelve nights.

TOM (*Gently*) Your pride kept you from coming over here? You could have talked to Mary.

ANNA I am talking to Mary now. You are both one to me. I would not have told Mary without telling you. I don't want to tell you anything that you can't tell Mary.

TOM (*Deeply moved*) Thank you.

ANNA You perhaps wonder why I came over now? I'll tell you. I could not stand it any longer, so I rang up Archie at his hotel. I know he has been staying at the St. Regis, so this afternoon I telephoned him there. They said he checked out today and left no forwarding address. What am I going to do?

TOM What about Zita? Would she be at the St. Regis too?

ANNA She might, she might not. They know us there. She could be in a suite with him and they would not suspect anything wrong.

TOM I don't think Archie would do that.

ANNA You like Archie, don't you?

TOM Yes, I do.

ANNA Men do. They really like him.

TOM (*Slightly annoyed*) Don't women?

ANNA Never for very long.

TOM You do. You love him.

ANNA (*Wearily*) Perhaps.

TOM Just a second. (*He looks in the New York phone book and dials O and speaks:*) Plaza 3-4500.

ANNA No! No! What are you going to do?

TOM (*Holding up his hand*) Just a minute . . . Is Miss Zita Schmidt registered, or Miss Zita Douglas? . . . I see. Thank you. (*He hangs up*) They know her, all right. No, she hasn't been there for quite some time. Mr. Archie Douglas has been there but checked out today.

ANNA Why did you do that?

TOM   I wanted to make sure about Zita. Did you ask for her when you phoned?

ANNA   No.

TOM   Why not?

ANNA   I was ashamed.

TOM   You didn't want to know. If she was there, you didn't want to know it.

ANNA   But I don't know anything now. She could be staying some other place but still be with Archie.

TOM   That's true. I think the important thing is to find her. I can see why you wouldn't want to call her friends, but how'd it be if *I* called a few places where she's likely to be, and I'll just say it's Tom McGarry calling. Nobody will know who Tom McGarry is.

CLAIBORNE   (*Entering with magazines*)   Good afternoon, Mrs. Douglas.

ANNA   Good afternoon, Claiborne.

CLAIBORNE   I could only find *seven* installments. The fourth one, I can't imagine what happened to it unless it's in your room.

TOM   Never mind now, Claiborne.

CLAIBORNE   Anyway I think the gentleman's coming. A car's coming up the driveway.

TOM   Thanks. (*She leaves*) The gentleman is Henry Countryman coming to ask about that play.

ANNA   (*Nervously*)   Then I must leave.

TOM   Not before he gets here.
    (HENRY *appears from Right*)

HENRY   Why hello, Anna.

ANNA   Henry darling.

HENRY   Doctor McGarry.

TOM   How are you, Mr. Countryman. (*They shake hands*)

ANNA   I must be going.

HENRY   I saw Archie one day last week, just to wave to, in 21.

ANNA   Yes, he told me. 21? I thought it was the Colony.

HENRY   No, I'm quite sure it was 21.

ANNA   I may have got mixed up.

HENRY   I was only in town overnight. I'm sure it was 21.

ANNA   Such serious discussion over such unimportant matters. When you are finished with Dr. McGarry come over to me for a drink if you feel like it, Henry.

HENRY   I may take you up on that. (*She leaves*) That's a great woman, Doctor. I could tell you things about her that would amaze you.

TOM   I'll bet you could.

HENRY   Sometimes I wish I'd studied medicine. I think I'd have been pretty good, you know. Possibly not as a surgeon, but in the mental field, for instance. For instance, people seem to like to tell me things. I'm the repository for more confidences than you can imagine. People in the theater, you know, they're not very self-reliant, believe it or not. They probably haven't any more troubles than other people, but they exaggerate them, and they're always looking for someone to confide in, and let me tell you, a good many of them come to Old Papa Countryman.

TOM   I should think they would.

HENRY   And not only the ones that are in my plays. Others as well. For instance, Anna there. In the strictest confidence, of course?

TOM   Of course.

HENRY   Well, she's been having a bit of trouble lately.

TOM   Oh?

HENRY   Mabel and I had asked Anna and Archie to come over and dine with us one night last week, and they accepted. But then at the very last minute—or practically—the afternoon of the day they were coming—she telephoned me and begged off.

TOM Mm-hmm?

HENRY She was worried, not about herself but about Archie. She told me—this is all in confidence, of course?

TOM Oh, yes.

HENRY She told me that Archie was in one of his moods of depression, and he can get into the blackest depression of anyone I know. So Anna suggested a trip to New York. Told him to go to town and buy a few neckties, take a pretty girl to lunch, get a bit tight.

TOM I see. Change of atmosphere.

HENRY Exactly. She knows how to handle him. When I told her a moment ago that I'd seen Archie, that was my way of telling her—well, that I approved of her suggestion. If I hadn't approved of it I wouldn't have said anything about it. Do you see what I mean?

TOM In a way. Not quite. But I think I do.

HENRY If I hadn't said anything about seeing Archie, that would have meant a tacit disapproval.

TOM Oh, now I understand.

HENRY You see, they not only confide in me. They also want my approval. I'm not a hell of a lot older than most of these people, but they do treat me like a father sometimes. By the way, is Archie back?

TOM I don't know. I haven't seen him, but of course that doesn't mean anything. I don't get around as much as most people, and I've been reading the play.

HENRY Ah, now we come to it. Good. I much prefer to have you mention it first and not me. What is your reaction—now that isn't as abrupt as it may seem. My full question is: what is your reaction percentage-wise as a hit, as a prestige play, and so on. First, what chance would you say it had of being a hit?

TOM   Percentage-wise?

HENRY   Yes.

TOM   Oh—eighty percent.

HENRY   Eighty percent is very close to what I estimated. What about prestige?

TOM   Percentage-wise?

HENRY   Yes.

TOM   Up in the nineties. Maybe as high as ninety-five percent.

HENRY   Really, now that's good to hear. I said ninety-five, but I was afraid I was going a little too high. Mabel, my wife, *she* thinks ninety-five too, but she's an admirer of Bellini's. Thinks he's *the* coming playwright, first one she's been enthusiastic about since Christopher Fry. She puts Bellini alongside Williams right now, and she thinks this play puts him *very close* to Fry. Now what about your personal enjoyment of the play, just reading it, how would you grade it?

TOM   Frankly, about seventy-five percent. Some of it's obscure and I had to go back and read over a couple of places.

HENRY   (*Chuckling*) That's all right. I did too. I don't mind that a bit. I don't even think that hurts at the box office. Not nowadays. Look at Tom Eliot and *The Cocktail Party*. We went to see that twice here and once in London, and I still have a few points I'd like cleared up, but that does no harm. I'm sure I'm no stupider than a great many people that liked it here, and a great many people did like it. I'm very glad you said seventy-five percent, because it makes your opinion even more valuable. It means I'm not getting the opinion of a terrific highbrow. I know you're a man of superior intelligence, Doctor, but frankly I was just a touch worried that you might be too highbrow.

TOM   Not me. I'm average, just average.

HENRY   No. No. But you're not a pundit. And I think you understand my problems with this play. You know I'll give it a good production. I never let down on *that*. Don't forget I've lost a couple of fortunes in the theater as well as made them.

TOM   Oh, I think everybody knows a Henry Countryman production, what that means.

HENRY   Thank you. I'm just as proud of some of my failures as I am some of my successes. Well, not to go on blowing my own horn . . . I believe you said eighty percent was your figure for its success at the box office.

TOM   Eighty percent.

HENRY   When you arrived at that figure you had in mind a top production, naturally. No expense spared, and so on. But did you particularly have in mind any actors or actresses?

TOM   (*A longish pause*)   Well, that's hard to say. Naturally I began to visualize various people in the more important parts.

HENRY   (*Excitedly*)   Naturally, naturally. Now will you tell me the first two who come to your mind? Thinking back on the man and the woman in this play, which actor and which actress do you see in those parts? I want you to be absolutely frank.

TOM   (*Deliberately*)   Anna Root for the woman, Archie Douglas for the man.

HENRY   (*Jumping to his feet*)   Wonderful! Wonderful! By God, Doctor, you said exactly what I was hoping you'd say! Those two, together for the first time. I tell you, man, oh—let me shake your hand! (*They shake hands*) You've no idea how this pleases me. (*He sits down*) Let me tell you about this play. I had first refusal on it—that means, I saw it first. You know. First refusal. Well, I read it through twice in one day, but I wasn't through the second reading before I realized what my big problem was going to be. Casting those two parts. Well of course there were some obvious ones—Alfred and Lynn, Rex and Lilli, and so on. Established couples. And it had to be a couple. I was convinced of that. But the established ones, either they weren't available, or they didn't quite fill the bill. And time was getting short. I had to give this Bellini an answer. He's an impatient little pansy. So I put him off. Doubled his advance and even raised his royalty, just so I could hold on to this play. I didn't want anyone else to do it. But I knew I'd have to let it go if I didn't come up with the right man and woman, and then out of the blue, so to speak, Anna had that dinner party a few weeks ago—the night I met you—and I could hardly eat that good dinner. I knew Anna and Archie were just right for the play, but I wasn't sure how Bellini would react. So I telephoned him in Rome, and the little son of a bitch is away somewhere in Africa. I couldn't find out where in Africa, and Africa's a hell of a big place. But I got my spies working, some of those curious little people in Rome that have sponged off me for years, and I finally got one to tell me where Bellini was. He wasn't in Africa at all. He just gave out that story. He was in Portugal, Estoril, Portugal, with some of his little playmates. Well, I called him there and he'd just started back to Rome, by motor. He'll be there day after tomorrow or the next day, or the day after, and do you know something, I'm going to be there to meet him! I'm going to fly to Rome and say, "Look here, young man. I have the right people for your play," and I won't leave till he says yes.

TOM   You anticipate trouble?

HENRY   I always anticipate trouble with playwrights. He has the right to approve or disapprove the principal actors in this play.

TOM   Does he know American actors—and English?

HENRY   This fellow knows every actor, every actress alive.

He's been in this country. Speaks perfect English. He knows his rights, too, and he has a very tough agent. I don't want to deal with the agent. I want to handle this personally. And you made up my mind for me.

TOM   I did?

HENRY   Well—at least you gave me the impetus. When I spoke to his friends in Portugal I just about decided to fly to Rome, and I had my office start making the arrangements. But you did give me the final impetus. I got the idea for casting Anna and Archie that night and Mabel, my wife, she saw exactly what I meant. But your opinion had a great deal to do with it, at least it was what they call the final convincer.

TOM   Well, I'm very pleased.

HENRY   I can't *tell* you how pleased I am. I have a notion to call Mabel. She was very much interested in what you were going to say.

TOM   Here's the phone.

HENRY   (*After a quick hesitation*)   No. I can't allow a word of this to get out, not till after I've seen Bellini. And I must ask for your solemn word of honor that you won't say a word to anybody. Not even Mrs. McGarry.

TOM   I'm bound to tell Mrs. McGarry, but she's a doctor's wife. She keeps secrets.

HENRY   Well, Mrs. McGarry. But emphasize to her how much it may mean to Anna and Archie. If they knew they were being considered and then I wasn't able to convince Bellini—this would break their hearts. It would really wreck them.

TOM   I can promise for Mary and me. We won't say a word to anyone.

HENRY   Please don't. For their sake as much as mine. You know what they said the other night, they were looking for a play to do together. Little did they know.

TOM   Little did they know.

HENRY Another favor, Doctor. They knew I was going to give you the play.

TOM Yes.

HENRY Don't let them pump you. If they try to ask you any questions about the play, you tell them—tell them, very casually, tell them you thought it was an amusing play. But not for Broadway. That's always a good out. Amusing, but not for Broadway. If they want any details you just say you're sworn to secrecy. That'll hold them till I get back from Rome, and then I'll certainly tell them that you had them in mind all the time.

TOM (*Laughing*) Do you think I can act that well?

HENRY Of course you can. You medicoes are acting all the time. If you're anything like my doctor, he gives a performance every time I go to his office. Performance worth six-sixty, though. *Not* what I pay him. (*He rises, and* TOM *hands him the script, which has been lying on table. They shake hands*) I'm going to bring you a present from Rome. You like leather, don't you?

TOM I don't want a present. This was a pleasure.

HENRY I know just what I want to get you. I know an Italian leather man. I think he's the best in the world, myself. I'll call you as soon as I get back. Maybe I'll call you from Rome, if you're interested.

TOM Of course I am. Have a good trip, a successful trip.

HENRY If it isn't successful I may not *be* back. I may strangle a certain Italian playwright.

TOM Good luck, the best.

HENRY Thank you. Thank you for everything.

(*He exits and* TOM *waits a moment, rings the silver bell, and calls out:* "Claiborne")

(CLAIBORNE *enters*)

CLAIBORNE Ready for your iced tea?

TOM Not for the time being. Claiborne, go out in the kitchen and watch to see when Mr. Countryman's car gets out of sight. (*She goes out, but her voice is heard:*)

CLAIBORNE   Almost all the way down the driveway. Now he's turning. He's turning towards Southampton. Now he's on the road. Now he's going, getting moving, now he's really moving, really moving.

TOM   Okay, thanks. (*He dials three digits on the phone*) Mrs. McGarry, please . . . Mary? . . . I just wanted to tell you. This is Top Secret . . . You know who I mean by Henry, the man that was coming to see me this afternoon? . . . Right . . . Well, I just wanted to tell you. He wants Anna and Archie for that job. You get what I'm driving at? . . . Good. . . . See you. (*He puts hand on phone cradle and dials three digits*) This is Dr. McGarry. Can you come over? I have some news. Good. (*Smiling*) Yes, I can see you. . . . (*Hangs up*) Just bring some ice, Claiborne. Never mind the iced tea. Just a bucket of ice and a pitcher of water.

(*He lights his pipe and* CLAIBORNE *brings the ice bucket and water, puts them on portable bar and exits.* ANNA *enters from terrace*)

TOM   Would you like a drink, or is it too early?

ANNA   I don't think I want a drink. Shall I fix you one?

TOM   Yes, if you don't mind. Scotch whiskey, plain water, in a tall glass. (*She goes to bar*) You told Mary you had read that Bellini play.

ANNA   (*At the bar, back to him*)   Yes.

TOM   Do you remember the scene where the donkey cart breaks down, in the village?

ANNA   Donkey cart in the village?

TOM   The wheel of the cart is supposed to break.

ANNA   No. Is this the new Bellini, or an old one? Is this the play that Henry is going to do?

TOM   Yes.

ANNA   (*Shaking her head*)   There is no such scene in the play.

TOM   I know there isn't. I just wanted to be sure you'd read it.

ANNA   (*Handing him his drink*)   Oh. I read the play. Of that you may be quite certain. Five hundred dollars, bribe money. (*She smiles wearily*) You don't trust me.

TOM   Well, I wanted to be absolutely sure. You don't always tell the truth, do you?

ANNA   (*Standing near him*)   Who does? What have you to tell me?

TOM   I don't always tell the truth, but I've very seldom broken my word of honor. I am now about to break my word of honor. In the simplest possible language, Henry Countryman—

ANNA   Oh, no! Oh, no!

TOM   . . . Yes. Wants you and Archie for the play.

ANNA   Oh, God!

(*She raises her eyes, but her hands fall to her sides limply. He looks away from her and takes a sip of his drink, not intruding on her emotion*)

TOM   I gave him my word of honor I wouldn't say anything to read the play. I suppose that makes a little difference. Countryman is flying to Rome to talk to Bellini, to get Bellini's approval of you and Archie.

ANNA   When?

TOM   Why, tomorrow, I think. Maybe tonight. He'll be in Rome day after tomorrow.

ANNA   (*Pleading, possibly to God*)   Where is Archie?

TOM   I have some friends in the state police—but that wouldn't do any good. I could call The Players club.

ANNA   He never goes there. He says it's too far downtown.

TOM   Isn't it worth a call?

ANNA   No.

TOM   I could call 21.

ANNA   He checked out of his hotel. He's left New York, of that I'm sure.

TOM I think what I'll do—you help me make a list of all the places he's likely to be, and I'll call every one of them and leave my name. He may not want to call back if you leave *your* name, but when he sees *my* name it'll arouse his curiosity.

ANNA All right. 21, El Morocco, Voisin, the Colony, Sardi's, Chambord, Passy, Pavillon, the Links Club— Robbie Thomas is a member there.

TOM (*With pencil and paper*) Not quite so fast, please. After the Colony?

ANNA Voisin.

TOM I have that. Voisin, Colony, and the other ones I have are 21 and El Morocco.

ANNA Oh, what's the use?

TOM Well, there's just a chance, you know.
(*Here* ZITA *enters from Right. She is momentarily surprised to see* ANNA, *but she is not embarrassed*)

ZITA Hello, Mother. Good afternoon, Dr. McGarry. Is Mrs. McGarry at home?

ANNA Hello, Zita.

TOM She's at the Library.

ANNA Is Archie with you?

ZITA He's in that house.

ANNA Is he all right?

ZITA Is he sober, is that what you mean? That's what it sounded like. Yes, he's sober. He doesn't get tight.

ANNA I'll see you later, Doctor. Thank you very much.

ZITA (*As* ANNA *is leaving*) I hope you're not going to make a fuss.

ANNA (*With a heavy attempt at lightness*) What about, Zita? (*She exits, terrace door*)

ZITA Do you expect Mrs. McGarry back soon?

TOM I don't know. She has no set time. But if you'd like to wait—

ZITA (*Over the last three words*) Would you mind if I waited here? I could sit out on the terrace if you're busy.

TOM   You're not disturbing me. Would you like a drink? I'm having a touch of Scotch.

ZITA   I don't like the taste of liquor. I simply don't like the taste. It isn't any moral scruple. (*She looks up at him quickly*)

TOM (*Inquiring about her look*)   What?

ZITA   I imagine you're thinking I have no moral scruples.

TOM   I wasn't thinking anything of the kind.

ZITA   You know I've been away.

TOM   I noticed you haven't been around.

ZITA   Has Mother been in and out of here?

TOM   This afternoon? She was here earlier, yes.

ZITA   I meant the last week or so.

TOM   No. But I think that's the kind of question to ask your mother, not me. If you want to know what she's been doing, ask her.
(*She is quite self-possessed, and more mature than she has appeared to be heretofore, but the transformation is not complete*)

ZITA   Do you expect Mrs. McGarry, in—an hour, say?

TOM   Well, if she comes home before she goes to get the mail and papers, yes. But if she stays at the Library, or in the village, no. Would you like to talk to her on the phone? There's a phone in the bedroom. You can close the door. The number is three oh seven.

ZITA   Thanks.
(*She goes to bedroom at Left, closing the door behind her.* TOM *takes a sip of his drink and* ARCHIE *comes in from Right, the terrace door*)

ARCHIE   Hul-lo, Tom. (*They shake hands*) It is good to see you again.

TOM Good to see you, Archie. We've missed you.

ARCHIE Yes. Mm. That's awfully good news about Henry Countryman's play, isn't it? (*He looks around, puzzled*)

TOM Very good. Congratulations.

ARCHIE Thanks. Thanks very much. Wasn't Zita here a moment ago?

TOM She's in the bedroom, telephoning Mary.

ARCHIE Oh, yes. Well, what have you been doing with yourself?

TOM What have I been doing with myself? Same old things. Reading. Listening to the radio. Going on and off the wagon. Playing my usual poker, and bridge. Did some painting since the last time I saw you.

ARCHIE Oh, yes. Good? Did you like what you did? The painting?

TOM It was all right.

ARCHIE Like to have a look at it, if I may.
(ZITA *re-enters*)

ARCHIE Hello, Zita.

ZITA Hello, Archie. (*To* TOM) She left.

TOM Then she's probably on her way home. Let's have a drink on the terrace. I've been in this house all day and I'd like to get one breath of fresh air before the rain starts.

ARCHIE Good idea. Shall I give you a push?

TOM Okay.
(ARCHIE *gives the wheel chair a push and when* TOM *is safely on the terrace* ARCHIE, *remaining inside momentarily, speaks softly to* ZITA)

ARCHIE I've got to talk to you. Don't have any conversation with Anna till I've had a chance to talk to you. This is terribly important, do you hear?

ZITA All right.
(ARCHIE *goes out to terrace,* ZITA *sits in the living room,*

silent until MARY *comes in from kitchen, slightly taken aback to find* ZITA *there, but glad to see her*)

MARY   Why, Zita. What a pleasant surprise.
(*They embrace*)

ZITA   I don't know how pleasant, but I guess it's a surprise all right.

MARY   We missed you. Did you have a nice trip?

ZITA   You know where I was, don't you?

MARY   No, I don't. But nobody does. Nobody.

ZITA   You're trying to tell me that Mother doesn't know.

MARY   Yes, I'm telling you exactly that. She does not know where you've been.

ZITA   She will in a little while.

MARY   I see.

(*A silent pause as they study each other*)

ZITA   Maybe nobody knows where I've been, but you've all guessed.

MARY   There's been some guessing. What did you expect?

ZITA   Well—the guessing can stop. I've been with Archie. You knew that, didn't you?

MARY   I suppose I did. But I repeat: nobody *really* knows. If you and Archie want to cook up a story, and it's a good enough story, your mother will have to believe it. And she wants to believe it now.

ZITA   But we don't want to cook up a story. I'm going away with Archie, and we came back to tell Mother. We're going away tonight. I came to get a few things.

MARY   But you can't! Not now, Zita.

ZITA   But I can, and I am, and I will. Now, tonight.

MARY   Child! Listen to me! Have you seen your mother?

ZITA   We said cordial how-do-you-do's, here.

MARY   You don't know about the play? Henry Countryman wants your mother and Archie for that new play.

ZITA   Well, he'll have to do it without Archie. We're not

going to spend another night in that house. We love each other, and we're going to get a whole new start.

MARY A new start? Do you know that the minute you leave here with Archie—that's the end for both of you? Anyway, Archie.

ZITA In the theater, maybe. But he's through with the theater anyway. He hates it, he's through with it and the people in it.

MARY You're out of your mind—

ZITA Thank you.

MARY I don't mean that, but what can Archie do?

ZITA Lots of things. He's an able-bodied man.

MARY What things?

ZITA Any number of things. Wall Street. Or work in a store, if necessary.

MARY Do you know how old he is?

ZITA I know how old he is. He can get a job in a hotel or a night club as a sort of a manager. And I can work. I can get a job in a publishing house. A friend—

MARY Publishing houses are not taking on new people. They are laying off people. I know that to be a fact.

ZITA Stop talking about it, please, Mrs. McGarry. This is all decided. It wasn't just decided—this afternoon. I came to say goodbye to you because you were very kind to me this summer. I came here first to give Archie a chance to speak to Mother.

MARY And he's already spoken to your mother?

ZITA Of course he has.

(MARY *looks out at* TOM *and* ARCHIE *chatting, and* ARCHIE's *manner is not that of a man who has just told his wife he is running away with her daughter*)

MARY Has he told you all about it? What she said?

ZITA He hasn't had a chance to.

MARY I'll give him a chance to, now.

(*She goes out on terrace,* ARCHIE *rises and they greet each other, politely, without details of their greeting being audible, then* ARCHIE *enters the living room. He looks at* ZITA, *hesitating before speaking*)

ARCHIE   Thank God I have this chance to talk to you.

ZITA   Thank Mary. What about? What's up, darling?

ARCHIE   (*Sitting beside her on sofa*)   You see, darling—

ZITA   It's something about that play. I know that much.

ARCHIE   Yes. Apparently Henry Countryman wants Anna and me to do that Italian play.

ZITA   (*Not believing her own words*)   But *you're* not going to.
(*He hesitates, looking straight ahead*)

ARCHIE   I haven't told her I wouldn't.

ZITA   That means—you didn't tell her we were going away.

ARCHIE   No. I didn't tell her.

ZITA   (*Beginning to understand, but with sympathy for him*)   You haven't quite made up your mind, darling.

ARCHIE   That's not quite it. I haven't had time to think it all through, but I feel this: I feel that this isn't the time to tell her. She doesn't know for certain that we've been together, and she wants to believe we haven't.

ZITA   That's what Mrs. McGarry said.

ARCHIE   I could do the play—think of the money—it's bound to be a hit. I feel it in my bones. And once the thing's a success I could tell Anna that I was in love with you.

ZITA   (*Helping him along*)   The success is all she cares about.

ARCHIE   I believe that. I do, I believe that.

ZITA   And when would that be? When do we tell her?

ARCHIE   Well, if we commenced rehearsals in say, October. I imagine Henry'd want about five weeks rehearsals, taking us into November. Play a week in New Haven and two or three, most likely three weeks in Boston. It's quite possible we could open in New York very early in December. You and I could have our Christmas together.

ZITA   What about her?

ARCHIE   Oh—she could look at her good notices. This is really quite a break for us, as a matter of fact. I could be saving money all the while . . . Don't you agree, it's better to start out with a *little* something in the bank?

ZITA   It's more comfortable. (*Rising*) Did you take my bag out of the car?

ARCHIE   No, I didn't. But I will.

ZITA   No, you stay here with McGarrys. I have to cook up some explanation.

ARCHIE   Tell her you've been off with some boy, that'll be realistic. How about the boy with the motorboats?

ZITA   I'll think of something.

(ARCHIE *tries to kiss her, and at first she draws away, then does kiss him, and goes out the Left door. He watches her leave, then goes out to the terrace, but at that moment the rain begins to come down, and there is a scurrying by* TOM *and* MARY *to come inside, followed by* ARCHIE. *They are in a semi-frivolous mood as people are when surprised by rainfall*)

MARY   You're all right Tom? Shirt dry?

TOM   Damn rain. I've been sitting in the house all day. I'll be losing my healthy bronzed look. The bronzed Viking from County Clare.

ARCHIE (*Taking off his jacket*)   Mind, Mary?

MARY   Not at all.

ARCHIE   Say, how about those chairs and things?

MARY   Oh, we leave them out all summer, rain or shine,

day or night. Here comes Anna with a raincoat over her head.

(*They look to Right and in a moment* ANNA *appears, laughing. She goes directly to* ARCHIE *and kisses his cheek lovingly, then puts down her mackintosh. She speaks to* MARY:)

ANNA My child has just made a naughty confession, but she's twenty years old, and if it's the boy I think it is— he's nice. Uninteresting, but nice. Archie, did you know it all along?

ARCHIE My lips are sealed.

ANNA Mine are not. (*To the* MC GARRYS) Zita is having an affair.

MARY I'm not surprised at anything these days.

TOM That's a profound remark.

(*At this moment there is a report offstage, slightly muffled*)

ANNA Oh, thunder.

TOM No. (*He says it casually, but positively, knowingly*)

ARCHIE (*Rather keenly*) No, that didn't sound like thunder. *That wasn't thunder!*

(*He gets up and runs from the room, out the terrace door Right, and they sit transfixed with the growing knowledge of what the sound was. They sit for a slow count of four and then there is a second report, exactly similar to the first. Then* ROSE, *the* DOUGLAS'S *colored cook, appears at the terrace door*)

ROSE (*Gently*) Mrs. Douglas?

CURTAIN

THE
CHAMPAGNE
POOL

ACT ONE

SCENE ONE

An apartment hotel off Park Avenue, midday. At rise a handsome woman, JOYCE CHILTON, *is silently reading a playscript, wearing glasses. As she reads, Room Service is wheeling away the luncheon table. Sitting in the room with* JOYCE CHILTON *is* FRANK WILSON, *a year or so younger or older than* JOYCE CHILTON. *He is a fairly well-known novelist and the author of the playscript* JOYCE *is reading.*

When Room Service has closed the door JOYCE *takes off her glasses and speaks.*

JOYCE   As I told you on the phone, I like your play.

FRANK   Good.

JOYCE   Well, don't act surprised. I told you I liked it yesterday.

FRANK   I am surprised. Pleased is the better word. I was surprised yesterday, and I'm pleased that you still like it today.

JOYCE   (*Looking at him carefully*)   Are you one of those?

FRANK   One of those what?

JOYCE   Am I going to have to look for hidden meanings in everything you say?

FRANK   No.

JOYCE   I'm not so sure. Even the way you say no isn't just a plain no. I've read all your novels and some of your short stories, and I'm a fan of yours. But Levine tells me this is your first play.

FRANK   The first play that's got as far as this. By that I mean, the first play I've finished and allowed anyone to see.

JOYCE   Well, you have one hell of a lot to learn about writing plays. In the first place, if you wrote this play for *me*, you've got to give me an entrance.

FRANK   I do give you an entrance. Quite a good one, I thought.

JOYCE   You thought. Mr. Wilson, I am Joyce Chilton. I'm not—well, never mind *who* I'm not. But I'll tell you *what* I'm not. I'm not the kind of actress who is standing Up Left gazing out the window as the curtain rises. That's what you have here. "As the Curtain rises, Sandra is gazing out the window." That, my friend, is for the birds. There are certain actresses who like to gaze out the window, who have been gazing out the window in every God damn play they've been in for the past thirty-five years. For my money, they are gazing out the window when there is no window in the set. They pose for publicity pictures and by God they're gazing out the window, although in at least one case that I can think of, the entire action of the play takes place in an underground air-raid shelter. I'm thinking of one particular actress, of course. (*She looks at him suspiciously*) Has she seen this play?

FRANK   Miss Chilton, you are the first actress to see this play.

JOYCE   Yes, you've said that before.

FRANK   You can ask Mort Levine.

JOYCE   I'd believe Mort Levine before I'd believe you. I don't know you, but I know Levine. That son of a bitch wouldn't dare lie to me. All right, I suppose unconsciously you wrote this play for someone else, a certain other actress. And Levine persuaded you I'd be better for the part.

FRANK   That's true.

JOYCE   What?

FRANK   The last part is true. I didn't write my play for any actress. I don't believe in writing vehicles.

JOYCE   Oh, have *you* got a lot to *learn*.

FRANK   But Mort did persuade me to let you have first look, because he thinks you'd be ideal for Sandra.

JOYCE   What do you think?

FRANK   I agree with him.

JOYCE   Come out and say it. You think I'd be *ideal*.

FRANK   Yes, I do.

JOYCE   Well, don't be so stingy with your compliments. I'll do your play.

FRANK   I'm glad to hear it.

JOYCE   There you go again. There's a hidden meaning.

FRANK   Yes, there's a hidden meaning. Not too well hidden, I guess.

JOYCE   What is it? Say it.

FRANK   Well, you said you'd do my play. But I seem to detect a mental reservation.

JOYCE   Uh-huh. Well, you're right. I'll do it if you make certain changes.

FRANK   Beginning with your entrance.

JOYCE   You're damn right beginning with my entrance. When Joyce Chilton comes on, she *sweeps* on. One son of a bitch, a critic, of course, once said that I charge on. Okay. I do. As long as I've been in the theater— and it's easy to find out how long that is—I've always symbolized one thing more than everything else. Vitality. Now let me show you something. (*She goes to the window and gazes out)* Now let me show you something else. (*She goes out of the room and closes the door behind her, then flings open the door, smiles at* FRANK WILSON *as though he were a character in a play, and sweeps toward him, then, still acting, says to the character as she abruptly halts:* "Oh, Larry, I forgot, I'm not speaking to you") Which do you like better?

FRANK   You're right. The second way is better.

JOYCE   Well then why didn't you write it that way?

FRANK   Well, for one thing, Larry has left her for another woman.

JOYCE   And you think the best way to show that is to have her gawking out the window. Mr. Wilson, you've been married twice, right?

FRANK   Yes.

JOYCE   I looked you up in *Who's Who*. I gather from certain passages in your books that there have been more than two women in your life. In other words, you've slept with quite a few.

FRANK   More than two.

JOYCE   And in your experience with women is it your idea that if a dull bastard like this Larry in your play —if he walked out on Sandra, do you really think Sandra would waste her time moping at a window? If *I* were Sandra I'd be on that telephone so fast—but in the first place I wouldn't have married Larry in the first place. If I were Sandra I might have had an affair with this Larry, but marry him, no. Now I know what you're thinking. You're thinking about sex. That Larry was so good in the hay that Sandra married him for sex.

FRANK   Yes, I make that point in the play.

JOYCE   You state the point, but you don't make it. I don't believe it. I don't believe it for one minute. It doesn't necessarily take brains to be a swordsman. Some of the—well, some of the most notorious swordsmen in

New York are about as stupid as they can get. But this man is a clod. A dull clod. And if I understand Sandra she might get in the hay with him once, but I doubt if there'd be a repeat performance.

FRANK   Why do you think he's so dull? I think he's a pretty nice guy.

JOYCE   Oh, you like him, do you?

FRANK   Yes, I do. At least I ended up liking him.

JOYCE   I see. Then you must have ended up disliking Sandra.

FRANK   Very much.

JOYCE   A real bitch, huh?

FRANK   Not an obvious one. Not a stereotyped character, I hope. But yes, a real bitch.

JOYCE   Do you mind if I ask you a question?

FRANK   Go right ahead.

JOYCE   Is Sandra really your first wife?

FRANK   No.

JOYCE   Really? It was just a guess.

FRANK   (*After a tiny pause*)   She's my *second* wife.

JOYCE   Oh! Ah! Are you still living with her?

FRANK   Hell, no. We parted company two years ago. You must have been reading an old *Who's Who*.

JOYCE   I see. Then you're divorced.

FRANK   Been divorced for over a year.

JOYCE   Well isn't that nice? I mean, how convenient.

FRANK   Why so?

JOYCE   Well, they say perfectly awful things about me, of course.

FRANK   You don't mind that, do you?

JOYCE   No. Because some of them are true. But some of them aren't. You probably heard that I had an affair with Sidney Renwick a year or so ago.

FRANK   Yes, I heard that.

JOYCE   Well, I didn't. As soon as I agreed to do a play with him everybody said uh-oh, those two, Joyce Chilton and Sidney Renwick. Well, there was absolutely nothing. Sidney was having a big thing with the ingenue and I covered up for them, but everybody said I was the one. So you see some of the things you heard about me aren't true. Sidney's ex-wife is supposed to be one of my best friends and she was so sure that Sidney and I would be sleeping together that she went off and had a quiet little affair of her own. You never heard that, did you?

FRANK   No.

JOYCE   Of course not. The only one you heard about was me. I was just this minute thinking, Sidney'd be very good for Larry.

FRANK   Yes, he would. He's a good actor.

JOYCE   Oh, for God's sake. Sidney Renwick a good actor!

FRANK   I've always liked him I thought he was excellent in—

JOYCE   (*Over him*)   Always *liked* him. Of *course*. I *adore* Sidney. But Mr. Wilson, please don't ever let anyone that knows anything about acting hear you say that Sidney's a good actor.

FRANK   He gets damn good reviews.

JOYCE   Oh, I want him in your play. I think he'd be perfect. All I'm saying is, Sidney is just Sidney. The theater is so full of pansies or if they're not swishing all over the place they're that new group, that all look like window-cleaners. On my word. And Sidney looks well and dresses well. Had a bath, and shaved, and at the same time you believe he's interested in the women in the play. But an actor—no. Do you know how Sidney gets by? On his appearance, and taking direction. Sidney's very clever that way. He knows he's not an actor.

I think he secretly hates being an actor. But he has sense enough to know that if he lets the director handle all the brain part, and does exactly what he's told, he can rely on his appearance to get him through. And of course he's a quick study. Directors like that, and so do playwrights. But there's never anything creative about Sidney's performances. Never. You can get him for a thousand a week, too. He needs a play after those two dogs last season, and I know he has nothing for next season. And Sidney and I are awfully good together. I've been in four plays with him. I feel *comfortable* with Sidney. Promise me you'll send him your play and at least let him read for you.

FRANK   I'm all for him. Do you know his phone number?

JOYCE   I have it here somewhere. And Levine always knows how to reach him. Now I'm afraid we have to break this up. I'm having a permanent at two-thirty. But darling, you'll have lunch here tomorrow? Same time? I know we have a play here. I'm convinced of it. (*He rises and by his expression it can be inferred that he is somewhat troubled*)

CURTAIN

SCENE TWO

The next afternoon, a small restaurant, now deserted except for SIDNEY RENWICK *sitting alone in the post-luncheon-pre-cocktail-hour lull. He is an attractive, well-dressed man of indeterminate early middle age.* FRANK WILSON *enters, and* RENWICK *rises. A waiter follows* WILSON.

SIDNEY   Mr. Frank Wilson?

FRANK   Yes, Mr. Renwick.

SIDNEY   Sidney Renwick.

FRANK   Oh, I knew that, of course.

SIDNEY   I'm having coffee. Will you have a drink?

FRANK   I don't think so, thanks. Coffee for me.
(*The hovering waiter nods and goes*)

SIDNEY   Well, sir, I read your play, Mr. Wilson.

FRANK   So soon?

SIDNEY   So soon? The messenger brought it to my apartment last night and I almost telephoned you at three o'clock this morning. I've only read one of your novels, the first one, I guess, and I liked it very much. But why haven't you been writing plays? Mr. Wilson, *this* is a *play*.
(*The waiter serves the coffee*)

FRANK   Thank you.

SIDNEY   Holy smokes, man, you should have been writing plays forever. What are you smiling at?

FRANK   I had a favorite uncle that used to say "Holy smokes." I don't think I've heard anyone say it since he died.

SIDNEY   You must be about my age. Thirty-eight?

FRANK   No, I'm forty-one.

SIDNEY   Three years. You're the only man I can think of that's caught our generation. Were you in the army?

FRANK   Yes.

SIDNEY   So was I. Special Services. Training films and stuff like that. I ended up a PFC. Were you an officer?

FRANK   Yes. First lieutenant. I was doing about the same thing you were, but writing them instead of acting them. Why?

SIDNEY   Well, I was just trying to find out how you happen to have caught the disillusionment and so forth. In your play, Larry's really very typical of our generation.

FRANK   Yes, I think he is.

SIDNEY   Sense of values and so forth. A fundamentally decent fellow, but having a very hard time adjusting. Have you been through analysis?

FRANK   No.

SIDNEY   Neither have I. (*He laughs*) I don't like to play to small audiences.

FRANK   Very good.

SIDNEY   Well, let's talk about Larry.

FRANK   All right.

SIDNEY   It's quite a fat part, of course. An actor's dream. I guess I'm onstage eighty percent of the time.

FRANK   Just about, I guess.

SIDNEY   Luckily I'm a quick study. You know what that means?

FRANK   It means that you learn your lines quickly.

SIDNEY   It means something else, too. I was referring to the fact that when you have an actor that's a quick study, it gives you more time to polish, polish, polish. You don't have to worry about his learning new lines.

FRANK   I suppose not.

SIDNEY   Absolutely not. That way, the author can bring in a new scene and you're in business right away, instead of having to cope with actors that haven't learned the new lines.

FRANK   Yes, that's true.

SIDNEY   For instance, I could be up in this part by Saturday, but maybe when you saw a run-through you'd want to do a lot of rewriting. It's always that way. Then the way the theater operates today, the creative director has come to be at least one of the most important factors. Who have you got to direct this?

FRANK   We haven't got anybody yet. *Signed.*

SIDNEY   Oh, you haven't? Well, you know who the only man that can direct this play is.

FRANK   Joe Rasmussen. That's who we—

SIDNEY   Joe Rasmussen? Oh, no. Oh, Mr. Wilson. Do you know him? I mean, is he a personal friend of yours?

FRANK   No, I've never met him, but he directed one of my favorite plays.

SIDNEY   What play was that? *The Valid Resentment*?

FRANK   Yes.

SIDNEY   Mr. Wilson, Joe Rasmussen almost ruined *The Valid Resentment. I know.* You talk to Axel Schmidt, who only wrote the play. Get *him* to tell you about Mr. Joe Rasmussen. Do you remember that scene in *The Valid Resentment,* it's in the second act, where What's Her Name plays the whole scene in a bra and panties?

FRANK   Sure.

SIDNEY   You know whose idea that was? Joe Rasmussen's. The soldier is supposed to carry that scene. It's the big scene in the whole play, where Axel Schmidt is really eloquent about war. Pure poetry, it was. Strindbergian it was. Better than Berthold Brecht. And how does Mr. Joe Rasmussen handle it? He has this broad with a pair of jugs you could hang your hat on squirming around like What's Her Name in *Tobacco Road.* That's the Rasmussen touch. Oh, boy.

FRANK   That was explained to me.

SIDNEY   How? How could anybody explain it? *I* can *explain* it. Rasmussen was laying the dame, that's all the explanation I need.

FRANK   Well, maybe, but there was another explanation aside from that.

SIDNEY   I'd like to hear it. I'd really like to hear it.

FRANK   Well, the way it was explained to me, during the soldier's speech, the girl is supposed to be so deeply moved by what the soldier is saying that she reacts sexually.

SIDNEY   You're not kidding.

FRANK   Because she's an earthy, primitive woman, and sex is one of the few things that can stir her, or at least is one of the basic forms of expression she has. She doesn't comprehend what the soldier is saying, but she feels it, senses it.

SIDNEY   Yeah. Yeah. And meanwhile, who the hell is paying any attention to what the soldier is saying?

FRANK   I did.

SIDNEY   You did? You weren't distracted?

FRANK   I was distracted, yes. But I really think the girl added something to the scene.

SIDNEY   Well, she ruined it for me . . . Shirley Tanner. I used to know her when I was in radio. She played a 12-year-old girl paralyzed with polio, and that took acting. Not on her part. On mine. I was playing Dr. Mc-Dowell, the earnest young general practitioner, and there'd be Shirley in a sweater, standing beside me at the mike. Supposed to be twelve years old, and permanently crippled. And every day when we were signing off Shirley would give three big bumps, N—B—C. Bump. That's where Joe Rasmussen first knew her, but boy he had to get in line. I have nothing against Shirley. Hell, she was a very useful and obliging girl. But she didn't belong in *The Valid Resentment*. I understand you've got Joyce Chilton signed.

FRANK   Not signed, but the contracts are being worked out.

SIDNEY   What does *she* say about Rasmussen?

FRANK   She likes him. Admires him.

SIDNEY   She does?

FRANK   Yes, I just had lunch with her. I might as well tell you, you'll hear it. She'll sign if we get Rasmussen.

SIDNEY Oh, then you're committed to Rasmussen? I didn't realize it had gone that far.

FRANK Well, he's being very tough about percentages. He wants twenty percent.

SIDNEY They all do, ever since Kazan got it from *Streetcar*. How far apart are you?

FRANK Ten percent. Stanley Stanton has offered him ten, and he wants twenty.

SIDNEY Well, that's none of my business, thank God. He may be worth it, if you want him that much and if Chilton wants him that much, *and* if you want Chilton that much. (*He is noticeably subdued*) I was just wondering, what's with Joyce Chilton and Joe Rasmussen.

FRANK I have no idea. But we want you. Stanton wants you, and Miss Chilton wants you, and so do I.

SIDNEY (*Brightening a little*) That's very good to hear. The only thing is, Mr. Wilson, whoever plays Larry, whether it's me or whoever it is, you've got to protect that character. I mean the character of Larry. There's a big demand for leading men these days, and you're not going to get anybody good to play Larry if Joyce Chilton and Joe Rasmussen start butchering that part. I can work with Joe Rasmussen. I've known him for years. As I said, I used to know him back in radio when he was trying to be a writer, and boy did that stuff stink. We used to send him out for coffee, for God's sake. He was one of the writers on the show, but they took him off the writing and made him a sort of assistant director, and his job was to get us coffee. Oh, I know Joe. But just you remember what I'm telling you. Watch him. And watch Joyce Chilton. And watch the two of them. I'll give you a friendly tip right now, for free. Joyce Chilton is not going to like your opening scene. Where you have Sandra staring out the window?

Oh, no. Not Joyce. You're going to have to throw that out and build up Joyce's entrance.

FRANK   (*Beginning to learn guile*)   Oh, do you think so?

SIDNEY   I would like to make you a small bet.

FRANK   Hmm.

CURTAIN

SCENE THREE

The same restaurant, the next day at about the same time in the afternoon. FRANK WILSON *is sitting alone. A badly dressed little man about* WILSON'S *age enters. He is wearing a cheap suit, no vest, black four-in-hand tie, loafers. His trouser cuffs almost cover the loafers. He enters slowly, and speaks to* FRANK (*he is, of course,* JOE RASMUSSEN).

JOE   (*Pointing his finger*)   Are you Wilson?

FRANK   That's right. Are you Joe Rasmussen?

JOE   (*Over him*)   Joe Rasmussen. Waiter. Hey, a cup of tea and a big piece of Danish with about a quarter a pound of butter. Cream and sugar with the tea. Where you from, Wilson?

FRANK   Indianapolis, Indiana. Why?

JOE   Yeah. Is that what it's like in Indiana? Those people in your books? What a cultural Sahara that is. If your picture is valid, that is. And I guess it is. I guess so. You convinced me it's a valid picture. What crap. What a way to live. A cultural vacuum. James Whitcomb Riley. Booth Tarkington. Meredith Nicholson. George Ade. (*He shakes his head*)

FRANK   Theodore Dreiser.

JOE   Don't give me Dreiser.

FRANK   Ring Lardner.

JOE   They didn't write in Indiana.

FRANK   Where are *you* from?

JOE   What does it matter where I'm from?

FRANK   Well, it seemed to matter to you where I was from. Forget it.

JOE   You want to know the awful truth, I was born in New Rochelle, New York.

FRANK   And you went to Harvard.

JOE   How do you know that?

FRANK   It's in all your publicity. You don't mention New Rochelle, but you always do Harvard.

JOE   Well, I'm thinking of dropping Harvard.

FRANK   Have a seat.

JOE   I'm restless. I don't want to sit down. I just walked all the way down from the Hayden Planetarium. The God damn thing was closed. All the way from 81st Street and Central Park West. (*He sits down*)

FRANK   Closed? Why was it closed?

JOE   I don't know. Oh, they're painting or some God damn thing. They wouldn't let me in.

FRANK   They ought to know better than that.
    (JOE *looks at him, puzzled, unused to sarcasm*)

JOE   What's the matter, don't you like me, Wilson?

FRANK   Not so far.

JOE   Stick around. I get worse.
    (*He sits at right angles to the table, not facing* FRANK WILSON. *He sprawls, with his legs spread out*)

JOE   You know, there is something very immoral about a joint like this when there are no people in it. I get a feeling of—I can almost smell the seductions that were started here two hours ago. Like over there at that table, probably some advertising jerk making a fast pitch at some model. Nothing in it for either one of them. No love, no honest lust. But just because he's an advertising jerk he has to seduce a model, and because she's a model she has to expect it of him. Over there, some fairy trying to make a date with some handsome Italian waiter. I don't like this joint. But I don't like any joints. People ought to stop eating in public. You got too God damn many scenes with people eating!

FRANK   Only two. The breakfast scene and the scene in the diner.

JOE   That's what I said. Two scenes with people eating. That's too many. I'm through with directing scenes where people are eating or drinking. Everybody in the audience knows it isn't whiskey. They're all wondering, is it ginger ale or is it cold tea? Illusion, gone. I had one actor though. I fell in love with him for one reason. He was supposed to feel faint and drink a glass of water. Well, the play had a long run and I guess we were in our fortieth week and I discovered this guy, instead of drinking water, he was drinking vodka. Any time I got a part for him, he's got it. Because you know what he did? He drank that vodka the way a fainting man would drink water. Not fast, the way they do in the movies and plays. But a little bit at a time. And it was his idea, it wasn't mine. I said to him, "Harry, you beautiful lush, you boozed your way into my heart." I hear you used to be quite a boozer, Wilson.

FRANK   Is that what you heard?

JOE   That's what I heard. I heard that's why your wife left you.

FRANK   Wrong.

JOE   Well, put me straight, then.

FRANK   Why the hell should I? It's none of your God damn business.

JOE   Everything I express the slightest interest in is my business. I make it my business. If she didn't leave you for booze, why did she leave you? I want to know why this Sandra dame in your play is such a bitch. Larry leaves *her*, in the play, but I understand your wife left *you*. All right. I'll get it out of you sometime.

FRANK   I don't think so.

JOE   You want me to direct your play, don't you?

FRANK   (*With dignity*)   I want you to direct my play.

JOE   (*Imitating him*)   "I want you to direct my play." What a reading. Pomposity will get you nowhere, Wilson. A former drunken newspaper reporter from Hicksville U. S. A. is no good trying to be Colonel Blimp, so knock it off. I don't mind your hostility, but don't be a God damn phoney. You're too good a writer for that.

FRANK   You're sweet to say so.

JOE   That's better. Sarcasm is okay. But don't draw yourself up like a dowager, or a butler. You've never been around the theater at all, have you?

FRANK   No.

JOE   How did you happen to write a play instead of using the characters in a novel?

FRANK   Because I've always liked to go to the theater and I always wanted to write a play.

JOE   Wilson, you're all right. If you knew the crap I get when I ask that question. I've worked with two novelists that wrote plays. One was a good play, the other stank. I asked both novelists that question. One said he did it for the money.

FRANK   He probably did.

JOE   Sure he did. I know he did. But in being so frank, so candid, he was trying to pretend to me that his frankness covered a great aesthetic process. Crap! The other novelist, he wrote the turkey. His answer was a windy thing about dimensions and depth and audible impact versus the visual. Oh, dear me. I went right to work and sabotaged that play. I didn't want that son of a bitch writing for the theater.

FRANK   You deliberately sabotaged his play?

JOE   Are you shocked? Did you ever review a bad novel?

FRANK   Yes.

JOE   You blasted it, didn't you?

FRANK   I panned it.

JOE   Well then don't be shocked at me, Wilson. You were doing the same thing I did, only I was doing it better. I got that son of a bitch out of the theater and I'd like to get every other son of a bitch out of the theater that shouldn't be in it.

FRANK   And you're the judge of who should be in and who shouldn't?

JOE   Do you know of a better judge? You don't, because there isn't any. Wait till you see me work, kid.

FRANK   *Kid?*

JOE   Kid. To me you're a kid. In this business you're a kid. You got lucky and wrote a good play, but in the theater I'm grandpa and you're a kid. Who uh you got in mind for Larry?

FRANK   I've talked to Sidney Renwick—

JOE   Who told you about Sidney Renwick?

FRANK   I didn't have to be told about him. I know his work.

JOE   Who *told* you about him? Sidney Renwick aint an actor that comes to anybody's mind quick. Sidney Renwick is an actor that you make a list of all the leading men. Then you go through the whole list and when you come to the R's you see Renwick's name and you say to yourself, he might not be bad. That's how plays end up with Sidney Renwick in them.

FRANK   Maybe, but not in this case.

JOE　You're not gonna sit there and swear to me that you thought of Sidney Renwick unassisted.

FRANK　I was assisted.

JOE　Who by?

FRANK　Joyce Chilton.

JOE　Really? She suggested Renwick?

FRANK　She did.

JOE　Gimme a minute to think.

FRANK　Take as long as you like.

JOE　Sidney Renwick is the ideal man for the part. *I* know that. I thought of him as soon as I finished reading your first scene. But that aint why Chilton suggested him. They been in three or four plays together, but he was never the leading man. Not that Joyce is so choosy. Let me think a minute. They were in a play together about eight or ten years ago. He played her brother. Yeah, I guess that's when it was.

FRANK　When what was?

JOE　It must of been then.

FRANK　What must have been then?

JOE　That she found out she could handle Sidney.

FRANK　I must apologize to Miss Chilton for my thoughts. I was beginning to suspect that you were trying to figure out when they had slept together.

JOE　Well, that's when they did, I guess. But it don't always work out that Joyce can handle a man just because she slept with him. Every four or five years she falls in love with some guy that she can't handle and then you got a happy woman. (*He studies* FRANK, *then shakes his head*) No.

FRANK　No what?

JOE　You're not sleeping with Chilton, are you?

FRANK　No.

JOE　Anyway, not yet. Do you go for her?

FRANK Sure.

JOE Yeah, but big?

FRANK No, not big. At least, as you say, not yet.

JOE That's good. Personally, I'm not going to go to bed with her till after we open in New York. And if you're smart, you won't either.

FRANK For all you know, I may have other arrangements.

JOE Pomposity again. You mean you *have* a girl?

FRANK There again, Rasmussen, that's none of your God damn business.

JOE But you're wrong. It is my business. If you're going to make changes in this play, I gotta know if Joyce Chilton dictated them from a bed in the Boston Ritz.

FRANK Never fear. If I make changes that's not how they'll be made, or why.

JOE Well, we're all right if you stick to that. We can get a sexy girl to play the maid and you can work it out with her. But never lay the leading lady before you open in New York. I had a hell of a time with the leading lady in *The Valid Resentment*. She wanted me to gang up with her against Schmidt, Axel Schmidt, the author. But I crossed her. I got a little broad named Shirley Tanner. Oomp. I put her in the play and I was banging her till we opened on Broadway. That way I was protected from the leading lady and her blandishments. You think these things are unimportant, but you'll learn. We'll get a sexy little broad for the maid. We could get Shirley Tanner, but she isn't a maid type, and anyway I can hear screams from Chilton the minute she saw Tanner. You know, a woman can measure thirty-eight inches bust measurement, but if she sees a woman with *thirty-nine* bust measurement she says it's disgusting. I never knew it to fail.
(*Waiter serves pastry and tea*)

JOE   Take it back, I changed my mind. (*Hands waiter a five-dollar bill*) I don't want to be at a disadvantage with you, Wilson. Talking with my mouth full. And I gotta go to the dentist. I got a coupla teeth I gotta take care of before we go into rehearsal. That play I told you I sabotaged. On top of everything else I had a wisdom tooth that was murdering me. Maybe that's why I sabotaged his play. Who the hell cares if we open the seventh of October? Who the hell cares if we ever open?

FRANK   Well, I do, for one. And quite a few other people.

JOE   No. The last play with a big idea was called *Wings Over Europe*.

FRANK   I don't think I ever heard of it.

JOE   Produced by the Guild in 1928. It ran ninety performances. Written by Robert Nichols and Maurice Browne.

FRANK   How old were *you* in 1928?

JOE   I was six years old in 1928. What kind of a question is that? How old was I when *Hamlet* was first put on? How old were you when *The Animal Kingdom* was first put on? Maybe you were ten years old, I don't know. But I can tell from this play of yours that you read *The Animal Kingdom*. Maybe you saw it, I don't know, but your play is the same idea as Philip Barry's. So don't give me that how old was I in 1928.

FRANK   Ignoring your implied accusation of plagiarism, what was *Wings Over Europe* all about?

JOE   It was about the splitting of the atom.

FRANK   That far back?

JOE   That far back. 1928. See? So don't be so touchy when I call you kid. In this business I'm grandpa. Wilson, how long does it take you to write a novel?

FRANK   About two years.

JOE   In two years I can read seven hundred plays. And I have.

FRANK   You've read seven hundred plays?

JOE   I've read over three thousand plays. I read seven hundred in two years when I was at Harvard. But what the hell am I doing, trying to impress you? I don't have to impress anybody.

FRANK   Nobody asked you to try. So why do you?

JOE   Yeah, I should have got over that a long time ago, but I didn't. Where'd you get that necktie?

FRANK   (*Looking down*)   This? I think I got this at Tripler's.

JOE   Finish your coffee. Tripler's is only around the corner. I want to get one like that.

FRANK   (*Rising*)   I'll buy you one.

JOE   (*Touched*)   You will?

CURTAIN

SCENE FOUR

The office of STANLEY STANTON, *theatrical manager.* STAN-TON *is about thirty-five, a law school graduate, publicity hound, who got into the theater by way of clients of the big law firm in which he started out. He has had two hits and three flops, but the flops have not hurt him financially. He is a huckster-type smoothie, and his office is on Madison Avenue, small but impressive. He is standing as* FRANK WILSON *enters. The time is afternoon, the day following the preceding scene.*

STANLEY   Good afternoon, Frank.

FRANK   Hello, Stanley. (*Takes out a cigarette case, and* STANLEY *holds a lighter for him*) Thank you.

STANLEY   My pleasure. Make yourself comfortable, and prepare yourself for a shock.

FRANK   A shock?

STANLEY   Yes. (*He points to a pile of papers*) All signed. Joyce Chilton. Sidney Renwick. And Joe Rasmussen.

FRANK   That's the kind of shock I don't mind.

STANLEY   No, I shouldn't think you would. I expected the negotiations to last over a week. But do you know who expedited the whole thing?

FRANK   No.

STANLEY   You did.

FRANK   I did? I didn't do a damn thing.

STANLEY   Maybe you don't think you did, but all three of them like your play and they all like you. Joyce said she trusted you. Renwick said he trusted you and respected you. And Joe Rasmussen—what did you do there? He's supposed to be the stormy petrel of the American theater. A tough baby to get along with. But do you know what he said? You like me to quote his exact words?

FRANK   Yes.

STANLEY   His exact words were, "I'll marry him if he'll have me." Meaning you. Of course that's the way Joe talks. Nothing homosexual about Joe, you realize that. He didn't mean anything by it that you could take exception to. It was Joe's idea of expressing exceptional admiration. How did you do it?

FRANK   I bought him a necktie.

STANLEY   (*Laughing weakly*) Heh heh heh. All right, if you don't want to reveal your secret. But I wish I knew the name of your haberdasher.

FRANK   All I did was listen to him, and I didn't yes him.

STANLEY   How do you mean you didn't yes him? I'd like to figure out a way to handle Joe. I've never worked with him before, but I've always wanted to. With Joe staging our play, we're in business, even if it did mean giving him a mortgage on my mother.

FRANK   What *did* you give him?

STANLEY   What he asked for. Twenty percent, or five thousand dollars a week, whichever was greater. I'm not going to make a nickel on this play, Frank. With me it's a labor of love. I'm frankly stagestruck and I admit it.

FRANK   Well, I'm glad to hear it, Stanley. I'll remember that later in case you want *me* to take a cut.

STANLEY   Heh heh heh heh. Well, what else have I got for you. We have a theater. As soon as I signed Joe Rasmussen and the other two, I got right on the phone and I got the promise of a theater. We open the eighth of October. Start rehearsals in August and I want to take this play to Detroit. I don't want those wise guys going to Philly or New Haven and coming back that same night before Sardi's closes, putting the blast on your play. I want to open in Detroit and then to Boston, and if we need any more time, maybe we run a week of rehearsals here in New York. You know how that works? Paid audiences, previews. Lousy audiences, but we pick up a dollar. And sometimes they like it, you know. You can't always tell about audiences.

FRANK   No, I guess not. You can't always tell about plays, either.

STANLEY   Oho. Vooze avay ray-zone, Frank. Vooze *avay*. If you could tell about audiences and plays, I'd settle for that any day. You can have a uranium mine. I'll settle for that talent. See what else. This afternoon I got an appointment to confer with Mary Lee Pastor. You know her work?

FRANK   I know who she is. The stage designer.

STANLEY   Right. She's the biggest fag in show business, but—

FRANK   You mean Lesbian.

STANLEY   Not her. She's so masculine, I think she's a fag.

FRANK   Oh.

STANLEY   But she'll steal from anybody. You want a traditional set, she'll give it to you. You want moderne, she'll give you moderne. She has no ideas of her own, but she has got taste. Why shouldn't she? She has the same taste as the best designers in the business because she copies from them. But I'll say this for her. She's cheap. She won't go over the budget.

FRANK   I hope she, or maybe I mean you—I hope we don't skimp on the set for the second and third acts. I'd like to see that giving the impression of affluence.

STANLEY   I know, Frank. That's the word you used. Affluence. Don't worry. Excuse me. (*His intercom buzzer has sounded and he speaks into it*) Yeah? What? She's here in the office? Well, tell her to come in. Joyce Chilton in my reception room.
    (JOYCE CHILTON *enters, sweeps in, walks to* FRANK WILSON *and halts, saying:* "Oh, Larry, I forgot, I'm not speaking to you." *She smiles at* WILSON, *and says, in her natural voice,* "Hello, darling.")

STANLEY (*On his feet*)   What's this hello I'm not speaking to you?

JOYCE   Private joke, darling, isn't it, Frank?

FRANK   Very private.

JOYCE (*Sitting down, taking a cigarette, which* STANLEY *lights for her*)   Thank you, darling.

STANLEY   My pleasure.

JOYCE   What am I interrupting? You don't have to be polite.

STANLEY   I was just telling Frank, I have an appointment this afternoon to confer with Mary Lee Pastor.

JOYCE   Oh, you're going to have *her* do the sets? Who are you going to have her steal from this time?

STANLEY   Well, since you put it that way, Donald Oenslager, probably.

JOYCE   Good. She steals from him very nicely. She has more trouble stealing from Jo Mielziner, although that's not saying she doesn't try. But speaking of Mary Lee Pastor, that's in the general area of what I dropped in about.

STANLEY   (*To Frank*)   You remember what I said about me not making a nickel on this show.

JOYCE   Make it on your next, darling. This man has made two fortunes from two plays that didn't cost him anything. Cheap actors. Cheap sets. That one in the girls' reformatory, the ugliest cheapest set I ever saw. Well, get ready to shell out now, sweetie. You have a play about affluent people this time. Affluence, such a *nice* word. Keep it in mind, Stanley dear. Not wealthy. Not rich. Affluent. Only a novelist would have thought of that word, Frank.

FRANK   Thank you.

STANLEY   *I* wish you'd have said wealthy. That word affluent is going to cost me plenty. All right, Joyce dear, as if I didn't know what was coming.

JOYCE   Well—there's a young man in Paris—

STANLEY   I've heard of him.

JOYCE   No you haven't. Not this one. This is another young man. This one has them all terrified, he's so talented. He's like that new painter that begins with a B. In fact, two B's, as in Miss Bardot.

FRANK   Bernard Buffet.

JOYCE   *Thank* you, dear! I should know his name. I have a painting of his that I've been offered thirty thousand for. Bernard Buffet of *course*. I have a thing about names.

STANLEY   I never knew you had a thing about thirty thousand dollars though.

JOYCE   No, I, uh, I have my practical side. But anyway, boys, this young man in Paris is having his first big show in August, and if I could be the first actress to wear two of his creations, he's going to be such a sensation that women would actually come to the theater just to see two of his originals. I have it all figured out, Stanley, that you could charge it off to publicity. *Vogue* and *Harper's Bazaar* would cooperate, I know they would. I'd give my soul to be the first to be dressed by this young man.

STANLEY   Would you give your body?

JOYCE   Be careful, Stanley, I have a witness. As a matter of fact, I *have* given my body, for a great deal less.

STANLEY   Then this guy, this designer, he must come pretty high.

JOYCE   What a *nice* compliment, Stanley. Even if you didn't mean it that way. Yes, he comes high.

STANLEY   Like how much for one dress?

JOYCE   Well, we won't know till August, but two thousand, three thousand, four, five, I don't know. I have no idea.

STANLEY   Honey, in the contract you signed this morning—

JOYCE   I know. You agreed to let me select two evening dresses at a cost not to exceed two thousand dollars. But I want to change that. We can have an exchange of letters. You're a lawyer, and you know how that can be done. Otherwise, what else is new?

STANLEY   Get her. Isn't she wonderful? She doesn't even wait for me to say yes.

JOYCE   Well you will say yes, won't you? You don't want me making my entrance in gunnysack, do you?

STANLEY   Gunnysack, at one thousand dollars a copy?

JOYCE   Honey—if you don't let this Paris person dress me, I can come on in gunnysack. Read the contract. You wrote it. It says, I can select two evening dresses not to exceed a total of two thousand dollars. But it doesn't say I *have* to spend *thirty dollars*. I have the right to select my costumes, and all you do is pay for them, up to two thousand dollars.

STANLEY   Well I'll be a son of a bitch.

JOYCE   I know, isn't it awful?

STANLEY   What would you do if you were in my place, Frank?

JOYCE   Don't answer that question, Frank. You may want me on your side later on, so be careful what you say now.

FRANK   Miss Chilton is the star. She's got to look her best.

JOYCE   Ah, now that's real gallantry. And it's all for the good of the play, isn't it, Frank?

FRANK   Of course it is.

JOYCE   Of course it is. Well, I didn't mean to interrupt anything. (*She rises*)

STANLEY   (*As his buzzer sounds*)   I haven't agreed to anything. Who is it? . . . Oh. Well, tell her I'll see her in a minute. Mary Lee Pastor.

JOYCE   Oh. Then, Frank, you'd better come with me. I think he's going to take it out on Mary Lee, and you don't want to see that, do you? She cries easily.

CURTAIN

SCENE FIVE

FRANK WILSON's *hotel room, strictly hotel room decor, relieved only by a portable typewriter and a few books, newspapers and magazines.* FRANK *is in shirtsleeves and slacks. The time is the late afternoon of the day following the preceding scene.* FRANK, *with his reading glasses on the top of his head, is swinging the telephone, obviously waiting for a call to be completed.*

FRANK (*Into telephone*) Hello . . . Yes. Hello, Stanley . . . Uh-huh . . . Stanley, I'm going to hang up on you now . . . We might as well get this settled at the very beginning.
When you want to speak to me on the telephone, don't tell your secretary to get Mr. Wilson on the phone and then keep me waiting. Make the call yourself. It only takes about thirty seconds of your valuable time, and maybe my time is valuable, too. I think it is.
(*He gently puts the phone back in the cradle, and sighs with relief over the fact that he has declared himself. He lights a cigarette, puts his feet up on a chair and clasps his hands behind his neck. The phone rings and he looks at his wrist watch*)

FRANK (*Sweetly*) Hello . . . Yes, Stanley . . . Uh-huh . . . I know that . . . I know all that, Stanley . . . Uh-huh . . . Uh-huh . . . Sure . . . Well, my point is this, Stanley, and it's a very simple one. I'm not working for you. At the very least, we're partners in a joint enterprise. If I were working for you, as an employee, being paid a salary, I would have to hold still for this what I consider discourtesy. But I'm not working for you, I'm not your employee. And I don't intend to sit here holding the phone while you get around to speaking to me . . .

Now wait a minute. I haven't finished.

When I call you, my name is announced to you. I have no secretary, and even if I did have, I would never allow my secretary to say "Put Mr. Stanton on the wire." I consider that disrespectful . . . Oh, I know you didn't. I know that, Stanley. But the fact is, it is disrespectful. You would never let your secretary say "Put Mr. Baruch, or Governor Rockefeller, on the line." Well, at this point in your life I am probably just as important as Mr. Baruch or Governor Rockefeller, therefore entitled to the same respect.

I'm not even going to insist that my time is as valuable to me as yours is to you. But from now on, if I answer the telephone and it's your secretary asking me to hold the wire, I'm going to hang up. And when the phone rings again, I won't answer, because I'll know it's you doing what you should have done in the first place.

Is that clear? . . . Good . . . Good. What *did* you call me about? . . . *What?* . . . You want to know if I'm free for lunch Friday? You mean you have your secretary keep me on the line while you're getting around to asking me if I'm free for lunch? Is that the way you always invite people to lunch? In that case, I am not free for lunch. I'll go to your office, if you want to talk about the play, but I'll be damned if I'll have lunch with you.

(*Hangs up, and he hears a voice shouting,* "Bravo, bravo!" *followed by a "Dragnet" knock on the door. He opens the door, and* JOE RASMUSSEN *enters*)

JOE That's the way to handle those people. Good work.

FRANK You heard it all?

JOE Every word. I always listen outsida room before I

knock. Hell, I often listen outsida rooms that I don't know the people. And I'll read your mail, too. If you don't want me to read your mail, don't leave it lying around where I can get at it. The best way to handle guys like Stanton, don't be in when he phones. Always tell his secretary you'll call him back.

FRANK   Yes, but I answer the phone myself, and she knows my voice.

JOE   Lie to her.

FRANK   Yes, but she always says, "Mr. Wilson?" and I say it is, and then she says, "Hold on, please, for Mr. Stanton."

JOE   Then you say to her, "I just decided I'm not Mr. Wilson. Tell that fathead boss of yours I'll have Mr. Wilson call him." I wanta show you sumpn. (*Picks up the phone and gives the number* "Murray Hill 8-3640") Is this the office of Mr. Stanley Stanton? . . . *The* Stanley Stanton? . . . Well put the fathead on the phone. This is Joe Rasmussen . . . Stanton, this is your old friend Singin' Sam, the Barbasol Man . . . I'm all right . . . Where am I? Why I'm over here at the Racquet Club having a cocktail with Papa. Where the hell else would I be at this time of day? Hello, there, Worthington. Hello, there Schuyler. Good afternoon, Sir Dudley. Just saying hello to the mob, Stanley. Pardon . . . What I called you about, Stanley. Our author, Frank Wilson, he's headed for a nervous breakdown. So don't cross him . . . Oh, you did? When did you suspect it? (*He holds the phone so that* FRANK *can listen along with him*) . . . You don't say . . . Persecution complex, Stanley. That's what I think . . . Schizo, eh? Yeah. Yeah . . . Well, yeah. Always. It's always those quiet easygoing guys . . . Tension, yeah. That's right . . . No, no violence, not at this stage. That comes at a more advanced stage. TLC now, you know. Tender loving care. We don't

give a damn after the eighth of October, but we gotta
nurse him along till then . . . Well, I thought I'd tell
you, but I see you already guessed it. All right, Stan
boy. (*He hangs up*)
Well, I guess we got *his* ulcer started. I don't mean
that. He's a thick-skinned, insensitive, unimaginative,
complacent horse-twat. And I happen to know he isn't
using a nickel of his own money to put on your play.
He took a nice capital gains on his two hits and put the
money in tax-exempts. He got the backing for this play
at ha' past eleven yesterday morning, as soon as he got
me and Chilton signed. You know why he's producing
your play instead of a better producer? Because your
agent, Levine, knew that Stanton could get the money
quicker than anybody else. Right now he's hot. It goes
like that, in waves. Some years everybody pushes money
at guys like Stanton. He's oversubscribed in a week.
Other years he won't be able to promote five thousand
dollars with John Wilkes Booth in *Our American
Cousin*. But he's set for life. If he quits being a producer, he goes back to being a theatrical lawyer, with
a big reputation for knowing all about the theater. He
don't know any more about the theater than I do about
raising bees. There's money in honey, that's all I know.
And that's as much as he knows about the theater.
Well, tomorrow we look at some actors. Gimme a drink.
Gimme a Scotch and water. Tomorrow will break your
heart. Tomorrow we got about ten actors reading for
the part of the judge. So far the casting has been easy.
You got your star, a good-looking broad that can act
when she wants to. You got your leading man. He's
what one critic used to call a cigarette-case actor. He
carries a long gold cigarette case in his inside coat
pocket and whenever you don't know what to do with
Sidney Renwick, you let him take out his cigarette case,
fondle it, take out a cigarette, tap it on the case and
steal a little suspense there while he takes his time

lighting up. It don't work so good in London. In London your audience can smoke in most of the theaters. But in New York everybody's dying for a cigarette and they all watch Renwick while he puts the cigarette in his kisser, puts the case back in his pocket, then reaches in several pockets to find his lighter. I've seen Renwick steal a little more with the lighter bit. He pats his pockets. No lighter. Then he'll take a lighter off a coffee table and you'd think he was lighting the candles for a church wedding. But he's good. He's all right. He's a quick study, and he's no booze problem, and he's right for Larry. So you had no trouble casting so far. But wait till tomorrow. Ten old men, maybe five of them you never saw before in your life. Maybe two of them you remember from old movies, former leading men. They know we're looking for a man to play a judge, so tomorrow you're going to see more dignity than you'll ever see in the United States Supreme Court. Good manners. And charm. The first man we have read, you're going to want to say, sign him. The second man will be just as good. You'll want to sign him. And maybe the first man is the one that eventually gets the part, but you have to let them all read. If you don't, you're a no-good, heartless son of a bitch. I learned my lesson the hard way. We were casting a play and we wanted a woman to play a cook. The first one that read for us, I said sign her. Some old lady come up to me and said, "You bastard, we come here with our hopes up and you don't even give us a chance to read. You don't even let us go home and dream that maybe you'll phone in the morning." Well, she didn't phone in the morning. She did a dive out the window of her apartment. Tomorrow you're going to look at these old guys and wonder where they all were. Where have they been? How have they been living? The ingenues, and the juveniles. They're young, they eat, they shack up with one another. But old men and old women that you know haven't been in a play in five, ten, fifteen years. Some you never saw. But they belong to Equity. Now they're not all people that saved their money. Actors do save their money, and when I was in radio I used to work with men and women that had been stars, big stars, too. Radio was a life-saver for them. They got good money and they were working, they were seeing their friends and knifing each other in the back and hating the directors and having a wonderful time. It was radio, so all that mattered was their voices and their timing. They didn't even have to remember lines. And it didn't make any difference if they had bags under their eyes or the old wattles were hanging down over their collars. Or if they got fat, or they had to walk with a cane. Nobody saw them except the other people on the show. Of course I never saw a one of them that wouldn't pass up a guaranteed thirteen weeks on radio for a chance to get back on Broadway. But that's another matter. As long as they stayed in radio they were eating and working and saving a little. But tomorrow I'll see old actors that I never even knew in radio. I don't know where they've been. And only one of them is going to get a job tomorrow.

FRANK   Hmm.

JOE   You might as well toughen up, Wilson. That's the way it's going to be for all the other parts too. You got this hardly more than a walk-on, Larry's mother. There'll be at least twenty women wanting that part. I'll tell you now what's going to happen. There'll be one old dame, she won't stand with the others. She'll keep off to one side, because she figures she'd be lost in the crowd, and we'll notice her. Then she'll disappear, and you know where she'll be? She'll be out front, looking for you. The author. You'll be sitting there in the dark, watching the people onstage. Then you'll feel a hand on your arm. "Oh, *there* you are, Mr. Wilson. I've brought this copy of your latest novel I wish you'd autograph. Will you say something just a tiny bit— personal? My name is Mary Smith, but don't just say 'to Mary Smith, Sincerely, Frank Wilson.' I do so love this novel and that's *really* why I want to be in your play." And all the time she'll be sizing you up, trying to decide whether you'd go for the real pitch. And that can be something, my friend. If she's young enough, say around fifty, she'll offer you various Oriental pleasures herself. If she's older, she probably will say she has a niece or even a daughter that's dying to meet you. And all she wants is a bit part in your play. It's all she does want, too. She isn't out to blackmail you or take you for a bundle. Maybe she doesn't even need the money the job pays. My advice to you, this being your first play, don't sit alone when we're casting. Always have somebody with you. They'll try to get you off alone, but don't go.

FRANK   Are you married?

JOE   I been married to the same girl for a year and a half. Wife Number Three. She's gonna be sore as hell you didn't know she was my wife. Angela Kirkbride.

FRANK   Oh, the poet. I didn't know she was your wife.

JOE   Well, she don't always remember it, but neither do I. Angie's a good dame. She's kind of a mutt for looks, but she's got a hell of a shape. I don't even have a hell of a shape. And we both got divorced to get married, so there must be something there. We have all our fights over politics. She liked Dewey.

FRANK   She did?

JOE   Not did. Does. She says if you're gonna be a champion of the underdog, *be* a champion of the underdog. And she means it. She wrote in Thomas W. Dewey the last election.

FRANK   Thomas *E.* Dewey.

JOE (*Gleefully*) She didn't *know* that. Ah, she's a good dame. I think I'll call her up. (*Says* "New Canaan 4-1111," *into the phone*) Notice I'm wearing the tie you gave me?

FRANK Yes. It's damn good looking.

JOE Sincere. Isn't that what they call it? Hello, hello . . . Hello, Lupe? This is Johnny. Awoo-awoo. What are you doing? Huh? . . . I'm having a drink with a guy here . . . The Bellevue-Stratford. I know it's in Philly. (She says that proves I'm in New York.) . . . Yes, I'm in New York. I'm with the author. Tell him *what?* No, I can't tell him that. And I won't let you tell him. You don't know him well enough . . . No, he may have one stashed away in the can, but otherwise I haven't seen any. (Have we got any women with us?) . . . What are you gonna do tonight? . . . What the hell do you wanta wash your hair for? Why don't you cut it off and wear a wig . . . A what? . . . How do you spell it? . . . She says to ask you if you know what a merkin is.

FRANK (*Nodding*) Uh-huh.

JOE Yeah, he knows, but I don't . . . She says don't tell me, make me look it up . . . Listen, the hell with your hair. Why don't you drive in and we'll have dinner some place. I'll take you to that French place over on the West Side . . . No, you come here. I gotta be here all day tomorrow . . . You know what you're missing, don't you? . . . What? . . . (*He laughs*) You son of a bitch . . . All right. Will you meet me? All right. (*He hangs up*) The hell with you, Wilson. I'm taking the 6-12. Son of a bitch. What a dame. (*Pointing his finger at* FRANK) And she's really quite ugly.

(FRANK *watches him go, follows him to the door and listens to see if* JOE *is there, suddenly swings open the door and* JOE *is there, sheepish but trying to hide it*)

JOE (*Thinking quickly*)   Aha, I knew it.

FRANK   You knew what?

JOE   I knew you wouldn't get right back to the type-writer.

FRANK   You were waiting to see who I telephoned.

JOE   How can you say that, about a— Who *are* you gonna telephone?

FRANK   You're going to miss your train. Beat it. (*He closes the door and goes to his typewriter, types one word— Sandra—and then aloud*) Oh—Larry—but I'm not speaking to you. (*He types it*)

CURTAIN

SCENE SIX

This scene takes in a conversation in which the principals are in two bedrooms that are separated by more than twenty city blocks: JOYCE's *bedroom in her apartment, and* FRANK's *bedroom in the hotel. The time is some hours after the preceding scene.* JOYCE *is in bed, watching TV; she turns down the volume with the remote-control gadget in her hand, and calls* FRANK's *hotel. The phone in* FRANK's *room is heard, ringing several times. As he wakes up a pinspot goes on him and we see that he is in pajamas, and that the floor of his room is littered with crumpled paper, evidence of his rewriting.*

FRANK (*Sleepily*)   Who the hell . . . Hello?

JOYCE   Oh, I'm sorry. You were asleep.

FRANK   Wha'?

JOYCE It's your leading lady, but you go back to sleep. If you *were* asleep. I'm not sure I'm convinced. You're so convincing that I a little bit suspect you.

FRANK Wait till I light a cigarette.

JOYCE Now I believe you. If you were faking you'd never think of that bit.

FRANK Dear lady, I'm not an actor.

JOYCE Oh, but you are. All authors are actors, except that they act with words instead of making faces and putting on makeup, the way we poor souls do.

FRANK I could demolish that analogy if I were fully awake.

JOYCE Oh, now don't be mean, Frank. Don't be mean. You're so good with words, and I can't even write a coherent letter. That's why I telephoned you, by the way.

FRANK You want me to write a coherent letter for you?

JOYCE No. You see I was sitting here, cozy in bed, enjoying my comfort, and when I feel good like that I like to share it. Don't be obvious.

FRANK (*Before she can stop him*) Share your bed?

JOYCE I said, don't be obvious. I no sooner said that than I realized what you'd say. No, honey, I'm alone, as I often am, in spite of what you've heard to the contrary. The only company I have is my hot water bottle. Well?

FRANK Well, what?

JOYCE Aren't you going to say you're envious of my hot water bottle?

FRANK A *little* obvious, especially after you just warned me not to be. Anyway, exactly where is the hot water bottle?

JOYCE Under my feet.

FRANK Which is exactly where I don't want to be.

JOYCE   I could put it some place else.

FRANK   Now you're talkin'.

JOYCE   Oh, I get it. You don't want to be—

FRANK   *Under* your *feet*. That's right.

JOYCE   Really, you're so mean, I'm almost tempted not to tell you why I called you. And it was nice, too.

FRANK   Dear lady, you know as well as I do that nothing short of a power failure would keep you from telling me whatever it is you want to tell me.

JOYCE   I suppose so. When I want to do something nice I can be very determined. A friend of mine once told me I was ruthlessly kind. Rather cute.

FRANK   Pretty cute. It follows in the great tradition of Oliver Herford's remark about his wife. She had a whim of iron, you remember?

JOYCE   I thought Mark Twain said that.

FRANK   No. What you thought Mark Twain said was actually said by Charles Dudley Warner.

JOYCE   What was that?

FRANK   Uh—the report of the weather is greatly exaggerated. Everybody talks about my death, but nobody does anything about it.

JOYCE   You're con-*fusing* me. And I really hate to be confused. I'm a very simple-minded girl. *Gal.* At my age when you call yourself a girl it's better to pronounce it gal. Then those other bitches won't be able to say, "Get her."

FRANK   Is that supposed to be the statement of a simple-minded gal? You're about as simple-minded as an IBM computer. But you're not fooling me.

JOYCE   Oh, dear. You're making it almost impossible to tell you what I wanted to. You're going to suspect me of something.

FRANK   Well, try me.

JOYCE You promise you won't suspect me of something?

FRANK I promise you I will, then if I'm wrong, you're in the clear.

JOYCE Well—you know, I have this house in Connecticut.

FRANK No, I didn't know.

JOYCE Well, I have. You don't think this dingy little apartment is all I have to show for—for my years as a star.

FRANK I did kind of wonder about that.

JOYCE Well I should think you would. Surely you gave me credit for having some self-respect.

FRANK Self-respect? How does that enter into it?

JOYCE Well, after all, I've been married twice, and both my husbands were *affluent* men. Love that word. So when they wanted a divorce, or I did, I forget which— you surely don't think I was going to let the bastards get away without paying. I have too much—

FRANK (*With her*) Too much self-respect.

JOYCE Too much self-respect for that. Exactly.

FRANK And that's how you happen to have this house in Connecticut.

JOYCE Among other things. It's a dear. I hate to leave it for a minute except when I have to come out and earn my living, like now.

FRANK Well, we don't go into rehearsal till August.

JOYCE I know, but I have to go to London and then of course I want to be in Paris before the fashion shows. That I *have* to do. So my adorable little house will be empty till I get back from Paris. Would you like to stay there?

FRANK In your house? What for?

JOYCE To work on our play. You'd be absolutely undisturbed. I have a German couple that live there all year round, perfect servants and used to the ways of people like us. The wife is a wonderful cook and the husband is good at all sorts of things. He's a carpenter, he can do plumbing when necessary. He can even shoe a horse.

FRANK   If you hadn't said that I wouldn't be interested.

JOYCE   Said what?

FRANK   That he can shoe a horse.

JOYCE   Oh, you're mad! You're divinely mad. You're just like me. I adore a mad sense of humor.

FRANK   How much would this house cost me, including the old smithy?

JOYCE   Cost you? I'm not trying to rent my house. I wouldn't let a stranger set foot in it. I want to give it to you, for the whole month of July and part of August. *If* you wanted to pay the help, I pay my couple six hundred and the gardener gets sixty a week. But the other expenses don't amount to much. I have an arrangement with some kind of a service, they come and clean out the swimming-pool. That's not much.

FRANK   They probably find a diamond bracelet every now and then.

JOYCE   Only once, a diamond wrist-watch, and they returned it to me. How did you know?

FRANK   Oh, I'm just mad, I guess.

JOYCE   You wouldn't have to join the club unless you really wanted to. If you do, I can speak to Ralph and see if he can't get you a summer membership.

FRANK   *Don't* speak to Ralph. Who *is* Ralph?

JOYCE   My first husband, silly. He lives down the road. Ralph McAneny.

FRANK   Well, then go on speaking to him. We're civilized people, I hope. But don't say anything about my joining the club. In fact, Joyce, I think I'll just stay here, thanking you very much for your kind offer.

JOYCE   You mean you don't want my house?

FRANK   It's nothing against you or your house, but—

JOYCE   Surely it isn't the money. You write best-sellers.

FRANK   Sure it *is*. You've heard of alimony. And isn't that the foolish question of the year. Well, I don't *get* it. I *pay* it. You see the difference? You get it, and I pay it.

JOYCE   (*A lament*)   Oh, Frank, *why* did you get married?

FRANK   It's what they call a good question, but a little late.

JOYCE   Do both your exes get alimony?

FRANK   No, only one. But she has a *hell* of a lot of self-respect.

JOYCE   You'd be near Joe Rasmussen. He lives only about ten miles away. He and that female Dracula. Oh, I do wish you'd take the house, Frank. If it really is the money—I have to pay the servants anyway, and the other expenses.

FRANK   I somehow inferred that.

JOYCE   I *was* chiselling a little, but in fairness to myself, I could rent the house for two or three thousand.

FRANK   In July?

JOYCE   Well, August *is* the best month, of course. How did you know that?

FRANK   I'm the man that pays, remember?

JOYCE   I'll tell you what I'll do. Would you go halves on the servants and the upkeep? Or let's make it a flat sum. Can you afford to pay me a thousand for all of July and the first two weeks in August?

FRANK   Let me think. I'm paying four-fifty here. Half of four-fifty. I'd be paying six-seventy-five here. That would be three-and-a-quarter more than I'm paying now.

JOYCE   You'd be paying the food bills for the servants, too.

FRANK   You're very honest. I might have overlooked that.

JOYCE   But in the long run even that would be cheaper than having your meals in restaurants.

FRANK   Oh, what the hell. All right. It's a deal. A thousand bucks.

JOYCE   I'm so glad. You won't regret it, either. Now I can go away feeling that my lovely house is in safe hands.

FRANK   What about a lease and inventory and all that stuff?

JOYCE   I'd rather not. Because what I'd really like you to do, instead of paying me rent, why don't you just buy me a present?

FRANK   Like what, for instance?

JOYCE   Oh—just cash. Ten one-hundred-dollar bills.

FRANK   It's so much simpler that way.

JOYCE   I think so, don't you?

FRANK   Yes. It just occurred to me.

JOYCE   What?

FRANK   I'll bet that hot water bottle feels like a solid block of ice.

JOYCE   Why it does. How did you know?

FRANK   Oh, you know me. Mad.

(*She looks frowningly at the telephone*)

JOYCE   Goodnight.

FRANK   Goodnight.

SCENE SEVEN

STANTON'S *office, a few days later.* STANTON *is behind his desk; sitting in the office with him are* FRANK WILSON, JOE RASMUSSEN *and* SIDNEY RENWICK. *They are killing time while waiting for the arrival of* JOYCE CHILTON. RASMUSSEN *is reading a comic book,* RENWICK *is reading the* Journal-American.

STANLEY   What are you reading, Joe?

JOE   This? This is a comic book. You want it when I'm finished with it?

STANLEY   No thanks. I don't have any children.

JOE   What's with children? I got two, but not old enough to read. This is indigenous art.

STANLEY   Is that why you read them?

JOE   No, but it's why you ought to. I don't have to worry about art. People write about me and my art, so now I don't have to worry about it no more. The Art of Joe Rasmussen. From Belasco to Rasmussen. Don't you ever read those articles?

STANLEY   Oh, sure, I read them.

JOE   The stormy petrel of the American Theater, by Nigel Tenney, in the *New Statesman*? Hey, Frank?

FRANK   Uh-huh. I saw that one.

JOE   Look, ma, I'm a bird. A stormy petrel. You read the one about me in the *Manchester Guardian*?

FRANK   It isn't the *Manchester Guardian* any more, Joe.

JOE   What is it then?

FRANK   Just the *Guardian,* without the Manchester. They've extended their guardianship.

JOE   Suits me. Everybody says I need a guardian. Where the hell is that broad?

STANLEY   (*Knowing he means* JOYCE)   She said she'd be a little late.

JOE   That figures, but I'd like to get to the ball game, there's a double-header today. Frank, you wanta go the ball game with me? I got a box.

FRANK   You what?

JOE   It aint my box. It belongs to Universal Airlines but I use it all the time. Press agent's a pal of mine.

STANLEY   What can you do for Universal Airlines?

JOE   Opening night seats for all the plays I work on. The press agent offers them to his boss, the boss offers them to the president of the American Gadget Corporation, and the president of the American Gadget Corporation gives them to somebody else. Very seldom you can parlay a favor as much as that. Everybody's happy, and I get box seats for the ball games. Wuddia say, Frank?

FRANK   Not today, Joe, thanks.

JOE   Whennia moving to Connecticut?

FRANK   Next week.

STANLEY   Oh, you're moving to Connecticut?

JOE   Don't tell him where if you don't feel like it. I shouldn't of opened my big mouth.

FRANK   I thought I told you. I'm renting Joyce's house while she's abroad.

JOE   Boy, could I make a bad gag out of that.

STANLEY   You must be renting it for ten years.

JOE   That's the kind of a gag I meant. I'm glad you said it, Stanley. Thanks.

STANLEY   My pleasure, Joe. I hear it's a charming estate. It's near you, isn't it, Joe?

JOE It's near enough, but far enough away so Frank won't be able to throw rocks at me when we start working.

STANLEY Within easy motoring distance, though?

JOE Easy for Frank. I got my license suspended for two years.

SIDNEY What for, Joe?

JOE The usual thing.

SIDNEY Reckless driving?

JOE No, I wasn't driving recklessly. I was just drunk. I'm much more careful when I'm drunk, but try and tell *them* that.

SIDNEY Then do you have to depend on Angela?

JOE Yeah. And if the State of Connecticut had any idea how *she* drives a car they'd gimme back my license. Oh, here she is. All rise, gentlemen. Madame Schumann-Heink.

JOYCE I'll hit you right over the head with this umbrella. Madame Schumann-Heink.

JOE You better not come to rehearsals this late.

JOYCE Now don't get tough with me, Joe. You can say anything you please after the twelfth of August, but until then you be your own sweet, dear, gentlemanly self. Hello, Frank. Hello, Stanley. Hello, Sidney.

STANLEY I only wanted we five to get together this one time before we scatter to the four winds, you might say.

JOE Yeah, and what the hell for?

STANLEY Well, I thought it would be a good idea to have us all together—

JOYCE While we're all still speaking.

STANLEY Oh, I don't think this company is going to have that kind of trouble. We're a small group, and we all respect one another's ability. I don't foresee any of the usual difficulties. Of course there'll be some, there always are. But in my opinion, I've gotten together about as talented a group of people as any manager on Broadway. We have a *great* star, one of the very few that has a real personal following. Our leading man, Sidney, you couldn't find a better leading man than Sidney Renwick. We have a terrific script, a real challenge, if you know what I mean. And last but by no means least, there isn't a manager on Broadway that wouldn't give his eye teeth to have Joe Rasmussen work for him. And in addition to those here—you notice that the ones that are here today are the ones that get billing—we're also going to have people in the smaller parts that will be chosen for their excellent acting ability, and that goes for the set designer and the costume people, lighting, and so on. (*He pauses and the others are modestly silent*)

JOE (*Who has been making notes on his comic book*) You forgot something, Stanley.

STANLEY   What was that, Joe?

JOE   Who's gonna handle your insurance?

STANLEY   I have a very good— Oh, you're kidding.

JOE   Why should I kid? You might as well give us the whole picture along with the rest of this crap. Now *I* got a few notes. We got a pretty good play by Frank Wilson, a novelist that doesn't know his ass from first base in the theater. His play needs work, as all plays need work, and that work has to be done by Frank and me. Nobody else. If anybody has any suggestions to make to Frank or me, put them in writing and we'll flush them down the can. If you want to *see* them flushed down the can, I'll be glad to pull the chain in your presence. But you'll all be saving a lot of time if you just drop your suggestions down the donnicker yourself. We start rehearsals on the twelfth of August. If anybody has to have their appendix out, have it done now. Or the dentist, or anything like that. If you have any money troubles, go to Stanton, but if you have any other beefs, come to me. You'll have to, because Stanton won't be around while we're rehearsing. (*This is news to* STANTON, *who frowns but remains quiet*) You got anything more to say, Stanton?

STANLEY Well—

JOE (*Not giving him a chance*) Okay. Have a nice trip, Joyce. Don't eat too much. You too, Sidney, wherever you're off to. Frank, I'll see you next week. (*Looks at his watch*) I'll catch some of the first game.

(*They all look at each other in silence as the curtain descends*)

ACT TWO

SCENE ONE

Interior, JOYCE CHILTON'S *house in Connecticut, a week later. It is a surprisingly sensible room, book-lined, unchintzy, with a large globe, dictionary stand, and a sturdy card table on which* FRANK WILSON *has placed his typewriter and paper. He is staring blankly at the typewriter at rise, which is simultaneous with the entrance of* BRUNO, *the manservant, bearing a small tray on which are a cup and saucer, coffee vacuum, cream pitcher and sugar bowl.*

BRUNO   Chentleman. Is half past ten o'clock.

FRANK   Thank you.

BRUNO   (*Puts the coffee things on a table and stands waiting to be recognized*)   Chentleman.

FRANK   What is it, Bruno? And why don't you call me Mr. Wilson?

BRUNO   Yes sir.

FRANK   We're in the country. Let's be informal. (*He is aware that* BRUNO *will not understand this small frivolity*) Is there something on your mind?

BRUNO   On my mind is—you wish two cups for coffee?

FRANK   No, one will do. Why would I want two cups?

BRUNO   I hear somebody else talking.

FRANK   No.

BRUNO   (*Doggedly*)   I hear somebody.

FRANK   Oh, I know. I've had that trouble before. That was me you heard.

BRUNO   No, it was a woman's woice I hear.

FRANK   That was me.

BRUNO   (*With an unpleasant smile*)   No. Excuse me, was a woman.

FRANK   Like this? "Darling, if you leave me this time, it's for good." Is that what you heard?

BRUNO   (*Baffled and annoyed*)   Ja. Yes sir.

FRANK   That was me. Do you know what dialog is?

BRUNO   No sir.

FRANK   (*Going to bookshelf, takes down a small book*) See if they have a word for it in German.

BRUNO   In German is words for everything. Long words.

FRANK   (*Looking at dictionary*)   How right you are. Yes. Here. Zwie-gesprach. Zwiegesprach, ja?

BRUNO   (*Nodding*)   Ja ja. Zwiegesprach. Unterhaltung. Conwersation.

FRANK   I guess so. I ought to explain. I am a writer. (BRUNO *nods*) You dig that. Well, I am writing a play. Rewriting it, actually. (BRUNO *nods*) Which Miss Chilton is going to act in. (BRUNO *nods*) In a play, in this play, she speaks words. (BRUNO *nods*) And other people speak words to her. (BRUNO *nods*) Those words are called dialog. Zwieges-whatever.

BRUNO   Zwiegesprach. Ja.

FRANK   Now when I am writing those words—pay attention, now—when I am writing those words, I say them aloud first. Like "Darling, if you leave me this time, it's for good." Which incidentally is all the words I wrote since eight o'clock this morning, but that's neither here nor there. I'm sorry, Bruno, I'm confusing you. The words you heard, that you thought were being spoken by a woman—*I* was speaking. I want the words to sound right, so I say them out loud.

BRUNO (*Dawn*) Ahhhhhhhhhhhhhh.

FRANK There was no one else here. Only me. You understand the word thorough?

BRUNO Yes sir. We Germans are wery thorough.

FRANK I thought you'd know that word. Well, I'm thorough, too. I try out these words before putting them on paper.

BRUNO Oh, yes. That's good. That's thorough. But Wilson is not a German name.

FRANK No, that's quite true. But Americans can be thorough, too. (BRUNO *smiles skeptically, superiorly*) I could recall several instances of it but no use reviving what might be rather unpleasant memories.

BRUNO Too fast.

FRANK Nothing, really. In any event, now you understand why you thought you heard a woman's voice?

BRUNO Yes sir. Was Mr. Wilson speaking. Not a woman.

FRANK Right. And it will happen again. In fact, the more you hear it, the better I'm working. If you don't hear it, I'm not going very well.

BRUNO (*Interested in anything technical*) When you are working, you are talking. When you are talking, you are working?

FRANK I couldn't have put it better. Well, yes I could improve on that. When I am talking to *myself*, I am working. When I am working, I am talking to myself.

BRUNO (*Giving up*) Coffee is getting cold. Is coming lady and gentleman for lunch?

FRANK Right. We'll be three for lunch.

BRUNO Werry good, sir. Cocktails at half past twelve?

FRANK   No cocktails. Oh, clam juice, or tomato juice maybe.

BRUNO   (*Frowning*)   But we serve lunch at one o'clock. Elsa prepares a soufflé.

FRANK   We'll be prompt.

BRUNO   Wery good, sir.

FRANK   Oh, Bruno.

BRUNO   Yes sir?

FRANK   Tell me about this room. It's the kind of room I'd like for myself, but I'm surprised that Miss Chilton — She didn't go to any extra trouble for me, did she?

BRUNO   No sir. These furnitures and decorations, they was all new when Miss Chilton got married the second time. She bought everything for a surprise, but Mr. Robinson, he never like this room. He liked modern furnitures. He was surprised but he didn't like the surprise.

FRANK   Then why didn't he change it? He had plenty of money.

BRUNO   Plenty of money, but he didn't stay long in this house. They was married two winters and one summer. Most of the time they was in New York.

FRANK   I see. Well, it's a very comfortable room.

BRUNO   Even more comfortable in the winter, with the TV.

FRANK   Oh, you like it too?

BRUNO   Sure. Anything else, Mr. Wilson?

FRANK   That'll be all, thanks. My guests should be here —oh, probably around twelve-thirty.

BRUNO   Is that them? Is a station wagon in the dri'way.

FRANK   (*Looking at his wrist watch*)   It couldn't be. And yet, all things considered, it could. (*He looks out the French window and shrugs*)

FRANK   (*Calling out*)   Come in this way, Joe. Joe?

(JOE RASMUSSEN *and his wife* ANGELA KIRKBRIDE RAS-
MUSSEN *enter through the French window at Left.* JOE
*is wearing a loud sports shirt and blue shorts and es-
padrilles; she, possessed of a notable figure, is wearing a
black shirt and black toreador pants and Japanese slippers*)

JOE Hello, Frank, this is Angela. If you're gonna be
formal, call her Miss Kirkbride. She don't like to be
called Mrs. Rasmussen. Frank is liable to be formal till
he likes you, then he relaxes.

ANGELA (*To* FRANK) Be formal then. I want to be able
to tell when you start liking me, if you ever do.

FRANK Good morning, Miss Kirkbride. How are you,
Angie kid?

ANGELA Don't rush things. I'd just as lief call you Mr.
Wilson till I like *you*. (*Turning to* JOE) And listen,
you, don't go around saying I don't like being called
Mrs. Rasmussen. I do so like it.

JOE That's not what you told me.

ANGELA I changed my mind.

JOE When? Yesterday?

ANGELA This morning, on the way over.

JOE You should have told me. I can't *always* read your
mind. *Most* of the time . . .

ANGELA Do you know something? You never read my
mind, never since I've known you. You don't even read
my poetry.

JOE I did try. After that, reading your mind was easy.
Frank, you comfortable here? Or are you *used* to
luxury?

ANGELA God damn novelists, best-sellers.

JOE I wouldn't be comfortable in a place like this, but
maybe you're used to it.

ANGELA *Look* at this place! Are they for real, those books?

JOE   Pinch them and find out.

ANGELA   Yeah, that's the way *you* find out. That woman last night, you're lucky her husband didn't flatten you. You're lucky I didn't.

JOE   You jealous?

ANGELA   No, I wasn't jealous. I was just sore at you. (*To* FRANK) He said to this crashing bore, a Wall Street type, "My wife's are for real. Are your wife's for real?" Can I have some of that coffee, if nobody's drinking it?

FRANK   I'll ring for some.

ANGELA   (*Holding her hands to her ears*)   Ooh. That line grates on me. "I'll ring for some." Ugh. It conjures up all those plays I used to go to with my aunt. My aunt that I was named after. Bad enough to be named after her, but when I was discovered secretly writing plays when I was ten years old, Aunt Angie used to take me to matinees. Her idea of encouraging the nascent playwright, the first author in the Kirkbride family. In every single God damn one of those plays there was a character that said, "I'll ring for some."

JOE   That's crap, and you know it. I've read over three thousand plays and I never saw that line. I've seen the line, "I'll ring," but never the line, "I'll ring for some." Go ahead and ring for some, Frank.

FRANK   (*Doing so*)   If it doesn't turn your wife's stomach.

JOE   (*Laughing*)   Show him how you can really turn your stomach.

ANGELA   Oh, shut up.

JOE   (*Still laughing*)   You can't top her. Hey, Frank. I found out what a merkin is.

ANGELA   Oh, shut up or I'll leave you and you'll have to take a taxi. Eight dollars.

BRUNO   (*At doorway, Right*)   Yes sir.

FRANK   Some coffee, please, Bruno. Anything else, anybody? No. Just coffee for three.

BRUNO Yes sir. (*Leaves*)

JOE What happened to *him* at Nuremberg? He must of copped a plea. You hear anything from La Cheelton?

FRANK I don't expect to.

JOE Well, get ready, because you will. She went by boat, didn't she? Then you can expect a long letter any day now. Suggestions. Four or five days on a boat will give her plenty of time to put that mind to work. And that means suggestions.

ANGELA I read your play twice. I have some suggestions.

JOE (*To her*) I have one for *you, too*. Butt out, and stay out.

ANGELA (*Ignoring him haughtily*) Don't have What's Her Name, Sandra, standing at the window. Not if you're going to have Joyce Chilton for your leading lady. She has to *breeze* on. The way you have it, it's a static beginning. (FRANK *and* JOE *look at each other, and* JOE *shakes his head negatively, to indicate that he has not spoken to* ANGELA *about this*) You don't want that, not with Joyce Chilton. I've seen her in a dozen plays, and if you once lose that animation, she dies on you. She always has to have little bits of business, otherwise it's too much of an effort for her to come alive again. Vitality like that, you know, it's a blessing, maybe, but it creates problems. And you have several places in your play where she has nothing to say or do, and it's going to be up to this guy (*Indicating* JOE) to goose her back into action again.

JOE She's right, Frank.

FRANK I'm inclined to agree with her.

ANGELA Well then I'll shut up.

JOE There's no fun in it for her now. She was looking for an argument. (ANGELA *stretches out on a sofa and lights a cigarette, ignoring the men and deep in her own thoughts*) But don't listen to anything else she tells you. Don't listen. You don't have to be polite to Angie.

ANGELA   Yeah, you found that out, a long time ago, you ill-mannered Boy Scout. He was a Boy Scout till he was sixteen years old.

JOE   Then I changed into a Girl Scout. You want to know something about that woman over there?

ANGELA   You be care—ful.

JOE   You want to know how she found out I was a Boy Scout? On our honeymoon—the real one, not the out-of-town tryout—we went to some little town in Pennsylvania, I even forget the name of it. You know why?

FRANK   No.

JOE   Because it was near some bird sanctuary. She didn't *tell* me that. She said we went there because *I* liked Pennsylvania Dutch cooking. "When did I ever say I liked Pennsylvania Dutch cooking?" I asked her. "I can tell," she said. Well, I did like it. I mean it was all right if you like everything cooked in dough.

ANGELA   You never eat anything but pastry. His favorite food is a chocolate eclair.

JOE   (*Hesitating*) And Danish. I like Danish and once in a while a Napoleon if it's fresh.

ANGELA   Anything sweet and heavy, it's a wonder he has a tooth in his mouth.

JOE   (*Back to* FRANK) You see what she's trying to do, Frank? Trying to divert me from the story of our honeymoon.

ANGELA   *Your* story of our honeymoon.

JOE   Sure my story. There was nothing new about the rest of it except that we were married.

ANGELA   That was news in itself. The first time I went out with him he said any time I wanted to get married, he knew the captain of the Staten Island ferry.

JOE   Get it right! The excursion to Sandy Hook. Anyway, we were there three days, this little hotel near
Reading P A, and I was reading plays, and she'd take
the car so's not to disturb me. Not to disturb me! She
could hardly wait to get out of the room. You know
why? To go take a look at some hawks. You know?
Hawks!

ANGELA   It just occurred to me that it wasn't much of a
change, leaving you to look at some hawks.

JOE   All that time she was making like a female Dylan
Thomas, actually she was a bird-watcher. A Girl Scout.
Tell you something else she was—a member of the
East Orange Junior League.

ANGELA   The Junior League of The Oranges.

JOE   Tell him where your Aunt Angela used to take you
to lunch before the matinee.

ANGELA   The Colony Club. Now *you* tell him about your
merit badges.

JOE   Woodcraft, and first aid. I got a merit badge in
first aid because I was the one they used as a patient.
They were always bandaging me up and putting me in
splints. You should of seen me making like an accident
victim.

ANGELA   *That's* what I wanted him to say. You realize
now what you've got directing your play, Mr. Wilson.
A ham. A ham actor from way back.

JOE   I was good. Watch.
(*He lies on the floor, imitating a woman with a broken
leg, groaning, "Don't touch it! God, let me die!" At this
point* BRUNO *enters and places the coffee things on a
table, then scornfully, silently marches out*)

ANGELA   (*As casually as possible*)   Let him die. Or let's
pretend he's a horse and shoot him.
(JOE *gets laboriously to his feet*)

JOE   So anyway, you know how it is, Frank. A lot of men

find out a lot of things about their wives on their honeymoon. But I found out that *mine* was a *bird*-watcher.

ANGELA   That's what a honeymoon is for, isn't it? To find
out things you didn't know before?

JOE   Yeah, well like I said, by that time we were pretty
well acquainted.

FRANK (*To* ANGELA)   When did you find out he'd been
a Boy Scout?

ANGELA   Through a big lie. That's how I usually find
things out about him. Some big lie.

JOE   I was testing her. I could never read any of her
poetry and we used to argue about that. So I told her,
I said I wrote better poetry than that when I was fourteen years old. "Do you still have any of it?" she asked
me. And I said I'd look in my scrapbook when I was a
Boy Scout.

ANGELA   And the next day he had a piece of paper that
he'd written on, imitating a fourteen-year-old boy's
handwriting. "I got a merit badge for poetry when I
was a Scout," he said, and this was one of his poems.

JOE   I wanted to see if she knew *anything* about poetry.

ANGELA   And this is what he'd written:

> If I can stop one heart from breaking,
> I shall not live in vain;
> If I can ease one life the aching,
> Or cool one pain,
> Or help one fainting robin,
> Unto his nest again,
> I shall not live in vain.

FRANK   Well, I don't want to go out on a limb, but that's
pretty good for a Boy Scout. In fact it sounds like a
poem a Boy Scout would write. Of course you didn't
write it, Joe?

JOE   Will you tell him, or shall I?

ANGELA   It was written by that well-known Boy Scout,
Emily Dickinson.

JOE She recognized it right away.

ANGELA Anybody would that knew anything about poetry.

FRANK I didn't, but I don't know anything about poetry.

ANGELA Neither does Mr. Rasmussen, or he wouldn't have copied anything as obvious as that.

JOE It sounded very Scouty to me.

ANGELA The Harvard man speaking.

JOE (*Loftily*) There are a few gaps in my cultural background. I admit it.

ANGELA He spent all his time at Harvard reading plays.

FRANK So he told me. Three thousand of them.

ANGELA He told me two thousand. He knows who played the maid in a revival of *Private Lives* in 1935 . . .

JOE That I know for sure. Nobody. For openers, there *was* no maid in *Private Lives*—

ANGELA Or who won the World Series in—1936.

JOE (*Eagerly*) Another easy one. The Yankees beat the Giants in a six-game series. I saw every game except the fifth, the game Schumacher won 5 to 4. Maybe it was 6 to 5. No, it was 5 to 4. I had a sadistic uncle a Yankee fan, took me to all the other games but not that one. I wonder, was the fix in on that game and he knew it?

ANGELA Didn't anybody warn you, Mr. Wilson?

FRANK What about?

ANGELA Him. About him. I was watching you, and you don't know whether he was kidding or not. He wasn't. He half believes that his uncle would fix a World Series game just to annoy him.

JOE Well, you know my uncle. Wouldn't he?

ANGELA If he could, yes, but let's be sensible.

JOE Too late now. That was damn near thirty years ago. (*Shakes his head*) I'll never be able to see that game.

ANGELA (*To* FRANK) See what I mean? The question

keeps coming back to me, Mr. Wilson. Why did you want to get Joseph to direct your play? It isn't his kind of play at all.

JOE   Yeah, I wanted to ask you that, too, Frank.

ANGELA   I'll be truthful with you, I told Joseph not to do it.

JOE   She did. She said I had nothing to gain and everything to lose.

ANGELA   Let me tell him myself. You don't have to tattle. I said your play was all right, nothing special. Good characters and good dialog, but not a play.

JOE   Show the man the bruises where I hit you when you said that.

ANGELA   But how could an author like what Joseph did with *Valid Resentment* and then think he would be good for a play like yours?

FRANK   Do you really want to know, Mrs. Rasmussen, or is this all academic?

ANGELA   I'd sort of like to know. If it doesn't take too long.

FRANK   It won't. I saw other plays Joe directed, besides *The Valid Resentment,* and two movies he did. He couldn't possibly know anything about the South, from personal experience, and yet *Georgia Boy* was absolutely convincing. I've spent a lot of time in the South. The play he did four or five years ago—

JOE   *Perihelion.*

FRANK   *Perihelion, that* was laid in the year Two Thousand Five Hundred, but I got personally involved with those people.

ANGELA   In other words you're saying, or leading up to saying that he's enough of an artist, and all that jazz. Okay, that's a valid reason.

FRANK   Thanks. But it isn't the principal reason.

JOE (*Gleefully*) I knew he was holding back. Go ahead, Frank. Tell her.

FRANK I wanted Joe to direct this play because a man that hates his guts told me that your husband has a thing about failure. He can't stand anything but un-qualified success, and therefore works twice as hard as anyone has to, only because he wants the play to be a success.

JOE Axel Schmidt told you that?

FRANK Yes, it was Axel.

JOE I didn't know you knew him.

FRANK I don't. I called him up when Stanton said he was going to try to get you.

JOE If I'd of known that I wouldn't of taken your play.

FRANK I don't apologize for trying to find out what I could. You did the same thing to me.

JOE How do you know I did?

FRANK I assume you did. Just a guess.

JOE You assume correctly.

FRANK Sure. I'm new in the theater, Joe, but never lose sight of the fact that I've had a lot of experience with book publishers and there's only one difference between them and theatrical managers.

JOE What's that?

FRANK A book publisher gets to his office at ten o'clock, the theatrical manager gets to his at eleven.

JOE (*To* ANGELA) Well, did he answer your question to your satisfaction?

ANGELA He was a little too glib, but he makes a lot of sense. You *are* success-prone.

FRANK I can't take the credit for that. Axel Schmidt told me that.

JOE Yeah, but you knew when to believe Axel and when

not to. He can be the biggest God damn liar I ever knew.

FRANK   Maybe I'll be before this is over.

ANGELA   You've got plenty of competition in that department. My little Joseph, here.

JOE   Don't forget Joyce Chilton. And I'll bet Sidney Renwick—no, not very convincing. Sidney's a natural-born liar, but since I used to know Sidney in radio, somebody gave him a Gentleman's Manual, How to be a Gentleman in Twenty-four Easy Lessons, and the part where it says a gentleman shouldn't lie, that threw Sidney.

ANGELA   Don't tell me there *is* such a book.

JOE   No, but I'm thinking of writing one. It'd be easy. Just study Sidney, and whatever he does, a gentleman would do the opposite.

ANGELA   If he heard you say that he'd cut his throat.

JOE   No. Slit his veins, in a tub of warm water. You haven't been following Sidney.

ANGELA   No, that would be like man bites dog.

JOE   She's pretty sharp this morning, for a dame that was up all night writing a poem.

ANGELA   Oh, shut up. You don't have to tell everything you know.

JOE   God, you'd think I said she was entertaining the fleet. I only said you—

ANGELA   My writing is my own business, and I don't want it talked about. I mean that, Joe.

JOE   When she calls me Joe, I make for the shelter. All right, Angie. I'm sorry. (*He has gone too far and knows it*) Frank, did you do anything about that third scene? You know, where Sandra in the flashback has a line, "Darling, if you leave me now, don't come back"? Have you been thinking about that? You see, if she says, "Don't come back," that is a peremptory line. You see what

I mean? A peremptory line is almost the same as an order. It closes out any further discussion, and that isn't the way she feels at that particular moment, Frank. She wants to leave it open. She wants to talk, to discuss their troubles. And she doesn't want to give him an excuse to walk out.

FRANK Yes, I changed the line. The way I have it now is, "Darling, if you leave me this time, it's for good."

JOE Better. Much better. Puts it squarely up to him without being an ultimatum. In other words, she's saying, "If you leave me now, I have no other choice but to let you go. You make the decision, I don't." Much better, Frank. Thank you. (FRANK *is a little surprised and pleased by the "thank you" but does not let* JOE *know it*) Then Larry hesitates. You see, Frank, the kind of dumb-head Larry is, he wouldn't have hesitated for the other line, but now when he hesitates, that's valid. It gets through his skull that Sandra doesn't really want him to leave, and that she'll do almost anything to keep him from walking out.

FRANK Almost anything, Joe. But later on, don't forget, she realizes that she's had it as far as Larry is concerned . . .

JOE Right. Right. But that's later on, when she's had time to think. In this scene she hasn't had much time to think. You know, everything happens pretty fast in this scene.

FRANK (*Nodding*) Yeah. Yeah.

JOE Oh, I agree with you absolutely that she's had it as far as Larry's concerned. But we know that before she's supposed to know it. And we God damn sure want the *audience* to know it. This is a pretty honest dame, and we want the audience to be with her, or actually a little ahead of her. Not too much, but a little. You know, pulling for her, even though they know what mistakes she's going to make. Or *because* they know what mistakes she's going to make. Right?

FRANK   Right.

JOE   At the same time, Frank, don't let me prejudice you when I call Larry a dumbhead. *I* don't like him, but I don't like any of those office guys. I don't like anybody that works in an office, rich or poor, Catholic or Jew, I just don't like office guys. Saloon guys, factory guys, farm guys—but not office guys. That's a blind prejudice I have. But in this play, Larry is an office guy, and I'm going to help you make the audience like him. We have to have that. And Frank, that's where your play is weak. The dame, Sandra, we're ready to open tonight, as far as the Sandra character is concerned. We don't want to tinker with her. I'll watch you to see that *you* don't, and you watch me in case I start trying to improve her. (ANGELA *rises quietly, smiles happily at the men at work, and slips out apparently unnoticed by the men in their absorption*) In case you didn't notice it, we're now free to make any comments on women that we feel like. (JOE *leans back and lights a cigarette*) Let me tell you about this broad Sandra. I knew a dame just like her in. . . . .

CURTAIN

SCENE TWO

Same as Scene One; after lunch. JOE, ANGELA *and* FRANK *have just finished lunch, are entering the room and assuming post-luncheon attitudes.*

JOE I'll say this for you, Frank. You got yourself a good cook, or does she go with the house?

FRANK Too good. Yes, she goes with the lease. But I'm not going to be able to eat that kind of food and start work right after lunch.

ANGELA I was almost ashamed to eat that food, dressed the way we are.

JOE I noticed that. Shyness overcame you as soon as you saw what we were getting.

ANGELA Don't be sarcastic.

JOE Sarcastic? Not sarcastic. You were so shy that the only way you could cover it was by compulsive eating, sometimes called making a pig of yourself.

FRANK We were going so well, I was hoping we'd be able to work through till five or six.

JOE You don't think you can?

FRANK Not unless I take a nap. Do you realize that we three put away a chicken curry this big.

ANGELA Not to mention Joseph, with at least four rolls with butter and chutney.

FRANK I didn't eat any of the rolls.

JOE Honey, buy some chutney. I think I'll have that instead of marmalade.

ANGELA One of these days you're going to end up with diabetes.

JOE Well, what the hell, I'm going to end up with something. Everybody does. And you keep forgetting, I'm part Turkish, and we Turks eat a lot of sweets.

FRANK I didn't know that, Joe. I've never known a Turk. There was one at college, but he was a senior my freshman year, so I never got to know him.

ANGELA (*To* JOE) Go ahead. Tell him about it.

JOE She doesn't believe me, but my grandmother was raped by a Turk.

FRANK   How did that happen?

JOE   The usual way. He knocked her down and pulled up her skirt, and—

FRANK   I didn't mean that. I meant the circumstances.

ANGELA   He's a little bit shaky on the circumstances. In the first place, the whole story is a God damn lie, and in the second place he invented it as an excuse for eating candy and pastry all the time, and in the third place, he'd like to have a harem.

JOE   Little does she know. Her idea of a harem is a lot of broads sitting around on pillows and eating coffee with a spoon. I belong to the modern Turks and I don't have my harem all in one place. Hey, Fatima, come on over and tickle my feet.

ANGELA   (*Ignoring him*)   I wonder if I could get into one of Joyce Chilton's bathing suits. I'd kind of like to go for a swim.

JOE   Frank?

FRANK   What?

JOE   Could she get into one of Joyce's bathing suits?

FRANK   Oh no, Joe. No you don't.

JOE   He doesn't think you could.

ANGELA   If we were home I wouldn't need a suit.

JOE   Well you need one here, with that butler.

ANGELA   Oh, I know, I know. Frank, couldn't you give them the afternoon off, Bruno and his wife, and I could— No, I guess not.

JOE   No. Now let's see the next thing that comes from that agile mind. You don't know this about her, but she's going to spend the next couple hours figuring out ways how she can go for a swim. Then by that time we'll be ready to go home. But once she gets an idea, boy . . . She hates to give up.

ANGELA   If Frank takes a nap, I could get undressed here

and you could go and get me a big towel. I'm sure Miss Joyce Chilton has those six-by-four towels.

FRANK If you don't mind I think I will take a nap for about a half an hour. Joe, do you want to come up and see if there are any big towels?

ANGELA You have no objection if I go in bareskin?

FRANK No, none at all. Why should I? Frankly, I'd enjoy it. In fact, I think I'll take a nap and then join you in the pool when I wake up.

ANGELA But you have swimming trunks.

FRANK Yes, I have trunks.

ANGELA Well I'm not going in bare and you come in wearing trunks.

FRANK What difference does it make? We're all grown-up men and women.

ANGELA (*To* JOE) Well, say something.

JOE Wuddia want me to say?

ANGELA Well, you don't want me going in the pool bare if Frank's there in trunks, do you?

JOE Why not? Why are you so anxious to have him go in bare-ass?

ANGELA I didn't *say* that.

JOE Yeah, but it's logical. What's the objection to him wearing trunks? The objection is you want him to go in bare-ass.

ANGELA No it isn't, and I didn't imply it.

JOE Didn't she, Frank?

FRANK Well, it would seem that way.

ANGELA Oh shut up, the two of you. (*She storms out and the men exchange grins*)

JOE You're getting wise to her. You played it smarter than I did. She always wants to do the opposite. The trouble is, so do I, and I give her an argument instead of letting her have her way. You still want to take a nap?

FRANK　I guess not. Let's just sit and gab, and if we happen to get around to the play, okay. I just don't feel like working at the moment.

JOE　All right. (BRUNO *brings in coffee and departs*) I wonder where we'll all be one year from today. What will you do if your play's a big hit? You know, like a year's run?

FRANK　I've thought about that.

JOE　I wouldn't want to have anything to do with you if you hadn't. Show business—take dreaming and hoping out of it and you got the worst bunch of cutthroats and chisellers and phonies and hypocrites. You have them anyway, but what makes them different in show business than any other business, once or twice a year they take a big dive in the dark, and they hope the pool is full of champagne. If the God damn pool is empty—smacko! But that's what it is if you have a hit. Champagne, you're over your head in it. What will you do?

FRANK　Right away, or a year from now?

JOE　First, right away.

FRANK　Well, I'd buy presents for everybody.

JOE　Except Stanton. Don't buy *him* anything. He'll rob you in little ways that you won't know about. Like if you go away he'll sell your house seats to the brokers and split the take. So don't buy him any presents.

FRANK　All right. No present for Stanton. Then I think I'll buy myself a boat.

JOE　What kind of a boat?

FRANK　Oh, a schooner, or a yawl.

JOE　You'll buy it right away?

FRANK　Yes. They're cheaper in October.

JOE But you have to pay storage all winter.

FRANK Oh, no. I'd take off for the South, the Inland
Route, and I'd spend all next winter on the boat, going
from place to place in the Caribbean.

JOE You know how to sail a boat?

FRANK Not a big one, but I can learn. I have a kid
brother that knows a lot more about it than I do. I'll
take him along.

JOE What will he do? Quit his job?

FRANK If he hasn't been fired. Boats are all he cares
about.

JOE Yeah, but you're doing this as much for him as for
yourself. I want to know what you'd do for yourself.
What would you buy for yourself?

FRANK Well, the trouble is, Joe, I don't exactly know.
I've made a lot of money, and spent it, so it isn't as
if I were having it for the first time. That experience
I went through in Hollywood, 1946. I had a house
bigger than this. A couple like Bruno and his wife. A
Bentley. And a Renoir. Don't forget I had three best-
sellers in five years, all sold to pictures for big money,
and I wrote the screen plays for two of my books.

JOE Taxes.

FRANK Sure. That's why I'm broke now, taxes and alimony. But I lived rich for a while, so that's out of my
system. I guess what I want is the satisfaction of seeing
a play I wrote on Broadway—

JOE *And a hit.*

FRANK Yes, and a hit. But honestly that isn't as important to me as it ought to be.

JOE It better be. If you don't have that zing, boy, you're
gonna have a lot of headaches for nothing. You're going
to dive into that pool and it's gonna be empty.

FRANK I don't think of this as a pool that I'm diving

into. To me it's an idea I had, with some things I wanted to say about married life, and I could say them in a play, or I could say them in a novel. It's a play because I did it that way.

JOE   No, there's more to it than that or you wouldn't have written a good play.

FRANK   Beginner's luck, Joe. I'm not even sure what the word dramaturgy really means.

JOE   If you want to know what I think, I think you're a better playwright than a novelist. I hope you have a hit so that you'll be hooked, and won't want to go back to writing novels. You know why the movies bought your novels? *I* do. Because regardless of whether they were novels, dramaturgically speaking they are naturals. Only you do it by accident. All you need is a hit, to get you started.

FRANK   I sure as hell don't intend to go on writing plays if this is a flop.

JOE   You don't now. Wait till we get in rehearsal. Wait'll you see your first run-through. And wait till that night in Philly or New Haven or wherever we open. (*Terror begins to show on his face*) Frank.

FRANK   (*Innocently*)   What?

JOE   Did you just hear something? A voice?

FRANK   I'm not sure.

JOE   Listen.

FRANK   Yes. I hear a voice.

JOE   Are you expecting anybody? You son of a bitch, are you holding out on me?

FRANK   On my word of honor—

JOE   If you knew about this and didn't tell me—

FRANK   Joe, take it easy. Now I don't hear *anybody*.

JOE   Oh-ho-ho-ho-ho-ho-ho. Oh, no.

(JOYCE CHILTON *appears in the doorway at Right. She*

is beaming, sure of her welcome, beautifully dressed in a suit, carrying a small airline bag in one hand and a jewel box in the other. She frames herself in the doorway)

JOYCE Oh, *yes.* As the great Durante would say— innnnnnnn poisson. (*Advancing on* FRANK *and* JOE, *kissing them both*) Dear Frank. Dear Joe. Aren't you glad to see me, and surprised? I'm so glad to see you.

JOE (*Stupefied*) Hello, Joyce.

FRANK (*Mystified, but responsive to her vitality*) Hello, Joyce. How did you do this?

JOYCE Wasn't I the impulsive one? Sit down now and I'll tell you *all* about it. Let me see now, where to begin. Last Tuesday, or was it Wednesday. No it wasn't a matinee day, it was Tuesday, I got on board that *dear* Queen Elizabeth. They're so wonderful to me on the Queen Elizabeth and they had all sorts of things planned for me, but I told them, no, no gayety, no festivities this trip. And I virtually locked myself in my little suite and spent every waking minute with— guess what?

JOE Frank's play.

JOYCE Well, you'd know that, Joe, because you're in the profession, but Frank is so modest, he'd never think of it. Yes, I had practically all my meals served in my room and I went over your play with a fine-tooth comb. And I've made so many notes. They're all here. (*She holds up the little airline bag*) Oh, did you know the *Irish* have an airline? Just think of that. They *are* trying to catch up with the modern world. Movie studios all over Ireland, I'm told. And an airline.

JOE The next thing, they'll have an atom bomb, and then look out.

JOYCE I don't know about that, but we've got to stop thinking of them as a backward people. Airlines and movie studios and everything. Anyway, I read and read and read and made notes, notes, notes, and it was all I could do, Frank, to restrain myself from calling you on the ship-to-shore telephone. But then I thought of the expense and inconvenience to you, dear. You might have been able to deduct it, but they're so unpredictable about what they'll allow and won't allow. So I realized the last day on the Queen Elizabeth— I was just bursting with ideas, and there was only one thing for me to do and that was turn around and come right back home. So I took an automobile to the London Airport, with all my luggage still on the Queen Elizabeth, and I couldn't get a thing on the New York plane, but fortunately I was recognized and this perfectly charming Englishman telephoned to the Shannon Airport, that's in Ireland—whurr the Rivvah Shannon flo-ows—and he found out that there was a vacancy or a cancellation or something on one of these Irish planes. So I flew to Shannon and from there to Idlewild, arrived safe and sound this morning, and here I am. Isn't it all exciting? Sarah Bernhardt couldn't have done that.

FRANK   No. Well, welcome home, Joyce. Welcome home.

JOYCE   Thank you, dear. Has everything been all right?

FRANK   Just fine. Perfect.

JOYCE   (*Something on her mind*)   I didn't come at the wrong *time*, did I?

FRANK   No. Why?

JOYCE   Well—I'm as broad-minded as it's possible to be. But didn't I see Shirley *Tanner* in my pool, naked as the day she was born? You could do better than that, Frank. You're an attractive man, and the nicest women go for intellectuals these days. Every man to his taste, but I wish you'd get her out of here. You know, (*She holds her hands in front of but at a distance from her bosom*) enough's enough.

JOE (*To* FRANK) Don't interrupt her.

JOYCE (*Turning to* JOE) Oh, *you* brought her. That's right, you did have a thing with her, didn't you? Back for retakes, eh? But do you think it's fair to Bruno to have this Rhine maiden sloshing around without any clothes on?

FRANK Joyce, the girl in the pool is Joe's wife. Angela Kirkbride. *Joe's wife.*

JOYCE (*Deadpan*) Hmm. Never at a loss for words, they say about me. (*Thinks of something and brightens*) Well, I'm so glad it is Mrs. Rasmussen and not Shirley Tanner.

FRANK I should say this, Joyce. Joe and I are just as much surprised to hear that Angela's in the pool as you were to see her.

JOE She crossed us. We thought we had her talked out of it.

JOYCE No matter. Nothing, really. Of course she could have borrowed a bathing suit from Bruno's wife. However, no harm done, and it's more or less the custom over your way, nude bathing, isn't it? (*She smiles, oversweetly*) Don't let's tell Mrs. Rasmussen about the men at the golf club. It would spoil it for her.

JOE What men at the golf club?

JOYCE Oh, that crowd of men on the seventeenth tee.

JOE (*In a hurry*) Where do you keep your towels?

JOYCE The large bath towels are in the bathhouse. (*As he exits*) I'm not sure they'll cover your wife, though.

JOE They'll cover enough of her. (JOE *leaves them alone*)

JOYCE (*Sitting down, taking out a cigarette, which* FRANK *lights for her*) Ah, journey's end. Do you love my house as much as I do?

FRANK Well, in the short time I've been here, I've gotten very fond of it.

JOYCE   I'm so glad. Do you like this room?

FRANK   I certainly do.

JOYCE   That's good. I was a little afraid. I spent two whole days before I sailed, doing this room over especially for you. Most of the old pieces belonged to my grandfather and I had them in storage, but I got them out because I had a hunch they were the kind of things you'd like. You know, I feel very much at home in New England. My ancestors were sea captains, you know. That globe. The harpoon. The ship model, and some of these chairs. They've all been in the family since time immemorial. It's all a bit masculine for as feminine a person as I am, but I wanted you to have one room where you'd feel—at home. So I want you to know, Mr. Frank Wilson, I spent two whole days getting this room ready for you.

FRANK   Whatever time you spent, it was well worth it.

JOYCE   Well then I'm well rewarded. I suppose you're wondering how my return affects our deal. Well, that's more or less up to you.

FRANK   Oh, I'll move back to town. That's all right.

JOYCE   No, now wait a second. It really all depends on— Oh, let's not be evasive. Have you got a girl, a mistress, that would make a stink if you stayed here? In other words, what *is* your situation in that department?

FRANK   Oh, I'm not committed to any one person. Free-lancing.

JOYCE   Sure, I understand. Well then no one's going to object if you stay here.

FRANK   No girl friend of mine is going to object. What about you, though?

JOYCE   Uh—between engagements, so to speak. You see, Frank, I've reached that very peculiar position where if I have lunch with a man, everybody jumps to conclusions. Whereas, on the other hand, if an author is staying at my house and working on a play that I'm going to be in—well, they jump to conclusions then, too, but in the latter case there's always a lingering doubt. They wonder if I'd be so open about it. You see what I mean? If I'm seen having *lunch* with a man, I might as well be as naked as that channel swimmer out in my pool. Why didn't she cover herself with grease? An awful lot of lard there to start with.

FRANK Yeah. She's all girl. But about the living arrangements.

JOYCE Naturally you have some things you want to say.

FRANK Well, yes, I have. The trouble is, I don't know what to say.

JOYCE Would you like a little help? You're thinking, what if this gal and I keep it Platonic for a week or so and then dear old propinquity takes over?

FRANK Yes, that's one thought I had.

JOYCE And—this is you thinking—am I smart to get mixed up with her at all when I'm supposed to be rewriting a play. Can I live in this house with her without making a pass, and if I make a pass, how is that going to affect my play? Maybe I'd better go back to the hotel till I finish the play, and *then* make a pitch.

FRANK All very true, very accurate.

JOYCE But there's more. You must have been wondering, just these past few minutes, whether it might not be a good idea to make the big pitch right away.

FRANK Yes, I thought that.

JOYCE Well, so far you've honestly admitted everything. But have you given any thought to the possibility that I'm not interested in going to bed with you? Tell me the truth, Frank.

FRANK No, I frankly thought it would be all up to me.

JOYCE (*Quietly*) Yes, that's my reputation. It isn't fair, you know. I'm not all that promiscuous. I had an affair with Sidney Renwick years ago, and not a soul knew about it. I was already a star and he was a love-sick juvenile, getting kicked around, underpaid, not very talented, and no self-confidence whatsoever. He cried on my shoulder one night in Boston, and I was nice to him. I slept with him every night for a week, and I've never even kissed him since then. I would no more sleep with Sidney again than I would with Stanley Stanton, who incidentally is getting ready to make the big pitch. Sidney was young, pitiful, and quite sweet, and I'll say this for Sidney. He never talked. It would have been very easy for young Mr. Renwick to blab it around that he was having an affair with Joyce Chilton, but he never did. People have made guesses that he's slept with me, but they know in their hearts that they're only guesses, because they've guessed at the wrong times. I had an affair with Robert W. McAtherton.

FRANK   You couldn't have. You don't go back that far.

JOYCE   I did, though. He was my dramatic coach when I was nineteen. He was close to sixty, or maybe he *was* sixty. But I worshipped that man. That voice, that wonderful voice. Do you remember his Othello?

FRANK   I never saw him.

JOYCE   You missed one of the truly great. I paid him fifteen dollars an hour, when I was making sixty dollars a week. Forty-five dollars a week I paid him and it was worth every cent of it, even if I did have to eat on a dollar a day. *He* didn't seduce me. I just adored him so that I was there for the taking, and gladly. He was ashamed. Oh, he was so ashamed. "My child, I need your money more than I do your love," he said. So he wouldn't touch me during our lessons. I'd go to his room at night, but most of the time he was dead drunk, sometimes lying on the floor, and I'd go away without his knowing I'd ever been there. That's how he died, you remember. In a furnished room on Fifty-fourth Street. One of the great artists of all time. And a wonderful, wonderful lover. (*She is silent, and he reaches over and puts his hand gently on hers*) I am thinking of a line. It's Iago's line, but Robert Mc-Atherton loved it. "Reputation is an idle and most false imposition; oft got without merit, and lost without deserving: you have lost no reputation at all, unless you repute yourself such a loser." I think I have it right.

FRANK Did you ever play Shakespeare, Joyce?

JOYCE (*Bitterly, but only faintly so*) Hah! For twenty years, when I come on there's a buzz goes through the audience. The women commenting on my costume. Then quiet while they wait to laugh at my first funny line. No, the spell of Mr. Shakespeare's words would be broken if I ever said them.

FRANK It wasn't just now.

JOYCE That's because you're nice. You listen. You have heart, and that communicates, you know. Nobody'd ever go to see me in Shakespeare, and really why should they? I've been as lucky as any actress ever was. I was an ingénue till I was thirty, and the critics were very nice about that. I was a star, but I was still doing ingénue parts. Then I made the transition from ingénue to soignée leading woman, sophisticated parts. Upper-class adultery. And I was a draw. Aided and abetted, of course, by publicity. Two big front-page love affairs and two, uh, affluent marriages, if that's a proper use of my new favorite word. I'm a star, and I'm rich. Those are the two things I wanted to be, and I am. (*Slightly defiantly*) And we start rehearsals in August. What else could I want?

FRANK I'm sure I don't know, Joyce. But whatever it is, I hope you get it.

JOYCE You do, don't you? And you're making all sorts of guesses as to what it is. You wouldn't guess anything as obvious as love, or children.

FRANK   Such obvious things occurred to me, but I'd hesitate to mention them.

JOYCE   Children are out of the question and have been for a long time. Physically. But that still leaves love.

FRANK   All right then, *is* it love?

JOYCE   Why of course. But what man would trust me to love him? I don't mean what man would count on my being faithful to him. I mean just what I said. Trust me to love him. A man old enough to marry me, he's probably pretty cautious about love. He isn't going to let himself love a woman who won't give him the same kind of love in return. At my age and at his age, we could have a pleasant enough arrangement without marriage or without love. The arrangement could be based on deep affection, or deep affection might develop from the arrangement. But that is still something short of love. I want to be in love again and for the final, last time, and I think I could be. But I haven't seen any signs of it, in myself or in any man. And as I think about it now, no man *should* trust me to love him. As I was telling you about Sidney, and then about Mr. McAtherton, as I was talking to you about Sidney I was in love with him, and when I was talking about Mr. McAtherton, I loved *him*. That's what this damn business I'm in has done to me. Why should any man trust me to love him, when I can quick-change like that?

FRANK   Well, at least you're aware of your—

JOYCE   My what?

FRANK   Well—your tendency to vacillate. You're honest enough with yourself to realize that you can love one man at a time, but that the time isn't going to last very long.

JOYCE   It doesn't last five minutes. For the past week I've been very much in love with Larry, in your play.

FRANK   *You've* been, or *Sandra?*

JOYCE   Why—*I* was—or *was* it Sandra? I don't know. I thought it was me as Sandra, but now that you ask the question, I'm not so sure. I guess it was me, because I'm not quite Sandra, not yet. (*She suddenly turns to him*) Are you Larry?

FRANK   More than you are Sandra. Basically, Larry is me.

JOYCE   You're kind of rough on yourself in the play, aren't you?

FRANK   That's one of the reasons why it's a play and not a novel. In a play I get a better look at myself, and it's high time I did. I was married to two pretty good women, and I've done a lot of very embarrassing thinking about them and about those marriages.

JOYCE   Why are you embarrassed?

FRANK   Well—self-castigation is a form of self-pity, of course. But it seems to me that I did as much as Geraldine did to louse up my first marriage, and then I did the same thing all over again with Lucy, my second wife.

JOYCE   What were the things?

FRANK   One thing, really. I never made the effort, or took the time, to look at things from her point of view.

JOYCE   Oh, well. That's masculine. Or anyway, human.

FRANK   It's both, and I'm convinced it's what louses up marriage. The dominant, male breadwinner, and the dominant female housewife are so God damn busy being what they are that they never have time for anything else.

JOYCE   Yes, but what were they before they were married? I agree with you, but here are the two of us, you and I, liking each other very much—

FRANK   Very much.

JOYCE   Almost to the point of love.

FRANK (*Smiling a little*)   Yes.

JOYCE   Yes. I love you dearly at this moment, Frank, and you love me, don't you?

FRANK   Dearly.

JOYCE   And you wouldn't think of trying to dominate me, or I, you. But if we got married, you were the breadwinner and I was the housewife, it wouldn't be any time at all before your job and your life made you want to dominate, and my kitchen and my life made me want to dominate.

FRANK   Well, yes. So I guess the only solution is to abolish marriage.

JOYCE   You're being funny, but a lot of people have, and a lot more would if they could.

FRANK   Yes, but I'm not yet ready to advocate that in a play. Or at all. It may not be even the semi-perfect state, but it's the only game in town. No, not the only game in town. But it's the best arrangement so far.

JOYCE   Well then you and I'd better not try it.

FRANK   You mean together?

JOYCE   Or separately. No marriage for you, no marriage for me.

FRANK   I have no intention of trying it. By the way, is any of this in your notes?

JOYCE   Oh, heavens no. My notes are—well, why does Sidney have to be onstage so much?

FRANK   You're not going to cut me out of my own play, are you?

JOYCE   Oh, I can see you're going to make trouble for the star. I love you dearly, Frank.

FRANK   I love you dearly, too, Joyce.

JOYCE   Will you stay?

FRANK   Here? Sure. As long as we love each other *dearly*, we're safe.

JOYCE (*Rising*) Anyway, you won't go away before I've had a bath. I suppose that will be the next big thing in airplanes: a bathtub.

FRANK They go so fast nowadays you haven't got time to get dirty.

JOYCE My baths have nothing to do with cleanliness. I have some deep-rooted guilt complex that makes me take three or four baths a day. I used to think it was wanting to be clean, but that was all straightened out for me by my second husband. He used to psycho-analyze me while I was waiting for him to climb in the hay. Oh, such dirty thoughts as he used to put in my simple little brain.

(*She pats* FRANK's *cheek and exits, and* JOE RASMUSSEN *appears in French doorway at Left, then saunters in*)

FRANK (*Slightly annoyed*) I suppose you were listening.

JOE I sent Angie home. I didn't figure this would be a good time for her and the Duchess to swap insults. We got more important things to talk about. Yeah, I was listening. I told you I always listen, and I read mail too. I told you that. (*Languidly sprawls on a chair*) You know what John Drew said? John Drew said more actors were ruined by a good voice than were ever ruined by booze.

FRANK I don't like you to listen in on my private con-versations.

JOE (*Ignoring* FRANK's *remark*) This poor dame. You know I'm getting to like her. I used to think she'd open up her drawers like a cash register. But she really went for Robert W. McAtherton. That isn't why I like her, going for McAtherton. What I like is that she was so naïve about it. She thinks of herself as a nice little stagestruck kid that was kind to an old broken-down actor. She likes that image of herself, and I like her for liking that image of herself. If she knew the truth, McAtherton was a lecherous old bum.

FRANK   How do you know that? You're younger than Joyce. You probably were in high school when she was taking lessons from him.

JOE   (*Angrily*) Anything I say about the theater, it's reliable. Did you ever hear of Annie Laurie Menzies, pronounced Ming-ees? No.

FRANK   No.

JOE   Annie Laurie was McAtherton's third wife, he was married five times. I had her in a play once. I knew all about the legend of Robert W. McAtherton, so I used to pump her about him. That line about, "I need your money more than I need your love," he used that on every little stagestruck broad.

FRANK   Well, if you ever tell that to Joyce I'll give you a punch in the nose.

JOE   I don't want any punch in the nose, but that aint why I'm not gonna tell her. I believe in illusions. Hell, I'm in the illusion business. But now that I know that about Joyce, I would appreciate it if you would consider putting in a scene in the second act. You know where Sandra has the talk with Larry's father. She wants to find out from the old guy what's the matter with Larry.

FRANK   (*Deciding not to sulk*) Yeah.

JOE   If you have no objection, I wish you'd consider writing the scene from the angle of Sandra. Uh, the way it is now, all she does is ask the old guy a lot of questions, and he answers them. But instead of that, she still asks the questions and he still answers them, but in the new version, she also sees things about the old man that are some of the good things and the bad things in Larry. In other words, the old guy is an older edition of Larry. That is, if you have no objections. I don't ask you to make changes without giving you a reason. All right, the reason for this change. First of all, this change wouldn't mean any changes in the *charac-*

ters of Sandra or the father. Second, knowing what I do now about Joyce and McAtherton, I could get one hell of a scene out of her. And it'll only add maybe three minutes to your second act.

FRANK   I like it.

JOE   (*Rather to himself*)   Yeah, I like it. (*Soliloquizing*) Maybe we can work something out. If I went after her myself, you'd probably get sore, because you're getting a little stuck on her. And Angie would be sore as hell at me and when she's sore at me she can be a real bitch. It's hard for me to work when Angie's sore at me. We have to work something out. I wish you were a little older, then it would take care of itself. Or if you were a fairy. I worked with a lot of fairies in my time and they can give you a lot of trouble, but they don't give you trouble over women.

FRANK   (*Sarcastically*)   No, that's what a fairy is, isn't it?

JOE   I got one solution, but I don't know if Joyce would hold still for it. What do you think? Do you think Joyce would let me move in here?

FRANK   I gather that all this is aimed at keeping me from having an affair with Joyce. Well, with your big ears, you heard what she said. She isn't interested.

(JOE *looks at him as at a sweet but stupid child*)

JOE   I think I'll ask her. Yeah, that's what I'll do. How can she refuse? If she refuses, she's admitting that she wants to sleep with you. That's the only reason she *could* refuse. I really got her on a spot. (*He goes to doorway at Right and calls out*) Hey, Joyce!

FRANK   She can't hear you, she's taking a bath.

JOE   When she comes down I'll ask her. She can't say no to that request.

FRANK   What are you planning to do, chaperone us, like a Spanish duenna?

JOE   What else? She comes back here with a suitcase full

of notes that she thought up a week ago. You don't know it yet, but every God damn one of those notes is very carefully thought out. This dame is a real pro, you know. There's nothing silly about her. You know what she did on the Queen Elizabeth? I'll show you. She played every scene. Not only the ones she's in, but those she aint in. Upstairs in her suitcase she has a brand new play. Right now there's stuff in your play that you never thought of. Where you have her Down Left, listening to a speech by Renwick, I bet you she has herself Up Right so that Renwick will have to turn his back to the audience. Here, I'll show you. (*He demonstrates, using* FRANK *for* RENWICK)

FRANK   Everybody knows that much about the theater.

JOE   You didn't when you wrote it. I know that. Because the only two times that Renwick or Larry has long speeches, you have Joyce Down Left. As soon as I saw that I knew there'd be trouble, and she spotted it, you can be damn sure. (FRANK *shrugs, and is silent*) I could collect some money off you if you wanted to make some bets. I'll bet you I can tell you two lines she wants cut out, and I could damn near tell you what she's gonna suggest for substitutes. You got a line, First Act, Second Scene, where Larry tells his father that he has decided to leave Sandra because she's frigid.

FRANK   (*Nodding*) "Frigid and calculating."

JOE   Right. Now I'll tell you about that line. Joyce doesn't realize that when the guy calls her frigid, he's admitting that he's had trouble keeping her aroused. You intended that line to characterize Larry, didn't you?

FRANK   Yes, of course.

JOE   Sure. But Joyce Chilton, this dame upstairs, she's not going to let anybody call *her* frigid. The only thing it means to her is that the audience might think Joyce Chilton is frigid. Not Sandra. Joyce herself. Joyce Chil-

ton is always going to be in there protecting Joyce
Chilton, and the hell with you and your play. For
that reason, the reference to the son at Yale has got
to go. A son at Yale pegs her age, and she won't let
you do that. A woman with a son at Yale has got to
be somewhere around forty-five, and I will bet you
fifty dollars to twenty that she's going to argue with you
that the son ought to be in prep school, not college.
Frank, she knows I'm tough, and she knows I know
my way around in this business. So when we're in
rehearsal, if I have her doing something she doesn't
want to do, standing one way, sitting another way,
giving an actor a piece of business—she's not gonna
argue with *me*. She's gonna get you to change lines that
will let her do what *she* wants to do. In other words,
destroy what I've made her do, get rid of it. What
you've gotta do with this dame is go right up and slap
her in the kisser right at the very beginning. And you
can't do that if you're sleeping with her. At least *you*
can't. (*He laughs*) I could, but you can't. You aren't
built that way.

FRANK What do you mean, slap her in the kisser? Exactly what?

JOE I mean, the first change she suggests, no matter
even if it's a good one, you got to say, "When I want
a suggestion, I'll ask for it." Just between you and me,
if it's any good, we can put it in later. But not when
she asks you to.

FRANK Well, I might as well be frank with you. That's
what I always intended to do. Not only with her, but
with you, too.

JOE Sure. But you don't care if *I* hate you. Every author
I ever had anything to do with, they all say to themselves, "Joe Rasmussen is going to direct my play, but
I'll be a son of a bitch if I'll let him rewrite it." Isn't
that what you said to yourself?

FRANK   Yes, I said it, and I mean it. Frankness will get you nowhere.

JOE   Oh, I get around your objections in my own way. I never *tell* you to change something. I always *ask* you. I can't change a word of your play, myself. I know the rules of the Dramatists Guild. I'm a member of it. But you'll have so much confidence in me by the end of next week that I won't have any trouble with you. You'll figure it out for yourself, so I don't mind telling you. I like your play and I want it to be a hit. I don't want to look beautiful in any two-thousand dollar dress from a French couturier. If you wanta give me a coupla six dollar neckties, okay. But I'm success-prone. That's all I want. I have to make up for years of running out for coffee for what I call nothing-people, guys like Sidney Renwick. You know, Frank, this probably never occurred to you, because you're an author, a conscientious, honest writer. But don't be misled by that old saying "The play's the thing." The play *is* the thing, but not just those words you wrote. Not just your dialog and your plot. I'll give you an illustration. You saw *The Valid Resentment.* You remember the scene with the soldier and Shirley Tanner?

FRANK   Sure.

JOE   Axel wrote a kind of an editorial about war in that scene. It was good, as an editorial, and he was sore at me because I didn't let the soldier stand in the center of the apron, for God's sake, and intone those words like a prayer. But what Axel didn't know was that in one performance in New Haven we did it his way. He wasn't there. I got him called back to New York on some phony pretext. We did the scene his way, with the soldier facing the audience and making his appeal. It was a bomb. It was the only time that scene didn't get a hand. It just laid there like a fried egg. After that we did it my way, and it never failed to get a hand. That's what I contribute. The *whole* play's the thing, Frank, and not just your words. I still have more respect for the words than I do for any actor or any director, or costume designer or the guy that does the sets. But don't you be pig-headed, or you won't get that schooner. (*Languidly he goes to doorway and calls*) Hey, Joyce, I got something I wanta ask you. You wanta take in another boarder?

(*Her voice is heard but the words are inaudible*)

FRANK   What did she say?

JOE   She said she'd be right down. She heard me, but she's giving herself a chance to think. Watch this.

FRANK   I wouldn't miss it.

(JOYCE *enters in lounging pajamas, cool and soignée. She puts the back of her hand to her nose, then holds it to* JOE'S *nose*)

JOYCE   Mm. Doesn't that smell good? Shannon Airport.

FRANK   Shannon Number Five?

JOYCE   No, it's—oh. A tiny little joke. Very cute. I hope you boys, you *gentlemen*, haven't just been sitting here making little jokes instead of working. (*Turns to* JOE) You especially, Joe Rasmussen. I don't blame Frank for wanting to relax a little.

JOE (*To* FRANK)   Here it comes.

JOYCE   But you. I was almost sure I heard you just now ask me if I wanted to take in another boarder. If I'm wrong, forgive me.

JOE (*To* FRANK)   I told you this was no silly dame. You can't fool around with her.

JOYCE (*Over-graciously*)   You can, but not during office hours. We've got to be serious, you know. That's why I gave up my trip to Europe, that I've been looking forward to all year. It'll be August before you know it, and we won't have a thing done. We won't really be ready to go into rehearsal, and that will put us back a month or so and we're just liable to lose that theater. Joe, you know how tough it is to get a theater these days.

JOE (*To* FRANK)   See? This is not a silly dame.

JOYCE   Why do you keep saying that, Joe? You know I'm not a silly dame, at least not about my work. Frank didn't say I was a silly dame, I'm sure.

FRANK   Nope. Never.

JOYCE   Frank knows I'm not. Frank and I have made a lot of progress toward a better mutual understanding, while you were out there drying off your wife. Where is she, by the way?

JOE   I sent her home. I got a new tactic. It used to be the brush-off, but now it's the dry-off. I dried her off and—

JOYCE (*Over him*)   Jokes. You see what I mean?
(*She pushes a wall button to summon a servant, talking while doing so*) I gave up my European trip— Oh, Bruno, will you go up to my room, please, and bring down a little green bag about so big. I think I left it on the chair by the window. A little green bag.

JOE   Takes me back to Harvard, the little green bag.

BRUNO   Madam. (*He goes*)

JOE   You all through with the pep talk, Joyce?

JOYCE   For the moment, yes, I guess so.

JOE   It was very good. It's what stage magicians call misdirection. You know, they make you look at this hand while they're doing something with this one. But magicians all tell me that they have a hard time fooling children. "I know where it went," the kids say. "You still got it in your left hand." Well, I got the mind of a child, too. A very simple fellow.

FRANK *and* JOYCE   Oh, sure. My, yes. Childlike.

JOE   And consequently, I don't fall for misdirection.

JOYCE (*As* BRUNO *hands her the bag and goes*) What ever are you talking about, Joe? Thank you, Bruno.

JOE I'm merely talking about you trying to get us off the subject.

JOYCE What is the subject?

JOE I asked you a question. I ask it again. Do you have anything against me staying here and working with Frank? . . . I'll pay you.

JOYCE Oh, you meant that seriously? I thought you *must* be joking. Why of course I have no objection, and I wouldn't dream of taking a cent from you. But aren't there other objections? Your wife, for one. She might not like your staying here—or have you got it worked out that she was to move in, too? I have no objection to anything, Joe, but I do wish you'd let me in on things. If we're going to start a little artists' colony here, all right, but give me some warning. Who else are we going to have? I draw the line at Shirley Tanner, by the way.

FRANK We—

JOE (*Silencing him*) She hasn't finished.

JOYCE I think I'll have to put up some kind of a high fence around the pool, or the golf club people will start making noises. And I know there's some kind of zoning law about having boarding houses in certain areas. Also, if we have more than a certain number of people living here, the Township will make me put up a fire escape. That's going to be hideous, a fire escape on this nice old salt-box. Maybe they'd let me install one of those ropes in every bedroom instead of an ugly, rusty old fire escape. And where are we all going to eat? Ten people is the most I can seat in my diningroom. I've tried twelve, and it's just too crowded. So—when do you propose to start this project? I'd like to see a list of the people, if you don't mind.

JOE (*Tears off a corner of a magazine page and scribbles on it, handing it to* JOYCE)   Here's your list.

JOYCE (*Reading*)   Me. M, e. This is your list? Just you?

JOE   That's all—but congratulations on a very good ad lib performance. She was good, wasn't she, Frank?

JOYCE   Well if I was good, don't just sit on your hands. This isn't a benefit. (*The two men applaud*) Thank you. You're serious about this? You really want to come here and live?

JOE   Yeah, really live. I would like to come here and work close with this guy.

JOYCE   What would you do, Joe? Go home weekends? Listen, I don't mind having a *ménage à trois*, as long as your wife isn't going to. But I don't see why you don't get her to come here, too. Have you spoken to her about it?

JOE   I don't have to speak to her about it. I know what she'd say.

JOYCE   She could sue me for depriving her of your services. That's the legal term for it, I believe.

JOE   Then you're against me living here?

JOYCE   I didn't say that, but it's my house and I'll get the blame for everything that happens here.

JOE   Not everything. Angela would only blame you if you and I were shacked up. She don't care what happens to Frank.

JOYCE (*Quickly*)   But you do?

JOE   No. Only what happens to his play.

JOYCE   And you think the best way to protect his play is to come here and work with him. That's the only reason you want to stay here?

JOE   What other reason could I have, Joyce? I *certainly* don't want to stay here so I can chaperone you and

Frank, like as if I was a Spanish duenna. How would I look with a big high comb on the back of my head?

JOYCE I'd never notice it. I never get beyond those piercing eyes of yours. All right, what time do you like to have breakfast?

JOE Preferably after a good night's sleep.

JOYCE You can have the room next to Frank's. It's on the other side of the hall from mine. And so, that's settled. I feel a little bit as though I were being led around by the nose. But then I suppose I should start getting used to that.

JOE I always heard you were very good at taking direction.

JOYCE You never heard any such thing, but we're still at the polite stage, are we not? And that's a good time to bring up a few points. By the way, are the three of us going to work together or just you two?

JOE We'll listen to everything you have to say.

JOYCE If that isn't the ying-yang answer of the week. (*She opens her airline bag and takes out a piece of paper. She reads it silently, then looks up*) Frank, this is such a minor point that I'm not going to make an issue of it. I know you wrote this before I met you, and when you didn't have me in mind for the part of Sandra. But (*She holds the paper suspended over the wastebasket, ready to drop it*) in the scene where Larry and his father are talking, you have Larry say that Sandra is frigid. You really don't want an actor to say that Joyce Chilton is frigid. How unrealistic can you get?

JOE Your cue, Frank.

CURTAIN

ACT THREE

SCENE ONE

Late in August, the scene is a bare stage, with a few bent-wood chairs and two or three standing lamps with naked bulbs. Down Left JOE RASMUSSEN *is straddling a chair, with his chin resting on the back of the chair. Behind him, perhaps six feet away, sits* FRANK WILSON. *On the floor beside each man is a playscript, lying open, face down. They are watching* SIDNEY RENWICK *and* JOYCE CHILTON *rehearsing a scene.* SIDNEY *is in tan cotton slacks and matching sport shirt;* JOYCE *is in a similar but feminine outfit, plus a foulard scarf at her throat, and she holds her "sides" in her left hand.*

JOYCE *(Playing Sandra)* "The trouble with you, Larry, is that you've gone through life having your own way."

SIDNEY *(Playing Larry, and without sides; he is up in the part)* "One of the troubles with us, Sandra, is that you really believe that. You think I've had it soft all my life?"

JOYCE "And you have."

SIDNEY "Not really. It just looks that way because I don't dramatize everything that happens to me."

JOYCE "And I suppose I *do*."

277

SIDNEY   "Well, don't you?"

JOYCE   (*Stepping out of the character Sandra*)   Where am I when he says that?

JOE   Right where you are. You stay there till he crosses to answer the telephone.

JOYCE   But I don't feel right just standing here, Joe.

JOE   You're not supposed to feel right. You're supposed to be God damn uncomfortable standing there, building up your irritation till you explode. You want to move *around*, but that's wrong for the mood of the scene. Don't you see that, Joyce? (*He gets up to demonstrate*) You're here, and it's like your feet were nailed to the floor.

JOYCE   I sound like a Strasbourg goose, being fattened up for pâté de foie gras.

JOE   Cut out the jokes, please, Miss Chilton. We're at work. You're standing here, having this argument with your husband. You keep arguing till you can't take it any longer, and then you let go. Bang! But if you're moving around during his speeches, restless, the explosion isn't an explosion at all. It's a continuing action. I don't want that. I want you to save it up for your next line. You know what your next line is?

JOYCE   Of course I do.

JOE   (*Standing away*)   That's good. Cue, please, Sidney.

SIDNEY   (*As Larry*)   "Well, don't you?"

JOYCE   (*As Sandra*)   "Well if I didn't there'd be damn little excitement around this house."

JOE   (*Imitating telephone*)   Linga-linga-ling.
    (SIDNEY *crosses to Stage Right and picks up an imaginary telephone*)

JOE   (*Pointing his finger*)   Now, Joyce!

JOYCE   (*As Sandra*)   "Don't answer it!"

JOE   Okay. Stop here, please.
    (SIDNEY *and* JOYCE *stand apart, paying no attention to*

each other. JOYCE *takes out her compact.* JOE *goes to* FRANK)

JOE (*Looks at his wrist watch*) Shall we knock off now?

FRANK All right.

JOE (*To* JOYCE *and* SIDNEY) It's a quarter to twelve. Can you have your lunch and be back here at one o'clock?

SIDNEY I can.

JOYCE I *can,* but I want you to know, I have to break a lunch date. My appointment was for one o'clock, when most people have lunch.

JOE I asked you not to make any lunch dates.

JOYCE I'll be here, but I just want you to know.

JOE I'll put a gold star in your book. One o'clock, *on stage,* please. That gives you an hour and a quarter, and you beat the crowd at Sardi's.

JOYCE (*Haughtily*) I never have any trouble getting a table at Sardi's. Or anywhere else. Come on Sidney, I'll treat you.
(*They leave the stage*)

OFFSTAGE VOICE OF A STAGEHAND You want us to knock off too, Mr. Rasmussen?

JOE Go ahead, but leave the lights on, please. You hungry, Frank?

FRANK Not very, and it's cooler in here than it is outside.

JOE Yeah, and it aint only the ventilation.

FRANK I know.

JOE Trouble, you got to expect.

FRANK (*Handing him a Thermos*) Here.

JOE What's in that?

FRANK Iced tea.

JOE (*Pouring a drink into the cuplike cap*) Thanks. Tastes good. Hemlock would taste better. I don't know what the hell to do with this dame. She's fighting me all the way, but she's very careful to avoid one big fight.

FRANK   I noticed that.

JOE   Like she won't refuse to be here at one o'clock, but she'll let you know she's doing you a favor. The hell of it is, this all started as soon as we went into rehearsal. At her house she was pleasant and friendly. I should of known it couldn't last.

FRANK   She's a different person, there's no doubt about that.

JOE   I had her all wrong. I figured she'd make all the trouble while we were at her house, and get it out of her system. She had plenty of reason to get sore then.

FRANK   You mean rejecting all her ideas?

JOE   Yeah. And the way we did it. The time I said to her, "Stick to your dancing, Mabel."

FRANK   I didn't hear you say that.

JOE   Yeah. Remember when she wanted you to take out "frigid," and she was holding that piece of paper over the wastebasket.

FRANK   Sure. And you took *all* her notes and dropped them in the basket.

JOE   That's when I said "Stick to your dancing, Mabel."

FRANK   I guess I didn't hear what you said because I was waiting to see what she'd do.

JOE   So was I. And what did she do? Nothing.

FRANK   You're wrong, Joe. She did something. She rescued her notes from the wastebasket.

JOE   But she never mentioned them again. That's where I was stupid. I'm not used to being around dames like Joyce, not in the home, not socially. My women are all the same. I like them saftig, noisy, belligerent, and playful. And heavy sleepers.

FRANK   Of the earth, earthy.

JOE   Yeah, but that was about a man. Aint that from the Bible? I want a broad that's a woman, female, not feminine. Like Angie, and Shirley Tanner, and sixty-five others all like them. Angie never holds a grudge. But this Chilton dame, she had us in her house for three weeks, for God's sake. The perfect hostess, and all the while she was waiting till we got on this stage, to teach us a lesson in high-powered bitchery. Well, are you learning?

FRANK   Yes, I'm learning. And I'm finding out that I never want to be a director.

JOE   *I* never want to be a *writer*. I couldn't stand it, to watch a dame screwing up my lines by giving them the wrong reading.

FRANK   She may get over it. Don't give up.

JOE   Give up? I'd cut my throat before I gave up. I got two reasons I won't give up. The first reason, I got an idea, Frank, that this whole thing is my fault. I knew too much. I was a wise guy. I advised you to stay out of the hay with this dame till after we opened in New York.

FRANK   You did.

JOE   I didn't want the changes in your play dictated from a pillow in the Boston Ritz, remember?

FRANK (*Nodding*)   Very well.

JOE   But if I had to do over again, Frank, I'd tell you to jump in the kip with her, the first night she came home from Europe. You should of given her a nice reception while she was all excited. And that's what she was excited about, Frank. A dame like Joyce don't get excited about any play. Not that excited, enough to give up her trip to Europe. Going over she suddenly realized she wanted to sleep with you, so that's what she came home to do. And I loused it up. And she knew I loused it up, and that's why she's giving me a bad time now.

FRANK   Joe, that's all very complimentary, but you could be just as wrong about her now as you were before.

JOE   I don't think so. I think this is pretty good second-guessing.

FRANK   No, Joe. I think she meant it when she said she loves me dearly, and that means Platonic.

JOE   There's no such thing as Platonic. Not if you got all your equipment.

FRANK   I didn't say it was Platonic with me. I never said *that*.

JOE   Platonic is the house detective. Platonic is no place to go. Platonic is an ugly dame that don't appeal to you —but six months on the polar ice cap and that ugly dame begins to look pretty good. That's what I think of Platonic.

FRANK   I'm inclined to agree with you. But Platonic is also the wrong time and the wrong place. Her house last month was the wrong time and the wrong place.

JOE   I'd like to think so, to get myself off the hook.

FRANK   You said you had another reason for not wanting to give up on Joyce.

JOE   (*Slowly*)   A good reason. The best reason, as far as I'm concerned. You know who Joyce's public is? They're the people that really get a bang out of Lynn Fontanne looking the way she does at her age. They're the people that wish Ina Claire would come back to the theater. They're the people that cry when they hear certain Cole Porter tunes. They're the people that write in for tickets as soon as they see the first ad for a play by Ratigan or Coward. I'm not talking about the opening-night people, and I'm not only talking about women. I'm talking about men *and* women, that saw Helen Hayes in *Coquette*, and Gertie Lawrence in *Oh, Kay!* Vivienne Segal in *Pal Joey*. Not art people. Oh, a little arty, maybe. They like to say Shavian when Shaw's name comes up, and maybe they *heard about* Stanislavski. But I'm talking about men and women I see at the summer theaters and I never see them in the Broadway houses. They started going to the theater when their parents took them to the Hippodrome, and they saw Joley and Ed Wynn, and Clark and McCullough. They were Theater Guild subscribers, and they always read Robert Benchley.

FRANK   You amaze me.

JOE   I know I do. And I know why. My reputation is for directing nose-pickers and ass-scratchers, in plays about prison camps and dope peddlers. They were good plays, too, some of them, although let's face it. *Tobacco Road,* which opened in 1933, paved the way, you might say. Then we had Odets and the Odets imitators. When I was at Harvard I wrote a play that was such a steal from *Awake and Sing!* that I got embarrassed and called it a parody. But it wasn't Odets, it was pure Rasmussen, which is crap. Crap, crap, crap. Dreadful. Then I worked in radio and was assistant stage manager and finally got to be a director. And a success. I'm a success. But the theater isn't all nose-pickers and ass-scratchers, any more than it's all Shakespeare. I was one of those that helped to tie a can to Philip Barry and S. N. Behrman. We drove them out of the theater, with their society comedies and Valentina dresses. But now I want them back, Frank. I want you to become a modern version of Philip Barry, and I want to bring back those people that go to see Joyce Chilton. Do you know what the word theater means? In Greek? It comes from the word—I can spell it but I can't pronounce it. Theta epsilon alpha omicron theta alpha iota. It means to see, to view. That's all it means. When I looked that up it frightened me. You know why? Because those bastards I used to work for don't know it, but they have a legitimate right to call that box a theater! Will you ever call your TV set a theater?

FRANK No.

JOE Well, we better be careful or it's the only theater we'll have left. So I'm not going to give up on Joyce Chilton, and I'm not going to give up on you. Let's go eat, so we'll have the strength to cope with that bitch.

CURTAIN

SCENE TWO

The same bare stage, a week or so later. JOYCE *and* SIDNEY *are in summery clothes but now they are wearing a dress and a suit; the coat of* SIDNEY's *suit is hanging on one of the chairs, along with his necktie.* JOE *and* FRANK *are sitting in approximately the same places as before, but now their playscripts are resting on top of identical attaché cases.* JOE *and* FRANK *are wearing the pants of suits, and the jackets are hanging on the backs of their chairs.* SIDNEY *and* JOYCE *are in the midst of a scene from the play.*

JOYCE (*As Sandra*) "It may be just as bad as before, Larry."

SIDNEY (*As Larry*) "I know that, Sandra."

JOYCE "I don't think I've changed."

SIDNEY "I didn't want you to change. I only wanted you to change back to what you were in the beginning." (JOE *looks up at* JOYCE)

JOYCE (*To* JOE) You're not going to make me read the last line?

JOE   Why not?

JOYCE   You know damn well why not. You've been around the theater long enough to know.

JOE (*To* FRANK)   It's supposed to be bad luck to say the last line in rehearsal.
(FRANK *nods; he knows that*)

JOE (*To* JOYCE)   That's a superstition I can't afford.

JOYCE   I've never said the last line in rehearsal, all the years I've been in the theater. And I'm not going to start now. God knows, we need all the luck we can get.

JOE   We could fix that. With Frank's permission, we could give Sidney the last line.

JOYCE   Sidney wouldn't read the line either. Would you, Sidney?
(SIDNEY *would give anything to have the last line, does not want to go against* JOE, *but is even more fearful of going against* JOYCE)

SIDNEY   Joe, if she feels so strongly. . . ?

JOE   All right, Sidney.

JOYCE   I may say, in all my years in the theater, all the bitchery and skulduggery, to try to bribe an artist by giving him a line that belongs to another fellow-artist. That's a new low. Sidney, no matter what happens, I want to say in front of these two *gentlemen,* and for anybody else that's listening, that took guts.
(SIDNEY *shrugs, not wishing to take bows for something he may regret, and not eager to give further offense to* JOE *and* FRANK)

JOE   Well, Sidney, she seems to be implying that she didn't think you had any. But you two can discuss that between yourselves. (*To* JOYCE *and* SIDNEY *and including* FRANK) I always give reasons for things. Miss Chilton, I wanted you to say that last line because this isn't pantomime. I wanted you to say the line so that you could feel it and act it, and I want to see how you feel it and act it. I wanted to hear your voice when you speak the words.

JOYCE You'll hear my voice next Thursday night in Boston.

JOE Will I? If I'm in the last row of the balcony will I hear your voice?

JOYCE I can be heard in the Winter Garden, and without a microphone. Nobody has any trouble hearing me. *I'm* an *actress*.

JOE Well, that's what we hired.

JOYCE Now you just watch your step, Mr. Joe Rasmussen. I've taken an awful lot from you. I could go to Equity right now with some of the things you've said to me these last couple of weeks.

JOE But you won't, will you, Miss Chilton? How many times you been late for rehearsal? How long'd it take you to get up in the part? And calling me a bastard in front of actors and stagehands and electricians. (*He pulls out a notebook*) I not only got the dates here, I got the actual times you called me insulting names. So you don't want to go to Equity. Let's just keep all that in the family. But let's not make any more threats about going to Equity. All right. We don't read the last line, and congratulations on your guts, Sidney. So ends our last rehearsal in New York City. (*Looks at notebook*) The entire company meets tomorrow afternoon at two'clock at the theater in Boston. We're not going to be able to rehearse in the theater tomorrow, because they'll be hanging scenery, but the next day we're going to have a run-through starting three o'clock in the afternoon, with scenery and costumes. (*From out front, stepping over the orchestra pit, now appears* STANLEY STANTON) Oh, what the hell.

(STANTON *is buoyant, full of good will, with the Madison Avenue hearty smile*)

STANLEY Joe, I know you'll forgive this little intrusion. You've got to admit I've been pretty punctilious about respecting your wishes. This is the first time I've set foot in the theater since you started rehearsals, but I infer from what I just heard that I—

JOE How longa you been here, Mr. Stanton?

STANLEY I just got here. Why?

JOE I just wondered.

STANLEY We're having a run-through the day *after* tomorrow? What about tomorrow?

JOE (*Relieved at this indication that* STANTON *has not been in the theater long enough to have listened to the spat with* JOYCE) Tomorrow we meet at two o'clock, at the theater. But they'll be hanging scenery, so we won't be able to rehearse. It's just a meeting of the company.

STANLEY I see. Well, I was hoping the entire company would still be here when I got here this afternoon, but I'll save my little speech for tomorrow then. However, it won't do any harm to—

(JOE *puts a cigarette in his mouth and* STANLEY *lights it.* JOE· *thanks him*)

STANLEY My pleasure. As I say, it won't do any harm to say these things to the, uh, well the *hard core* of this production. Our gracious star, Joyce Chilton. Our excellent leading man, Sidney. Our famous author, Frank Wilson, and last but not least the man responsible for whipping the whole production into shape.

JOYCE Did you say whipping, Stanley?

STANLEY (*Forced laughter*) Well, yes, but perhaps that was an unfortunate turn of phrase. If so, Joe, I apologize, although I've always heard that you're a stern taskmaster. Heh heh heh. I'll only keep you a moment longer. I just wanted to say that in my opinion we've got a smashing good company and a smashing good script, as the English say. And while keeping all our fingers crossed, I'd almost be willing to bet that we have a smashing big hit. I was hoping we'd be able to open in Detroit because I was born in Lansing, Michigan, and I'd have packed the house with relatives, also friends, but our director persuaded me otherwise, and you have to admit, Joe, I've gone along with all your suggestions whenever I could. Joyce is going to be the best-dressed actress on Broadway. Not that she hasn't always been, but this time I have reason to know that she's the most expensively dressed one too. Heh heh. I'm taking a full-page ad in next Sunday's *Times* and *Tribune*, two full-page ads, and I understand both papers are sending reporters up to Boston for interviews with our author and our director. As you know, *Life* magazine had photographers all over the place last week, taking pictures, but from past experience I don't count too much on them. They certainly throw their money around.

FRANK   Not to mention their weight.

STANLEY   Yes, that's true, Frank, but publicity is publicity, and a good spread in *Life* is worth the inconvenience. What else did I have in mind? Oh, yes. I'm letting *Harper's Bazaar* have an exclusive on Joyce's costumes for the November issue. And Frank, the Garroway show would like to do some tape interviews with you and Joe. By the way, I'm budgeting I-won't-say-how-much for spot announcements on radio when we open in New York, and I'm working out a tentative deal for some local commercials on TV. And speaking of TV, Joyce, I told the people on the Jack Paar show that you'd agreed to appear the night we open in New York. I hope all your accommodations please you in Boston. Those here now will be at the Ritz, of course. I got a separate room for Mrs. Rasmussen, Joe, as you requested. Joyce, there'll be a limousine to meet you at the Back Bay station tonight and it'll be at your disposal while we're in Boston.

JOYCE   Oh, thank you, Stanley. You didn't have to do that.

STANLEY   My pleasure. Oh, and Joe, I had a very nice letter from that Professor at Harvard, thanking me for the opening night seats. He said to tell you he'd like to see you if you have time.

JOE   For him I'll *make* time.

STANLEY   Well, I have to catch a plane, and I guess the rest of you have things to do before you take the train. So—good luck to all of us, and see you in Beantown tomorrow. (*He leaves through the wings, to a chorus of thank-yous and goodbyes*)

JOE   Ben Bernie used to have a gag, he'd say I want to introduce Colonel Mannie Prager, our arranger. He arranges the chairs. I hope you took notice, Frank. He mentioned everything but your play, so that oughta keep you from getting a swelled head. Sidney, what's the matter?

SIDNEY   I don't know. All of a sudden I want to be sick. It always happens just before I open in a show. As soon as I get the feeling that we're really going to face an audience. I'll be all right.

JOE   You'll be wonderful. (*To* JOYCE) And so will you, God damn it.

JOYCE   (*Unreconciled*)   Thank you. If there's nothing else . . . ?

JOE   (*To* FRANK)   You got anything to say to the star?

FRANK   (*Rising*)   See you tomorrow in Boston. You too, Sidney.

SIDNEY   Don't *worry* about me.

JOE   You had your appendix out?

SIDNEY   When I was fifteen.

JOE   Good. So long.
   (SIDNEY *and* JOYCE *depart*)

JOE   "They make a handsome couple." That's a line from your play.

FRANK   And not a very good line. I've been thinking about taking it out.

JOE   Leave it in. It's a morale-builder. Joyce and Sidney are standing in the wings when the maid reads that line, and they love to hear it. They always listen for it. Opening night it may even get a hand from loyal Joyce Chilton fans. How do you feel, Frank?

FRANK   I feel all right, I guess.

JOE   You'll never feel this way again.

FRANK   How do you mean, Joe? I don't really feel *any-thing*.

JOE   That's what I mean. All what you've been going through the last four or five months—getting somebody to produce your play, casting the play, signing the director, little announcements in the papers, you and me working together, starting rehearsals, our troubles with Joyce, and that irritating bastard Stanton—all that is nothing. You remember those thirteen weeks basic in the Army? That's all that this amounts to up to now. You're through with your basic, and it turns out to be nothing, doesn't it? You don't really feel anything.

FRANK   That's right.

JOE   Well, I'll tell you what's gonna happen. Twenty-four hours from now, this time tomorrow, you'll be in another city, and New York will seem like some place a thousand miles away that you left a year ago. You'll go to this meeting tomorrow afternoon, in a theater where you've probably never been before. A lot of men will be working, hanging scenery. They won't know you, and you won't know them. But some time during the afternoon you'll think to yourself,

"Here's seven or eight men come from New York to Boston, what for? To hang scenery for my play. My play. Guys I don't know and never expect to know, but they're getting damn good pay and they come all the way to Boston to hang scenery for my play." Then you'll look around at the people in the company. A bunch of well known actors and actresses, *they're* here in Boston because I wrote a play. A big star like Joyce Chilton is in Boston because I wrote a play. Then maybe you go out in the lobby of the theater and there's two or three people near the ticket window, and you hear somebody say, "Can I have two nice seats in the balcony for Saturday matinee?" And you think to yourself, "My God, they know about my play already. There's a woman from Dorchester, wants to go to the Saturday matinee." You go to your room at the hotel, you look in the Boston papers and you see the ads. Your play. All this time in New York you never realized that Boston knew about your play. You go down to the dining room for dinner. The headwaiter won't know *you*, but over near the window Joyce and probably Sidney and Stanton will be having dinner, and people will be staring at them. "That's Joyce Chilton. That's Sidney Renwick." Slowly it dawns on you. All of Boston knows about your play. Never mind if a lot of them are still on vacation. It's a big town. Anybody on Beacon Hill wants to go to the theater, they're going to see your play. If the president of Harvard wants to go to the theater, it's your play. And tomorrow night when you go to bed you won't be able to sleep. You'll lie there thinking back on how it all started with an idea you had five years ago. You'll go through embarrassment, humility, pride, apprehension. And finally you'll get to sleep. But after tomorrow, whenever you see the word theater in print, you're going to react. No matter what happens with this play, for the rest of your life you're stuck. You're hooked. Today, now, while I'm talking to you, you're not hooked yet. But after tomorrow in Boston you'll never be the same. You're like a virgin, like a sophomore in his first varsity game. Well, virgin, enjoy your last moments of innocence. And I want to say this, Frank, I want to welcome you to the fold. You've seen what it's like, and a lot of it is disgusting to a guy like yourself, with ideals and ethics. And you'll see more and worse. But I hope you don't get so disgusted that you'll give up. You won't. When you go out in the lobby and hear that woman from Dorchester. "Can you let me have two nice seats for the Saturday matinee?" Brahms, my friend. Beethoven's *Ninth*. Tschaikovsky's *Romeo and Juliet*. (*He hums and pantomimes playing the fiddle through the Tschaikovsky*) The sweetest music there is. "Two nice seats for the Saturday matinee."

FRANK   I have a present for you, Joe. I was going to save it for Boston, but I think I'll give it to you now. (*He opens his attaché case and takes out a small parcel and hands it to* JOE, *who shows pleasure while opening it*)

JOE   A present. If there's anything I like to get it's a present. This is for me? Me with a gold cigarette case? You're out of your mind. You crazy son of a bitch, you're out of your mind.

FRANK   Read what it says.

JOE   "To Joe Rasmussen, who took me for a dip in the Champagne Pool." You remembered that? The champagne pool. You know, Frank, I never had one of these, and I never wanted one till now. But I'll never part with this. Thanks.

FRANK   You're welcome, Joe.
       (JOE *looks down at the case, looks up at* FRANK, *then suddenly turns away and walks briskly offstage, for once inarticulate.* FRANK *watches him until he is out of sight, then stands alone in the center of the stage, facing up,*

and slowly turns his head from left to right, gazing at the bare walls, taking in the flies, etc.)

CURTAIN

SCENE THREE

FRANK'S *sitting room in the Boston hotel. Late on opening night. At rise the door at Right is opened and* FRANK *allows* ANGELA *to pass in ahead of him. She is quietly well-dressed in a blue linen dress, looking more like the former East Orange Junior Leaguer than previously. She takes out a cigarette, which* FRANK *lights for her.*

ANGELA   Thank you.

FRANK   My pleasure. Good God! Did you hear that? That's what association with Stanton will do.

ANGELA   I hope we're not going to have him here.

FRANK   No. Joe's the only one I'm expecting here.

ANGELA   What time did you say the papers come out?

FRANK   We'll get the first review in about a half an hour, I think. How about a drink?

ANGELA   I don't think so, thanks. All right. If it'll give you something to do. A light Scotch and soda, or plain water, whatever you have.
(FRANK *prepares her drink*)

FRANK   Have you been through a lot of these?

ANGELA   I guess about five. Maybe six. I think five out of town, and one play Joe opened cold in New York.

FRANK   Then you've really been through ten or twelve of them, counting New York.

ANGELA   Or even more. Philadelphia, New Haven, Washington. You know, some plays Joe's had, tried out in three or four towns before New York. Wilmington. Princeton.

FRANK   So then it's an old story to you.

ANGELA   No. It's never an old story. You do the same things and say the same things, every time, but it's a new story every time.

FRANK   Yes, I guess it would be if you have a rooting interest in the show. Have you ever written any plays?

ANGELA   About thirty-five. Plays come easy to me, because there's never the slightest possibility that any one of them will ever get produced, so I can write a play in the time it takes me to write a poem. The kind of playwriting *I* do is really very enjoyable. When *you* write a play, you have to think of the sets, and the limitations of the theater. But you see, I don't let those things bother me. For instance, I wrote a play in which the stage would have to be two miles deep.

FRANK   Two miles? From the apron to the wall?

ANGELA   No wall. In my play, this particular play, in the fifth act—

FRANK   The *fifth* act?

ANGELA   It's an eight-act play and each act is two hours long, except the fifth act. That's a little longer. That takes longer because as the act begins, you see, or you're supposed to see, General Sheridan in the distance. His horse drops dead and he has to walk the last two miles. Naturally it's in verse.

FRANK   Well, naturally.

ANGELA   It's a sort of serious parody of Thomas Buchanan Read's poem. I wrote another play that shows the orchestra in Radio City Music Hall, you know how it comes up on an elevator?

FRANK   Yes.

ANGELA   Well in this play, the elevator doesn't stop. It keeps going up, up, up, until it's out of sight. A kind of a switch on the Sheridan play. Naturally that's with music. The orchestra keeps playing *Poet and Peasant* until you can't hear it any more.

FRANK   Your plays would present production problems.

ANGELA   So much so, that I have no such problems. Once I wrote a play in three acts. A conventional play about incest. But then I copied it all down in reverse. You know, for instance a line of dialog that went, "How are you today, my dear?" became, "Dear my today you, are how?" You'd be astonished at the rhythms I got. I think I could very easily learn to talk backwards. We all ought to try it. It would make us think before we speak.

FRANK   It would, wouldn't it?

ANGELA   Yes, it would slow down communication, which is becoming much too rapid. One of the great troubles with the world today is that people communicate too God damn fast. (*She smiles*) Now, of course, you wish the Boston papers would communicate a little faster.

FRANK   Yes, I do.

ANGELA   I don't think you have anything to worry about.

FRANK   You don't? Why?

ANGELA   I have ways of telling when a play's going to be a hit.

FRANK   Well, I wish you'd tell me.

ANGELA   They wouldn't make sense to you. They don't to Joe.

FRANK   I'd still like to know what they are.

ANGELA   Well—if somebody starts coughing and the audience glare at him, that play is going to fold.

FRANK   I would have thought the opposite.

ANGELA   That's Joe's reaction. But you're both wrong. If they glare at the cougher they're only looking for an excuse to be distracted. If they really cared about the play they'd strain their ears to listen to the actors and the hell with the cougher.

FRANK   Well, it makes sense when you explain it.

ANGELA   (*Continuing*)   I'm not as a rule favorably impressed when there are cries of "author, author."

FRANK   Why not?

ANGELA   You and I left the theater too soon, so we don't know whether there were any tonight. But when the audience calls for the author, they're *thinking*. A play shouldn't start them thinking so soon. They should be applauding the actors, not the author. They should still be identifying with the actors, the characters in the play, not the intellect that created them. On an opening night the author has about the same standing as the groom at a big society wedding. Who needs him? I think you have a hit because frankly, when I read your play, it sort of lay there, flat. But with the actors playing it, tonight, especially Miss Joyce Chilton, I liked it. And isn't that the purpose of a play? The hell with how flat it seems when you read it. It's when those actors take over. You may not think much of that theory, but wait till you've been around a while.

(*There is a knock on the door*)

FRANK   The morning papers!

ANGELA   No, that's Joe.

(FRANK *opens the door, and it is* JOE. *He has a sloppily folded newspaper in his hand, which he tosses into a chair.* ANGELA *and* FRANK *both go to retrieve it*)

JOE   Nothing in there about us. Yogi hit two home runs. One with one on, one with two.

ANGELA   Who wants to hear about baseball at a time like this?

JOE   What are you drinkin'?

ANGELA   A light Scotch and soda.

FRANK Don't pick on her, Joe. She's been a godsend to me, getting my mind off the play. Don't think I don't appreciate it, Angela.

ANGELA You knew that's what I was doing?

FRANK Of course I knew. At least I caught on when you told me about Sheridan.

JOE Richard Brinsley Sheridan?

FRANK Phil.

JOE There was another Richard Brinsley Sheridan. You ever know that? He was a West Point football player and got killed in the Yale game. Who is Phil Sheridan? I don't place him. (*Not waiting for an answer*) How about that Joyce? Did she give a performance, or didn't she?

FRANK Angela was just saying.

JOE (*To* ANGELA) How did the cough test work? I didn't notice any coughers tonight. My wife has this test.

FRANK I know. She told me.

JOE You mean you two were just talking? Not even a little necking? I wouldn't be sore, Frank. If I was alone on opening night with a dame like Angie, the only thing'd distract me would be a little necking. You know, around the edges, so to speak. Opening nights don't count. Opening nights, and a death in the family.

ANGELA He really wouldn't, Frank. He wouldn't have minded. Neither would I.

FRANK (*Half seriously*) Now you're telling me. No, you did enough for me, Angela.

JOE Frank, you didn't answer my question.

FRANK Which question was that, Joe?

JOE How about Joyce? Did she come through, or didn't she?

FRANK She certainly did.

JOE If you're gonna hand out any more gold cigarette

cases, you better order one for her. Just on the strength of tonight's performance. God *damn* it she was a trouper. As late as yesterday she was still going up in her lines in two scenes. But not tonight. Word perfect, and I caught the second act from a last-row seat in the balcony. Heard every word, beautifully modulated.

FRANK   She was wonderful.

JOE   Did you stay for the final curtain?

FRANK   I couldn't, Joe.

ANGELA   I tried to make him stay, but he was getting pale.

JOE   Then you didn't see the curtain calls. You know what that dame did? You know how we rehearsed the curtain calls? The whole cast, then Joyce and Sidney, then Joyce alone? She wouldn't take a call alone. She grabbed hold of Sidney's hand and wouldn't go on if he didn't go on with her.

FRANK   No kidding?

ANGELA   Joyce Chilton?

JOE   Joyce Chilton. (*All three are silent, thinking about this phenomenon. They raise their eyebrows, then shrug it off*) She's coming here.

FRANK   Here?

JOE   She told me she wanted to thank you, and where would you be? You don't mind, do you?

FRANK   Hell, no. I chickened out, and I want to apologize for not going backstage.
(*A knock on the door*)

JOE   That'll be Joyce. Now let's give her a good hand, let's go all out.
(*He opens the door, and* JOYCE *is there, radiant but subdued, and standing behind her is* SIDNEY, *slightly in a fog but grinning. Led by* JOE, FRANK *and* ANGELA *applaud and cry* "Brava! Bravissima!" *and* JOYCE *makes*

a slow entrance. She goes to FRANK *and kisses him on the cheek, then to* JOE *and rubs her cheek against his.* SIDNEY *hangs back, still foggy, still grinning*)

JOYCE   One of the great nights of my life, Frank. Joe. Thank you both. And thank this man, too.
(*She points to* SIDNEY)

JOE   (*Politely but somewhat perfunctorily*)   Sidney, you were great.

FRANK   (*As restrained as Joe*)   Yes, you really were, Sidney.

SIDNEY   Hell, the part was actor-proof.
(*His remark is lost in the next speech*)

JOYCE   Stanley said he'd wait and bring the papers.

JOE   At last, a use for Stanley. I knew we needed him for something.
(*There is an insistent banging on the door, and* JOE *opens it to admit* STANLEY, *carrying some newspapers*)

STANLEY   Here they are. I grabbed these off the truck, literally.

JOE   How are they?

STANLEY   Don't know. Haven't had a chance to read them.
(*He starts distributing them: one to* JOYCE, *one to* JOE, *one to* FRANK, *and keeps one for himself. There are no more, which leaves* SIDNEY *and* ANGELA *paperless. The others flip through the papers to the review, and start reading it silently to themselves. Almost simultaneously all four look up and across the room at* SIDNEY, *then back to their papers, then up at* SIDNEY *again, who is gazing at them with a half-hopeful, half-apprehensive fixed grin on his face. The first to speak is* JOE)

JOE   Ho-ly Ka-*zan!* Joyce. You wanta read it?

JOYCE   If I can without crying. Crying for joy, that is. By Malcolm Parker. He's the one that was supposed to get Atkinson's job on the *Times*. Very tough. I heard the *Times* decided he was too tough.

JOE   Joyce, will you read the God damn notice?

JOYCE   By Malcolm Parker. "The news this morning is all good, for not only has the enterprising Stanley Stanton persuaded Frank Wilson, best-selling novelist, to write, and the captivating Miss Joyce Chilton to act in, the interesting new play at the Plymouth theater, but he has also lured the hard-hitting Joe Rasmussen to abandon the monotony of his recent work." (*She pauses, and she, and the others who have been reading with her, look up and slowly look across at* SIDNEY, *who is grinning and hanging on every word. She continues*) "But as if those blessings were not enough, Boston theatergoers were treated last night to one of the finest, most sensitive, knowledgeable performances it ever has been this reviewer's privilege to witness. Not since the late lamented Walter Huston has an actor taken over a play with such quiet authority as was demonstrated by Mr. Sidney Renwick in the new offering by Mr. Wilson. Mr. Renwick, who has been best known for a series of adequate performances in drawing-room comedies, proves unmistakably this reviewer's oft-re-peated contention that Broadway type-casting is one of the greatest obstacles to progress in the theater today. Under Mr. Rasmussen's surprisingly deft direction, Mr. Renwick's interpretation of Larry Worthington, a confused and questioning modern husband, could not be improved upon. In plain language, Mr. Renwick is exactly right, and he has carved out a new career for himself after years of wasting his talents on frothy, light comedy. Miss Joyce Chilton—" (JOYCE *halts her reading*) I can't go on. Somebody else take over. (*She looks at* SIDNEY, *who has covered his face with his hands*)

JOE   (*To no one in particular*)   You want me to take over? All right. Happy to. "Miss Joyce Chilton, ever a favorite in Boston as elsewhere, plays Sandra, the wife of Larry Worthington, with the sure incisiveness that we have come to expect of this actress. Radiant in costumes that brought forth murmurs of admiration from the audience, Miss Chilton adds another faultless performance to her list of successes. She plays without the brittleness that in this reviewer's opinion has marred some of her other characterizations. A new warmth has been infused, without which the character Sandra Worthington would have been wholly unsympathetic. Miss Chilton's graciousness extended even to the curtain calls following last night's opening, when, obviously at her insistence, Mr. Renwick was literally pulled on stage. Miss Chilton stood to one side and led the applause for her fellow artist. Although a newcomer to the theater, Mr. Wilson writes with—"

FRANK   Joe, if you don't mind.

JOE   I want to read it.

FRANK   No, please don't. This is their night.
(*All are looking at* SIDNEY. JOYCE *is sitting on his lap, holding his head to her bosom*)

SIDNEY   I don't know what to *say*.

JOE (*Humorously*)   Frank, quick. Think of something for him to say. That's why we came to Boston.

FRANK   I'm trying to think of something for myself to say. Thanks to all of you doesn't seem enough.

SIDNEY   If half of what Malcolm Parker says is true, who directed me? Who wrote the play? And *this* girl—this isn't the first time I cried on her shoulder, and right here in this town. You remember, Joyce?

JOYCE   I couldn't forget that, Sidney.

ANGELA   I've got a sensible suggestion. Joyce, why don't you and Sidney get the hell out of here where you belong?

JOYCE (*Rising*)   Come on, Sidney. She's right.

(*He puts his arm around her shoulder and they leave
quietly, no one speaks*)

STANLEY (*Slapping the review with the tips of his fingers
and shaking his head*)   I'll be a son of a bitch.

JOE   Louse up your plans, Stanton?

STANLEY   Well, yes. It does.

JOE   Why don't you take the limousine away from her?
She won't need it here.

STANLEY   Oh, hell, that would be cheap. (*He looks at the
newspaper, squinting a little*) Roberta Sloane. The girl
that plays the maid. Do you happen to know where she's
staying, Joe?

JOE   She's at the Brunswick. Good luck.

STANLEY (*Rising*)   Well, people, I guess all I can say is
thanks, too.

JOE   Nothing really, Stanton. Nothing but a small for-
tune.

STANLEY   Yeah. Well, goodnight, all.

JOE (*Looking at* FRANK *and at* ANGELA)   We got an odd
number here, and that's no way to celebrate. You like
that Roberta Sloane, don't you, Frank?

FRANK (*Annoyed*)   Yes. She's pretty cute. Why did you
have to tell Stanton—

JOE   All I did was send him to the Brunswick.

FRANK   That's what I mean.

JOE (*Confidentially*)   She is staying—at the Hilton.
Gimme the phone.

CURTAIN

VERONIQUE

ACT ONE

SCENE ONE

The scene is a basement apartment in Greenwich Village in the late Twenties. The time of day is late afternoon. There is an air of disorder about the apartment. An unmade studio couch is at Left against the wall. There are a few chairs helter-skelter. Two windows, barred, are cut out of the wall up Right and Left, and between the windows, a kitchen sink and gas stove, not part of a unit. Above the sink and stove, two shelves on which rest utensils and cups, saucers, and dishes, which are not part of a set. There is an open coffee can. On the window sill at Left, a half-empty milk bottle, and beside it a half-consumed loaf of bread. The entrance to the apartment is through a door cut out of the wall up Right. Along that wall, a davenport with a couple of pillows. Down Right, another door is cut out of the wall, opening on to a bathroom. Hanging or stuck on the walls are several steamship line posters and some unframed reproductions of Modigliani, Picasso, Kuniyoshi, Grant Wood, in no order or sense. Up Center is a cheap office table on which is a typewriter, with a stack of paper still in the wrapping, although the wrapping has been torn open. Beside the paper is an empty coffee can, used as an ash tray. Beside

*the table, a cheap bridge lamp. On an end table beside
the davenport rests a telephone. On a coffee table in
front of the davenport, a half empty gin bottle from a
cordial shop.*

*At rise a man is standing at the gas stove, making
coffee. This man is named* TOWNSEND RINGWALD. *He is
in his thirties. He is wearing grey flannel slacks that have
not been pressed in weeks, a white Brooks shirt open at
the neck, a pair of leather bedroom slippers. He has a
pair of horn-rim glasses pushed back on the top of his
head. He needs a shave. While the coffee is brewing he
peers out the window, trying to get a look at the sky to
see what kind of day it is, but although there is a yard
on the other side of the windows, the yard area is hemmed
in by the neighboring buildings, and it is an apartment
that sees little daylight.*

RINGWALD, *satisfied that the coffee is ready, pours himself a cup, puts in sugar and cream. He picks up the loaf
of bread, but changes his mind about having a slice of it,
and instead takes the coffee and sits at the table and lights
a cigarette, smoking and sipping coffee as he reads the stuff
that is still in the typewriter.*

*He reads critically, becoming absorbed, and now properly
seats himself at the typewriter and writes a few words
rapidly. While he is so engaged there is a knock on the
door.*

RINGWALD   Come in.

(*The door is opened and a young woman in sweater
and skirt enters. She carries no bag and is not attired for
the street. Her name is* VERONIQUE MC CULLOUGH)

RINGWALD   Hello, Rat Face.

(*She is too pretty for the epithet, but it does caricature
her prettiness*)

VERONIQUE   Hello—Horse Face.

RINGWALD   Well, after this brisk exchange of compliments, what do you want?

VERONIQUE   I thought I could smell the coffee, so I thought I'd drop in for a cup.

RINGWALD   All right. Have a cup.

VERONIQUE   Were you working? I don't want to disturb you.

RINGWALD   It's nothing. I'm just finishing up a review.

VERONIQUE   Who for? Are you going to get paid for it?

RINGWALD   I'll get six dollars. Maybe seven-fifty, if they don't cut it.

VERONIQUE   Do you get to sign your name to it?

RINGWALD   No. It's just a mystery story.

VERONIQUE   You don't even get to sign your initials?

RINGWALD   No. There's no glory. Only money. Six dollars, maybe seven and a half.

VERONIQUE   You make your coffee so *strong*.

RINGWALD   Thin it out if it's too strong.

VERONIQUE   Oh, I like it this way.

RINGWALD   You can't keep the note of complaint out of your voice. Sit down. Have a cigarette.

VERONIQUE   I don't want to disturb you.

RINGWALD   That calls for several obvious remarks. I don't think I'll make them.

VERONIQUE   *I* worked today.

RINGWALD   Did you? At what?

VERONIQUE   Modeling, of course.

RINGWALD   Did you get paid?

VERONIQUE   I certainly did.

RINGWALD   Did you get paid a lot? Enough to give me a little something on account?

VERONIQUE   I can give you *some*. But not the whole fifteen dollars.

RINGWALD   The whole fifteen dollars is actually twenty-five dollars, Veronique.

VERONIQUE   Oh, the other ten. That's right. It is twenty-five. Well, I can give you *five*.

RINGWALD   All right. It helps.

VERONIQUE   I haven't got it with me, though.

RINGWALD   That's all right. Just finish your coffee and run upstairs and get it.

VERONIQUE   All right, as soon as I finish my coffee and smoke a cigarette. May I use your phone?

RINGWALD   It's been shut off. Temporarily disconnected.

VERONIQUE   So's mine. This building is full of disconnected phones.

RINGWALD   Oh, it wasn't the smell of my coffee that brought you here.

VERONIQUE   I didn't say it was the only thing. But when I smelt the coffee I knew you were in.

RINGWALD   Who else's phone is disconnected?

VERONIQUE   The boys'.

RINGWALD   The boys let their phone get shut off? What *ever* will they *do*?

VERONIQUE   I know. Earl says it's a tragedy.

RINGWALD   Well, for him I guess it is. When his window's open I can hear him dishing all day.

VERONIQUE   How much do you owe?

RINGWALD   It isn't so much a question of how much I owe as how long I've owed it. My bill's around thirty dollars.

VERONIQUE   I think they're a bunch of crooks at the phone company. I get charged for calls I never made. I never called anybody in Idaho. I don't know anybody in Idaho. Actually I'm not even sure where Idaho is. I get Idaho mixed with Iowa.

RINGWALD   Don't they teach American geography in Canada?

VERONIQUE   They teach it, but I don't even know Canadian geography. Geography is just a big, boring waste of time. If you want to go some place, go to the railway station and buy a ticket. Let them worry about where it is, and how to get there. When I came to New York two years ago, I left Montreal at night and the next morning I was in New York. I don't know what states I passed through and I don't care. The engineer knew the way, that's what he gets paid for.

RINGWALD   That may be a very sensible way to look at it.

VERONIQUE   (*Pleased with herself*)   Even more so on the ocean. My family took me abroad when I was fourteen, and it's even harder to know the way from Montreal to Liverpool, England. On the ocean there's nobody to ask. At least if the engineer of a train gets lost he can ask at the next station. You see what I mean?

RINGWALD   Yes, dear. Just put your trust in the man up front.

VERONIQUE   That sounds religious.

RINGWALD   It was meant to.

VERONIQUE   But you're not a Catholic.

RINGWALD   No, I most certainly am not a Catholic. But you are, I suppose. I never thought to ask.

VERONIQUE   Devout. I don't believe in some of the stuff, but I love my religion. I cry on Good Friday, but then I'm so happy at Easter. When do you think you'll have your phone connected again?

RINGWALD   Search me, I don't know.

VERONIQUE   Because I was thinking, if you—

RINGWALD   Can I finish it for you? If I got my phone reconnected, you'd put off having yours reconnected. As a matter of fact, Veronique, on my bill there are two long distance calls to Montreal. I've never called Montreal.

VERONIQUE   There, just what I told you a minute ago. I never called Iowa, either. But I guess I did call Montreal on your phone. But I asked you if I could and you said it was all right. You knew I came from Montreal.

RINGWALD   Yes, I did. But I didn't assume that whenever you used my phone you'd call home.

VERONIQUE   Actually I didn't call home. I called a friend of mine that my parents don't approve of. A man about your age, and married. You're not married, are you, Townsend?

RINGWALD   I was, but I'm not. I told you that.

VERONIQUE   Divorced. We can't get divorced, that's why I haven't got married. We have to be *sure*. *You* can get married and if it doesn't work out, you just get a divorce. But it's against our religion. If it hadn't been for that I probably would have been married three or four times by now. Oh, at least . . . You don't seem very cheerful today, Townsend.

RINGWALD   Do I ever seem very cheerful? I don't think I ever radiate cheer.

VERONIQUE   No, but sometimes you're more cheerful than others.

RINGWALD   That may well be true.

VERONIQUE   Oh, it is. I've seen you when you had enough to drink and you were loads of fun. If you have a hangover, why don't you take a drink? You have some gin there, I see.

RINGWALD   No hangover.

VERONIQUE   I haven't got exactly a hangover, but it's almost six o'clock and I haven't had a thing to drink all day.

RINGWALD   Help yourself, but I have nothing to go with it.

VERONIQUE   Not even any Angostura Bitters? You usually have a bottle of Angostura.

RINGWALD   I guess there's some Angostura there.

VERONIQUE   There is, I can recognize the bottle from here. Townsend?

RINGWALD   What?

VERONIQUE   Let's get just a little plastered? Just enough to forget our troubles.

RINGWALD   Too early, and I have a lot of work to do.

VERONIQUE   I thought you were finished.

RINGWALD   I've finished the review I was writing, but I have other work and I'm way behind.

VERONIQUE   Oh, your play. But you've been working on *that* ever since I've known you. I feel like getting just a little tight and then going over to Mario's. I'd love some spaghetti and red wine. How much do you owe Mario?

RINGWALD   About seventy-five or eighty dollars.

VERONIQUE   That's all right, as long as it's under a hundred. He told me. He said if you pay him a little every once in a while, just keep it under a hundred. But he doesn't like it when people that owe him money stop coming in. He told me that.

RINGWALD   He tells everybody that. But I haven't even got enough money for a tip.

VERONIQUE   I have. What do you tip? A dollar?

RINGWALD   As a rule.

VERONIQUE   That's for two. Well, have you got fifty cents?

RINGWALD   Just about.

VERONIQUE   Well, you can sign for the dinner and each of us leave fifty cents, that's a dollar. Mario *told* me he doesn't like people staying away because they owe him money.

RINGWALD   You have a gin and Angostura.

VERONIQUE   Not alone. I don't want to drink alone,

Townsend. When a girl starts drinking alone, that's one of the signs you have to look out for.

RINGWALD   I don't want a drink.

VERONIQUE   Well do you mind if I have one? That's not really drinking alone, if you're here with me.

RINGWALD   Go ahead. Help yourself.
(*She pours gin and a dash of Angostura into a tumbler*)

VERONIQUE   Cheero, Townsend.

RINGWALD   Cheery-ho, and *à votre santé*.

VERONIQUE   Thank you, my dear. *J'oublie toujours que vous parlez Français.*

RINGWALD   *J'oublie toujours que je parle Français.* In fact, *ça me fait du bien d'oublier que je jarle Français.*

VERONIQUE   No, I think it's nice to hear French spoken in the states. Maybe some day you'll all speak French.

RINGWALD   When the Canadians take over.

VERONIQUE   Well, you were originally Canadians, in a way, weren't you? Weren't you under the King, the same as we are? And then you broke away.

RINGWALD   You always have a fresh slant on things, Veronique.

VERONIQUE   I know, isn't it strange? Because I didn't have much schooling. I was terrible in school. Terrible. But everybody says I have a good mind.

RINGWALD   I have a good mind to . . .

VERONIQUE   What?

RINGWALD   (*Reading the line differently*)   Nothing. I was just saying I have a good mind, too.

VERONIQUE   Oh, yes. There's no doubt about it. I can always tell your reviews, even without the initials. You have a flair, Townsend. You really have.
(*There is a knock on the door*)

VERONIQUE   (*To Ringwald*)   Who's that?

RINGWALD   We'll see. Come in!

(*A woman, thirtyish, in a good but not new suit, appears in the doorway. She is* MARY LEONARD)

MARY   Am I intruding?

RINGWALD   Yes, but we'll find a place for you. Miss Leonard, Miss McCullough. Mary, Veronique.

MARY   Hello. Veronique McCullough. French and Scotch?

VERONIQUE   French and Scotch-Irish. Canadian.

MARY   A dismounted Canadian. Were you sent down to apprehend our friend here?

RINGWALD   Yes, and she always gets her man, if that's what you're getting around to.

MARY   I was. Can I have some of that, whatever it is?

RINGWALD   Help yourself.

MARY   It must be awful, if you're staying away from it.

RINGWALD   It's gin and bitters, and you're familiar with it. Do you want a cigarette?

MARY   (*Helping herself to gin without bitters*)   I have some, thanks. You're a show girl, aren't you?

VERONIQUE   I have been. I'm modeling now.

MARY   You were in an Earl Carroll show.

VERONIQUE   Oh, you remember me?

MARY   Yes I do, and I'm not a Les.

RINGWALD   Since when?

MARY   Since you came into my life and showed me all that I was missing. How's that for an answer? Why aren't you drinking?

RINGWALD   It's a good thing I'm not, or there wouldn't be enough to go around.

MARY   There isn't going to be anyway. I brought you a cheque.

RINGWALD   Miss Leonard works for my agent.

MARY   Miss Leonard *is* your agent. You don't make enough money to have Keith Singleton handle you personally.

RINGWALD   What's the cheque for?

MARY   For summer stock. Do you want me to tell the amount in front of our Canadian friend?

RINGWALD   Sure. Impress her.

MARY   Two hundred dollars less commission, less a hundred dollars borrowed from the office. Total, net, eighty dollars.

VERONIQUE   Just enough to pay Mario!

RINGWALD   You're supposed to ask how I earned this magnificent windfall.

VERONIQUE   Oh. How did you?

MARY   He wrote a play once. It was called *Perihelion,* and they do it in summer stock because it only needs five actors and a lot of porch furniture.

RINGWALD   *And* it was a good play.

MARY   It wasn't a bad play. And it was a comedy.

VERONIQUE   I heard of it. I didn't know you wrote it, though.

MARY   He wrote it years ago, in 1922. Unfortunately, he hasn't written anything since.

VERONIQUE   Why yes he has.

MARY   Nothing that didn't close in Atlantic City. He went Greenwich Village on us. No more comedies. Eugene O'Neill. When I think of the money this man is passing up it makes me cry.

RINGWALD   Let's see you cry, Mary.

MARY   (*Over him*)   I wouldn't mind if he didn't like money, but he does. You should have seen him when *Perihelion* was a hit. A racing car, and a closetful of clothes—and an apartment full of girls. Parties, parties. And he could have it all again if he'd write another comedy.

VERONIQUE   Then I think he's entitled to a lot of credit. I thought he lived this way because he had to.

MARY   Oh, he has to, but he wouldn't for long. And it isn't the honest way, you know. It isn't honest to go around borrowing money, and not paying bills, *when* you have the ability to *do* something. It's just stubbornness. Ever since he saw *The Hairy Ape*—

RINGWALD   *Anna Christie.*

MARY   No, it was *The Hairy Ape* that really did it to you. But we don't have to argue that point. In fact, I don't want to argue with you at all. I just want to tell this voluptuous young woman that you don't have to live poor.

VERONIQUE   What are you telling *me* for?

MARY   (*Looks pointedly at her figure*)   Because I assume that you have some influence.

VERONIQUE   Not so far.

MARY   How long have you known each other?

VERONIQUE   I don't know. About six months, I guess. Whenever I moved here.

MARY   Here? You live here? (*She looks around for signs of a woman's occupancy*)

VERONIQUE   Upstairs.

MARY   (*Genuinely baffled*)   Well—but you've been living in the same building six months, and you have no influence?

RINGWALD   Mary, what's come over you? This delicacy, this tact. Why don't you come right out with it?

MARY   All right, I will. Don't you and Townsend go to bed together?

VERONIQUE   Well, not always.

MARY   Then you must have someone else.

VERONIQUE   Well, don't act surprised. You didn't *ask* me *that*.

MARY   I see. Townsend is just a neighbor.

VERONIQUE   Sort of.

MARY   And once in a while you bring him a nice cup of hot soup.

VERONIQUE   I guess you could put it that way.

MARY   I do put it that way.

VERONIQUE   (*No fool*) The same way that—for instance you could have *mailed* him that cheque.

RINGWALD   Score one for the Canadian team.

VERONIQUE   I was here first, but maybe I'm the one that's intruding, Miss Leonard.

MARY   Believe me, kid, you were *not* here first. Not by about ten years.

VERONIQUE   Well, I'm here now.

MARY   So I see, but not having much influence.

VERONIQUE   I never tried to influence you, did I, Townsend?

RINGWALD   Not in any way that affects my professional life. You do try to influence me, though.

MARY   (*Eager*) How, for instance?

RINGWALD   Well, just before you made your timely arrival, Veronique wanted me to get a little drunk with her.

MARY   And you resisted her wiles? Why?

RINGWALD   Because I want to work on the fourth act of my play.

MARY   That should be easy. Just cut it off. (*She makes a downward-with-cleaver gesture*)

RINGWALD   No, that's the easy way, Mary.

MARY   If I'd been ten minutes later—no not ten minutes. You don't get tight in ten minutes. If I'd been a couple of hours later—

RINGWALD   Or better yet, not come at all.

MARY   Or not come at all, you and Miss Canada would be cementing relations.

RINGWALD   I don't know, but that's extremely well put.

VERONIQUE   When you love a person as much as I love Townsend you don't have to cement relations.

RINGWALD (*Amazed*)   This is a new one on me. As much as you love me, Veronique?

VERONIQUE   Well, I love you more than I love most people.

RINGWALD (*Relieved*)   Oh.

MARY   That was quick. Bing—romance! Bang—friendship! Don't you wish they were all over as quickly as that?

RINGWALD   Sometimes they are, but I don't always catch on.

VERONIQUE   I have the rest of a bottle of gin upstairs.

MARY   Get it.

VERONIQUE   I might as well, don't you think? We'll need it.

RINGWALD   Why do you think we'll need it?

VERONIQUE   Because aren't you going to take us out to dinner? Miss Leonard isn't going to leave you with me, and I'm certainly not going to leave you with her.

MARY   If we all get enough gin in us nobody'll have to leave.

VERONIQUE   Are you planning something?

MARY   I'm not planning anything, but you never can tell. You get the gin.

VERONIQUE   I'll only be a minute.

MARY   That won't give us much time.

VERONIQUE   No it won't, will it? (*She exits*)

MARY   She's no fool.

RINGWALD   No.

MARY   Well, but she's so quick.

RINGWALD   You helped her out a little. You started out by saying you weren't a Les.

MARY   I had to. I could tell it was what she was thinking.

RINGWALD   Maybe you had a glint in your eye.

MARY   Maybe I did. Well, she doesn't seem shocked.

RINGWALD   She isn't shocked. She's so far ahead of you and me that she's kind of innocent.

MARY   I've heard *that* before.

RINGWALD   I don't claim it as an original remark. Just a comment on Veronique's morals.

MARY   Well, I guess you learn fast in an Earl Carroll show. And she was beautiful, absolutely beautiful. Somebody taught her to look out over the audience.

RINGWALD   Nobody taught her anything. She was born knowing those things.

MARY   But what's she doing living in a dump like this? Is she by any chance really in love with you?

RINGWALD   Hell, no.

MARY   Well then, what's doing here when she could be living on Central Park West?

RINGWALD   That's exactly where she did live for a while.

MARY   A lot of those girls get the idea that they can paint. Can she paint?

RINGWALD   No. And she hasn't any money beyond what she gets modeling. Her phone is turned off, for instance.

MARY   So is yours, by the way.

RINGWALD   I know. It's been off for over a week.

MARY   Do you want me to go home?

RINGWALD   That depends.

MARY   On her?

RINGWALD   On you.

MARY   Why? If it doesn't mean anything to her, if she's

so damn sophisticated that she's sort of innocent. Are
you getting protective, Townsend?

RINGWALD   She can take care of herself.

MARY   Then let her.

RINGWALD   You know, Mary, you're absolutely corrupt.
You came down here to get laid, but as soon as you saw
her, you have other schemes.

MARY   If you'd pay your phone bill you could avoid such
complications.

RINGWALD   If I wrote the kind of crap you want me to
write I could have a butler to answer my phone. And I
cold be swimming in the blue Mediterranean. And I'd
have Veronique with me, at least for a couple of weeks.

MARY   And that's what you want. A butler, and the South
of France, and girls like Veronique for a couple of
weeks. This is the real crap, Townsend. This filthy
place. Unpaid phone bills. Scrabbling for eighty dollars
and writing nasty little five-dollar book reviews. You're
stubborn. You're in over your depth. That's really it.
You're in over your depth. You'll never be O'Neill or
anywhere near him. Your whole scheme is based on
envy of better writers than you are.

RINGWALD   Enjoy yourself.

MARY   I intend to. You live in this dump, writing un-
producible bad plays, and you keep telling yourself
that you're an artist. You're not. You're an envious,
jealous coward, not an artist. You can go on for the rest
of your life, living from hand to mouth and telling yourself how artistic you are. But all that time you're a
yellow coward, because you won't admit to your own
limitations. You're an extremely competent hack, putting on artistic airs.

RINGWALD   You're going great.

MARY   And loving it. This five-act play, for God's sake. I
suppose you read in the paper that Eugene O'Neill is

writing a five-act play. Of course you did. But his will be
out before yours will. And his will be good. Philip Barry
has two hits, comedies, and that's another reason why
you're a coward. You're afraid a comedy by you won't
be as successful as Barry's comedies, and you wouldn't
be able to stand that, would you? You had a hit before
Barry had a hit, and now he's nudged you out of the
way.

RINGWALD   I'm not conscious of being nudged by anybody. Except you, Mary. You want me to give up what
I'm doing, for which I've already given up a great deal.
And the thing that inspired this outburst, you want me
to give up Veronique McCullough so that you can have
her.

MARY   You had to say that, didn't you? You can't deny
that everything I said about you and your work is true,
but you can sweep it all under the rug because I am
what I am. Dear of you, Townsend. Well, I didn't
always know that I was bi-sexual. You can take some
credit for that, if you like. (*She rises and exits angrily,
sadly*)

CURTAIN

SCENE TWO

*Same as Scene One. The next day. Townsend Ringwald,
attired as before, is pouring coffee. He takes a sip, and
while he is doing so the telephone rings. He does a slow
take of surprise as he realizes that the phone is on again.
At the sound of the telephone bell, Veronique, on the
studio couch, attired in a pair of Ringwald's pajamas,*

wakes up and slowly brings herself up on her elbows as Ringwald goes to the phone.

RINGWALD   Hello. Oh, hello, Mary. First I want to ask you something. Did you have the phone service restored? You did. Why? Well, I think that's probably a good idea. What's on your mind now? I don't know. How much can you get for it? That seems like a lot of money, do you think they'll pay it? I don't know, Mary. I leave those things for you to decide. You and your boss Mr. Singleton. Is this important enough for Singleton? His personal attention? Well, get all you can, because obviously from your remarks yesterday you never expect to get any more. That is exactly (*Looking over at* VERONIQUE) none of your business. You might try having her phone service restored. Goodbye. (*Hangs up*) Do you want some coffee?

VERONIQUE   I'd like a cup of coffee.

RINGWALD   Piece of toast? I have no butter, but you can have some strawberry jam.

VERONIQUE   All right. (*She studies him, waiting for him to disclose the details of the telephone call. He is making up his mind how much he will disclose, meanwhile getting her coffee, etc.*)

RINGWALD   The agency paid my phone bill.

VERONIQUE   You must be getting valuable again.

RINGWALD   I'm not so sure about that. After our fight yesterday Mary decided it'd be better to communicate by phone instead of coming down here.

VERONIQUE   What did she want to know about me?

RINGWALD   Wanted to know if you were here. I told her it was none of her business.

VERONIQUE   I don't care if she knows. I didn't keep it secret yesterday.

RINGWALD   It's still none of her business.

VERONIQUE What else did she have to say? What seemed like a lot of money?

RINGWALD A movie company wants to buy the rights to my play.

VERONIQUE *Perihelion?*

RINGWALD The only one they ever heard of, yes. They think it would make a picture for Ann Harding.

VERONIQUE Oh, boy. Then they'll pay a lot for it.

RINGWALD So it would seem.

VERONIQUE You won't tell me how much?

RINGWALD They're offering fifteen thousand.

VERONIQUE They'll go to twenty-five.

RINGWALD That's what Mary thinks. God, twenty-five thousand, less twenty-five hundred commission. Twenty-two thousand five hundred dollars. I haven't had that much money since 1922. I haven't got it yet, but you're probably right, you and Mary. I have a feeling they'll buy it and pay twenty-five thousand. And Mary said she can get me a job writing the scenario, five hundred a week with a three months' guarantee. Twelve times five hundred. Six thousand dollars.

VERONIQUE When would you leave?

RINGWALD I'm not going to leave. I'll sell the movie rights, but I won't go to Hollywood.

VERONIQUE Not even if they offered you a thousand a week?

RINGWALD I was offered a thousand a week a few years ago, to go out and write subtitles. I turned it down then. You see, Mary forgets these things. She forgets that I gave things up in order to write what I wanted to write.

VERONIQUE I wish I could have been here when you were having your fight. She got under your skin, didn't she?

RINGWALD She always can. She knows all my soft spots.

VERONIQUE   I didn't know you had any.

RINGWALD   I don't know how you can say that. I'm just a big pan of mush where you're concerned. You can twist me around your little finger.

VERONIQUE   Hah!

(*He sits on the edge of her bed as she sips coffee*)

RINGWALD   Why do you live in the Village?

VERONIQUE   Why do I live in the Village? Why do you live in the Village?

RINGWALD   Because for me it's one step above a flophouse on the Bowery. The Bowery is better suited to my income, but I couldn't have a typewriter there, and I couldn't have privacy in a flophouse. This lousy dump is a luxury for me. But you could do so much better.

VERONIQUE   You mean being kept, uptown?

RINGWALD   Yes.

VERONIQUE   You're a writer. Did you ever stop to think of what it means, being kept? It doesn't only mean somebody's keeping you in the lap of luxury. They're also keeping you from doing what you want to do. A man doesn't just give you a fur coat and pay your rent to go to bed with you. They want to know where you are all the time, who you're with. And a woman is just as bad if not worse.

RINGWALD   You've been kept by a woman?

VERONIQUE   For a couple of weeks.

RINGWALD   Who?

VERONIQUE   (*Shaking her head*)   Don't ask me to mention any names. Anyway, you wouldn't know her. She wasn't in show business. She didn't exactly keep me. She got me to live with her while her parents were abroad.

RINGWALD   A society girl.

VERONIQUE   Big. Prominent. Sent me flowers to the theater, just initials on the card. I thought it was a man till I found out otherwise.

RINGWALD   A dyke, huh? But you've been around, you knew what to expect. Did you like her? You must have.

VERONIQUE   She was good-looking. At first I thought she wanted me for her boy friend. I had that happen to me. But she wanted me for herself, and believe me, nobody else. No other man, woman or child. She wouldn't even let the maid bring me my breakfast in the morning, and every night we went out with the same two pansies. We'd go to Tony's and Harlem. Oh, did they ever know her in Harlem!

RINGWALD   If I tell you her initials will you tell me if I'm right?

VERONIQUE   Yes.

RINGWALD   A. W.

VERONIQUE   Oh, you know her?

RINGWALD   Of course. Have you seen her lately? She isn't so good-looking any more. She's gotten fat and very mannish.

VERONIQUE   No, I haven't seen her.

RINGWALD   Is that why you live here? To get away from people like her?

VERONIQUE   If you mean Lesses, there are plenty of them down here.

RINGWALD   I know that. No, I meant people that keep you.

VERONIQUE   I'd let you keep me if you had the money. It's hard to say why I live here. I came to New York to get away from Montreal and my parents, but they're just as strict uptown, only in a different way. Here at least you don't have to take orders from anybody.

RINGWALD   Now we're getting somewhere. You live here because you want to be your own boss.

VERONIQUE   Yes, but even that's not the whole thing. That doesn't quite express it.

RINGWALD   Then I'll try another way. Independence. What everybody comes here for.

VERONIQUE   That's closer to it. Independence. Except that you get awfully lonesome being independent. But I'm not lonesome here, very often. I can come in and see you. And the queers, Wilmer and Earl. They're always good for laughs—when they're not fighting with each other.

RINGWALD   But you don't miss having pretty clothes and all that?

VERONIQUE   Well, if I want them I know how I can get them. If I want them bad enough.

RINGWALD   And money?

VERONIQUE   Money is part of that. I wouldn't know what else to do with money except spend it on clothes and stuff.

RINGWALD   Where does marriage fit in with your plans, or does it?

VERONIQUE   Well—I told you I have to be sure. And I won't marry a man that asks too many questions.

RINGWALD   That lets me out.

VERONIQUE   Oh, you and I would never marry each other. And I don't mind you asking questions. You ask out of curiosity. But some men would try to find out all about me so they could throw it up to me later on.

RINGWALD   By the sound of that I would guess that someone has done that.

VERONIQUE   Yes. A young fellow. He got me to tell him everything about myself, I didn't hardly hold back a thing. And after that he made my life miserable. So it doesn't pay to answer a lot of questions. He can take you for what you are, what he sees with his two eyes.

RINGWALD   Every man is going to ask you questions, Veronique.

VERONIQUE   So it seems. But when I tell them something I don't want them to hold it against me. I don't ask them anything. Of course men tell you without you asking them. With one exception.

RINGWALD   And who's the one exception?

VERONIQUE   You. You never volunteer any information about yourself. I always have to ask you.

RINGWALD   Do you like that, or don't you?

VERONIQUE   I don't like it or I don't dislike it. It's just your way. We all have different ways. That's what makes us different people. Maybe you like something in one person that you don't like in someone else. (*She stops to listen to the sound of angry voices*) Wilmer and Earl. Just listen to them. Wilmer's going to walk out on Earl.

RINGWALD   He's threatened to do that before.

VERONIQUE   Yes, but this time he's serious. He told me. Earl is drinking too much and Wilmer says he isn't going to put up with much more.

RINGWALD   I've heard that before, only the last time Earl was complaining about Wilmer.

VERONIQUE   But this is different. Earl's been on a bender, hasn't worked for two or three weeks, and he stole some money from Wilmer. (*There are more angry cries from above*) Listen to them.

RINGWALD   Has Wilmer got a job?

VERONIQUE   Wilmer's making plenty. He's playing piano in a speakeasy. But Earl's been on this bender and stole some money from Wilmer, and then the other night Wilmer came home and Earl had taken two of his suits and hocked them. New suits, worth seventy dollars apiece, and Earl hocked them for twenty dollars. I don't blame Wilmer for being cross. He needs wardrobe in his work. (*The door bursts open*) Hello, Wilmer.

(WILMER, *a slight man in his thirties, wearing shirt and trousers, stares at them*)

WILMER (*Tearfully*) Look what he did to me, that bitch. He scratched my face.

VERONIQUE Gee, he did.

RINGWALD Here, let me put something on it.

WILMER No iodine! I don't want to look like an Indian.

RINGWALD I have some peroxide.

WILMER I'm going to have him arrested. He stole my watch that was left to me by my father. My gold watch. I'm going to swear out a warrant.

RINGWALD (*Busy with peroxide*) He really gouged you.

WILMER Those long nails, the drunken bitch. How am I going to work tonight? I'll lose my job.

RINGWALD Maybe Veronique can cover it with makeup.

WILMER I'll get an infection and die of blood poisoning.

VERONIQUE Go to Stein's on Sixth Avenue, they know how to make you up so it won't show.

WILMER Even if I perspire? I perspire by the time I finish a set. You know I play forty-five minutes uninterrupted.

VERONIQUE Explain that at the drug store.

WILMER Tomorrow how am I going to shave? He's ruined my face, the thieving bitch. I could kill him. Townsend, could I trouble you for a drink to steady my nerves?

RINGWALD There's some gin.

WILMER Anything. I don't care what it is, just so it's strong.

VERONIQUE But don't get tight, Wilmer.

WILMER How can I get tight? He stole all my money and everything he could hock. If I lose my job I'll starve to death, literally. (*He looks at them craftily, and lowers his voice*) No I won't. I have some money saved up that he didn't know about. In the bank. He thinks he's so smart, stealing my father's watch and all. But wait till I blossom forth in a new wardrobe. It'll kill him, and especially when I tell him what I was saving up for.

RINGWALD Christmas?

WILMER Oh, hell, no. No, I was going to take him on a trip to Bermuda. He's been dying to go to Bermuda. I know why, too. He met a sailor boy from some British ship that's stationed in Bermuda. But now I'm going to spend every cent of that money on myself. Wouldn't you if you were me?

RINGWALD Absolutely, Wilmer. But when are you going to see him, Earl, I mean?

WILMER *Quién sabe?* He'll come crawling back on his hands and knees, begging my forgiveness.

RINGWALD And you'll take him back?

WILMER Oh, sure. He's so young. But I'm going to teach him a lesson, don't you think I'm not. He's only twenty-three years of age, ten years my junior. Is this Mario's gin?

RINGWALD Yes.

WILMER I thought it was. I wonder what proportions he uses. I can't get my gin to taste as good as this. Veronique, you always ought to wear boys' pajamas. There's something very appealing. Those silly fronts of yours in boys' pajamas. Townsend probably doesn't think so, he's such an old norm.

RINGWALD I think she's very appealing.

WILMER Yes, but we look at it different. To me she's hilarious, with those fronts. Oh, I'm beginning to feel human again. I just had to be among friends. It's awful to want to kill somebody. I could have stabbed him, the thieving little bitch. Can I have one of your Chesterfields, Townsend? Are you still working on your play? I hope it's a big, big success.

RINGWALD Thank you, Wilmer.

WILMER Did you know that Eugene O'Neill lived not far

from here? I think he lived in either forty-three, or forty-five, or forty-seven. At least that's what I was told. You know who I mean, of course. Eugene O'Neill, the playwright. They could be lying, though. Every damn little hole in the wall they say some famous person used to live there. It's supposed to make it more romantic. Personally I hate the Village, but there's one thing I hate worse and that's paying a lot of money for rent. What do you pay, Townsend? Twenty-five? Thirty?

RINGWALD   Thirty.

WILMER   I pay fifty, but I have the two rooms. You didn't see it since we fixed it up. One thing you got to give Earl, he can do wonders with a few cans of paint and a few yards of material. He has such imagination and taste, if you know what I mean. But he just will not hold a job. He no sooner gets a job than he starts criticizing. That's puke, he'll say. He said it to some of the most famous decorators in the profession. That's puke. Well, no wonder he can't hold a job. But you're going to hear from him. He has talent, that boy. Ask Veronique.

VERONIQUE   He has.

WILMER   Everybody that sees our apartment wants to get Earl to do theirs. And all the training he ever had was one year at Carnegie Tech. He told them it was puke, too, what they were teaching. And you wonder where he gets it from. His parents are common as dirt. The father works in a steel mill, and the mother is just a big fat sow. At least *my* mother gave music lessons, and I could play violin when I was six years of age. Piano when I was seven, before I could span an octave. I wish I could let *my* nails grow, but I can't. Well, kids, thanks for coming to my rescue. Stein's on Sixth Avenue, Veronique?

VERONIQUE   Corner of 47th and Sixth.

WILMER   You're very sweet, the two of you. Real sweet. (*He exits bouncing*)

VERONIQUE   I hope Earl didn't hear all that.

RINGWALD   How could he?

VERONIQUE   Oh, do you know where I bet he is right this minute? In my apartment. He often goes there when they have fights. He knows where the extra key is, up on the transom. One night I had a friend of mine come home with me, and then when he went home about four o'clock, Earl came out from under the bed.

RINGWALD (*Laughs*)   Were you sore?

VERONIQUE   Of course I was sore. Wilmer's right. Earl is a bitch. He stole things from me, too, you know. Nothing worth much, but handkerchiefs. Scarves. If he sees something he likes, he takes it. Steals it. He reads letters that are lying around. Douses himself with my perfume, when I have any. He stole a pair of shoes of mine to go to a drag. Just took them without asking, and denied it, swore up and down and I marched right up to his closet and there they were. I paid twelve dollars for them, and I could never wear them again because he stretched them. He's a damn nuisance.

RINGWALD   Then why do you hope he didn't overhear us talking?

VERONIQUE   Because he'll make trouble for Wilmer. Wilmer's an old queen, and don't believe what he says about his age. He's forty, not thirty-three. But of the two of them he's the nicer one. Earl is a damn *nuisance*. (*Deliberately louder*) I said Earl is a damn nuisance . . . Maybe he isn't there. I guess I ought to start putting some clothes on. Do you mind if I make a phone call?

RINGWALD   Go ahead. Not to Montreal, though.

VERONIQUE (*Picking up phone*)   Local. To see if I have a job. Chickering 8191. Hello, this is Veronique

McCullough. Will you see if there're any calls for me,
please? . . . Who? . . . How much will he pay? . . .
What's the address again? . . . Thank you. Goodbye.
Well, I work tomorrow. The R. & B. Company, 780
Seventh Avenue. Lingerie. It's a wholesale house, which
means if you want to see me tomorrow night, speak up
now, because those buyers will want to take me out,
spend somebody else's money on me, and get a free lay.
And if I want to work there again, those are the condi-
tions.

RINGWALD   Have dinner with me. When did you start
modeling lingerie?

VERONIQUE   I always have, for photographers. But this is
the slack season for them, so I said I'd take jobs in the
wholesale houses. It's five dollars an hour, less commission. The next time I work for them they'll double it,
if I'm nice to the buyer I go out with. But if I'm *not*
nice to the buyer there won't *be* any next time. This
isn't my regular agency. This is just a little pimp that
has a list of show girls that are out of work. No questions asked. The wholesaler pays him, he pays me. If my
work is satisfactory, he charges them double the next
time I go on a job. No questions asked, no trouble with
the police. The only one that can have any trouble with
the police is me, in case the Vice Squad catches me in
bed with the buyer. Or I could get pregnant or catch a
disease. Or draw some buyer that likes to beat up girls,
or a Jack the Ripper. They had a Jack the Ripper case
last year, it was hushed up because the girl didn't die.
She'd be better off if she had died.

RINGWALD   Aren't you looking for a job in a show?

VERONIQUE   There's nobody casting now. Oh, plays, but
I can't act. All I can do is walk. (*She demonstrates a
show-girl walk and turn*)

RINGWALD   Mary Leonard said that someone must have

taught you to look out over the audience. What did she mean exactly?

VERONIQUE   Oh, that. Well you know some girls, show girls, how they smile down at the people in the first couple of rows? (*Demonstrates*) Not me. I look at the back of the house. Austere. That's why some of the kids used to call me The Duchess. But you'd be surprised. I got more letters and people wanting to be introduced to me.

RINGWALD   How did you happen to do that? Did someone tell you?

VERONIQUE   Nobody told me. I'm just a little near-sighted, that's all. And of course if you look hard to get, why they try to get you. Mr. Carroll picked me out of a line of girls because he said I looked like a nun. I don't look like any nun that I ever saw.

RINGWALD   But oddly enough I understand exactly what he meant.

VERONIQUE   So do I. Now. Horse Face?

RINGWALD   What?

VERONIQUE   Were you married to Mary Leonard?

RINGWALD   What makes you ask that?

VERONIQUE   Were you?

RINGWALD   No.

VERONIQUE   Why do you lie to me?

RINGWALD   (*Pauses, looks at the floor, then at her*)   Apparently I can't lie to you, very successfully. Yes, Mary and I were married in 1917, so that I could stay out of the army. But I was drafted anyway. We only lived together about three months, I was drafted, and when I got out of the army in 1919 we didn't go back together again. She got a divorce and married someone else, and I stayed single.

VERONIQUE   Is she still married?

RINGWALD   No. The man she married committed suicide.

VERONIQUE   Why?

RINGWALD   Why? Say, you're asking a lot of questions.

VERONIQUE   I told you, I always have to. You never volunteer anything about yourself.

RINGWALD   But why are you so interested in my career as a husband? You never were before.

VERONIQUE   Oh, I was interested, but I never saw Mary Leonard till yesterday, and she made me wonder. She's older than you are.

RINGWALD   A few years, not much.

VERONIQUE   Why did her husband commit suicide?

RINGWALD   Back to that.

VERONIQUE   Not back to it. We were never away from it.

RINGWALD   You're persistent, aren't you, Rat Face?

VERONIQUE   I'm not bright like you are, that's why I have to concentrate on one thing at a time. Why did her husband commit suicide?

RINGWALD   Let's see if I can remember what he put in the note.

VERONIQUE   Yes. Tell me that first, and then tell me why he really did it.

RINGWALD   (*Looks at her in genuine alarm; she is even shrewder than he thought*) Why do you say that? Have you any information about it?

VERONIQUE   I never heard of him till now. But I hardly ever believe what people put in suicide notes. They're always blaming other people, or the world. And sometimes they make it very nasty for other people.

RINGWALD   (*Still alarmed*) That's what he did.

VERONIQUE   Who did he make it nasty for? Her? . . . You?

RINGWALD   . . . Yes. I wasn't going to tell you the truth about his note, but I will. He said: "I give you back to Townsend. You belong with one another."

VERONIQUE   Oh, what a bitch! "Belong *with* one another" not "*To* one another." *With*.

RINGWALD   Oh, you got that, did you?

VERONIQUE   Where did he do it? How?

RINGWALD   He jumped out of a window. They were
living at the Algonquin.

VERONIQUE   What was he? A writer?

RINGWALD   I guess you could call him a writer.

VERONIQUE   Well, either a man's a writer or he isn't a
writer.

RINGWALD   Not quite. We have plenty of guys living
down here that call themselves writers, but if they've
ever written anything they've kept it a deep dark secret.

VERONIQUE   He was one of those?

RINGWALD   Very much so. One of our leading non-writing
writers. He was always around where writers were, and
I believe he put some money in Horace Liveright's firm.

VERONIQUE   Oh, he had money.

RINGWALD   *Her* money. Mary's. No, you mustn't get him
confused with patrons of the arts. Some of them are
very useful, but this fellow had no such redeeming
feature.

VERONIQUE   What was his name?

RINGWALD   Morgan Hanscom.

VERONIQUE   And he didn't do anything. Just call himself
a writer.

RINGWALD   Well, he wasn't exactly *idle*, though. He'd go
to parties and insult publishers that Mary had to do
business with. Or better yet, get one of her clients off
in a corner and tell him what was wrong with his latest
book or play.

VERONIQUE   Why did she put up with him? She had the
money. I guess he really loved her. He did commit
suicide over her. That's why she put up with him.

RINGWALD   He didn't commit suicide over Mary, he didn't give a damn about her except as a bankroll.

VERONIQUE   Then why *did* he kill himself?

RINGWALD   What would make a man like that kill himself?

VERONIQUE   Money.

RINGWALD   Right. Money, and the trouble he got into over it. Mary's boss, Keith Singleton, confronted him with a bad cheque, a forgery of Singleton's signature, and gave him twenty-four hours to make good. Singleton naturally hated Hanscom for antagonizing publishers and clients and people like that. Hanscom had cost Singleton a lot of money, and Singleton was delighted that he finally had something on him. "Twenty-four hours, or I go to the police," said Singleton. Well, Hanscom had only one person to turn to besides Mary.

VERONIQUE   Who? I bet I can guess.

RINGWALD   (*Nodding*) Me. He called me up and asked me if I'd lend him a thousand dollars right away. Well, I had a thousand dollars all right, but I wondered why he hadn't gone to Mary, and I said so. "Listen, you've been sleeping with Mary and I never complained," he said. Screamed, is what he did. Screamed into the phone. And I said, "Are you complaining now, or blackmailing me?" And he screamed some more and hung up. Then I guess he sat down and wrote his farewell message. And that was what got into the papers. Nothing about the forgery. Just "I give you back to Townsend. You belong with one another." The afternoon papers couldn't come right out and mention my last name, but everybody knew who he meant. Then a couple of the morning papers did get my last name into print. They said that Miss Leonard was formerly married to Townsend Ringwald, the playwright, who was questioned by police. You see, the cops found out that Hanscom had telephoned me a short while before he jumped out the window.

VERONIQUE   What did you tell them?

RINGWALD   Simply told them he'd tried to borrow some money, which was the truth, and all I knew at the time.

VERONIQUE   Were you sleeping with her?

RINGWALD   Well, now, what a question.

VERONIQUE   Were you?

RINGWALD   Of course.

VERONIQUE   I'm glad you were.

RINGWALD   Why?

VERONIQUE   Because you stood up to a blackmailer. If you hadn't been sleeping with her, then you'd have just been stingy. But you were sleeping with her, and he was trying to blackmail you.

RINGWALD   (*Smiles and shakes his head*)   Your own slant, as always. Not many people took that attitude.

VERONIQUE   What do you care?

RINGWALD   I don't now. I did then. When you have a hit on Broadway you're vulnerable.

VERONIQUE   Now you're the one that's taking a new slant.

RINGWALD   It's true, though. It was my first and only hit, and I was trying my hardest to prove that success hadn't gone to my head. Of course it had, but I didn't admit it, even to myself. I was polite to people I despised, and I lent money to people that despised me. I was nice to everybody, without taking time to realize that the only thing that can cure you of success is more success. (*Pauses*) I've had two failures since my first and only success. I knew they weren't going to be financial successes, but they weren't the other kind, either. That's what hurt. That's why I'm a son of a bitch.

VERONIQUE   Explain that to me. Why?

RINGWALD   You have to follow your first success with

another one, the sooner the better. If it doesn't make money, that's all right, provided you did what you started out to do and can honestly say to yourself that this financial flop is an artistic success. But I couldn't say that. My two financial flops were also artistic flops. And I know it. Mary Leonard knows it, too, and won't let me forget it. She's wrong about me in some things. I don't care about making money again. That isn't the way I want to live any more. The cars and the parties. But I hate her for believing I do. Someone that knew me as well as she once did, to go on believing that I'm afraid of Philip Barry and Michael Arlen. Christ, I'm afraid of O'Neill, I'm afraid of Sidney Howard. Elmer Rice. No, not afraid of them. In awe of them. Maybe there's envy in my admiration of what they're doing, but it's not *mean* envy. And I'm *not* afraid of Phil Barry or Michael Arlen or George Kelly. What I am afraid of is Townsend Ringwald, the playwright. The way my name always appears in the papers. Townsend Ringwald, the playwright. I won't consider myself Townsend Ringwald the playwright until they can print my name Townsend Ringwald without having to add, the playwright.

VERONIQUE Well, keep trying.

RINGWALD (*Smiling wryly*) Oh, I will. Because Mary Leonard and all the rest of them forget one thing.

VERONIQUE What?

RINGWALD That before I wrote *Perihelion* I had written two *comedies* that never saw the light of day.

VERONIQUE Then maybe the play you're writing will be a success.

RINGWALD (*Significantly*) I'll let you know. One way or the other.

VERONIQUE Don't talk like that, Townsend.

(*She goes to him, puts her arms around him and they kiss. It is an affectionate kiss rather than a prelude to anything else*)

RINGWALD   Don't you start telling me how I should talk.

VERONIQUE   I won't any more.

RINGWALD   I don't take direction very easily. Mary Leonard found that out.

VERONIQUE   Her trouble is that she didn't find it out.

RINGWALD   I stand corrected, you are absolutely right. What would you think of living here?

VERONIQUE   (*Smiles*)   You want me nearer than two flights away?

RINGWALD   Yes, I do.

VERONIQUE   (*Shakes her head*)   No, Townsend.

RINGWALD   (*Looking about*)   There isn't much room. And no privacy.

VERONIQUE   You need privacy more than I do, to work. No, that isn't why I say no. A lot of people come down to the Village so they can live with somebody, but I didn't. Just the opposite. I'm even a little, a tiny bit worried that you *want* me to live with you. I'm flattered, yes. But a little worried. We don't want that, Townsend. Keep it the way it is, me two flights up. You here. I don't want you to give up your other girls.

RINGWALD   Because you don't want to give up your other men?

VERONIQUE   Just now there doesn't happen to be another man, not really. But that's not saying there won't be, and then I'd have to move back upstairs.

RINGWALD   You're not saying what you really mean.

VERONIQUE   You say it for me.

RINGWALD   The thing that worries you is that my wanting you to live here is the first sign of possessiveness. Is that it?

VERONIQUE   Yes. That's supposed to go with love, I know. But the trouble is I've had the possessiveness part of it. People have been possessive toward me, but I've never been in love. And maybe I never will be, because I'm on my guard against the possessiveness and I don't let people love me. Or me them. First it was my parents, and then a boy in Montreal, and then another boy in Montreal—only he was a man. And then since I came to New York two men and one girl. Every damn one of them started out being possessive. You're just a little slower than the others, Townsend.

RINGWALD   I was just thinking . . . If *you* had suggested that *I* move two flights up, my reaction probably would have been the same as yours.

VERONIQUE   Notice I didn't suggest it?

RINGWALD   (*On an impulse*) I'm going to get some money. (*Goes to the phone*) Bogardus 3150 . . . Miss Leonard, please. Mr. Ringwald calling . . . Oh, hello, Bessie . . . No, I never get to see you, either. You're too far uptown . . . Thanks . . . Mary, Townsend. Listen, if the movie offer is as good as you think, how are my chances of getting some money now? . . . Well, how about $200? . . . No, I don't want five. Two is all I want. I'm out of hock to Mario, and I'd like to pay some rent . . . Good, thanks. And send cash, not a cheque. Goodbye. (*Hangs up*) Very interesting. She said they've got Warner Brothers up to twenty thousand, and she thinks they'll go to twenty-five when they hear from the coast. Nothing happens for years, then everything happens all at once. She's sending me two hundred cash by messenger. I've never borrowed any money from her, meaning Keith Singleton.

VERONIQUE   Why are you doing it now?

RINGWALD   I haven't wanted to buy anything for anybody for a long time. I want to buy something for you.

VERONIQUE   (*Shakes her head*) No. That's almost the same as moving down two flights.

RINGWALD   Oh, but it isn't. I'm a month behind in the rent, so I'm going to pay that and get a month ahead.

There's sixty dollars. And even if I spent all the rest on a present for you—which I'm not going to do—it wouldn't be a sable coat.

VERONIQUE   I don't want a present, but if you want to buy me one I guess I can't stop you.

RINGWALD   I owe money at the delicatessen, around fifty dollars. I have five shirts at the Chinaman's that he won't give me till I pay him the fifteen dollars I owe him. You can see your present getting smaller and smaller.

VERONIQUE   Yes, but this time tomorrow you *will* be able to buy me a sable coat. This is all pretending, Townsend. You could buy me a sable coat today, because you're going to get that twenty-five thousand and you know it.

RINGWALD   That's just the point. I'm going to keep on pretending, and in some things I have a great knack for kidding myself. Do you know what Mary Leonard said?

VERONIQUE   No.

RINGWALD   She wanted me to take five hundred dollars and pay up and move out of here today. She thinks the smell of money has got me. She just won't learn.

VERONIQUE   Where are you going with all those clean shirts?

RINGWALD   Well, not to the opera. Do you realize that I don't even own a suit of clothes? These slacks and a jacket. When I had my shoes repaired I had to walk over to Sixth Avenue and back in my bedroom slippers, the only other shoes I had.

VERONIQUE   Townsend?

RINGWALD   What?

VERONIQUE   Why don't you give Mary Leonard the twenty-five thousand dollars?

RINGWALD   (*Looks at her carefully*)   I don't have to ask you if you're serious. You are.

VERONIQUE   She'd accept it, wouldn't she?

RINGWALD   Oh, I think she would. Yes.

VERONIQUE   Then why don't you give it to her? When the messenger arrives, take the two hundred dollars, but tomorrow give her the rest. Do you want to give me a present, Townsend? That's the best present you could give me.

RINGWALD   (*Half humorously*)   You sure you wouldn't rather have a set of sables?

VERONIQUE   It's also the best present you could give yourself. Pay her off, Townsend! Get rid of her! Get rid of all the things she says to you.

RINGWALD   You think it's as easy as that, do you?

VERONIQUE   It isn't easy, giving away twenty-five thousand dollars when it's all you have.

RINGWALD   Five years ago it wouldn't have been easy, but it is now. I've had five lean years and I'm used to it. And I'm not going to bribe Mary Leonard or my conscience with twenty-five thousand dollars that at this very moment doesn't exist. Oh, no, my dear. It isn't that easy. (*He goes to the table*) Today that money is in the Warner Brothers' bank account, in Los Angeles. Tomorrow it will be mine, even if I don't want it. I'll give it to *you*. But I won't give it to Mary.

VERONIQUE   All right. I'll take it.

RINGWALD   You really will?

VERONIQUE   You're damn right I will. (*Goes to phone*) Chickering 8191 . . . Hello, this is Veronique McCullough. Let me speak to Harry, please . . . Harry? This is Veronique. That job at 780 Seventh Avenue tomorrow? You're going to have to get another girl . . . I said, you're going to have to get another girl. (*She hangs up*) See what you did for me, Townsend?

(*He looks at her, puzzled, baffled, incredulous, and unwilling to yield to his chagrin*)

RINGWALD   The question is, what did I do for you?

CURTAIN, NOT TOO SLOWLY

SCENE THREE

Same as before, a week later. Townsend Ringwald is at his typewriter, in white shirt, same slacks and bedroom slippers as before. At rise he is taking a drag on a cigarette and examining the paper in the typewriter, going over what he has written. There is a knock on the door.

RINGWALD (*Slightly annoyed*)   Come in.
  (VERONIQUE *enters, wearing a fur coat*)

VERONIQUE   Well—how do you like it? (*She models the coat*)

RINGWALD   It's a nice coat. Is it sable?

VERONIQUE   Lord, no. It's mink. I didn't spend it all on a fur coat.

RINGWALD   Well, it's very snappy. I suppose you managed to get it wholesale?

VERONIQUE   Is that supposed to be a razz?

RINGWALD   You have friends on Seventh Avenue.

VERONIQUE   I have friends on Park, too, that would give it to me for free.

RINGWALD   Not quite free, of course. Well, would you like to sit down for a minute? Better take your new coat off first. (*She carefully takes off the coat and sits down*) Would you like a drink?

VERONIQUE   I'll have a gin and bitters.

RINGWALD   You're damn right you will, if you want a drink. (*He fixes a gin and bitters*) Here. When are you moving?

VERONIQUE   Who said I was moving?

RINGWALD   Wilmer.

VERONIQUE   I didn't say anything to Wilmer about moving.

RINGWALD   You didn't have to. He has a sick sense, sixth sense—my that's hard to say—sixth, sense about those things.

VERONIQUE   Well, his sick sense, sixth sense—it *is* hard to say—is wrong.

RINGWALD   You wouldn't give six cents for his sixth sense? You wouldn't give six cents for his sick sixth sense? Don't mind me, I'm a bit tired. What else have you been doing, besides deceiving Wilmer and buying fur coats?

VERONIQUE   Well, I've been looking at apartments in the Murray Hill section. I found two I quite liked.

RINGWALD   Then Wilmer was right.

VERONIQUE   Half right. I didn't take either one. (*She looks at* RINGWALD's *manuscript*) Page 411. You're working. The last time I looked you were in the three hundreds. Page 390, somewhere around there. How is it going?

RINGWALD   It's going very well. I didn't go out of the house all day yesterday or today. I had sour milk in my breakfast coffee.

VERONIQUE   Keep it on the window sill, it won't get sour so quickly.

RINGWALD   After two days it gets sour.

VERONIQUE   How long does it take *you?*

RINGWALD   Oh, I can turn sour over night.

VERONIQUE   So I noticed. What if I just took off my dress and lay down for a little while. Would you keep me company?

RINGWALD   I never refuse a lady. And of course I couldn't refuse you anything. I've certainly proved that.

VERONIQUE   Oh, I sent for my younger sister. She's never been to New York.

RINGWALD   It's the land of opportunity, I keep hearing. What does she specialize in?

VERONIQUE   As far as I know she's a virgin.

RINGWALD   Actually I didn't mean it that way, but thanks for the information. She pretty?

VERONIQUE   Petite. Much younger than I am. She's seventeen. She takes after my mother. I'm more like my father in looks.

RINGWALD   It's totally impossible for me to think of any man looking like you.

VERONIQUE   Let's lie down a while and make love, Townsend?

RINGWALD   No thanks.

VERONIQUE   Are you getting to like Wilmer?

RINGWALD   Well, I think he's getting to like me. He's been dropping in. I think he must have noticed that you *haven't* been dropping in. Or maybe it's his sick sixth sense.

VERONIQUE   Don't try to say that in front of Wilmer, or he may take it as a hint.

RINGWALD   That I was a piece of trade?

VERONIQUE   Yeth.

RINGWALD   (*As* WILMER *enters*) Why there he is now. Hello, Wilmer.

WILMER   Hello, kids. You dishing about me?

RINGWALD   We were.

WILMER   I thought you and this one were on the outs.

VERONIQUE   Wilmer, have you got a sixth sense?

WILMER   Have I got a what?

VERONIQUE   A sixth sense.

WILMER   Oh, what a camp! Have I got six cents? What are you doing, you big Canuck, camping in Italian? Youa gotta sixtha thents? Translate for me, Townsend?

RINGWALD   I can't.

WILMER (*Seeing coat*)   Oh, get her! Where did you ever get this gorgeous mackinaw, Veronique? What did you have to do for that?

VERONIQUE   Nothing.

WILMER   You mean just sit there? With an old man? Do you mind if I try it on?

VERONIQUE   It'll be big for you in the bust.

WILMER (*Trying on coat*)   I know, but ooh, it feels so— mm—how do I look? Can I wear it some time? I promise to take terribly good care of it. You know, I could win a prize with this. I have just the dress to wear with it, and I'd do my hair— No, I have a wig I paid forty dollars for would be just perfect with this. Come on, Veronique, tell us the history behind it. Every sordid detail. Who, where, what, and how many times.

VERONIQUE   If I told you the truth you wouldn't believe me.

WILMER   Well at least tell me was it a man or a woman?

VERONIQUE (*Looking at* RINGWALD)   Well, a man, but a woman was involved in it.

WILMER (*Knowingly, nodding*)   Oh, yes. Uh-huh. That old stunt. Do you know who it was, Townsend?

RINGWALD   Uh-huh.

WILMER   It wasn't that ex-wife of yours, was it? Not that

you'd tell me anyway. Townsend? Are you keeping a secret from me?

RINGWALD   Yep. Lots of them, Wilmer.

WILMER   Yeah. I'm not fooled, you know. The word gets around, you be surprised how quick it gets around. Honestly, inside of twenty-four hours every bitch in New York City knew Earl scratched me last week. Every bitch in town. They were flocking in, the joint where I work, just to get a good look. But I got that makeup you told me, Veronique. It's a wonderful thing to know about. Thanks a lot, really. You couldn't hardly tell my face was marred. Is that gin and bitters? I can smell it is. Can I have some, Townsend?

RINGWALD   Help yourself. Where's Earl?

WILMER   Oh, piss on Earl. He's off with some old queen, they're decorating a huge mansion on Long Island. You know how long that'll last. But do you know what he's getting, for four weeks' work? Six hundred dollars. Six hundred simoleans. I could garnishee that, you know. He owes me more than that. Oh, was he ever cross when he saw me in my new Saks Fifth Avenue. Livid! And of course my things won't fit him, at least my suits. Nasty thieving little bitch. Thanks for the slug, Townsend . . . Oh, say, you button your lip to me, but have I got something for you! Is Keith Singleton still your agent?

RINGWALD   Yes.

WILMER   Did you ever know about him?

RINGWALD   No.

WILMER   I didn't either. Neither did I. I thought I could tell one—across Grand Central station. But I never heard a whisper about Keith Singleton. Then lo and behold, he shows up at a friend of mine's party with— this is rocking the town—Eric Battersby. You know, Eric Battersby, the young English playwright? Eric

Battersby and Keith Singleton, the biggest, hottest thing in town. Keith won't let him out of his sight, flew into a *rage* when Eric danced with somebody else, slapped the other boy right in the face and made the most awful scene. Where have I been, not knowing about Keith Singleton? I must be slipping. Eric of course I've known for years, been on many parties with him and adore him, as who doesn't? But this overgrown schoolboy, Keith Singleton. Bulldog, bulldog, bow-wow-wow, Eli Yale. Swipes Eric right from under everybody's nose. Isn't Keith getting on a bit? He's surely fifty.

RINGWALD   He's more than fifty.

WILMER   He was so mean to Morgan Hanscom that time. You remember, Townsend? You were mixed up in that. Of course Morgie was a bitch, too. He hadn't oughta write that note, but he was desperate. She (*Meaning* VERONIQUE) don't know what the hell we're talking about.

RINGWALD   Yes she does.

WILMER   (*Eyeing them shrewdly*)   She does? You two got to the tell-all stage? I'd give a lot to listen in on that. You two.

RINGWALD   Why? There's nothing you don't seem to know.

WILMER   Oho-ho-ho-ho. What I know, and what two people tell one another, those are two entirely different things. You got one advantage, though, Townsend.

RINGWALD   What's that?

WILMER   No matter what you tell this one, you couldn't shock her. But I bet she's given you a couple jolts. That is, if you're both taking down your back hair. This is a terrible woman, Townsend.

VERONIQUE   Why am I so terrible? What did I ever do?

WILMER   What didn't you do is more like it.

VERONIQUE   Oh, sure, but what did I do that *you* think is terrible, Wilmer?

WILMER   That I think is terrible?

RINGWALD   Yes, what shocks you? Or offends your sense of the proprieties.

WILMER   You promise not to hit me?

RINGWALD   I won't hit you. Maybe Veronique will.

WILMER   (*Touching his scratches*)   No, I guess I won't.

VERONIQUE   Oh, go ahead. I won't hurt you.

WILMER   Listen, don't be so sure. This is something you think I don't know about. If she goes after me will you protect me, Townsend?

VERONIQUE   He won't have to.

WILMER   All right. . . . She's trying to break up Earl and I.

VERONIQUE   Oh, for God's sake.

WILMER   Oh, for God's sake? Did you give him a hundred dollars to sleep with you last—uh—Tuesday night? And where did you get a hundred dollars and a mink all of a sudden?

RINGWALD   You are an old bitch, Wilmer.

WILMER   Listen, anybody that tries to come between Earl and I, I'll come between them. She knows Earl is a little double-gaited, especially if there's a hundred dollars in it.

VERONIQUE   Do you think I'd give Earl a hundred dollars to sleep with me? Me? With all the people I know in this town?

WILMER   Yes I do, because you always hated me.

VERONIQUE   Granted, I have no use for you, Wilmer. But that's not why I gave Earl a hundred dollars.

WILMER   Make me believe that, just make me.

VERONIQUE   What's the use of trying?

WILMER   No use at all, but I'm going to get even with

you, Veronique. Ever since you moved here Earl's been horrible to me, perfectly horrible. And you're the cause of it. I know. Your type always tries to make trouble for boys like Earl. You always try to get them back to your ways, and then when they do go back, you ditch them. You're ruining Earl, that's what you're doing, and that's why I hate you. And you watch out, Veronique. I'm a bad hater.

VERONIQUE   Oh, go wash out your socks, you silly old woman.

WILMER (*To* RINGWALD)   This one won't bring you good luck, Townsend. Don't say I didn't warn you. (*He exits*)

VERONIQUE (*Anticipating* RINGWALD's *question*)   It's my money, isn't it? I can do what I like with it.

RINGWALD   Anything at all. But watch out for Wilmer.

VERONIQUE   Why? Will he ruin my reputation? Or are you worried about yours?

RINGWALD   My reputation isn't any better than yours. But if I were you, I'd lay off Earl.

VERONIQUE   You believe what Wilmer said?

RINGWALD   I don't know. I had you figured all wrong.

VERONIQUE   Yes. You didn't expect me to take that money.

RINGWALD   No, I guess I didn't.

VERONIQUE   Well, you can have it back. What's left of it.

RINGWALD   No, I don't want it back. So far it hasn't seemed to do you much good, and I've been working much better since I gave it to you. No, I don't want it back. And there are no strings to it.

VERONIQUE   No, but you're dying to know about the money I gave Earl.

RINGWALD   I admit that.

VERONIQUE   All right, I'll tell you.

RINGWALD   You don't have to.

VERONIQUE I know I don't have to, the money's all in my name. But I will. I gave Earl a hundred dollars, and he slept in my apartment. But we didn't go to bed together. Maybe Earl told Wilmer we did, but we didn't. Not that we *never* did. We did once, when I first moved here, but the kind of double-gaited that Earl is, it's not what *I* mean by double-gaited. Do you want me to tell you all about it?

RINGWALD (*Sensing that she will hate him if he gives an affirmative reply*) No. I can probably guess.

VERONIQUE It's a good thing you said no, Townsend, or I would have had *you* figured all wrong.

RINGWALD It was close between yes and no.

(VERONIQUE *smiles at that remark*)

VERONIQUE But no won-out. (*Author's note: this line has to be read so that it does not seem like "no one out"*) I gave him the money because he didn't want to have to arrive broke at his new job, the job he's doing on Long Island. He didn't want to have to ask for railroad fare and pocket money. Earl doesn't like girls. He likes me, but not girls. But he doesn't like Wilmer, either. Not any more. He wishes Wilmer would fall in love with someone else. (*She smiles*) He suggested you.

RINGWALD Did he make that suggestion to Wilmer?

VERONIQUE No. To me. But maybe he's planted the idea in Wilmer's little brain. He probably has.

RINGWALD He probably has. But I'm afraid it won't work.

VERONIQUE Why?

RINGWALD I still like girls better.

VERONIQUE Yes. I still like men better. I'd rather wake up with a man beside me. There's something sweet about waking up with a man—if you like him, that is. You had a good time and gave him a good time, and you're like two kids. You only get that with a man, at least I do. How I'll be ten years from now is another

story. 1938. By that time everybody'll be flying around
in aeroplanes, smashing into each other. And my mink
won't fit me, I'll be over thirty. My Daddy weighs fourteen stone, and I take after him.

(*He says nothing, he is only half listening to her, but
studying her, mystified, charmed by an elusive something, feeling tenderness as well. She catches him in
this study*)

VERONIQUE   What were you thinking?

RINGWALD   I wasn't thinking.

VERONIQUE (*Nods*)   I do that sometimes. Just look at a
person and enjoy them. I wish we could all do that more
often, instead of thinking how we can get the better of
somebody. That's what half of our thinking is, trying to
get the better of somebody in some way or other.

RINGWALD   I don't know about that.

VERONIQUE   That's what you do when you write, isn't it?
You're getting the better of your hero and heroine. Or
maybe you're only getting the better of yourself, but I'll
bet if you analyze it . . .

RINGWALD   Maybe. The struggle for existence. The sur-
vival of the fittest.

VERONIQUE   And writers especially. Writers just have to
think. Think, think, think, think. You never give your
minds a rest.

RINGWALD   I just did a moment ago.

VERONIQUE   Yes, but you had to think about not thinking.

RINGWALD   When do you rest *your* mind, Veronique?

VERONIQUE   Well, I can tell you when I don't. Not when
I listen to music. That's supposed to rest your mind, but
it doesn't mine. Or when I go to an art gallery.

RINGWALD   How about when you're making love?

VERONIQUE   Yes, if it's someone I like. It's nice to feel
that way and make him feel that way. I guess that rests

my mind. I have to think *some,* but the more I like a person the less I have to think.

RINGWALD   And how about when you drink?

VERONIQUE   Oh, God! I have ten thoughts at the same time when I drink. My mind is so busy, so active that it gets tired. That's why I can't drink as much as some people. I get tired and fall asleep from thinking. Just in the time it takes me to have three or four drinks I have every thought there ever was. I may not show it, but God, I'm thinking. And being near-sighted affects a person, don't forget. You have to guess sometimes what's going on, and you overhear little bits of conversation. My parents are glad I'm in New York.

RINGWALD   Why?

VERONIQUE   On account of my sister that's coming to visit me. At home I used to say to her don't spend so much time thinking, thinking, thinking. And they used to give me holy hell because she wasn't doing her home work.

RINGWALD   What does your father do?

VERONIQUE   He's a brakeman on the C. G. R. Canadian Government Railways.

RINGWALD   How could he afford to send you abroad when you were, what was it, fourteen?

VERONIQUE   Not on his pay. My mother does tapestries, she could make as much as he does. Maybe that's how I got my bad eyesight, from her straining her eyes. Maybe not, though. She learned it from my grandmother, and Grand'mère still doesn't wear glasses. I know how to do it but I never had the patience. . . . Did you ever kill a man?

RINGWALD   (*Nods slowly*)   Mm-hmm.

VERONIQUE   In the war?

RINGWALD   Mm-hmm.

VERONIQUE　You're wondering why I suddenly ask you that question?

RINGWALD　I know that there's some connection with what we've been talking about.

VERONIQUE　There is. That's supposed to be the worst thing you can do. Right?

RINGWALD　Well—all right. Yes.

VERONIQUE　That's when you're more animal than any other time.

RINGWALD　I suppose so.

VERONIQUE　I'm trying to think of the word.

RINGWALD　Atavistic.

VERONIQUE　No, I never knew that word. Basic, maybe.

RINGWALD　All right. Basic. When you're killing a man you're at your most basic.

VERONIQUE　Yes. My question is, what did you think at the time?

RINGWALD　I see. What did I think when I was at my most basic? (*He ponders*) Well, first of all, I killed more than one man. And I killed men on several occasions, under differing circumstances. The first time I ever killed anybody I killed three or four. I was firing a Lewis gun. A machine gun. There was another fellow and myself, Joe Cuccinelli. We were set up behind an overturned wagon. There were nine Germans, a corporal and eight privates, and their idea was to take a prisoner. Our idea was to keep them from taking a prisoner. My orders were to wait till they got close and then let them have it. And that's what I did. What was I thinking? Well, I think I was thinking how I'd hate to get shot in the nuts, and then I started to fire. You know the French word, *enfilade*. We pronounced it en-fill-aid. Spray fire. I missed the first German, got the next three, then swung back and I think I got one more. I remember feeling very good about it.

VERONIQUE   Were they all dead, the ones you shot?

RINGWALD   Well, if they weren't dead from my shooting
they soon were. Our fellows lobbed a few hand grenades
at them. Joe Cuccinelli and I moved to another position, quick. A minute later the Germans threw over
some mortar shells and blew that wagon to hell. What
I was thinking was that I hoped I'd always be that
lucky. And I was. You don't want to hear about the
other times I killed people. It was always the same. You
did your best to kill them. The circumstances were different, but the only difference in the thinking was in
wondering whether your luck wouldn't run out. That
was very important, because the machine gunners' cas-
ualty rate was higher than the average. For instance,
Cuccinelli was killed by a bullet that was surely meant
for me. He stopped feeding the belt, and there he was,
dead.

VERONIQUE   And what did you do?

RINGWALD   I picked up the gun and charged . . . The
hell I did. I hit the dirt and crawled away. That sniper
had the range, and he knew one of us was still alive. I
wasn't pressing my luck. An officer came back to see
why I wasn't firing, and the sniper got him. Lieutenant
Jones. He wasn't a bad fellow, so I went to help him
but there was nothing I could do for him except drag
him to cover. Which I did with a minimum of risk to
my own skin. And then it turned out I was dragging a
dead man. First Lieutenant Raymond L. Jones, from
Cornwall, New York. I went to see his mother after
the war. (*He pauses*) In Cornwall, just a few miles
upstate. You passed it on your way down from Montreal.

VERONIQUE   (*She is puzzled by these extra details*)   You
went to see his mother?

RINGWALD   (*Nods, and speaks rather slowly*)   Yes. In
1919. I went to see her. We had a few drinks together.
In fact, we both got plastered . . . Good and plastered.

I laid her. Right there in the living room. That was a hell of an experience. And I never told anyone that before, not even Mary Leonard.

VERONIQUE   Well, I guess you—I could see how that would happen.

RINGWALD   You don't like it, though. Neither do I. Obviously that's why I never told anybody before.

VERONIQUE   Well, truthfully, I don't. But I don't know why.

RINGWALD   I do. At least I think I do. I was going up there to pay a sentimental call on a little old lady. But she wasn't a little old lady, and that surprised me. I knew that as soon as I saw her. But even when she brought out a quart of whiskey I still kept saying to myself that this was Lieutenant Jones's mother. She had pictures of him all over the place. It was darn good whiskey, prewar.

VERONIQUE   Where was her husband, if she had one?

RINGWALD   He was at work. I never did see him. She drove me to the station, although she was in no condition to drive a car. She gave me some money, I forget how much, but a lot. I used to think about her and when her husband got home that afternoon and found her plastered. I was glad to get out of there. (*He looks at her*) I think you'll understand why I didn't like it. I hadn't been to church since I was about nineteen, the year I went to college. And all the way up to Cornwall I had the same feeling I'd occasionally get when I went to chapel. I was going to see a little old lady, a Gold Star Mother. And when I got there, instead of being in church with a little old lady, I was in a nice, middle-class front parlor with a pushover.

VERONIQUE   You make me sick.

RINGWALD   (*Surprised*)   Why?

VERONIQUE   You just do. I thought writers were supposed

to have understanding. Well, I hope you never try to write about a woman character. If you couldn't understand that poor woman you wouldn't understand anybody.

RINGWALD (*Fighting back*)   I understood her all right.

VERONIQUE   Did she ever try to get in touch with you again?

RINGWALD   No.

VERONIQUE   No, I'll bet she didn't. Her son's friend comes to see her, and she's touched. What can she do? She knows he's just out of the army, so she gives him a drink. Lots of drinks. She's what? Forty-five? Husband probably older than that. And the two of them have been grieving over their son. Nice young man comes to see her and she's so grateful that she's what you say, a pushover. But you never thought to ask yourself why she was a pushover. You make me sick, you men. You often used to wonder what happened when her husband came home. Did you ever stop to think of the other days too? Years of being ashamed of herself? Why, every time she'd look at those pictures of her son she must have felt ashamed of herself. God, you're horrible. And so pious. She spoiled it for you because she wasn't a little old lady. What did you do for her? And even now, all you can think of to call her is a pushover.

RINGWALD   I see you can always be depended upon to take the woman's side.

VERONIQUE (*Steadily*)   . . . Well, I don't hate women, the way you do.

RINGWALD   No.

VERONIQUE   Have you got a copy of your play? Not this one (*Indicating the manuscript on table*), the one that was a hit.

RINGWALD   *Perihelion?* Yes. Why?

VERONIQUE I'm going to have to read it.

RINGWALD I don't see why, but go ahead. Over there's a half a dozen copies, help yourself.

VERONIQUE Maybe after I read it I'll want to give you back your money.

RINGWALD Oh, now really, Veronique. You've taken money from people you didn't like.

VERONIQUE Sure I have, but I've never taken money from anybody I like till I took this money from you.

RINGWALD Aren't you a little confused? You're talking in circles. You don't take money from people you like, but you liked me when you took this twenty-two thousand three hundred dollars. Now you're going to read my play and dislike me, and therefore return the money.

VERONIQUE I'm not confused at all. It was a new experience to like the person that gave me so much money, and a nice experience. If I'm going to dislike you, I don't want to enjoy anything about you. You know, I've still got about eighteen thousand dollars in the bank. I could give that to Mary Leonard. And she'd take it, too.

RINGWALD In a flash. Before you could change your mind.

VERONIQUE Maybe I'll give it to her anyway. I wanted you to give it to her so you could get rid of her. Maybe I'll give it to her so I can get rid of you.

RINGWALD Keep the coat, though.

VERONIQUE Oh, I'll keep the coat. It's money I don't like. Oh—an afterthought. I'm going to keep some of the money for when my sister gets here.

RINGWALD Don't tell *me*. I didn't ask you for an accounting. It's Mary's money now.

VERONIQUE (*Holding up the play volume*) Not yet. I'm going to read this, and then maybe I'll read one of those plays that closed in Atlantic City.

RINGWALD   That was an exaggeration of Mary's. They never even got to Atlantic City.

VERONIQUE   (*Devilishly*)   I did.

QUICK CURTAIN

ACT TWO

SCENE ONE

Two flights up, VERONIQUE'S *apartment. A week or so later. It is inexpensively furnished, but with imagination and in the prevailing* moderne *mood. There are unframed pictures on the walls, the inevitable folding screen of varnished* New Yorker *covers, tubular chairs, strange dolls, masks, statuettes after Jacob Epstein, etc. In contrast with Ringwald's apartment, however, the atmosphere is neat, orderly. It is a one-room flat with studio couch against the wall at Left. Entrance is by a door cut through the wall at Right. The same stove and sink arrangement, behind the folding screen, as in* RINGWALD'S *apartment. The telephone is on a night table beside the studio couch. The bathroom is through a door in the wall at Right. The windows are half covered by full length, ceiling to floor, strips of bright colored material.*

It is late afternoon, early evening, and VERONIQUE *and her sister* JEAN *are getting ready to receive guests for cocktails.* JEAN *is "petite," not so much in stature as in a kind of frailty and daintiness that the word suggests, and which contrast with* VERONIQUE'S *tall, independent, self-sufficiency. It is not too much to say that* JEAN *is more French than her Scotch-Irish sister.*

JEAN (*In French. She is washing cocktail glasses*)   Where do you keep your tea-towels?

VERONIQUE (*In French*)   You'll find a dry one in the drawer under the gas burner.

JEAN (*Still in French*)   Here?

VERONIQUE (*In French*)   Yes. (*In English*) And by the way, only one of the people coming this afternoon speaks French. His name is Townsend Ringwald.

JEAN   Townsend Ringwall?

VERONIQUE   Yes, he's a writer. A playwright. He lives downstairs, in the basement.

JEAN   Is he a Canadian?

VERONIQUE   No. To tell you the truth I don't know where he's from. One of the western states, I guess, but I never asked him.

JEAN   Is he your lover?

VERONIQUE (*Lightly*)   Of course.

JEAN   Seriously?

VERONIQUE   Why must I have a lover?

JEAN (*Looking about the flat*)   This is a place where you would have a lover. It reminds me of Paris.

VERONIQUE   How could it remind you of Paris? You don't remember anything about Paris, you were too young. And our uncle didn't live in a place like this.

JEAN   That's just why I say, this is a place to have a lover. And you have lovers, Nique.

VERONIQUE   In two years you've learned a lot.

JEAN   Did you expect me not to?

VERONIQUE   Well—I guess I did, but it doesn't make sense. You *are* two years older. And so am I. And so is everybody. Have you got a lover?

JEAN   Not a real one. A boy at Loyola. A sophomore. Henri Duplessis? You remember him?

QUE Good Lord. He's in college? We are two
older, aren't we? Are you going to marry him?

Two years from now, when he takes his degree.

IE Will you have me for maid of honor?

course. Need you ask?

Well, I wasn't told.

old is Townsend Ringwall?

Older. Thirty-five, maybe.

JEAN Who else is coming?

VERONIQUE Just two others.

JEAN (*Quickly*) Men?

VERONIQUE (*Amused at her speed*) Yes. One is even
older than Ringwald. His name is Wilmer. Wilmer
Hightower. The other is Earl. Earl Fisher. He's about
my age. They also live in this house.

JEAN Are you the only girl that lives in this house?

VERONIQUE No. There are, one, two, three, four. Four
other girls. Or women. Two of them live on the top
story, across the hall from Wilmer and Earl. And the
others live on this story. But I haven't made friends with
either of them. You know, I've only been here about six
months.

JEAN But you've made friends with the men.

VERONIQUE You could put it another way. They've made
friends with me.

JEAN I beg your pardon.

VERONIQUE Granted.

JEAN Could I get a job on the stage, Nique?

VERONIQUE The first thing they'll ask you is what experience you've had.

JEAN What did *you* tell them?

VERONIQUE It was different with me. I didn't have to act,
or sing and dance.

JEAN   Oh, I know what you did. I saw your picture.

VERONIQUE   Where?

JEAN   In a magazine. *That* magazine. (*Pointing*) *Vanity Fair*. Could I do that?

VERONIQUE   I think you'd have to be taller. Did Papa and Mama see those pictures?

JEAN   No. They never heard of that magazine.

VERONIQUE   Not many have, in Montreal. Where did you see it?

JEAN   I saw it at one of the fraternity houses. At McGill.

VERONIQUE   Henri goes to Loyola.

JEAN   (*Petulantly*)   I know he does.

VERONIQUE   Oh.

JEAN   Well, why not? The McGill boys are more fun. Could you introduce me to the people that hired you?

VERONIQUE   It would be a waste of time now. All the girls are hired for the new shows. But next summer I could, when they're hiring show girls. That's what I was, a show girl. You don't wear much in the way of clothes.

JEAN   I saw your pictures.

VERONIQUE   Yes, and what if Henri and Mr. and Mrs. Duplessis saw *your* picture?

JEAN   (*Shrugs her shoulders*)   Maybe I wouldn't care. How tall do you have to be? I could wear higher heels.

VERONIQUE   Dearie, you're hardly unpacked and we've got these people coming. Don't try to do everything at once. Wait till you're here a few days. You may not like New York.

JEAN   (*Dramatically*)   I love it! All those mad people in the streets, hurrying somewhere. Those big beautiful limousines, coming down Fifth Avenue. And the buses. I want to ride on top of one of those buses. And that place you took me to lunch. That hotel. They all spoke French there. Better French than we speak.

VERONIQUE   The Brevoort. Tomorrow I'll take you to another place just like it, in the next street. The Lafayette. But that was a special treat, Jean. I don't go there every day.

JEAN   If I could go there once a year! Nique, I never want to go home. Two men flirted with me at lunch.

VERONIQUE   I saw them. You've had men flirt with you in Montreal.

JEAN   That's different. Here they meant it.

VERONIQUE   What did they mean?

JEAN   I don't have to tell you. You know what they meant.

VERONIQUE   They do in Montreal, too.

JEAN   (*Shakes her head*)   No. It isn't the same. These men were *bad*. At home, they're just flirty-flirty. But those men today—I was glad I was with *you*. I'd have been frightened, alone.

VERONIQUE   And you like being frightened?

JEAN   Yes. That is, I like to go to a first-class restaurant, where you'd never expect to be frightened. And know that two men are saying very wicked things about you. In Montreal—that's *home*. Am I tall enough to be a model?

VERONIQUE   Yes.

JEAN   I could start as a model, then next summer get a job on the stage.

VERONIQUE   All in good time.

JEAN   You sound like Grandmere.

VERONIQUE   That's good, because I meant to. Have you ever had a Martini cocktail?

JEAN   No.

VERONIQUE   Then only take one, and don't drink it too fast. Or would you rather have a glass of wine?

JEAN   I'll have what the others are having.

VERONIQUE   All right, but mind you. One. And drink it

slowly. This tube is anchovy paste, you can squeeze some on the biscuits. That's all they'll want.

(*There is a knock on the door. It is* WILMER)

WILMER   Hello, hello.

VERONIQUE   Hello, Wilmer. I wasn't sure you'd come.

WILMER   Oh, curiosity. I had to see what your sister was like. I'm Wilmer.

VERONIQUE   Jean, this is Mr. Wilmer Hightower.

WILMER   Just Wilmer, to my near and dear ones.

JEAN   I'm pleased to meet you.

WILMER   Oh, she's cute. She's the way you must have been, ages ago, Veronique. You're pretty, Jean. Are you in show business?

JEAN   Not yet.

WILMER   Well, you shouldn't have too much trouble— one way or another. Would you like to be like your big sister?

JEAN   Yes, very much.

WILMER   (*Clears his throat*)   Mm. Well, that shouldn't be too hard. In fact, very *easy*, if you know what I mean.

VERONIQUE   All right, Wilmer. All right. Where is Earl?

WILMER   Earl is my friend. Veronique is terribly interested in Earl. Why, he's coming. He's prettying up.

JEAN (*Mystified*)   What?

WILMER   He'll dazzle you with his coloring, Jean.

VERONIQUE (*Who has been stirring cocktails*)   Here. Let her find out for herself.

WILMER   But at the same time, he's very expensive. Isn't he, Veronique?

VERONIQUE   You ought to know.

WILMER   Oh. This is a good cocktail, Veronique. You can hardly taste anything but Mother's Downfall.

VERONIQUE   He means gin.

WILMER *(To Jean)* Aren't you having one, dear?

JEAN I guess so.

VERONIQUE Do you want yours now?

JEAN Yes.

WILMER Oh. Sister is protective, isn't she, Jean?

JEAN *(Taking cocktail)* Yes.

WILMER Well, welcome to the great big wicked city.

JEAN Thank you.

WILMER *(Knocks off his drink and extends empty glass)* As they say, my first today and God knows I need it. I won a prize last night—and without your coat.

VERONIQUE You could have had my coat.

JEAN Why would he need your coat?

WILMER I want to hear you explain that, Veronique.

VERONIQUE I know you do. You've been leading up to it. Wilmer is a fairy. Do you know what a fairy is?

JEAN Of course. But I thought they got mad if you called them one.

VERONIQUE Not Wilmer.

WILMER You weren't very subtle.

VERONIQUE Neither were you, so why should I be?

WILMER I thought you'd be more delicate in front of the kid sister from Montreal.

VERONIQUE You thought you had me on a spot, that's what you really thought.

WILMER And Jean's embarrassed, aren't you, Jean?

JEAN I don't know.

WILMER See? Jean's the one that's put on the spot, and you put her there. You shoulda been more delicate.

JEAN Oh, stop talking about me, please. *(She gulps her drink)*

VERONIQUE You're going to have to get used to a lot of things if you want to live in New York.

WILMER   Oh, good. Are you going to live in New York?

JEAN   I don't know.

VERONIQUE   You were sure a few minutes ago. You changing your mind already?

JEAN   I didn't say for sure I wanted to live here.

WILMER   Listen, Jean. This is *the* place. The rest of the country is Bridgeport.

JEAN   I don't come from this country.

WILMER   Well—Canada's practically. I did one-nighters in Canada. Toronto—that's Canada, isn't it? Hamilton. Niagara Falls. I was working for somebody named Jean, too. Jean Goldkette. I played piano with Jean.

JEAN   Is that what you do?

WILMER   Oh, not any more. I still play piano, but no more bands, thank you. No—thank—you. What a life *that* is. I get offers all the time, but who wants to live in a bus all their life? Not yours truly.

JEAN   Why do you have to live in a bus?

WILMER   Why do you have to live in a bus? Because you finish playing a job in Mahoney City, PA, at one o'clock in the morning and then you have to get in the bus and drive to Hagerstown, Maryland, a couple hundred miles away. And the night after that you're back somewhere near Mahoney City. What booking! It's absolutely ruinous to the disposition. And the money isn't good. Don't let anybody tell you the money's good. Listen, some weeks I make more from tips than my week's salary with a band. The other night I had a Cuban millionaire give me a hundred bucks just to play "A Media Luz." You know, that tango? Diddle-umpta dumpta dum. We got a regular comes to the joint twice or three times a week, and as soon as I see him I go into "On, Wisconsin." Good for five bucks every time. You can have playing with a band.

VERONIQUE   And at your age, too.

WILMER Never mind about my age, Veronique. Just give me another drink, please, and shut up about my age. I heard a good one. A boy that would tell his age would tell anything. What's keeping Earl? I didn't say who. I said what.

(*A knock on the door; it is* RINGWALD)

WILMER Oh, I thought you'd be Earl.

RINGWALD Ah, too bad, Wilmer.

VERONIQUE Hello, Townsend. I'd like you to meet my sister, Jean. Jean, this is Townsend Ringwald.

JEAN I'm pleased to meet you.

WILMER She's cute, isn't she?

RINGWALD I don't need your help, Wilmer. How do you do, Miss McCullough.

WILMER Everybody's picking on me. (*He sits down, away from the others*)

RINGWALD How was your trip?

JEAN On the train? I didn't see much. I came down on the sleeper.

WILMER Keep your eyes open next time, you'll see plenty.

RINGWALD Pay no attention to Wilmer.

JEAN (*With a smile*) How can you help it?

WILMER Now she's razzing me. I'll turn on you, Jean, and you'll be sorry.

RINGWALD Shut up, Wilmer. Has Veronique been showing you the town?

WILMER It's still daylight.

RINGWALD Oh, shut *up*, Wilmer.

WILMER Not going to be much of a party if I don't talk.

RINGWALD Well, let's give it a try.

WILMER And you don't have to be formal with Jean. Her big sister started out by telling her I was a fairy. So the ice is broken.

RINGWALD Maybe Jean would have figured that out for

herself. And anyway, you're not going to sue for damages, are you? (*To* JEAN) I take it you knew what a fairy was.

JEAN   Yes, but I was surprised when Nique came right out with it.

WILMER   Heavens, you weren't surprised that *she* knew? *That* one!

JEAN   If I knew, why shouldn't she know? She's older and more experienced.

WILMER   Oh, God, what an opening.

VERONIQUE   Well, we're all waiting.

WILMER   Yeah, that's the trouble with an opening like that. I pass.

RINGWALD   Good. Well, even if the ice *is* broken, Jean, it's all right if I ask you some plain ordinary questions.

JEAN   I wish you would. I'm not used to this kind of conversation.

WILMER   I'm squelched.

JEAN   I don't want to squelch anybody, I just don't want to have to think twice before I talk. Is that the way everybody talks in New York?

RINGWALD   Lord, no. But in this part of town there's quite a bit of it. At least when there's a Wilmer around. And the more Wilmers, the more of that kind of conversation goes on. Luckily they all talk at once, so you don't have to listen very carefully. In fact, you can't. Are you going to see any plays while you're here?

WILMER   (*Groaning*)   Oh, God. Ask her what she thinks of our skyscrapers.

JEAN   I haven't seen any very big ones.

RINGWALD   If you're not doing anything tomorrow I'll take you downtown. That's where the big ones are. Downtown.

WILMER   You better get in there, Veronique. He's moving fast.

VERONIQUE   Tomorrow we're going shopping, but any other day.

WILMER   While you're up, pour me another drinkie.

JEAN   They don't seem to affect *him*.

VERONIQUE   They will.

RINGWALD   And watch out for him when he bares his fangs. He's merciless.

WILMER   Maybe you don't think so, but don't you try my patience, Townsend Ringwald. I have a few saved up for you. Oh, there we are. (*As* EARL *enters*) And aren't we ravishing?

EARL   I'm sorry I'm late, Veronique. I just got in from Long Island, and I was all over paint and plaster.

VERONIQUE   My sister, Jean. This is Earl Fisher.

JEAN   I'm pleased to meet you.

EARL   How do you do, I'm sure. Hello, Town.

RINGWALD   Hello, Earl.

VERONIQUE   How's your job going, Earl?

EARL   (*Looks hesitatingly at* WILMER) Well—this was my last day.

WILMER   Your last *day?* What do you mean, your last day? You have three weeks to go.

EARL   He fired me.

WILMER   You didn't tell me that upstairs. Why are you breaking this terrible news in front of these strangers?

EARL   Oh, Wilmer, shut up.

WILMER   I suppose you told him what he was doing was puke.

EARL   Well, it was. He ought to be ashamed to take the money.

WILMER   And since when are you so rich that you can

pass up six hundred dollars—unless our hostess has had a hand in this. Hand in it indeed.

RINGWALD   All right, Wilmer. Enough of that.

WILMER   *You!* Where do *you* come in? Don't you start acting gallant. Who do you think you're kidding? Well, *her* (*He means* JEAN) but she'll find out quick enough.

RINGWALD   (*To* VERONIQUE)   Shall I throw him out?

VERONIQUE   Yes.

WILMER   Don't you touch me. I'll go of my own accord. (*To* EARL) And as for you, you'll find your things out in the hall. Start sponging off someone else for a change.

EARL   All right.

WILMER   All your things will be out in the hall. Don't even knock on the door. (*To* JEAN) Good afternoon to you, Miss McCullough. It's been a great pleasure, I'm sure. Just as much for me as it was for you. (*To all of them*) Huh. Cozy little group. I wonder who gets who.

(RINGWALD *starts to rise, and* WILMER *dashes to the door*)

WILMER   Don't you dare! Don't you dare! (*He exits*)

VERONIQUE   *Did* you lose your job, Earl?

EARL   I wouldn't kid about that. I had four hundred and fifty coming. He guaranteed me four weeks' work. But I just couldn't keep quiet. Really. You should *see* what he's doing with a lovely big room. He's making it into another Roxy. I wanted to scream and I finally did.

VERONIQUE   Earl's been working for a decorator, on Long Island.

EARL   Decorator. Townsend's little pigsty has more charm than— Oh, I give up.

RINGWALD   Did he pay you?

EARL   He sure did, honey. He got me out of there before I could say anything to the owner. Gave me a hundred and fifty. The awful part is, he knew I was right. He couldn't get really angry with me, and I don't mean for personal reasons. He was such a coward. He said when I was leaving, he said he was only doing what the owner wanted. Good heavens! Such a coward. Jean, don't you ever get into interior decorating.

JEAN   I won't. I don't know the first thing about it.

EARL   That doesn't stop some people. Town, I saw a friend of yours last night.

RINGWALD   Who?

EARL   Keith Singleton. He was at a party where I was. I danced—(*He checks himself, suddenly remembering* JEAN) with a friend of his.

VERONIQUE (*Gratefully*)   Earl, you haven't got a drink.

EARL   Oh, I don't even know if I want one. Just a little one. Liquor's going to be my downfall. I reveled in it last night at the party and didn't get home till practically dawn. You know how those parties are. They don't get started till very late, because the boys that are in shows all have to go home and change. (*To* JEAN) A sort of a costume party. Wilmer went as Jeanne Eagels, and I must give him credit, he deserved his prize. Then I finally got home and got about two hours' sleep before I had to drag my poor weary bones up to Penn Station and take the train to Long Island, feeling like the wrath of God. And of course this would be the day my employer picked to positively desecrate the big room. So I—I just let go. I don't know what I'm going to do next. Have this drink, I guess.
(JEAN *has been watching the others to get their reaction, but they are used to him*)

VERONIQUE   You'll find something to do.

EARL   Oh, I know. But I wish I didn't always have to work for someone else. I ought to have my own business, with my own studio. But it takes money, and I can't seem to get hold of any. Did you ever hear of an old witch named Mrs. J. Francis Krag? Filthy rich.

RINGWALD You ought to know about J. Francis Krag. He's a famous architect.

EARL He's alive?

RINGWALD He's pretty well along, but I think he's still alive.

EARL Oh. I met this new friend last night. Mrs. Krag is helping him financially, and I got to wishing I'd meet somebody like that that would help me financially.

RINGWALD Does it have to be an old witch? Why not a young witch?

EARL Listen, I'm not going to look at her teeth to see how old she is, as long as she has enough to help me financially.

JEAN Why does it have to be a woman? Why not a man?

EARL (*Looks at her quizzically*) Well, there's that, too. There's always that, Jean. Say, how much does this kid know? I been putting on an act for her, watching my language and all, but do I have to? (*Shakes his finger at* JEAN) I think you're a sly one. I think you know more than you let on.

RINGWALD Maybe she learns fast, Earl.

EARL That may be it. Anyway, she's a cute one. Are you going to get a job in New York, Jean?

JEAN Some day, I hope.

EARL (*Appraisingly*) What is she, about a twelve? Veronique, you could teach her to walk. In fact, *I* could. Stand up, Jean. Oh, no. No, no, no. Never that way. You're not defending the bridge at that Greek place.

RINGWALD Thermopylae?

EARL (*Ignores him*) You know, Jean. You're not daring people to charge. Don't stand with your legs dug in that way. Stand this way. One thigh crossed over the other so that you don't show a big gap at the crotch. You know, if you stand with your heels together. You're

modeling lon-jer-ray. If you stand with your heels together, well you make this gap right here, because being
a girl you aint got nothing there. One foot in front of
the other, one thigh crossing over, just enough to hide
that gap. Now you try it. If you could take off your
skirt I could show you better.

(JEAN, *hypnotized, starts to obey him, then looks at
the others*)

VERONIQUE   He's right. Go ahead.

JEAN   Yes, but what about—Mr. Ringwald?

EARL   Oh, honey, give him a cheap thrill. You're among
friends.

(JEAN *shrugs her shoulders and quickly gets out of her
skirt obediently and hands it to* EARL)

EARL   Oh, she won't have any trouble, Veronique. She
could get some hosiery work. Now stand the way I told
you. There, that's better. Shoulders back. You don't
have to be brazen, Jean. Just confident. Now walk
towards your sister. No, no, no, no. Don't shake it. It
shakes itself, honey. Show her, Veronique.

(VERONIQUE *demonstrates a show-girl walk*)

EARL   (*To* JEAN)   I hope you realize, Jean. Your sister is
being very big-hearted. (*To* VERONIQUE)   If this kid
was two inches taller she'd put you out of business.

VERONIQUE   I'm out of business.

EARL   (*Handing* JEAN *her skirt*)   All right, honey. You're
doing fine. Practice it, and inside of a week—

(*The door opens; it is* WILMER *with a suitcase*)

WILMER   Here's your junk, every last thing you own.

(*He sees* JEAN, *skirt in hand. He throws the suitcase
at* EARL, *then makes a rush at* VERONIQUE)

WILMER   I'll kill you, you bitch.

(RINGWALD *wards off* WILMER's *attack and receives some
slaps and kicks, but he is stronger than* WILMER *and
braces his arms.* EARL *goes to* JEAN, *to protect her from
possible attack by* WILMER)

WILMER Whores! Pimps! Dirty little whores. You pimp, you. I'll kill all of you!

RINGWALD (*Holding and pushing him*) Out, Wilmer. Out. (*Propels* WILMER *to the door, pushes him out and shoots the bolt*)

WILMER'S VOICE (*Offstage—banging on door*) I'm going to call the police! I'm going to call the Vice Squad.

RINGWALD Ah, shut up, you God damn fagot.
(*There is silence,* WILMER *presumably going away, and the silence is heavy, each person with his own thoughts. Then* VERONIQUE *notices* EARL *in a protective attitude toward* JEAN, *an arm around her.* RINGWALD, *with his back to the door, is looking at* VERONIQUE *and studying her reaction*)

VERONIQUE You better put your skirt on, Jean.
(EARL *sighs audibly. He is unaware of any significance in his instinctive defense of* JEAN. JEAN *is frightened by the outburst, is busy putting on her skirt*)

VERONIQUE Is he still out there?

RINGWALD (*Listens at door*) I don't know.

EARL No, I'm sure he isn't. He's probably half way to Mario's by now. I think I'll have a cigarette.

RINGWALD (*Opens door cautiously and closes it*) He's gone.

EARL Anybody else want a cigarette? Jean?

JEAN I guess so, yes, thanks. (EARL *lights it for her*) It was all my fault. I'm sorry.

VERONIQUE It wasn't anybody's fault.

RINGWALD Wilmer's.

VERONIQUE Oh, not even his. He can't help himself.

EARL Maybe, but after this I'll never go back. I'll never go back again.

RINGWALD (*To* VERONIQUE) Don't be so damn forgiving.

VERONIQUE Don't you tell me what to be. You have

killed people, and it didn't do anything to you. Wilmer —what he's going through is wanting to kill somebody. That's much worse.

RINGWALD You're welcome, Veronique.

VERONIQUE Oh, I'm supposed to thank you. All right, thank you. He wanted to kill me, but he couldn't have. I wouldn't have let him.

RINGWALD You may get a chance to prove that. Wilmer isn't through yet.

EARL He's right, Veronique. I never saw him like this before. This isn't just a tantrum. And he went after you, not after me. You're the one he blames.

VERONIQUE Well, he should. What did it look like? Jean's my sister, and we're getting ready for a party. That's what it looked like to Wilmer.

JEAN You ought to thank Mr. Ringwald. I thank Earl. He was going to protect me.

VERONIQUE Yes, I noticed. That's going to make Wilmer madder than anything, when he stops to think about it.

EARL It surprises *me*.

VERONIQUE Did he go to Mario's? Is that where you think he went?

EARL He always lights out for Mario's.

VERONIQUE Townsend, will you take me there?

RINGWALD What for? What good will that do? He'll think you've come to taunt him.

VERONIQUE I don't care what he thinks about that. Or about anything else. But if he's going to make any more trouble, let him make it with us instead of somebody else. Me, instead of somebody else. I'm not afraid of Wilmer.

EARL (*Quietly*) Veronique.

VERONIQUE What?

EARL   You better be. I honestly mean that. He hates you worse than anybody that ever lived.

JEAN   Why?

EARL   Oh—this and that. He thinks he has plenty of reason, and anyway, Wilmer doesn't need any reason. Wilmer's not all there.

JEAN   Oh, well that explains it.

RINGWALD   You've got advice from an expert, so forget about going to Mario's.

JEAN   Please don't go, Nique. I'll be afraid.

EARL   Afraid to be left with *me?*

JEAN   I don't *know* you, Earl.

EARL   No, I guess you don't.

(VERONIQUE *realizes that she had not given any thought to* JEAN *alone with* EARL. *She is strongly influenced by his instinctive rush to* JEAN's *defense*)

VERONIQUE   All right, I won't go. But you two, I wish you wouldn't say things that frighten Jean. In the first place I don't believe them. Wilmer's furious, but he's *not* dangerous.

EARL   Well—you have it your own way, Veronique, but I know him.

RINGWALD   When he's furious, he's dangerous. Everybody is, and especially a desperate old queen like Wilmer. Am I right, Earl?

EARL   *I'm* afraid of him. I admit it.

VERONIQUE   Well, I'm not. Now I say, let's the four of us go out to dinner.

JEAN   Yes, I'd like to go some place else for a while.

VERONIQUE   Let's go to that Basque place over on Bleecker Street. Wilmer won't be there. He's never been there that I know of.

EARL   My treat. I got paid today.

VERONIQUE   No, it's my party for Jean. (*Smiles at* RING-

WALD) Well—it's really Townsend's party. (*She puts her hand on his arm*) Don't mind what I say when I'm cross.

(*They put on coats and turn out the light and exit. When they have gone, the door opens.* WILMER. *He looks about him for a moment, then goes to* VERONIQUE's *wardrobe as the curtain descends*)

SCENE TWO

VERONIQUE's *apartment, a few hours later. At rise the door is opened and the light is switched on.* VERONIQUE, JEAN, EARL *and* RINGWALD *enter. They are all in good spirits, but nobody is drunk.*

JEAN   Oh, I like New York all over again. *That* place was like Paris, Nique.

VERONIQUE   She was in Paris when she was little.

JEAN   And Uncle took us to a place like that. I remember. Uncle and Aunt and Mama and you and I and all the cousins. It had a tile floor. I remember that. And they put a cushion on my chair. All the people knew each other, and it was the only time Uncle took us out.

VERONIQUE   You're right. I remember that.

EARL   I had an offer to go to Paris but Wilmer made me turn it down.

RINGWALD   Well, now you can go, if the offer's still good.

EARL   Oh, the offer's still good. I get plenty of offers. Jean, you had a good time. I'm so glad.

JEAN   I had a marvelous time. Earl, you're so funny. You make me laugh.

EARL   I got off a couple of good ones, didn't I? But don't forget Townsend, he's a wisecracker, too. Only his humor's more the dry kind. I'm just a camp, that's really what I am. But it gets laughs. It isn't what I say, it's the way I say it. It wouldn't sound funny coming from Townsend.

VERONIQUE *(To* JEAN*)*   Tomorrow you can wear my coat.

JEAN   Can I honestly? Oh, I can hardly wait to get one of my own.

EARL   Maybe she better find out how much they cost, eh, Veronique? What you have to pay for them, dearie.

VERONIQUE *(Slightly annoyed, but decides not to make a reply. She is standing in front of the wardrobe, hesitating about speaking, then opens the wardrobe door and reaches in for a hanger, gets hold of a hanger, then draws back)*   Oh, my God! Look at this!

RINGWALD *(Quickly alarmed)*   What?

VERONIQUE   Every one of my dresses. *(She tosses the fur coat on the couch and takes out a couple of dresses that have been cut to shreds. She holds them up for the others to see)* Every one of them.

EARL   He's been here.

RINGWALD   Good Lord. You know this is serious, Veronique.

VERONIQUE   Don't I *know* it's serious.

EARL   Let me have a look at one. *(He examines a dress. Nods)* Uh-huh. You know what he did it with? My shears, my heavy shears that I use for cutting wallpaper. He had himself a time doing this, all right. Look how evenly. Honestly, I don't want to exaggerate or anything, but if I were you I wouldn't sleep here tonight. *(He suddenly goes to the hall door, opens it, and reaches up on the outside transom. He returns)* He let himself in with the extra key.

VERONIQUE How did he know about it?

EARL Oh, I guess I told him. I'm sorry.

VERONIQUE Well, we can bolt the door.

RINGWALD I'm not one for calling in the cops, but—

VERONIQUE No. No, no, no. No police.

RINGWALD Now wait a minute.

EARL I think Townsend's right.

RINGWALD Now listen, I know a sergeant. Sergeant Hinchcomb, I knew when I was on the *Evening World*. He's over on Charles Street. I might be able to get him to pick up Wilmer on a drunk charge. At least I can try, and I won't have to say anything about this.

EARL *(Shaking his head)* He won't be drunk, Townsend. He'll be more sober than you or I.

RINGWALD The point is to get him locked up for the night. It's the best way to keep him out of trouble. Let me see if I can get Sergeant Hinchcomb.

VERONIQUE No, I don't want you to.

RINGWALD Don't be stubborn. Don't you see it'll be better for him?

EARL I don't know though, Townsend. Wilmer did thirty days on the Island one time. He told me he'd never go through that again.

RINGWALD Listen, all of you. He'd be a damned sight better off doing thirty days on a homo charge than what he faces if he goes after somebody with a pair of shears.

EARL He's only mad at one person, Townsend.

RINGWALD You think so? Well, why don't *you* go out and try to find him?

JEAN No!

RINGWALD   I say let's get the cops before he kills some-body.

VERONIQUE   (*Impatiently*) Oh, what for? He was angry at me and he got even by cutting up my dresses. That doesn't mean he's going to go around killing people.

RINGWALD   Unfortunately that's exactly what it does mean, but you're stupid.

JEAN   You shut up!

RINGWALD   *You* shut up, little girl. Keep out of this. (*To* VERONIQUE) Ask any psychiatrist the meaning of cutting up your dresses.

VERONIQUE   Any what?

RINGWALD   Psychiatrist. Don't you know what a psychiatrist is? Haven't you ever heard of psycho-analysis?

VERONIQUE   Oh, that. I wouldn't rely on anything *they* said.

RINGWALD   Or anyone else. I can see that. Well, do you remember a week or so ago, telling me about a girl that would be better off if she'd been killed?

VERONIQUE   No.

RINGWALD   You do! Think! The model.

VERONIQUE   (*Remembering*) Oh.

RINGWALD   They're the same thing. The same mentality.

VERONIQUE   I don't believe it.

RINGWALD   Listen to me. They're finding out more and more about criminals these days.

VERONIQUE   Yes, by beating them up.

RINGWALD   *Not* by beating them up, by getting them to talk. Getting them to brag, in some cases. And one thing they're finding out, you stubborn fool, if they go back into a murderer's past, they always find, or nearly always find, that something in his past gives at least a hint of how he's going to commit a murder.

VERONIQUE   Then why don't they stop them?

RINGWALD That's what I'm trying to do. Wilmer is psychopathic. Do you know what *that* is?

VERONIQUE Crazy.

RINGWALD Well, that'll do. Unbalanced. And right now that's what Wilmer is, and he's dangerous.

EARL He is, Veronique. Townsend's right.

VERONIQUE Oh, I know what you're saying. Voodoo. Sticking pins in dolls. What's His Name over on MacDougal Alley. Pierre, from Haiti. Listen, Townsend, I know all the queers and all the queer ways and things and everything queer, and I don't believe for one minute that Wilmer Hightower is out to kill me because he snipped my dresses with a scissors. (*Lightly*) I could kill *him*, what he did to those dresses.

JEAN Don't say that, Nique, even in fun.

VERONIQUE Well, you know I didn't mean it.

EARL (*To* JEAN) They're heavy, too, those shears. You know, they're made to cut through several thicknesses of wallpaper.

JEAN Like a tailor's. We have another uncle that's a tailor.

EARL Resembling a tailor's, yes. You could do a lot of damage just hitting a person. They could be a real deadly weapon.

RINGWALD If you won't let me call the cops, I have another suggestion.

VERONIQUE What?

RINGWALD You and your sister sleep in my apartment tonight.

EARL That pigsty! How anybody could sleep there—although I guess some have.

RINGWALD Look, Earl, save your campy humor for some other time.

EARL I apologize.

RINGWALD   The windows are barred, and there are two locks on the door.

JEAN   My first night in New York I didn't expect . . .

VERONIQUE   (*Favorably inclined*) Well, I don't know.

RINGWALD   Lock both locks. Put the table against the door, if you feel like it, and don't open the door for anyone but me or Earl.

EARL   Does that mean you and I are supposed to spend the night here?

RINGWALD   Yes, aren't you happy about that?

EARL   I am if you are, you rough tough old thing. Seriously, no. I don't want to be in this room tonight. He might come back and mistake me for Veronique. You can stay here, but I'll go up to the Y. M. I'll find some place. Seriously, I think you're right about the girls, though. Kids, you ought to stay in the pigsty, just for tonight.

RINGWALD   (*To* VERONIQUE) All right?

VERONIQUE   I guess so. It's much ado about nothing, but you've frightened Jean.

EARL   You know what's going to be funny. If tomorrow breakfast— Townsend.

RINGWALD   What?

EARL   I just had a hunch. Call the joint where he works, and see if he's there.

RINGWALD   A good hunch. Do you know the number?

EARL   If I think. Yes. Circle 4646.

RINGWALD   (*Into phone*) Circle 4646 . . . That's right . . . Hello, would you let me speak to Wilmer Hightower? . . . Wilmer, the piano player . . . He isn't? Did he say he'd be late or anything? It's personal . . . He didn't call at all . . . Thank you. They sounded a bit annoyed. He hasn't been there all night, and hasn't phoned.

EARL And you know Wilmer. He even went to work the night a certain person scratched him.

JEAN Who?

EARL (*Patting her head lightly*) Oh, a friend of his. Well, we know one place where he isn't.

VERONIQUE Let's try Mario's. I'll do it. Watkins 9244 . . . Hello, Mario? This is Veronique McCullough . . . Fine thank you. I wanted to ask you, is Wilmer there? Wilmer Hightower? . . . He hasn't . . . No, no thanks. In fact I'd rather you didn't. I just wanted to know if he was there. Thank you, Mario. Well, you heard that. Hasn't been there all evening. (*To* JEAN) Mario said to be sure and bring you in while you're in town. (*To all*) I told Mario not to tell Wilmer I called, in case he does come in.

EARL I was wrong about him going to Mario's.

RINGWALD Actually, in a way you were right.

EARL Why?

RINGWALD You said he always hightails it for Mario's when he's sore about something, but tonight he isn't just sore about something.

VERONIQUE There you go, making a mountain out of a molehill.

RINGWALD I'm interested in everything he does that isn't his usual routine. Where else would he be likely to go, Earl? Where was the party last night?

EARL (*Laughs*) Bryant Hall. No use calling there. It was a big one. They thought there might be a raid, it was so big. We don't often have big ones downtown, only Harlem. Friends. Friends. Who else? If he was real desperate there's a boy over on Eighth Street smokes muggles, but Wilmer gave them up. They don't go with gin. Anyway, I don't know the boy's name. Not his last name. His first name is Dale. Dale Something.

VERONIQUE I know him. Dale Faber.

EARL   That's it!

VERONIQUE   I'll see if his number's in the book.

EARL   He can get other things in addition to muggles.

JEAN   What are muggles?

EARL   Uh—a special brand of cigarette. They also go under the name of reefers.

VERONIQUE   Here it is. Watkins 1611. One six, one-one . . . Hello, could I speak to Wilmer? . . . I don't want to say his last name . . . Well, I don't want to say mine either, but I know you . . . He's a piano player. Middle-aged . . . I wanted to talk to him. It's important . . . No, I'm calling from a pay station. You can't call back . . . Well, why didn't you say that in the first place? (*Hanging up*) He hasn't been in for over a year. What shall we do, start with A and go through the whole book?

RINGWALD   No, but I'll bet he's not very far from here. In the Village somewhere.

VERONIQUE   Why? Have you got a hunch, too, like Earl's?

RINGWALD   Call it that.

EARL   You think he's roaming around somewhere, Townsend?

RINGWALD   I may be wrong. But if he's roaming around, Sergeant Hinchcomb could pick him up inside of an hour. Every cop on post has to phone in once an hour, all at different times. At this minute some cop is what they call boxing in. Phoning from a police box. And the streets down here aren't very crowded at this time of night. Why don't—

VERONIQUE   No. This whole thing isn't going to amount to anything. But Jean and I will sleep in your apartment, just so *you'll* stop fretting.

EARL   It isn't like him not to go to work, Veronique.

(*There is a knock on the door. They all look at each*

other, and RINGWALD *picks up a tall brass figure of a sitting cat and holds it behind his back*)

VERONIQUE   Come in, it's unlocked. No it isn't either. (*Unlocks and unbolts the door. A fiftyish woman in a man's bathrobe enters*)

WOMAN   I'm Hazel Pomeroy, from the floor above. Good evening, Miss McCullough, Mr. Ringwald. I have this letter for Mr. Fisher. Mr. Hightower asked me to give it to you when you came in, but I was in the midst of taking my bath.

VERONIQUE   Wouldn't you like a drink, Miss Pomeroy? This is my sister, from Montreal.

POMEROY   Oh, thanks very much, but I have to be up so early. You know, I teach. I'd love a drink some other time. Mr. Hightower wanted to be sure you got this tonight. He's so nice, Mr. Hightower. Whenever we have anything heavy to move.

EARL   Thank you. When did he give you this?

POMEROY   Oh, I guess it was around nine-thirty or ten. I didn't take notice to the time, but I was in the midst of correcting papers. Yes, about nine-thirty or ten. It must be important, because he gave me five dollars to stay awake till you all got in. Well, goodnight. Goodnight, everyone.

EARL   You wouldn't think it to look at her now, but she had an affair with the King of England.

RINGWALD   The Kaiser, not the King of England.

EARL   That's who I meant. The one with the moustache. She has pictures of them on a yacht together.

VERONIQUE   Open your letter!

EARL   I am, I am. Give her a few drinks and she'll tell you all about it. And I mean all. Kaiser Bill.

VERONIQUE   It takes you longer to open a letter.

EARL   It's my letter . . . (*He reads it, then rereads it*) It isn't very long. (*He finishes it, and is undecided whom to give it to. He decides to give it to* RINGWALD)

RINGWALD Do you want me to read it aloud?

EARL Well, I think it would be better if you did.

RINGWALD (*Reading*) "Earl," it says. And it's signed Wilmer. "Earl," he says, "You must leave there right away. I am not responsable." Spelt *a*-b-l-e. "My brain is going around and around and want to kill somebody." Underlined. "You know who." And the signature, Wilmer. I'll read it again. "Earl you must leave there right away. I am not responsable. My brain is going around and around and want to kill somebody. You know who. Wilmer."

VERONIQUE Well, we all know who. But that doesn't say he's going to do it.

RINGWALD *He* thinks he is. Quite convinced of it. This isn't a hysterical letter, Veronique. He doesn't say "I'm *going* to kill somebody." He says he *wants* to kill somebody. It's almost as though he were talking about somebody else, not himself. If he came right out and threatened you, Veronique, I wouldn't be so concerned. But he knows somebody, namely himself, is going to do something, and he wants Earl to be somewhere else when he does it. We'll take you and Jean down to my room and see that you're safe for the night. Then Earl, you might as well take his advice and go some place else. I'm convinced that he's somewhere in the neighborhood, waiting to see if you leave.

JEAN Why must Earl go? Maybe he'll attack Earl as soon as he sees him alone.

RINGWALD He doesn't want to attack Earl. Earl is really the only one he doesn't want to attack. Now let's do what I say, please?

EARL You take the girls down to your room. I want to see what he put in my suitcase. I'll wait till you come back.

RINGWALD (*Hesitates, then agrees*) All right. (*He and*

the girls, with their nightgowns, exit. EARL *goes to the phone and speaks softly into it*)

EARL   Watkins 6517. Six five one seven. (*In the silence a phone can be heard ringing not far away. Simultaneously with the cessation of the ringing Earl speaks softly*) You fool. I knew you were still in the building. Townsend wants to call the police. You get out of that apartment or you're going to be arrested . . . All right. I'll meet you wherever you say . . . Dale's? . . . You mean Dale Faber's on 8th Street? . . . All right. But go now, before Townsend has a chance to call the police. He's downstairs, the dames are spending the night in his room, and then he's coming back here. You get out right away, and be careful you don't run into him in the hall . . . No, I'm not cross. Not really . . . All right, Wilmer, but hurry.

(*He hangs up. He pours a shot of gin and drinks it. Lights a cigarette. Opens the wardrobe and takes out a mutilated dress and holds it up to examine it. He is doing that when* RINGWALD *returns*)

RINGWALD   They ought to be safe for the night.

EARL   I hope so.

RINGWALD   Yes. Jean took quite a shine to you.

EARL   (*Dispassionately*)   She's a nice kid. I didn't mind her at all.

RINGWALD   But you don't really like her.

EARL   Yes I do. I don't dislike her, but after all, Townsend. She's not built right for me.

RINGWALD   But you go for girls sometimes.

EARL   No, not really, but sometimes they go for me. Then they're sorry and they think it's my fault. It isn't my fault, it's theirs for getting hot pants. When I was a kid the other kids used to yell at me, "Earl got curls but don't like the girls." And they were right, I didn't. But they liked me, big ones and little ones. I didn't get started with boys, Townsend I got started with girls. You should of seen our neighborhood, where I grew up. There wasn't a house had a coat of paint on it. You couldn't see the sun for the smoke, even on a clear day. The smoke from the mills. And two big girls used to take turns at me. They were fourteen or fifteen, but I was only ten or eleven. They'd wait for me after school. They used to take me to the movies. *The Perils of Pauline.* I had a teacher in school and she used to try to protect me, but then she, she got just as bad. But at least she put up the money to pay for my year at Tech. That's how I went to Tech for a year. I was a whore that far back. I guess I was always a whore, from when I was about ten years of age. And can I tell them! Veronique better get that Jean back to Montreal. She's ready and willing, even if she doesn't know it. One thing about being a whore, though. You never worry.

RINGWALD   What?

EARL   You don't. You may have to take a cut, but you don't worry. Like tonight, I leave here and I got a dozen places I can go. The devil takes care of his own, my grandmother used to say. Goodnight, Townsend.

RINGWALD   Give us a ring in the morning.

EARL   All right. Some time tomorrow. (*Takes bag and exits, and* RINGWALD *goes to phone*)

RINGWALD   Spring 3100 . . . Connect me with the Charles Street Station-house? I want to speak to Sergeant Hinchcomb . . . Sergeant Hinchcomb, please . . . Hello, Hinch? This is Townsend Ringwald . . . Oh, fine. Fine . . . Hinch, I want to ask you a favor. (*The door opens. It is* VERONIQUE, *who looks angrily at* RINGWALD, *then crosses to him and puts her hand on the phone to disconnect it, speaking as she crosses*)

VERONIQUE   I knew you were going to do that.

CURTAIN

ACT THREE

SCENE ONE

Immediately following Act Two. Continuous action. At rise VERONIQUE's *hand is on the telephone.*

RINGWALD What's the matter with you, you damned fool!

VERONIQUE Give me that phone.
(*He keeps it from her grasp, then gives up*)

RINGWALD (*Disgusted*) Take it. Take it.

VERONIQUE What right have you to have the police mixing in our affairs.

RINGWALD None.

VERONIQUE Then why do you?

RINGWALD Because I don't think it is your affair. It's gone beyond that. Tomorrow he may be all right, but tonight he's not. He should be kept from—
(*Here there is a frightful scream from somewhere nearby, followed by another scream that ends abruptly*)

RINGWALD (*Quietly*) Did you leave my door open?

VERONIQUE Oh, no! Oh, no!
(*She starts to leave and he grabs her firmly, they tussle, and as they tussle* WILMER *enters*)

389

WILMER (*Looks with incredulous horror at* VERONIQUE)
I thought she was you. I thought she was you. I didn't
mean to kill *her*.
(VERONIQUE *breaks away and runs downstairs, and*
RINGWALD *deliberately punches* WILMER *in the chin,
knocking him out.* WILMER *collapses on the floor and*
RINGWALD *leaves him there*)

RINGWALD   You poor miserable son of a bitch. I hope
you don't wake up. (*He goes to the phone again*)
Spring 3100 . . . Sergeant Hinchcomb, Charles Street
station. It's important . . . Hello, Hinch. Townsend
Ringwald again . . . Yes, I know. I know we were . . .
Hinch, I have a homicide to report . . . Eighty-four
West Third Street. And I have the man that did it.
I knocked him out with a punch. It wasn't hard to . . .
No, he won't get away . . . A Canadian girl, named
Jean McCullough. Age about seventeen . . . Stabbing.
I think a pair of shears, paperhanger's shears. You'll
get all that . . . Oh, I can handle him. Anybody could,
now . . . Hinch? Don't let them rough him up too
much. He's an old fag. Not so old. His name is Wilmer
Hightower, and he's lying here on the floor. He'd be
better off if he never got up . . . Try to come yourself,
will you? I don't want your boys thinking I did it. Okay,
Hinch. The girl is in my apartment, the basement . . .
No, I didn't see it, Hinch. I'm upstairs in the girl's sister's apartment. Her name is Veronique McCullough. I'll
spell it when you get here . . . Oh, age about twenty-
four. Also from Montreal. Model. The sister just arrived
in New York this morning. Hinch, I know what you're
doing. You're tracing this call. Well, I'll give you the
number. It's Stuyvesant 4086. Under the name of
Veronique McCullough. Haven't you got it traced yet?
Okay. I'm going to hang up now. I'm going downstairs.
(*He hangs up, and as he does so* VERONIQUE *appears
in the doorway*)

VERONIQUE (*Shaking her head*)   Don't. (*She goes to him*

*slowly and he takes her in his arms, but she cannot take
her eyes off* WILMER)

VERONIQUE (*Wearily*) Is he dead?

RINGWALD No. I knocked him out. He'll come to in a
few seconds.

(MISS POMEROY *appears*)

MISS POMEROY I heard that scream. What happened to
Mr. Hightower?

RINGWALD He had an accident. Go away, please, Miss
Pomeroy. The police are coming.

MISS POMEROY Did you kill him?

RINGWALD Look at him. (WILMER *is coming to*) Miss
Pomeroy, the police'll be here any minute.

POMEROY I have nothing to be afraid of.

RINGWALD We want to be by ourselves.

POMEROY (*Haughtily*) Oh, well. (*She exits*)

(VERONIQUE *looks at* WILMER *with fascination, loathing
and pity*)

WILMER What are they going to do to me?

RINGWALD You'll have to wait and see.

WILMER I can get away!

RINGWALD No you can't, not if I can help it. And I can.

VERONIQUE Let him go.

RINGWALD Let him go! If you'd let me call the cops
earlier . . . I'm sorry. But—

VERONIQUE You ought to be on his side. You've killed
people. . . . Wilmer, what are you thinking about?

WILMER I can get away. I want to get away.

VERONIQUE You don't want to kill me any more?

WILMER (*Getting to his feet*) Townsend, you'll let me
go.

RINGWALD She would, but I won't.

WILMER You know what they'll do to me. They'll take

' me down in the cellar and turn the hose on me. That's what they do, the police.

VERONIQUE (*To* RINGWALD)   Is that what they do?

RINGWALD   That's one of the things. Sometimes.

WILMER   They'll make me stand in a corner for hours and hours. I know. I've been arrested.

VERONIQUE   Wilmer, are you sorry?

WILMER   I'm afraid.

VERONIQUE   Yes, but are you sorry?

WILMER   What are you asking me questions for?

VERONIQUE   I want to know if you're sorry you did that to Jean.

WILMER   She was a bitch, too, but not as bad a one as you are.

RINGWALD   Now he's beginning to rationalize.

VERONIQUE   You wanted to kill me, didn't you, Wilmer?

WILMER   *You* know that.

VERONIQUE   Then aren't you sorry you killed the wrong person?

WILMER   Maybe she wasn't the wrong person. Can I use the phone?

RINGWALD   No. What for?

WILMER   I want to call somebody.

RINGWALD   Who?

WILMER   If you let me use the phone you'll find out.

VERONIQUE   Let him use the phone.

RINGWALD   Tell me who you're going to call.

WILMER   I want to call Earl.

RINGWALD   Where is he?

WILMER   If you let me use the phone you'll find out. You want to find out where he is so you can tell the police. I don't want to use the phone.

RINGWALD You're absolutely right. But they'll find him. If I were you, Wilmer, I wouldn't hold out on the police when they ask you where Earl is. It's not going to look so good, his running away.

WILMER He didn't run away from anything.

RINGWALD You seem to know a lot about Earl and where he is.

WILMER Why shouldn't I? I talked to him not a half an hour ago.

RINGWALD How did you know he was here?

WILMER I didn't. He knew I was upstairs. Oh, he's clever, Earl.

RINGWALD You were hiding upstairs?

WILMER For hours.

RINGWALD And Earl knew it?

WILMER He called me, didn't he? I warned him, I sent him a note. So he warned me. You can't come between Earl and I. I told you that. That boy's loyal to me.

RINGWALD He told you where the girls were.

WILMER Of course he did. What did you think?

RINGWALD He told you where they were, and let you go and kill Jean.

WILMER That's not the way it was at all.

RINGWALD In other words, he practically put you up to it.

WILMER No he didn't!

RINGWALD Yes, that's the way it was, Wilmer. You may not think so, but that's the way it was. He practically put you up to it, but he made sure he was nowhere around.

WILMER (*Making a rush at* RINGWALD) No it wasn't! It—was—not. (RINGWALD *shoves him aside*) You want to get Earl in trouble on account of *her*. You're jealous of Earl because of her. Earl could have her any time he

wanted her, but he didn't want her. She was the one
that wanted him. She always did want him.

RINGWALD   Well, what if she did?

WILMER   What if she did? Her sister wouldn't be dead,
that's what-if-she-did.
(*A police siren, followed by another police siren and
various offstage male voices are heard.* WILMER *suddenly
becomes panic-stricken*)

WILMER   Where can I go? Help me. Help me, Townsend.
Veronique! *You* help me.

RINGWALD   (*Opening door and calling downstairs*)   We're
up here. Hinchcomb? Hinch? We're up here. Yes, he's
here.

VERONIQUE   (*To* WILMER)   I didn't try to take Earl away
from you, Wilmer.

CURTAIN

SCENE TWO

*The time is some years later, the scene, a luxurious apart-
ment on the upper East Side. At rise* TOWNSEND RINGWALD
*has his back to the audience as at rise in previous scenes,
but as he turns it is seen that he is wearing a well-cut
dinner jacket. He has two on-the-rocks drinks in his hands,
one of which he hands to* VERONIQUE, *who is dressed in
chic hostess pajamas. They are accustomed to prosperity
and to each other. He is whistling "The Lambeth Walk,"
and at the end of the chorus she sings:*

VERONIQUE   Doing the Lambeth Walk, hoy!

RINGWALD   Where shall we go tonight?

VERONIQUE   Well, let's *talk* about going to a *lot* of places, but let's not try any experimenting. We'll go to Morocco, where we're known.

RINGWALD   As a matter of fact, I wouldn't even know what other places to talk about any more.

VERONIQUE   The Stork.

RINGWALD   Yes. And Montparnasse.

VERONIQUE   Yes, Montparnasse. Larue, for that matter.

RINGWALD   Would you say we were in a rut?

VERONIQUE   If it's being in a rut to go to places you like, and stay away from places you don't like. Morocco's where I see the people I care about seeing. It's like the Savoy Grill. Everybody isn't there every night, but you have a better chance of running into people at Morocco, or the Savoy. So why waste time at the other places?

RINGWALD   I was thinking of where Eric might like to go.

VERONIQUE   Morocco of course. Although I guess we could take him to the Stork for a little while. Bea Lillie goes to the Stork, and Lord Beaverbrook. At least they were there the other night.

RINGWALD   I doubt if Eric and The Beaver would have much in common.

VERONIQUE   Well, but they're both English.

RINGWALD   Not really. Beaverbrook is one of your people. He's a Canuck.

VERONIQUE   Lord Beaverbrook is? I didn't know that. Are you sure?

RINGWALD   I'm sure. His name is Max Atkins. No, not Atkins. Aitken. He's from one of the Maritime provinces.

VERONIQUE   Now how do you know that? How do you keep up with those things?

RINGWALD   I do it when I'm supposed to be working. I often read every God damn word in *Time,* just to put off going to work.

VERONIQUE   All that stuff in the front, too?

RINGWALD   Everything. The Rh factor. Religion.

VERONIQUE   *Why* do you?

RINGWALD   I told you. To put off getting back to work.

VERONIQUE   Well, *I* don't. What is there in the papers except Hitler and Mussolini, and of course Roosevelt.

RINGWALD   Yes, and they're going to be for a long time to come.

VERONIQUE   Oh, you keep saying things like that, as if you knew something about it.

RINGWALD   I don't claim to have any inside information, but I think any damn fool knows we're headed for war. They're getting ready, and so are we.

VERONIQUE   Well, if enough people go on talking like that of *course* there'll be a war. You're talking yourselves into it.
(*There is a distant buzzer,* PEARL, *the maid, crosses from Left to Right and goes out to the foyer up Right. In a moment* ERIC FABER *enters, goes straight to* VERONIQUE *and embraces her without disturbing her coiffure*)

ERIC   Dear Veronique. And Townsend. (*The men shake hands*) A Bourbon on the rocks, before you have a chance to ask me. Don't I know someone else lives in this building?

RINGWALD   A lot of other people do live here.

ERIC   Well now surely Keith Singleton did use to live here?

RINGWALD   A long time ago, yes.

ERIC   I knew it. Leastaways I thought I did. He didn't *die* in this building?

RINGWALD   No, he died in the country.

ERIC   I always say, stay out of the country. Well, you two
appear to be living a healthy city life. You haven't put
your royalties into horses and guns and other such kid-
die nonsense. A steam yacht, possibly?

RINGWALD   Not even a steam yacht.

ERIC   Of course they're all Diesel now, aren't they? What
is Diesel? I'm not embarrassed to ask you, Townsend, as
I am so many people.

RINGWALD   I believe it's a fuel. A kind of oil instead of
gasoline. Or petrol.

ERIC   Yes, I think so. But it's German, isn't it?

RINGWALD   Well, as a matter of fact, a German named
Diesel invented the Diesel engine, and that takes Diesel
oil. It would be more accurate to say that the Diesel
engine came before the Diesel oil.

ERIC   (*Nodding politely*)   Mm. Well, thank you. Isn't it
nice to have Townsend to enlighten you on such
things?

VERONIQUE   Did he enlighten you?

ERIC   Well—a man called Diesel invented something
called Diesel, that's either a kind of petrol or a kind of
engine.

RINGWALD   Or both.

ERIC   Yes, but I can only take in one thing at a time. For
tonight, Herr Diesel is the inventor of the engine. What
do you think of the Germans, by the way? I haven't had
much chance to sound out American public opinion,
having disembarked only this morning.

RINGWALD   What do *you?* You're closer to it.

ERIC   Well you see, Townsend, I have so many friends
Germans. In fact, Nazis. It's getting to be less and less
the thing to say, at home, but there are still a great
many of us who understand their point of view, and at
least to a certain extent, sympathize. You're expanding

over here, but you have so much room. The Germans want to expand, but where to? We ourselves had to expand and we went all over the face of the earth, grabbing whole continents, you might say. My Nazi friends tell me that all they'd like to do is unite the German-speaking peoples, and that seems fair enough.

RINGWALD   I don't think Britain would do so well if they tried to unite all the English speaking peoples. They might hear from us, at least a feeble note of protest.

ERIC   You're having me on, Townsend, and I suspect that you're anti-Nazi. But you're not a Jew, at least I don't think you are.

RINGWALD   No, I'm not. In fact, I'm of German descent. Ringwald. But I fought against them twenty years ago.

ERIC   Well, I, of course, *was* a Jew. Leastaways, my grandfather was, then he became C. of E. Church of England. But I've always been sympathetic to Jews and my friends in the Nazi party have never raised the question. Hitler has nothing against the Jews, other than those who oppose him.

VERONIQUE   I was a Catholic. Doesn't anyone want to hear about that?

ERIC   Yes, tell us about it, Veronique. What was it like? Forgive me, but I did want to ask what you over here thought about the Germans. People, not Mr. Roosevelt. He seems very impatient, and some of us are afraid that he'll push us into a war and then leave us high and dry.

RINGWALD   I don't think he'll do that.

ERIC   I don't know. At home we hear that Mr. Roosevelt wants a war but that the American people don't. Therefore he could make some of our people count on you in the event of war, but then your people would refuse to go. Is that possible?

RINGWALD   The American people could vote him out of

office the year after next. They may anyway, on the third-term issue.

ERIC   The third-term issue. Shall we go back to Herr Diesel? Veronique, is that Schiap? It is, isn't it?

VERONIQUE   Yes. I went haywire last summer.

ERIC   Well, why not? Townsend is making so much money. Three big hits, and you sold them all to films, I read.

VERONIQUE   And he has another one for late this season.

RINGWALD   If I ever finish the revisions. But you have a hit in London, Eric. We saw it, and it's delightful. Deserves to be a hit.

ERIC   I was desolated not to be there when you were. I wish you could have been with me in Sweden, too. Have you been?

VERONIQUE   No, but we're going next year.

ERIC   You must. It's enchanting, Sweden, and I was mad for the people. They're the most beautiful people I've ever seen. Ever. Have you ever had an affair with a Swedish girl, Townsend?

RINGWALD   No.

ERIC   You must make him have an affair with a Swedish girl, Veronique. I don't want you to be stuffy about it. Promise me.

VERONIQUE   If he wants to, I won't stop him. Why, did *you?*

ERIC   Now, come. But in the first place they're beautiful, simply beautiful. And in the second place, a friend of mine told me that—this was an Englishman—who said that with the possible exception of a Japanese girl, no woman on earth is as good for a man's ego as a Swedish girl. And do you know why?

VERONIQUE   I can guess.

ERIC   No you can't. The reason is, that when she feels like ending the affair, she does, and usually before the man is ready to end it. Then he realizes that he was honored by her having an affair with him in the first place.

VERONIQUE   Why is that particularly Swedish? I'm a Canadian, half Irish and half French, and that's exactly how I feel about the whole thing.

ERIC   Oh. But you're you. I don't think of you as having any nationality.

VERONIQUE   You got out of that pretty nicely. Townsend, get into practice. I hear Swedish girls like to drink.
(RINGWALD *takes their glasses*)

ERIC   What are we doing tonight?

VERONIQUE   Dinner here, and then we'll take you on the town.

ERIC   Have you got someone for me?

VERONIQUE   Mary Leonard is coming.

ERIC   I adore Mary. Anyone else?

VERONIQUE   Yes. Do you remember Earl Fisher?

ERIC   Earl Fisher. Of course I remember him, and I wouldn't have to *remember* him. I think he's very nearly the best you have, if not the best. We have no one like him at home. If my play goes on here, I want him to do it. I'm going to insist on it.

RINGWALD   You can't have him till he's finished with my play. He does all my plays. He has to, I got him in into the theater, away from interior decorating.

ERIC   Didn't he do this flat?

VERONIQUE   Yes, but he doesn't do many. He hasn't got time. He does commercial work. Industrial, they call it. He has fifty people working for him.

RINGWALD   Sixty-five people, full time. The theater isn't where he makes his money. Is Jack doing your play over here?

ERIC   Not this one. Pollock and Chase are doing this one.

Fifteen percent, because they're just getting started and want an English name. Snobs, aren't they?

RINGWALD   The reason I asked, Earl Fisher won't work for Jack, but that's not saying he'll work for Pollock and Chase. But we'll go to work on him.

(*The buzzer again sounds. Maid crosses as before and admits* MARY LEONARD. *She is dressed by Valentina, her hair is all grey and cut very short*)

MARY   Eric darling.

ERIC   Mary, my dearest love.

(*They embrace*)

MARY   (*Rubbing cheeks with* VERONIQUE)   Hello, sweet. Hello, Townsend.

VERONIQUE   Mary, that's new.

MARY   Brand new. First time out. Townsend, I think I'd like a long drink. Scotch and plain water. We're not quick running in to dinner, are we?

VERONIQUE   Not for a half an hour or so. We're going out later.

MARY   You don't think I'd have worn this just to sit around, and I know I'm not going to impress Eric.

ERIC   But you do impress me. You've completely changed your type. You don't wear those deer-stalking costumes any more.

MARY   Referring to my expensive suits? I wore those as an economy, partly, and partly because when Keith was alive he didn't want any of us small fry to outshine him. He was the bird of paradise in his office.

ERIC   But now it's your office?

MARY   Now it's my office, and nobody that works for me can afford to outshine me. I see to that. (*She sips her drink*) Have you seen the afternoon papers?

VERONIQUE   No. Maybe Townsend has. What's in them?

RINGWALD   You mean about Czecho-Slovakia?

MARY   No. I mean about Wilmer Hightower.

VERONIQUE   What about him?

MARY   He's out on parole.

(VERONIQUE *sits back to consider the news*)

VERONIQUE   Parole. I forgot about parole.

MARY   There's just a little squib at the bottom of a column. I called his lawyer, the one he had at the trial, but he wasn't in his office.

VERONIQUE   Why did you call his lawyer?

MARY   Well, I don't imagine the poor bastard has many friends. He can't go back to playing the piano. Under the parole rules he's not supposed to return to his old job, or his old haunts, or even his old friends. I'm just afraid he might look up *some* of his old friends and get arrested for being naughty. Or he might pick up a sailor. The town's full of sailors. And if he gets into trouble, back he goes for violation of parole.

RINGWALD   I think you ought to stay out of it, though.

MARY   Well, you're entitled to think that. You're married to Veronique, and she certainly can't be expected to help him.

ERIC   Wilmer Hightower. He stabbed somebody! See, I remember.

VERONIQUE   He murdered my sister, Eric. And now he's free. Isn't *that* nice? Nine years in prison, with a lot of boy friends I'm sure, and now he's free. Townsend, did you know he was getting out?

RINGWALD   I didn't know he'd be eligible for parole so soon, but I haven't thought about him lately.

VERONIQUE   I have. Every day of my life. It was me that he wanted to kill.

(*The maid admits* EARL FISHER, *now no longer brash but smoothly dignified*)

EARL   Hello, dears. And Eric *Faber*. Do you remember me? I'm Earl Fisher.

ERIC (*With a new respect for* EARL *and his poise*)   Remember you? I tell everyone I used to know you.

EARL   Well, I do the same. And our paths almost crossed in Stockholm last summer. I missed you by one week. You'd just gone. I heard you had a perfectly grand time in Sweden.

ERIC   I've been telling the Ringwalds. Don't you agree with me that Townsend must have an affair with a Swedish girl?

EARL   Why?

ERIC   Well, it would do him good.

MARY   No, what Townsend needs is a flop. Another kind of flop, not one in the hay.

ERIC   In a curious roundabout way that's what I've been trying to tell him.

RINGWALD   I may be working on it.

MARY   No, not this one. You've got another hit, I'm positive, with or without Kate Hepburn, although with her, a bigger one.

EARL   You're not going to get Kate, I happen to know. Don't ask me any more, but give up on Kate. Have you seen the afternoon papers?

RINGWALD   About Wilmer Hightower? Mary was just telling us.

EARL   I think it's shocking. I really do. You know what's going to happen.

MARY   What? I don't.

EARL   Well, nothing good. Where can he go? He won't have any money. I think they give him ten dollars, and it's against the law for him to work at whatever he was doing before. Or to take a drink. Or hang around the places he used to know. And Wilmer's a good fifty, you know.

MARY   I called his lawyer.

EARL   You did? What for?

MARY   I wanted to find out what Wilmer's plans were.

EARL   That was rather cheeky of you.

MARY   Not at all. We're all doing well. Couldn't we give him some money? Not Veronique and Townsend, but some of the people he used to know.

RINGWALD   I'm under the impression that before they grant him a parole he has to prove that he has a job of some kind.

EARL   But all he could ever do was play the piano.

RINGWALD   Maybe he learned something in prison.

EARL   Ha *ha*. Nothing he didn't know before he went in, if you know what I mean. Prison would be awful for some people, but for Wilmer it would be sheer paradise. Think of being in such demand.

MARY   Didn't you ever write to him or anything?

EARL   Of course not. You must think me a terrible hypocrite, Mary Leonard. Veronique is one of my dearest friends. I was wishing he'd get the chair.

MARY   Well, I can see where he might have been better off.

PEARL   Miss Leonard, telephone for you. Mr. Emmett J. Cassidy.

MARY   The lawyer. Thank you. Veronique, could I take the call in here?

VERONIQUE   If you want to.

MARY   I do.

VERONIQUE   (*To maid*) Pearl, will you bring the telephone in here for Miss Leonard?

PEARL   Yes ma'am.

RINGWALD   Why do you want us all to be in on this?

MARY   I'm thinking more of Veronique than the rest of you. Thank you, Pearl. Hello, Mr. Cassidy. Thank you

for returning my call. I wanted to know about Wilmer
Hightower . . . Yes, I'm the literary agent, and I was a
friend of his. (*Puts her hand over the mouthpiece,
and says to the others:* "He said, 'Just a minute.' I
think he has Wilmer there with him.") Yes, hello,
Mr. Cassidy . . . Why of course I would. (MARY:
"He's putting Wilmer on." *At this* VERONIQUE *rises
and starts to leave, but* RINGWALD *gently puts his
hand on her shoulder to make her stay*) Hello,
Wilmer. How are you? . . . No, I'm—not at home.
I'm with some friends of mine. How are you?
. . . Yes, I imagine it does seem very strange. Where
are you staying? . . . Let me write that down. Three-
twenty-four West Eighty-fourth Street. Is that an apartment? . . . I didn't know they had boarding-houses
any more . . . Oh, I see. You have your meals—I see
. . . What kind of a job? . . . Well, it's something to
do for the time being, and meanwhile you can be looking for something better . . . No, it wouldn't embarrass
me to see you. Come to my office tomorrow afternoon
around five . . . All right, call me up any day next
week, and I'll let you know what's the best time . . .
Yes, I see them. I'm Townsend's agent, you know . . .
He has. He's done very well. He's working on a new one,
almost finished, and I think it's going to be a big success. Keep your fingers crossed . . . You'll what? Pray,
did you say? . . . You're a what? . . . That's what I
thought you said. When did *that* happen? . . . That
long ago? And you're still one? Then it took. It really
took . . . No, I wouldn't try to see her, Wilmer. You
can write to her, care of me, and I'll see she gets your
letter, but I wouldn't try to see her . . . I don't think
she'd want me to give you her address. You write her
care of my office, and if she wants to see you she'll let
you know, but I don't feel that I have the right to give
you her address. Their phone is unlisted . . . Any day
next week. I usually get to my office around ten in the

morning, and I have a business lunch with somebody every day, but I'm nearly always back by three o'clock. How are you fixed financially? . . . But why don't you let me lend you some? . . . But you don't want to go on doing that forever . . . You *have* changed . . . No, I don't think I have. Just older . . . No, as they say, I'm wedded to my business, and I'm not sure whether I'm the husband or the wife, but I'm wedded to it . . . You're not keeping me, but I'm probably keeping you. You probably want to talk to Mr. Cassidy, so you ring me up next week . . . Thank you, Wilmer. (*She hangs up, but her hand rests on the phone as she ponders the conversation*) You didn't want me to give him your address, did you?

VERONIQUE   No.

RINGWALD   What kind of a job's he got?

MARY   He's washing dishes in a cafeteria.

EARL   I could probably get him something better than that. In a factory, for instance, although I don't know what.

MARY   (*She is still in a deeply reflective mood*)   He doesn't want anything better. He doesn't want any money. He has a room in a boarding-house on the West Side. He played the organ in the prison chapel. (*She looks at* VERONIQUE)   He's turned Catholic. Five years ago. Got interested in religion through playing the organ, and turned Catholic five years ago. I wish you all could have heard him. You wouldn't have known it was Wilmer.

ERIC   I've heard that they lower their voices in prison.

MARY   It wasn't only that. Calmer. Serenity. *Gentle.*

VERONIQUE   (*Bitterly*)   Gentle.

MARY   Yes. I never would have recognized his voice—not exactly his voice, but his whole manner of speaking. I wouldn't have believed a voice could change that much.

I keep saying his voice. *Not* his voice. I wouldn't have believed a person could change as much as he has.

EARL   Did he say anything about me?

MARY   No, he only asked about Veronique and Townsend. He knew you had a lot of hits, Townsend, and he's going to pray your next one's a hit. Pray. That's how it came out that he'd turned Catholic. He wants very much to see you, Veronique.

EARL   He didn't ask about me at all?

MARY   No.

EARL   In a huff, I suppose, because I never sent him any goodies. Well, I'm glad I didn't.

MARY   He's not in a huff about anything, Earl. That's just it. Not in a huff. Content to wash dishes. And wanting very much to see Veronique.

RINGWALD   Veronique doesn't owe him anything. Most of all she doesn't owe him a quick easy forgiveness. And that's what he wants.

MARY   There I think you're right. Not quick or easy, but forgiveness, yes.

EARL   I agree with Townsend. Veronique doesn't owe him a thing. I think he has an nerve to even hope to see her. What I don't understand is your attitude, Mary. Why are you so Eleanor Roosevelt about all this?

MARY   Oh, I don't know. I guess it goes back a long way. Long before you were anybody, Earl. Before you ever came to New York, when you were back in Pittsburgh, PA, cutting out dolls' dresses, I suppose. But Townsend remembers. A husband of mine named Morgan Hanscom.

ERIC   Morgan Hanscom. I knew Morgan.

MARY   Yes, I guess you'd have known him.

ERIC   Forgotten he was your husband—if I ever knew it.

MARY   Yes, I've had two husbands. Nobody can ever call me an old maid.

EARL   That's one of the *last* things anybody'd call *you*, Mary.

MARY   No, you'd be surprised how many people don't know I was ever married. Not the *old* crowd, of course.

EARL   If you're trying to lord it over me, dearie, you've succeeded. I admit I'm younger than you and haven't been around as much, or as long. But what has your first husband got to do with Wilmer seeing Veronique? I fail to see any connection.

MARY   Maybe Townsend sees a connection.

RINGWALD   I do. But I'm not going to let Veronique see him.

EARL   I'm still just as much in the dark.

RINGWALD   Morgan Hanscom got into trouble, over money, and he committed suicide. Now Mary doesn't want Wilmer to commit suicide.

MARY   I don't think he will commit suicide. But his life now is going to be very different from the life in prison. I think he's one of the few people that prison did some good for. I know, I *know*, he's a better person for having been in prison. And I think that Veronique's forgiveness is very important to him.

RINGWALD   How could you tell all that from talking to him over the phone?

VERONIQUE   (*Interrupting*)   I'll see him.

RINGWALD   Of course you won't. I won't let you.

VERONIQUE   I'd love to see him.

MARY   (*Shrewdly*)   You want to destroy what's left, is that it?

VERONIQUE   You're very smart, Mary. Yes, that's what I want to do. I've been thinking how awful it's going to be, having him here in the same town. My first impulse was to go away, as soon as I heard he was here. But I've been thinking it over, and I'd love to see him.

EARL   Well, you can be sure Mary isn't going to let you, not on those terms.

MARY   You're quite wrong. I *want* them to see each other, on *any* terms. I don't expect Veronique to forgive him, but it's important to him to ask her forgiveness.

ERIC   Why, Mary?

MARY   Because this way it's a vacuum, his life. But if he can see her, even if she refuses to forgive him, he's going to keep trying, and as long as he's trying, he's living. Not living in a vacuum. And I know Veronique better than any of you do.

EARL   Better than Veronique knows Veronique, no doubt.

MARY   In some ways, yes. In at least one way.

EARL   Oh, dear. You frighten us. You know us all better than we know ourselves?

MARY   In some cases there isn't very much to know. When will you see him? When can I bring him here? I won't stay, but let me come with him and then disappear.

VERONIQUE   Tomorrow. The sooner the better.

CURTAIN

SCENE THREE

VERONIQUE RINGWALD'S *apartment, the next afternoon. At rise the doorbell is heard, the maid admits* MARY *and* WILMER HIGHTOWER. *They enter the living room and remain standing, awkwardly.* WILMER *is wearing the shabby suit given to paroled prisoners. He is definitely much older, calmer. He is wearing steel-rim glasses, a solid blue neck-*

tie, a wrinkled white shirt. He goes delightedly to the grand piano, runs his fingers soundlessly across the keyboard. He looks about the room, enjoying the touches of luxury. He stands in front of the portable bar, picks up a bottle of brandy, sniffs it, smiles, puts it back on the bar. His inspection of the apartment is pleasurable but at the same time remote; he has seen nothing like all this in nine years, and he is rediscovering it without participation in it. He and MARY *do not converse; they await* VERONIQUE's *entrance.*

VERONIQUE *now enters from a hallway off Left, and* MARY *is immediately startled by* VERONIQUE's *costume. It is so out of style and does not fit too well, and* MARY *accurately guesses what it is: the costume worn by Jean McCullough the night she was murdered.*

VERONIQUE   Hello, Mary. Wilmer. Will you sit down— or Mary, you said you weren't staying. Wilmer understands that, doesn't he?

MARY   Yes. I have my car downstairs. I could wait there, or if you wouldn't mind, I have quite a few phone calls to make. Could I go back to Townsend's study?

VERONIQUE   Yes, he's not using it.

MARY   I know that.

VERONIQUE   All right. You know where everything is, and you can ring if you want a drink or coffee or anything.

MARY   Thank you.

(*She goes to* RINGWALD's *study. When she has gone* VERONIQUE *speaks*)

VERONIQUE   Recognize my dress?

WILMER (*Smiling*)   Not the dress, but I know it goes back a few years. We got the magazines up there.

VERONIQUE (*Turning around*)   This one had a big rip in the back, but I had it repaired.

(WILMER *now realizes what the dress is and what she is doing to him*)

WILMER I didn't remember the dress, Veronique. I guess I should have.

VERONIQUE It doesn't surprise me, your forgetting.

WILMER There isn't much I forgot.

VERONIQUE There isn't *any*thing *I* forgot.

WILMER I understand that. I could tell, the way you looked at me at the trial, you weren't going to forget. You weren't going to let yourself forget.

VERONIQUE No, and I haven't. I know you're not supposed to take a drink, but go ahead. I won't report you.

WILMER No thanks.

VERONIQUE Isn't that going to be pretty tough on you, especially now, when you can go in anywhere and have a drink? No more Prohibition.

WILMER I don't think so. Of course I don't know. But it's so long since I've had a drink, I don't miss it.

VERONIQUE There's some coffee, if you want that.

WILMER Are you having some?

VERONIQUE No.

WILMER Then I won't. May I offer you a cigarette? (*He holds out a pack of Camels*)

VERONIQUE I'll wait. (*She waits only until he lights one for himself, then she takes one out of a silver box and lights it before he can*) What did you want to see me about, Wilmer?

WILMER Didn't Mary tell you? Didn't she even give you a hint?

VERONIQUE I haven't the slightest idea.

WILMER (*Incredulously*) Veronique? But what would I want to come here for?

VERONIQUE That's what I'm trying to find out.

WILMER (*Continuing his own thought*) What's the only thing I'd want to see you for?

VERONIQUE (*Unable to resist one more cruel shaft*)   I don't know. She said you didn't want money.

WILMER   Money? A pack of cigarettes, a bar of chocolate, a cake of soap, a new toothbrush. That's what I've been using money for, the past nine years. I wouldn't know what to do with money if I had it. There's only one thing I want, Veronique, and it doesn't look as though I'm going to get it.

VERONIQUE   And what's that?

WILMER   What I've been praying, the past five years. You used to be a Catholic, maybe you still are. Well, I'm one now. I was converted about six years ago. This Father DuBois, he was the Catholic chaplain then, and they didn't have a Catholic to play the organ, so he asked me to. And I said I would, and one thing led to another and pretty soon I was taking instructions. I was baptized and confirmed a little over five years ago, and ever since then I had a special intention. You know what a special intention is. And every day I asked God to grant me my special intention. Your forgiveness.

VERONIQUE   My forgiveness.

WILMER   The only thing I wanted to see you for, Veronique.

VERONIQUE   Well, your prayers were wasted.

WILMER   No prayers are wasted. If that isn't the way God wants it, I'm not going to receive your forgiveness, but the prayers aren't wasted, Veronique. You know that. You don't always get what you pray for, because it isn't always the will of God to grant it, but He hears your prayers.

VERONIQUE   You studied your catechism all right.

WILMER (*Proudly*)   Ask me any question in the catechism.

VERONIQUE   I learned my catechism in French.

WILMER   Well, ask me in English.

VERONIQUE   No, you know all the answers. That's you, you know all the answers. You always did. All the latest gossip, who was doing it to who. What kind of a man was your priest, the one whose name you mispronounce, DuBois?

WILMER   He pronounced it that way. He was a good man.

VERONIQUE   What else was he?

WILMER   He wasn't one of us.

VERONIQUE   Didn't you have any boy friends in prison?

WILMER   Yes, at first.

VERONIQUE   But you gave that up when you turned Catholic?

WILMER   . . . I tried to.

VERONIQUE   But you didn't succeed.

WILMER   Yes, I finally succeeded.

VERONIQUE   How long ago?

WILMER   How long since I've been with a man?

VERONIQUE   Yes. In other words, how much have you re-formed?

WILMER   About a year. I couldn't help myself. But that was the last time, over a year ago.

VERONIQUE   And now that you're out, how long do you think your reform will last?

WILMER   I don't know. . . . Don't do this to me, Veronique. Let me keep what I have.

VERONIQUE   What have you got?

WILMER   A place to go. The Church. My religion. *Your* religion.

VERONIQUE   You don't want me to kill that, do you?

WILMER   Oh, you can't kill it, but you can take it away from me.

VERONIQUE   How?

WILMER By—making me doubt it. I have doubts. Father DuBois said I'd have them, and I have. But when I have them I pray.

VERONIQUE And then everything's all right again.

WILMER No. But a year ago I gave in because I was having doubts. If I hadn't been having doubts I wouldn't have given in. Now you're starting up my doubts again, and I'm out on parole. Free. Free to walk around, ride in the subway, but what kind of freedom is that if it's going to get me in trouble again?

VERONIQUE You sound as though you were going right out and make a pass at the elevator boy.

WILMER Well, you know what happens if I do, and get caught.

VERONIQUE They'll send you back?

WILMER Yes. Is that what you want?

VERONIQUE It seems little enough, when I think of Jean. (*At the mention of* JEAN's *name his head drops for a moment, then he looks up again, beseechingly*)

WILMER If I go up again, back to prison, will that be enough for you? Will I be forgiven then?

VERONIQUE I don't know.

WILMER (*He shakes his head*) I can tell you, Veronique. It won't be enough for you, and do you know why?

VERONIQUE Why?

WILMER Because then you'll be the murderer, but you'll be a cold-blooded one, and you won't be able to sleep at night.

VERONIQUE You wanted to kill me in cold blood, but you killed my sister instead.

WILMER The person I wanted to kill I didn't kill. That makes killing your sister so much worse. The innocent one, I didn't hate her. What have I got, Veronique? Shall I tell you? Before I had my religion I had nothing

but hate for myself and you, and feeling guilty for
Jean. Then I learned to pray. Do you remember praying,
do you remember what it is to pray? You know what
prayer is? It's a sign of hope. And every night I'd pray
for forgiveness, God's forgiveness and yours. Did I
expect God to tell me I was forgiven? No. But I kept
on praying, and I looked forward to it every day, the
one time when I could really feel hope was when I was
asking God to forgive me. Then they told me I had
a chance for a parole, and I began to hope that if I
got out I could talk to you. Because God doesn't whisper
to you that He's forgiven you. But He can give a sign.
And the sign would be if you forgave me.

(*He takes a deep breath, rises, and goes to the foyer at
Right.* VERONIQUE, *against her will, is impelled to rise
to her feet but every inch she moves is an effort against
a downward pull. It requires all her physical strength,
but she gets to her feet and follows* WILMER, *who is now
in the foyer*)

VERONIQUE   Wilmer—don't go.

CURTAIN

THE
WAY IT
WAS

ACT ONE

SCENE ONE

The scene is a corner of a cheap dance hall. The time is 1922, the summer. A brassy band offstage is playing a one-step, loud and fast, couples are dancing. The young men are all badly dressed, except for one group of three. Most of the young men are dressed in the awkward style of the moment or, in a few cases, in very sharp cake-eater outfits. The exceptions are in the group who are Brooks Brothers of the day: three and four-button suits, buttoned-down collars, saddle straps. The young men are all about the same age—between sixteen and twenty-two. The girls are about the same age and younger. At Right there is a stand where soft drinks, candy, and cigarettes are sold and in front of it are the non-dancing young men of both classes, eyeing the talent. The music stops and the dancers stand and mop their brows and the young men lift their elbows to let some air in under their jackets.

A young man lights a cigarette and the Bouncer goes to him and says, "No smokin'." The Bouncer goes to another young man, who is about to light up, and says, "No smokin'. You wanta smoke go outside." . . . A young man rubs his belly against the belly of the girl he has been dancing with, and she slaps him . . . Two young men

*start a fight and are surrounded by the other young men,
and automatically all the girls go to one side and are left
to themselves until the Bouncer pushes in and grabs one
of the fighters and takes him out. The girls do not get excited by the fight; it is a not uncommon occurrence.*

*Among the girls there is one who stands out for her beauty
and distinction, in spite of her cheap clothes. She is* MARY.
*Among the young men there is one who stands out be-
cause he stands alone. He takes advantage of the fact that
she is momentarily without a young man and goes to her.
His name is* JOHNNY.

JOHNNY   Hello, Mary.

MARY   (*Not unfriendly*)   Hello, Johnny.

JOHNNY   Kin I have the next dance?

MARY   I have it.

JOHNNY   The one after that?

MARY   I have that one, too. You can't dance, Johnny.

JOHNNY   Well, you said you'd learn me.

MARY   But not here.

(*One of the Brooksy types joins them. He is* BOB
MC ADAMS)

BOB   Hello, Johnny. Mary, have you got the next?

MARY   All right.

(*The music starts up and* BOB *and* MARY *dance, doing
the toddle, while* JOHNNY, *not sore, but far from happy,
goes back to his post at the soft-drink counter and
watches the dancers, particularly* MARY *and* BOB. *The
lights fade down and a voice through a megaphone announces:* "Ladies and gentlemen, this dance will be a
Moonlight." *The lights go down except for a sickly
moon at Center*)

CURTAIN

SCENE TWO

It is the exterior of the McAdams Iron & Steel Company plant. The time is noon the next day. At Center, perhaps halfway up, is the entrance to the plant, and on either side, extending all the way to the arch, is a high fence, behind which are visible stacks and cranes and roof tops that are part of the plant. Over the open gateway is an arch on which is painted MC ADAMS IRON & STEEL CO.— BRIDGE & STRUCTURAL SHOP. *Men are sitting on the ground, their backs leaning against the wall, and other men are playing catch, two or three actually having catcher's mitts and pitcher's gloves. Two others are pitching quoits. Two older men, smoking pipes, are playing cards. Each man has a lunch pail near him or in his lap. They are all grimy and in work clothes. One of the ballplayers is* JOHNNY; *one of the men sitting against the fence is* BOB. JOHNNY *is obviously a good ballplayer.*

A WORKMAN   Johnny, you gonna pitch Sunday?

JOHNNY   I guess so.

ANOTHER WORKMAN   Hey, Johnny, I heard there was a scout lookin' at you from the International League.

JOHNNY   Maybe, I don't know.

SECOND WORKMAN (*Incredulously*)   You don't know?

JOHNNY   It don't make no difference. My old man says I gotta finish high school.

SECOND WORKMAN   He won't if Binghamton gives you fifty dollars a week.

JOHNNY   You don't know my old man.

FIRST WORKMAN   It aint your old man, it's your old lady. I hear she wants you to be a priest.

JOHNNY   (*Half humorously*)   I don't have no vocation. (*Here Mary walks by, carrying a large basket of groceries. She knows what is going to happen. It happens. The men notice her in various ways. A few of them whistle:* "Root te-toot, root-te-toot," *in time to her steps. Another says,* "Hyuh, Mary. Gettin' much?" *Another repeats the question. Another:* "How about a date, Mary?" *Another:* "Hey, Mary, you wanta go pickin' huckleberries?" *There is no real offense given or taken. They admire her. She expects to be whistled at. She says,* "Hello, Johnny . . . Hello, Bob . . . Hello, Les . . . Hello, Jake . . ." *to those she knows and makes a lightly contemptuous face at the others. When she has disappeared one workman says,* "How'd you like to dip your socks in her coffee?" *Another says,* "I'd give a week's pay to have a piece of that." *Another says,* "Hey, McAdams, that ought to be something for you," *to which* BOB *replies:* "I wouldn't mind," *to which the first speaker says,* "You never did?" *to which* BOB *says,* "I don't think anybody ever did." *To which another man says, in the then current slang,* "That's what they ALL say." *Here the end-of-lunch whistle blows and the men start going back to work.* JOHNNY *lingers*)

JOHNNY   (*To* BOB)   Hey, McAdams.

BOB   What?

JOHNNY   I wanta ask you something.

BOB   All right.

(JOHNNY *waits until they are alone*)

BOB   You better hurry up or we'll get docked.

JOHNNY   You should worry.

MC ADAMS   Listen, I need the money . . . What do you want?

JOHNNY (*Fumbling*) . . . Dancing . . . How old were you when you learned?

BOB I don't know. About seven. Seven or eight.

JOHNNY (*Dismayed*) Seven or *eight*. Did you learn that early?

BOB That's how old I was when I started dancing school.

JOHNNY Oh. You went to a school for it.

BOB Every God damn Saturday, till I went away to school.

JOHNNY It took that long. Other guys it didn't take that long.

BOB It doesn't take that long. You could learn in a couple of hours.

JOHNNY Could you show me how? Lunch hour, could you show me?

BOB I could show you how to waltz, but I wouldn't here. The other guys would give us the razz.

JOHNNY There's nobody in the oil shack doorn lunch hour.

BOB All you have to do is . . . Watch. (*He makes a square in the dirt and shows* JOHNNY *the primary waltz step.* JOHNNY *imitates him and is catching on when the foreman appears*)

FOREMAN What the hell are you two . . . ? Get back to work you God damn lazy bastards. You, McAdams, I'll turn you in to your old man.

BOB We're going, we're going. (*To* JOHNNY) You're an athlete. You could learn it in no time.

JOHNNY (*Disgustedly*) Athlete.

BOB If I could pitch a drop like yours—well, I'd still want to dance.

CURTAIN

SCENE THREE

A year later. The scene is a dance pavilion, open-air, and a great improvement over the previous dance hall, although still no Palais Royale. JOHNNY *and his partner, a petite redhead, have won the Charleston contest and receive the silver cup. The ceremonies concluded, the general dancing starts up again, and as* JOHNNY *and* RED *are about to dance* BOB MC ADAMS *comes up to* JOHNNY.

BOB   Hey, Johnny, congratulations.

JOHNNY   Hyuh, Bob. You didn't come back to the plant this summer.

BOB   No, I have to crack the books. I'm going to a tutoring school.

JOHNNY   A what?

BOB   Oh, I have to make up some studies.

JOHNNY   (*Holding up the cup*)   By rights you ought to get this . . . This is Bob McAdams. He showed me how to dance.

BOB   All I did was get you started. What's your name, little one?

RED   Will I tell him?

JOHNNY   Sure. Her name is Theresa McDonald, but Red is what we call her.

BOB   How about a dance, Red?

RED   Ask my escort.

BOB   All right, escort?

JOHNNY   Sure. I'll hold the baby (*Indicating cup*) while you dance with her.

BOB   Hey, a wisecrack.
    (JOHNNY *goes off and* BOB *and* RED *dance*)

BOB   Where you from, Red?

RED   That's for me to know and you to find out.

BOB   Are you Johnny's girl?

RED   I consider that a personal question.

BOB   So do I. I don't know what else you could consider it, Red.

RED   I consider the source of that remark.

BOB   You sound as if you were in a considerate mood tonight. Are you? If so, I have a car. Okay?

RED   Ask me no questions I'll tell you no lies.

BOB   You *are* Johnny's *girl?*

RED   (*Wearily*)   Nobody's Johnny's girl.

BOB   What happened to Mary Stukitis?

RED   Oh, you know Mary?

BOB   Casually.

RED   Johnny's got her on the brain.

BOB   Well, I don't blame him for that.

RED   (*Bitterly*)   She's a regular tramp.

BOB   Mary? No.

RED   Aah, you. You're like him. Making excuses for her.

BOB   No, I just said she wasn't a tramp.

RED   All right, where is she?

BOB   All right. *Where* is she?

RED   Her parents don't know. Or maybe they do. Maybe they just aint telling.

BOB   Oh, she isn't home any more?

RED   Since last Feb-uary. She left town with a traveling salesman.

BOB   Mary? I didn't know that. Did she get married?

RED   Huh. April she wrote to Johnny for money.

BOB   How do you know?

RED   How do I know. He got drunk and told me, that's how I know.

BOB   Johnny got drunk?

RED   He gets slopped all the time. You're the McAdams that your father owns the steel mill.

BOB   Check.

RED   I thought I reccanize your name. *That* McAdams.

BOB   Johnny gets fried, eh? What about basketball? What about baseball?

RED   Dancing, that's all he cares about any more. Him and I won four cups this year. We got an offer to go on the stage.

BOB   In a year's time? A year ago Johnny couldn't dance two steps.

RED   Don't take the credit. He's a natural dancer from the word go. All somebody had to do was start him. I guess it was you.

BOB   Are you going on the stage?

RED   We had an offer to, but my parents don't wish me to leave home. My parents are very strict.

BOB   Then I guess it's no use asking you again.

RED   What?

BOB   Oh, go for a ride. Drive up to the Stage Coach and have a highball.

RED   You gotta promise to bring me back in an hour. Anyway two hours.

BOB   Do you want to ask Johnny?

RED   Aw, the hell with Johnny. *He* never asks *me*.

CURTAIN

SCENE FOUR

*Philadelphia. A year later. Wanamaker's. One of the row
of boutiques on the main floor. The candy store, next to
the Redleaf of London store. Closing time in the afternoon. The last customer is leaving the Redleaf shop, while*
MARY *is wrapping candy for her last customer. The candy
customer leaves,* MARY *is alone, and she is joined by a
man from the Redleaf shop who has been waiting for*
MARY'S *customer to leave. He is a man in his thirties,
extremely well dressed, blasé as a man in a custom shop
can be. During the conversation that ensues other sales-
people cross the stage as they presumably leave for home.
The men among them give* MARY *the eye, say goodnight
to her, and among them are a couple of boys of the Wanamaker cadet corps in their blue caps and jackets, white
breeches and canvas leggings. The boys say* "Goodnight,
Miss Stewart," *indicating* MARY'S *change of name from
Stukitis. The name of the Redleaf salesman is* RALPH KIP-
LINGER. *When he saunters over to* MARY'S *shop, and
through part of the ensuing conversation, she is taking
trays of candy out of the display cases and putting them
away.*

RALPH KIPLINGER   Do you want to go home first?

MARY   Uh-huh.

RALPH   That suits me. I gotta go over to North Broad.
You know that friend of mine, the auto salesman?

MARY   Uh-huh.

RALPH   Well, you know I got him a polo coat at a re-

duction. A real Worumba, would have set him back
ninety-five bucks, full price. He's the same size as me,
so I got it for him at the employees' price. Oh, plus
I charged him ten dollars over what it would of cost
me, but even so.

MARY   Even so.

RALPH   He's a very neat dresser. He has to be. You know,
all those Main Line society people. I often get him
a good bargain. Well, do you know what he has for me
tonight?

MARY   No.

RALPH   Wait'll you see it. A yellow Marmon roadster.
Speedster. A Marmon speedster. Wait'll you see it. I
think it's the snappiest job in town. You know, he's
suppose to be giving me a demonstration.

MARY   Uh-huh.

RALPH   So I was thinking, I'll stop for you around ha'
past seven and instead of eating in the city, we go for
a ride. You ever been to the King of Prussia Inn?

MARY   No. I never even heard of it.

RALPH   Well, there's a lot you never heard of, Mary, but
you're learning fast. I'll give you credit. You know,
some of these headwaiters, I bet they wonder who you
are.

MARY   Headwaiters. What do I care about headwaiters?

RALPH   (*Smiling*)   Well, you don't have to care about
them, but you can't just start out with one of the
Drexels. Or would you rather have a Biddle?

MARY   (*Finishing her trays*)   There. Ralph, I got something to tell you.

RALPH   What?

MARY   I'm not going out with you tonight.

RALPH   Oh. The way you sounded, I thought you were
gonna tell me you were knocked up or something.

MARY   You're not going to have to worry about that any more.

RALPH   What do you mean by that?

MARY   Well, you remember you said we were never gonna get serious.

RALPH   Sure. I'm only separated. No divorce.

MARY   I'm quitting this job.

RALPH   All right. Listen, let's go to your apartment, I don't wanta talk here.

MARY   I moved.

RALPH   Wuddia mean you moved? When did you move?

MARY   The day before yesterday.

RALPH   Where to?

MARY   It wouldn't do you any good to tell you where to, Ralph.

RALPH   You mean you're telling me to take the air, just like that? Listen, I spent a hell of a lot of money on you.

MARY   Half of it was on you. More than half. I never cost you anything for liquor.

RALPH   Are you gonna give me back the diamond ring? I still owe on that.

MARY   No, I'm not gonna give you back the ring.

RALPH   I'll sue you.

MARY   Like hell you will.

RALPH   Who's the new boy friend?

MARY   You don't know him.

RALPH   How do you know I don't know him?

MARY   Because I saw you wait on him and you didn't know him.

RALPH   Was he a charge customer?

MARY   (*Nodding*)   Yes.

RALPH   How do you know?

MARY   Because then he bought some candy.

RALPH   (*Looking at her from a drawn back position*) Well, I'll be a son of a bitch. So you been two-timing me, you blonde-haired Lithuanian broad.

MARY   The both of us were two-timing one another, Ralph, so don't call me any names. Anyway I don't like to be called names. I'll give you a tray of chocolate creams right square in the face.

RALPH   It's a good thing you're quitting here, or I'd fix you.

MARY   Oh, I knew that all right.

RALPH   Is this bastard married?

MARY   Everybody's married that wants to take me out. Sure he's married.

RALPH   Mary, I wouldn't be surprised if you got somewhere.

MARY   I wouldn't either. But I wasn't getting anywhere with you, Ralph.

RALPH   (*Realistically*)   No, I guess not. This new bastard, he probably *owns* a Marmon, and *I* gotta *chisel* one.

MARY   Something like a Marmon, but not a Marmon.

RALPH   Well, so . . . But that don't say—you know, Mary, you two-timed me, you could two-time him.

MARY   Oh, no.

RALPH   Too good, huh?

MARY   It's everything I wanted so far. (*Then, after a pause*) Or I guess it is.

RALPH   So long, Mary Stukitis.

MARY   Goo' bye, Ralph Kiplinger.

RALPH   (*Calling after her*)   What's *his* name, Mary? (*She smiles and puts her fingers to her lips as she goes off*)

CURTAIN

SCENE FIVE

*A rehearsal hall in the Forties, a few months later. It is
furnished only with some bentwood chairs and an upright
piano. Two boys and two girls are doing backbends, etc.,
ad-libbing time steps. The pianist is improvising in the
manner of Rube Bloom. A rather tired blonde with a still
good figure is smoking a cigarette indolently, standing aloof
from the others. The operation seems to be in charge of a
man named* BILLY BRADFORD, *a fat queen of young-middle
age.*

BILLY   All right, you terribly talented people. We do
the Newport number.
*(The piano starts up and the boys and girls, who are
all in rehearsal costume, do a dreary society-type song-
and-dance, the lyric sung by the blonde, who is named*
KITTEN CLEVELAND. *During the number* BILLY *shouts
at the dancers:* "You, Blanche, get your canetta into
it, dear. Charles, stop camping. We're gonna play
Shamokin and they don't like uth there. They don't
underthtand uth. Allan, don't you know right from left?"
During the number JOHNNY *has entered the hall unob-
served and watches fascinated while the number is being
done. At the end of one chorus* BILLY *calls a halt.*
"Fifteen minutes out for lunch, and fifteen, that's all."
*A boy comes up to him and borrows a dollar. The others
wander out and* BILLY *for the first time notices* JOHNNY)

BILLY   Who are you? Get out of here.

JOHNNY   Didn't you get my letter?

BILLY   Didn't I get your letter? I should say not. Where did I know you?

JOHNNY   You didn't know me, but I sent you the, uh, enrollment fee, the ten dollars.

BILLY   *You* sent *me* ten dollars?

JOHNNY   When I answered the ad. You said to send you ten dollars enrollment fee.

KITTEN   Wait a minute. Are you looking for the Jack Weston Dancing Academy?

JOHNNY   Yeah. Is this the wrong floor?

KITTEN   No, it's the right floor. (*She and* BILLY *exchange glances*) Was Mr. Weston expecting you?

JOHNNY   Well, maybe he wasn't. In a way he was. Not this particular day, but when the new classes started.

KITTEN   Oh, well that may be some time. Right now the hall is—we rent the hall for rehearsals of our show.

BILLY   How much was Mr. Weston charging?

JOHNNY   A hundred and fifty for the course. Ten dollars enrollment fee and twenty dollars a week for the six weeks.

BILLY   That leaves twenty dollars. What happened to that?

JOHNNY   That's for registering your name so you can get jobs, *after* you complete the course.

BILLY   Oh. You had any show business experience at all? Can you dance? Do a time step for me.

JOHNNY   I don't know what it is. I won a lot of cups but I never had no lessons.

BILLY   What were the cups for?

JOHNNY   Ballroom dancing.

BILLY   Just for the fun of it, dance with Miss Cleveland. Miss Cleveland, you know, she's the former Ziegfield star and now she's the star of our own production.

JOHNNY   She is?

BILLY   I'll play the piano.

(*He goes to piano,* KITTEN *becomes* JOHNNY's *partner, and they dance. He is very sharpie, original, crude, but has something.* BILLY *finishes playing*)

BILLY   How would you like to get some practical experience?

JOHNNY   Fine, as soon as I learn the steps.

BILLY   Do you know what a tab show is? No, you wouldn't. Well, our production is what they call a tab show. You might say it's a condensed version of a Broadway musical comedy.

KITTEN   (*Warningly*)   Equity. Equity.

BILLY   I'll charge you the same money as Jack Weston would, only I'll get you experience right away, at the same time.

JOHNNY   I don't get it.

BILLY   You don't? I'll tell you what I'll do. I'll let you rehearse with us, or watch us, and I'll give you the same instruction course you'd get from Jack Weston. You have the money on you, don't you?

JOHNNY   Yeah, I just got here.

BILLY   Well, we open a week from Sunday, uptown. By that time you ought to learned enough to be an understudy. Can you sing?

JOHNNY   I can carry a tune.

BILLY   Uh-huh. Well, that's always in one's favor. You give me fifty dollars now and then at the end of next week, when we open at one of the big New York theaters uptown, another fifty. And then if you've lived up to expectations I'll take you on the road with us. That's the best experience you can get, you know. On the road. Where you staying in New York?

JOHNNY   I guess I'll go to the Y. M.

BILLY   All right. You be here at ten o'clock sharp tomorrow morning and we'll start. Okay?

JOHNNY Sure, I guess so.

BILLY All right, then, see you tomorrow. Ten sharp. Don't be late.

(JOHNNY *goes off, and* KITTEN *stares at* BILLY *disapprovingly*)

KITTEN You'll end up over on the Island with Mr. Jack Weston.

BILLY I been on the Island, honey. It aint so bad. Anyway I didn't take his money.

KITTEN Not yet. Tomorrow.

BILLY He does have something.

KITTEN Listen, he's innocent.

BILLY I didn't mean that. Honestly I didn't. Anyway, he's not my type.

KITTEN I didn't know you had a type.

BILLY Oh, dear, yes. But who are you to talk? Is he your type?

KITTEN Well, he *reminds* me of somebody.

BILLY That's all the excuse *you're* gonna need. All right, you can have him.

KITTEN Well, just to keep him away from you.

BILLY *Big* of you, dear. *Big* of you. Now let's see. After the Newport number you and I need some jokes, some funnies. Now what can we steal? Did you happen to catch Cleo Mayfield and Cecil Lean a couple weeks ago?

KITTEN I thought we were gonna be Julia Sanderson and Frank Crumit.

BILLY Watch your billing, dear. I think it's Frank Crumit and Julia Sanderson. No, I want you more on the order of Mayfield. Frank and Julia, they don't get the laughs the way Cecil and Cleo do.

KITTEN It won't make any difference when we get to Shamokin.

CURTAIN

SCENE SIX

Interior of a speakeasy, the Puncheon Grotto. It is late afternoon but before the cocktail crowd begins to arrive. It is, of course, a class joint, since it was the original 21. There is not room for very many people, and now the only person in the room besides the help is BOB MC ADAMS.

BOB Georgetti.

GEORGETTI (*Waiter*) Yes, Mr. McAdams. A Planter's Punch, sir?

BOB Another Planter's Punch.

(JOHNNY *enters and* BOB *greets him*)

BOB Hyuh, Johnny.

JOHNNY Hyuh, Bob. I got your message. (*He sits down with* BOB)

BOB I see you did. I was afraid you might have moved.

JOHNNY How did you ever find out where I was living?

BOB Easy. I called up and asked your mother.

JOHNNY Yeah, they have a phone now. The first good job I got I sent her the money. All her life she always wanted a phone, but my old man didn't want no phone. And he was right. We didn't know anybody that had one, so where was the advantage. But my old lady wanted it, so I made her a present of it. How's your family? Your parents? Your sister?

BOB   They're all pretty well, thanks. Connie got married last June.

JOHNNY   She did? Marry a guy from town?

BOB   No, fellow from Baltimore.

JOHNNY   Baltimore, eh? I guess everything's all right at the mill.

BOB   Oh, sure. The old man's running it by himself. What will you have?

JOHNNY   Nothing, thanks. I got a show tonight.

BOB   You sure have. From what I hear, you *are* the show.

JOHNNY   No. Don't believe all you hear. I got good notices, but I wouldn't be anywhere without the stars. They got four real stars in this show. I was afraid, you know, when I got those good notices, I was afraid the real stars—well, *you* know. Who the hell is this punk? But they were great. They all congratulated me. Well, one of them, but everybody always has trouble with her, and it don't mean anything. She squawks if it rains, and she squawks if it don't rain. What are you doing, Bob? I guess I should know, but I don't.

BOB   I just started working downtown. Wall Street.

JOHNNY   Bond salesman?

BOB   That's the idea. There's nothing for me at the mill. As a matter of fact my old gent doesn't want me at the mill. He said go out and get a job where the boss wasn't my father. So I got this job, or anyway he got it for me.

JOHNNY   You living in the city?

BOB   Yes, I have an apartment with two other guys. We just moved in. Over on 37th Street. Four rooms and bath. We got a two-months' concession on a two-year lease. After we get moved in properly we're going to have some parties, so you'll see it. Not bad. Near the Lexington Avenue subway, Princeton Club, a couple of good speakeasies. Grand Central, if you have to go away. Not bad.

JOHNNY This is a new place for me. I had a hard time getting in.

BOB Didn't you mention my name?

JOHNNY When they gave me a chance to, I did. I guess they didn't like my looks.

BOB Yeah, they're funny here. The first time I came here it was with my old gent. A lot of *his* friends come here. My favorite is Dan Moriarty's, but they don't allow women.

JOHNNY They must be the only ones that don't. You know, I can't get used to the idea of seeing a girl in a speakeasy. I mean, you know, a girl like your sister. Show people, that's different. I go to a joint down the street from here, Tony's. Not that I been going there very long, just since I been in honest-to-God Broadway shows. But—well, I don't know.

BOB You got anything good in the show?

JOHNNY (*Nodding*) Yeah. There's one. I got one lined up. I gave her a little lay when we were in New Haven, but nothing, you know, serious. If she has a date, all right, and if *I* have a date, all right.

BOB Yeah, I guess there must be plenty of it.

JOHNNY (*Nodding*) Yeah. Yeah.

BOB You know who I always thought you'd get together with?

JOHNNY Well, I can guess.

BOB Mary Stukitis.

JOHNNY If there would have been anybody it would have been her.

BOB Do you ever run into her?

JOHNNY Mary? No. The last I heard, I guess she was working in some store in Philadelphia, but that was two-three years ago. I played Philly a lot of times and I used to have the temptation to go to—what's the name of it?—Wanamaker's. See if I could find her.

But what chance would you have in a place that size, with I don't know, a thousand, two thousand clerks. But if it'da been anybody it'da been Mary. You know, Bob, I never told anybody this, but there doesn't a day go by without me thinking of Mary. And I guess I think of her on the average two, three, four times a day.

BOB   In other words, you're in love with her.

JOHNNY   But I'm not. You know I was never *out* with Mary? I tell you something else. I never even danced with her. You know why I'm a dancer now? Because of Mary. I got you to show me the waltz, remember?

BOB   Sure. I brag about it all the time.

JOHNNY   (*Smiling, pleased*)   Huh. But that's why I wanted to learn. And she blew town before I could show her I could dance.

(*A middle-aged man, quietly and expensively dressed, enters. The waiters and bartenders all address him respectfully:* "Good evening, Mr. Jones. Good evening, sir.")

JONES   (*Gently but commandingly*)   Emil. Georgetti. We'll be two, please.

BOB MC ADAMS   (*Recognizing him*)   Hello, Mr. Jones.

JONES   Oh, hello there. (*He half smiles and nods at* BOB, *then at* JOHNNY, *but without real recognition*)

BOB   (*Standing up, extending hand*)   I'm Bob McAdams.

JONES   (*Sincerely pleased*)   Oh, of course. Hello, Bob. Good to see you. Are you in New York now?

BOB   Yes sir, I just started.

JONES   How's that father of yours? Son of a gun owes me a letter. How's your mother?

BOB   Fine, thanks.

JONES   And Connie got married. I knew *that*. I was sorry I couldn't get up for the wedding.

BOB How's Mrs. Jones?

JONES Oh, very well thank you. The twins just got back from Europe. I s'pose you knew they were at Bryn Mawr.

BOB Yes, I did. This is my friend Johnny Anton.

JONES Oh, yes. How do you do. I thought I recognized you. I saw your show. Very *fine*. *Very* fine. Fact I saw it twice. Philadelphia, and here. Saw it last night, with a friend of mine.

JOHNNY Thank you.

JONES (*Politely ditching them*) Well, nice to see you, Bob. Regards to the family. Like to buy you a drink, but I'm waiting for somebody right this minute.

BOB That's all right. We have to go, too. I mean, we have to go. Check, please.

(JONES, *instead of sitting down, waits at the bar, watching them and the door uneasily until they have paid the bill and left*)

EMIL (*Bartender*) Sir, I bought some of that Aviation Corporation, thank you sir.

JONES (*Cautiously*) Well, now I didn't *tell* you to *buy* it. I think you'd be a fool *not* to, but that isn't the same as advising you, if you know what I mean.

EMIL I'll take my chances, Mr. Jones. Lady, sir.

(MARY STUKITIS-STEWART *enters and joins* JONES)

MARY Hello.

JONES Hello, my dear. Do you know who was just here?

MARY Yes. I *saw* them, but they didn't see *me*.

JONES Let's sit down. You want a Side Car?

MARY Yes.

JONES Damned Side Cars. What do you want to drink brandy for?

MARY What do I want to drink anything for?

JONES   Well, all right. A Side Car, please, and a Scotch and soda. You know young McAdams.

MARY   Sure. We come from the same town.

JONES   I know that, but I didn't know you knew him.

MARY   I used to live near the steel mill, and I danced with him a lot of times.

JONES   Is that all you did with him?

MARY   Oh, lay off.

JONES   Well, I just wanted to know. This place is getting too popular.

MARY   Yes, look at the crowds, every table packed.

JONES   You know what I mean.

MARY   Now, listen, last night we went to a show and the Central Park Casino.

JONES   That's different. That's *public*. This place is, *any* speakeasy, if I see a friend of mine having cocktails in a speakeasy, I know what I think.

MARY   And you're probably right.

JONES   Right or wrong, I don't like it.

MARY   Drink your drink, Denison, and you'll feel better.

JONES   Don't call me Denison. I'm sorry. I guess it's seeing those damn kids. McAdams, and the other one.

MARY   You know what?

JONES   What?

MARY   You didn't ask me about the other one. Johnny Antonelli.

JONES   Should I?

MARY   Well, you always do. Why make an exception of him?

JONES   Well, all right. If it'll make you feel any better, what about him?

MARY   I'm in love with him.

JONES   No, I know you're not that. I think you're telling

me the truth. I think you love me. But God damn it
you can certainly give me a bad time when you want
to. Why do you want to give me a bad time, Mary?
I always try to be nice to you. Maybe I don't always
succeed, but I try.

MARY   You can be sweet, I'll admit that.

JONES   Well, I should think you *would* admit it.

MARY   . . . Did you make a lot of money today?

JONES   Yes, I made quite a lot of money today. And so
did you.

MARY   Did I? How much?

JONES   More than your job pays you in a year.

MARY   Good. Then I'll buy you a present.

JONES   I don't want a present. The best present you can
give me is—let me relax.

MARY   All right, relax.

JONES   If you really want to give me a present, I know
one you can give me.

MARY   Quit my job.

JONES   Exactly.

MARY   No.

JONES   Why not? You have plenty of money, and you
get just as tired as I do. That's why we have these
spats. You walk around all day, taking off dresses,
putting on dresses, taking a lot of guff from fat slob
women. And you don't eat enough.

MARY   If I ate more I'd get to be one of those fat slob
women. Then you'd start looking for another Mary.

JONES   (*Sincerely*)   No I wouldn't. You're my girl, and
you know it.

MARY   Yes, but that gets us back to the same old place.
You're never going to get a divorce and even if you
did I wouldn't marry you. I wouldn't marry a divorced
man. It's against my religion.

JONES   So is having an affair with me against your religion. I know. I have a Catholic friend. I know quite
a bit about your religion.

MARY   You don't know anything about it. But I'm not
quitting my job. As long as I have my job I'm all right.
It's the same to me as your wife and family are to you.

JONES   Well, I guess I can't argue that.

MARY   I'll get older and they won't want me to model
any more, but by that time I'll be a vendeuse.

JONES   A what?

MARY   A vendeuse. Don't they teach French at Harvard?

JONES   God damn little to me, I must say.

MARY   A saleswoman.

JONES   Oh.

MARY   Or—I'll get married.

JONES   (*After a count of three*)   Mary, if you knew what
that does to me, when you say you'll get married. You
will. You'll get married. You ought to. According to
everything that's right, and decent, and that I was
brought up to believe. You know what kind of a man
I've been, I've told you often enough. I'm not very
proud of myself as a husband. As a father I guess I've
been all right, but not as a husband. But nevertheless
when you speak of marrying somebody, it's like a punch
in the guts that I wasn't expecting. I realize how much
you mean to me and how little everybody else has ever
meant. I've been happier with you than I've ever been.
And any thought of your not being in my life . . .
Do you realize that, Mary?

MARY   Why do you think I'm here?

JONES   (*With an attempt at humor*)   Because one day
I stopped at Wanamaker's, and bought a box of candy.

CURTAIN

SCENE SEVEN

The top of a Fifth Avenue bus, number 1 to 5. BOB
MC ADAMS *is sitting alone in one of the front seats. It is,
of course, one of the old open-top buses. He is letting the
wind blow on his face. The bus stops, we hear the con-
ductor's signal, and the bus starts again.* MARY, *who has
boarded the bus, appears at the back end. At first she
thinks she is alone, but then, seeing* MC ADAMS, *whom
she does not recognize from the rear, she takes a seat halfway up toward the front.* MC ADAMS, *enjoying life, turns
around and sees first, a girl, then, recognizing her,* MARY.

BOB MC ADAMS   Hey, Mary?

MARY   Who is it? . . . Bob. Bob McAdams!

BOB   This is swell. How are you. Come on, sit with me.
Where you headed for?

MARY   Home.

BOB   Home? I thought you lived in Philadelphia.

MARY   Not any more. You don't keep up to date. Do you
live in New York?

BOB   Sure. I've been living here almost a year. Do you
know who I see all the time? Johnny Antonelli. Johnny
Anton, of course.

MARY   I saw him in his show.

BOB   Didn't you go backstage? I have a lot of friends in
the show, thanks to Johnny, of course. But he'd be
disappointed if he knew you saw the show and didn't
go back.

MARY   I couldn't. I was always with somebody.

BOB   You say always?

MARY   I've seen it three times.

BOB   You better not let him find that out. What are you doing, I mean have you got a job?

MARY   Yes, I'm a model.

BOB   Where? Bergdorf Goodman's? I know a model there.

MARY   No, a smaller place. It's called Elise Brennan, you probably never heard of it.

BOB   No. Where do you live? Are you in the phone book?

MARY   (*After a fraction of a second's pause*)   Yes. Under the name of Mary Stewart. East 65th Street.

BOB   Mary Stewart. You know what happened to her.

MARY   She was beheaded.

BOB   Yes, I was going to say she lost her head. Stewart, eh? Well, that's not so far from Stukitis.

MARY   It's about as far as Lithuania to Scotland.

BOB   (*Laughing*)   Not bad. Listen, you're not married or anything, are you?

MARY   No, I'm still single. How about you?

BOB   Oh, me? Marriage is the farthest thing from my thoughts.

MARY   I'll bet.

BOB   Well listen, Mary, how about dinner some night? If I call you up are you going to be busy for the next six months or would you like to reminisce about the old home town?

MARY   Any time.

BOB   How about weekends?

MARY   (*Suspiciously*)   What do you mean?

BOB   Well, next Sunday, for instance. I share an apartment with these two friends of mine and we have a cocktail party almost every Sunday.

MARY Weekends I'm almost always free.

BOB Well good, how about this Sunday? I'll get Johnny to come.

MARY Oh. Well, I don't know.

BOB Why? Don't you want to see Johnny?

MARY Well, you don't have to have him on account of me.

BOB You'd rather he didn't come.

MARY Well—I wouldn't have much to say to him.

BOB Okay, we don't have to have him. You come, and then you and I go some place for dinner.

MARY All right, fine. I'd like to go out with you. Talk.

BOB Swell. And not just once or twice, huh?

MARY Well, there's one thing, though, Bob. I'm liable to break a date at the last minute.

BOB Who doesn't?

MARY Well, I just don't want you to get sore.

BOB Listen, don't get me wrong. I don't delude myself that you've been sitting here in New York waiting for good old Bob McAdams to take you out.

MARY Sixty-fourth Street. I get off here. Are you in the phone book?

BOB East Thirty-seventh Street. Any time after five-thirty.

CURTAIN

SCENE EIGHT

A large room in the Hotel Astor, the night of the Beaux Arts Ball. The room is crowded with people in costume, notable especially for the decolletage of the women. There is a makeshift bar, attended by bartenders, but there are scarcely any chairs, not enough to seat a fraction of the people. The door up Center is open most of the time, and when it is closed it gets opened by the curious, the tight, the misdirected, or the invited. A man is playing piano. The people in this party range in age from college boys to men well in middle age, but the women are mostly young.

A GIRL   Whose party is this?

A BOY (*Uncertainly*)   The, uh, Société de Ecole des Beaux Arts Architects. Anyway, it's the Beaux Arts Ball. Does that help you?

THE GIRL   No, I knew that much. I mean this party, where we are.

THE BOY   Oh. You mean *this* party. I don't know.

THE GIRL   Because actually, I don't know a soul.

THE BOY   Hell, I don't even know *you.*

THE GIRL   Oh, *well.* (*Her tone implies, "Let's fix that." She kisses him and they embrace warmly*)

ANOTHER BOY (*In white flannels and white shirt, with a red handkerchief around his head*)   What are you supposed to be?

THIRD BOY   A pirate.

ANOTHER BOY   Yes, but what pirate?

THIRD BOY   Billy the Kid.

ANOTHER BOY   No. Billy the Kid was a cowboy.

THIRD BOY   Are you sure?

ANOTHER BOY   I'm *almost positive.*

THIRD BOY   Then what am I?

ANOTHER BOY   Why don't you be an Indian?

THIRD BOY   That's a thought.

OLDER MAN   I think they must be having the pageant.

YOUNGISH WOMAN   Oh, really? Why?

OLDER MAN   Because it's time for it. I have to get down there, Mrs. Menken would never forgive me.

YOUNGISH WOMAN   You're fried. There is no Mrs. Menken.

OLDER MAN   I'm speaking of Mrs. S. Stanwood— Oh, Lord, every year, every year. Hello, Denny.

DENISON JONES   Hello, there, Crownie. Miss Stewart, Mr. Crowninshield. Pronounced Crunchel.

CROWNINSHIELD   Any relation to Will Stewart?

MARY   No relation to any Stewart.

CROWNINSHIELD   Oh, yes. A *nom de guerre.*

MARY   A *nom.* I don't know about the *de guerre.*

CROWNINSHIELD   Speaks French. How nice, my dear. Nice accent.

MARY   I learned it at school.

CROWNINSHIELD   Lausanne? Genève?

MARY   St. Mary Star of the Sea, Gibbsville, Pennsylvania.

CROWNINSHIELD   I must run. Pageant. Committee, y'know. Au vwah. (*He pats* MARY'S *bare arm*) See you later, Denny. (*He goes*)

JONES   You know who that was?

MARY   Sure.

JONES You know more people in this town than I do.

MARY No. I just don't know the *same* people.

JONES I'm not any happier about that than you are.

MARY I didn't say I was unhappy. Just a statement of fact. You have your Racquet Club friends, and I have my friends.

JONES You've met most of my Racquet Club friends.

MARY But not their wives.

JONES You wouldn't like *them,* the wives.

MARY What makes you think I like the husbands? Dull bunch of bastards.

JONES (*Loyally*) Well, I'm one of them.

MARY I'll say you are.

JONES (*Hurt*) Mary, we came here to have a good time. You wanted to come, I didn't particularly. I don't any more like quarreling in the midst of a party than I would making love. Look at those two. (*Indicates the first boy and girl, necking*)

MARY They're enjoying it.

JONES (*After a two-count, helplessly*) Would you enjoy it?

MARY I don't know. I don't know what I'd enjoy.

JONES . . . I'll get you a drink. Would you like some champagne?

MARY I don't want a drink. A drink isn't what I want.

JONES Yes it is. I know these moods. I'll get you a good stiff highball.

MARY You don't know these moods, and I don't want a drink.

(JONES *smiles patronizingly and leaves her. She is standing alone and* JOHNNY *enters, first unseen by her, but then as he moves through the crowd she sees him, joyfully, then* JOHNNY *sees her*)

MARY   Johnny! Johnny!

(JOHNNY, *slightly tight and on the prowl, full of confidence nowadays, goes quickly to her and they embrace, then she takes her head away without removing her arms, then she kisses him in an unmistakably abandoned way, and together they push through the crowd and out the door*)

CURTAIN

ACT TWO

SCENE ONE

MARY'S *apartment.* DENISON JONES, *still in some of his Beaux Arts Ball costume, is asleep in an armchair. It is dawning, not yet full daylight. A whiskey bottle and glass are on the coffee table in front of* JONES' *chair. The door of the apartment opens and* MARY *enters, wearing a man's trench coat buttoned all the way up. She sees* JONES, *looks at him for a moment, then takes off the trench coat and hangs it in the foyer closet, revealing herself still in ball costume. She goes off and comes back, now divested of her costume and wearing a dressing gown, and carrying a large glass of milk, which she puts on the coffee table in front of* JONES. *During the action he stirs a little, then when she puts the milk on the table he wakes up but does not get out of the chair.*

JONES Hello.

MARY Hello.

JONES You been home long?

MARY No.

JONES (*Rather pitifully*) The dance still going?

MARY I guess so.

JONES (*Looks at mantel clock*) Ten past six. What happened to you? I turned my back to get you a drink and the next thing I knew you were gone.

MARY I know. You better drink some of that milk.

JONES Where did you go?

MARY Who cares?

JONES I care. I care a great deal. I didn't say anything to get you sore at me, not *that* sore.

MARY I was fed up, and I left.

JONES What were you fed up with?

MARY Drink your milk. I got fed up because—I'll tell you why I was fed up. Whenever I get the blues you say, "Have a drink, that's what you need." Till I started going around with you I never knew the taste of liquor. Now I drink all the time. Drink doesn't solve any problems for me. Maybe it does for you, but not for me.

JONES We don't drink enough to do us any harm.

MARY Apple sauce. You couldn't eat a meal without a drink, and pretty soon I'll be just as bad.

JONES . . . Who brought you home?

MARY I came home alone, in a taxi.

JONES (*Relieved but unsatisfied*) You came home alone?

MARY Ask the doorman. You better get some sleep. You have to go back to Philadelphia today.

JONES Have you been to bed?

MARY (*Sticking to the literal truth*) I only got home a little while ago. Anyway, I'm not going to work today. I got the day off, I knew how late we'd be up.

JONES (*Clinging to the hope that things are okay*) I must look pretty silly. There's nothing worse than fancy dress in the daytime.

MARY (*Picking up whiskey bottle*) You through with this?

JONES Yes. Not permanently, of course.

MARY   Oh, I know that much. I want to put it away so I don't have to look at it.

JONES   . . . Mary, I'm sorry if I was stupid last night. It's pretty hard going for both of us.

MARY   I'm glad you realize that.

JONES   Realize it? I think about it all the time. But I must have been pretty obnoxious. You never actually walked out on me before. You go to bed. I'll sleep out here.

MARY   All right. Goodnight.

JONES   (*Goes to her and kisses her gently*)   I won't wake you up when I leave.

MARY   Thanks.

JONES   I'll be in New York Tuesday and I'll call you then, but I'm not spending the night. Wednesday I'm coming over again and I *will* spend the night.

MARY   All right.

JONES   I'm sorry about all this. I love you. You know that.

MARY   Yes.

JONES   Oh, and call Zimmermann Monday morning. I want you to get out of that stock. You've made about four thousand dollars out of it.

MARY   Have I?

JONES   Yes. I'm watching something else for you. I'll know more about it when I see you Wednesday.

MARY   When am I going to be able to spend some of this money?

JONES   When your account gets to fifty thousand.

MARY   That'll be never.

JONES   It'll be sooner than you think. Why, do you need money?

MARY   No.

JONES   I wish my wife would say that, just once. (*It is*

exactly the wrong thing for him to have said, and he almost immediately realizes it)

MARY   Well, goodnight, or good morning.

JONES   Goodnight. Oh, will you take the costumes back to Brooks?

MARY   (*Wearily*)   Sure.

CURTAIN

SCENE TWO

JOHNNY's *apartment, brand new, tubular modern. He is in the process of showing it for the first time to* BOB MC ADAMS.

JOHNNY   Well, here it is.

BOB   (*Looking about*)   Boy!

JOHNNY   Johnny Antonelli on Park Avenue. Who'da thunk it. Like the piano? That bar? Those chairs. The idea is if you get drunk you don't have far to fall.

BOB   Boy. This makes our place look like the stockyards. You must be making more money than I thought.

JOHNNY   They tore up the contract. I got an offer to dance in a supper club, it would have paid me an extra five hundred bucks a week, but Sid Harrison, you know, manager of our show, he said he'd give me three hundred if I didn't take any outside offers. So I said sure. But when the show closes my price goes up. I got an offer of a show next season. . . . You ever read The Vanity Fair?

BOB   The book or the magazine?

JOHNNY   The magazine.

BOB   Sure.

JOHNNY   They're gonna have an article about me. With pictures. I saw the article. It says I combine Jack Donahue and Fred Astaire. They're crazy. Those two guys know more about dancing than if I lived to be a hundred. You ever watch Astaire's hands. If I did that they'd say I was camping.

BOB   I guess it's because you're new, they have to compare you with somebody.

JOHNNY   You're right. I never thought of that. (*Looks about him*) I'll say one thing for show business. If I'da had my other ambition I wouldn't have a joint like this. If I was a rookie pitcher I'd be lucky to have two rooms. I bet Lefty Grove, Carl Hubbell, financially I'm better off than they are.

BOB   When are you going to christen the place?

JOHNNY   You mean with a party? In a couple weeks. In another way it was christened already.

BOB   Anybody I know?

JOHNNY   Yeah. Yeah, you know her—you know. I'd rather not say.

BOB   Check. Well, as they say in Harlem, I gotta take a run-out powder. Good luck in the new apartment, Johnny. And I'm proud of you, you deserve the whole thing.

(*At this point* JOHNNY *does a solo dance, a sort of parody of the Fred & Adele Astaire business of dancing on the furniture. The justification for the dance is in the previous speeches and the reason for it is to consume time while* BOB *is going down in the elevator and leaving the building. At the end of the dance* JOHNNY *smiles and shakes his head negatively in a kind of mute tribute to Astaire. The doorbell rings and* MARY *is admitted*)

JOHNNY (*Shyly*) Hello, Mary.

MARY Hello, Johnny.

(*They do not go to each other, he is taking his cue from her, and she is carefully not inviting an embrace*)

MARY I brought your trench coat.

JOHNNY That's all right. I'm just glad you came. But thanks. A few minutes earlier and you'd have seen Bob McAdams.

MARY That would have been great.

JOHNNY I thought you liked him. You used to.

MARY I do like him. But . . .

JOHNNY Can I get you anything?

MARY A match.

JOHNNY (*Producing a lighter*) I'll give you this instead of a match. It's gold. It has my initials on it, but I can put *from* in front of J. A.

MARY No thanks, Johnny. You keep that.

JOHNNY Are we gonna see each other, Mary? I know I'm seeing you now, but you know what I mean.

MARY (*Looking at the end of her cigarette*) It all depends on how much you want to, Johnny.

JOHNNY Well, I'll tell you how much I want to. Outside of you there's only two things in the world I care about. One is dancing, and the other is baseball. But if you said the word I'd quit dancing, I'd never go to a ball game, and I'd go back home and get a job in the mill, if that would make you happy.

MARY (*Nodding*) I had an idea that was the way it was. I just wanted to make sure you didn't think on account of the other night you had to . . .

JOHNNY What happened the other night never would have happened back home, would it?

MARY Not between you and me, no.

JOHNNY But I was always in love with you back home,

and I never been in love with anybody else. You know what, Mary?

MARY What?

JOHNNY I never even told anybody else I loved them.

MARY Never?

JOHNNY I know what you're thinking. You're thinking sometimes a person *has* to say it, even if he don't mean it. I never said it. You know how I got around it?

MARY How?

JOHNNY I'd say to them, "Baby, do you love me?"

MARY What if they asked you the same question?

JOHNNY (*Suddenly shy about his amours*) I don't like to talk about *that*.

MARY (*Teasingly*) Come on, what did you say?

JOHNNY Well, that all depended. If I was in—like if I—

MARY If you were *in bed* with one.

JOHNNY Yes. If I *was*—in bed with one. I'd have to say something nice. Wouldn't I?

MARY I think you ought to. What *did* you say?

JOHNNY You mean how did I get around saying I loved them?

MARY (*Good-humoredly*) Quit stalling, Johnny.

JOHNNY Well, if she asked me did I love her, sometimes I'd say, "How can I help it, baby?"

MARY (*Laughing*) You dog.

JOHNNY Or I'd say "How could you ask such a question?" Inferring, you know.

MARY Mm-hmm.

JOHNNY (*After a two-count*) What about you, Mary?

MARY . . . You're going to want to know everything, aren't you, Johnny?

JOHNNY . . . Yes. I could say no, but I'd be lying.

MARY There's somebody now.

JOHNNY   Well, I was sure of that. Pretty sure. One, huh?

MARY   Only one that has any claim on me.

JOHNNY   What claim does he have on you?

MARY   Well—nearly three years.

JOHNNY   What is he, married?

MARY   Married, and has a daughter as old as I am.

JOHNNY   The son of a bitch.

MARY   No, he's not a son of a bitch.

JOHNNY   What else is he? Does he sleep with his wife? If he does, he's a son of a bitch. What's he doing for you?

MARY   I never asked him to do anything for me.

JOHNNY   You have a job, you work. He isn't marrying you. And I'll bet he don't spend Christmas Day with you, or take you out with his friends' wives. You show me where he aint a son of a bitch.

MARY   If I thought he was a son of a bitch it wouldn't have lasted three years.

JOHNNY   Then I tell you what you better do, Mary. You better forget what I said. You better hold on to him.

MARY   (*Leaving*)   I guess maybe I'd better.

JOHNNY   (*As she goes out*)   Maybe his wife'll die. But don't count on it.

CURTAIN

SCENE THREE

The shop where MARY *is a model. Another model comes in and shows a dress, and among the few customers are*

BOB MC ADAMS *and a girl. Then* MARY *comes in, and when she does,* BOB *gets up.*

BOB   Hello, Mary. I told you I'd bring my sister in. Well, here she is. Jean, this is Mary Stewart.

MARY   I'm glad to know you. (*To* BOB) I'm not supposed to have conversation with the customers. (*To the attending saleswoman*) Is the boss around?

SALESWOMAN   He didn't come back after lunch.

BOB   He? I thought the boss was somebody named Elise Brennan.

MARY (*Smiling at the saleswoman*)   Elise Brennan is a man.

SALESWOMAN   Ooh, and what a man. If you *know* what I *mean*.

BOB   You'll shock my sister.

JEAN   Oh, sure. Innocent little Jean.

SALESWOMAN   I'll leave you. But don't sit down in the dress, Mary.

MARY (*To* JEAN)   Do you want to see anything in particular?

BOB   Show her everything. Alimony, Mary. Big settlement. Alimony. Don't you get a commission?

MARY   I split with her, the vendeuse, if I bring in a customer. But don't you buy anything here. I can get anything you want twenty percent off.

JEAN   Oh, no, thanks. You're entitled to your commission. (*The others in the shop conveniently leave*)

MARY   I'll be back in a minute. (*She goes off to change her dress*)

JEAN   Her father works in the mill?

BOB   Did. He died a couple of years ago.

JEAN   You'd certainly never think she ever lived on Slag Hill.

BOB   She lived at the *bottom* of Slag Hill. But her mother was quite a woman. She made Mary finish Catholic High, and take piano lessons, learn to sew.

JEAN   And she isn't married?

BOB   Not married, but there's somebody.

JEAN   She's being kept?

BOB   I don't know for sure. She's got somebody, but she keeps on working.

JEAN   The somebody isn't you, I take it.

BOB   Listen, don't think for one minute I wouldn't. But I never got to first base.

JEAN   You know, boys are lucky. Just think, now you used to know this girl, because Daddy made you work in the mill, and that's how you knew Johnny Antonelli. Oh, I've *got* to meet *him*.

BOB   You're going to.

JEAN   I'd like to see that show every night I'm in New York, just for him.

BOB   Don't count on brilliant conversation, because brilliantly he does not converse. And by the way, don't mention Johnny to Mary, or Mary to Johnny.

JEAN   Oh?

BOB   You mention one to the other and he or she gets sad, as the case may be. I don't know *why*, I don't know when, but something happened.

JEAN   It'd be almost too perfect if the two best products of the mill ever got together.

BOB   Yes, they pulled two good heats when they pulled those two.

JEAN   Is that some new dirty slang I haven't heard?

BOB   If you knew more about the mill you'd know what pulling a heat means.

JEAN   I'm sorry, but it sounds more like kennel talk.

BOB   (*Laughing*)   So it does.

MARY (*Re-entering*)   Are you going to be in New York for a while, Miss McAdams?

JEAN   Officially it's Mrs. McAdams Robertson, but I wish you'd call me Jean. After all, we grew up together, even if we didn't know it at the time.

MARY   Thanks, I will. Jean.

JEAN   To answer your question. I'm afraid not. Just two more days.

(*An exquisitely tailored man enters*)

MAN   Good afternoon, Miss Stewart. Good afternoon, Madam. Sir.

(*He flounces through the shop*)

MARY   The boss.

JEAN   Shall we stay around and buy a lot of things?

MARY   Oh, he'll stamp his foot but I'm not afraid of him.

JEAN   How would you like to have lunch with me tomorrow?

BOB   Oh, come on, Jean. Aren't you having lunch with Jonesey? Jonesey's a girl from Philadelphia, as dull as anything the Main Line ever produced, and that's covering a lot of dullness. Don't expose Mary to that.

JEAN   All right. How about the next day?

MARY   The next day *would* be *better*.

JEAN   Do you ever go to Michel's?

MARY   Sometimes.

JEAN   One o'clock?

MARY   Fine, thanks. Goodbye, goodbye, Bob.

CURTAIN

SCENE FOUR

MARY'S *flat. She is sitting with her knitting when* DENI-
SON JONES *lets himself in with his key, placing his bag just
inside the room, and going to her. She continues with her
knitting while he kisses her on the cheek.*

JONES   Knitting me a sweater?

MARY   It's for a girl that used to work in the shop.

JONES   A, uh, blessed event? What's that fellow's name?

MARY   Winchell. Walter Winchell.

JONES (*Stuffily*)   I think they used to say that when I was
a boy. Blessed event. I'm sorry I didn't get here yesterday, but I had to go to that funeral.

MARY   I know.

JONES   Jack Wellworth. It's getting so I hate to look at
the obituary column. Somebody I know always in it.
Not necessarily friends of mine, but I'm always recognizing names, don't you know. You'd have liked old
Jack.

MARY   Would I?

JONES   He *was* a close friend of mine. One of my ushers,
I was one of his. I guess Jack was as close to me as any
man I ever knew. I could tell him anything.

MARY   Did you tell him about me?
    (JONES *is silent*)

MARY   Did you?

JONES   Yes. I hope you don't mind. He's dead now. You
see, Jack had somewhat the same problem.

MARY   Problem? Am I a problem? I guess I am.

JONES   Problem was an unfortunate choice of words. What I meant to say, Jack was in love with someone other than his wife, and Nancy, his wife, wouldn't give him a divorce.

MARY   Did he ask her?

JONES   Did he ask her? I don't know that he ever actually put it to her in so many words, but it wouldn't have done him any good if he had. Not Nancy.

MARY   He just took it for granted.

JONES   Well, the way you *do*. A man gets to know his wife pretty well. He can pretty well tell whether she'd give him a divorce or not.

MARY   Yes, and sometimes it isn't worth going to all that trouble. Is it?

JONES   . . . Aren't we getting pretty close to home? Are you being bitter?

MARY   Bitter? No, not any more, Denny. A year or so ago, but not any more.

JONES   You told me time and time again you didn't want to marry me. *Wouldn't* marry me. But now, today, honestly dear, you sound very bitter.

MARY   Do I?

JONES   Everything I say is wrong. You have a quicker mind than I have. I've found that out.

MARY   That's because I'm a Lithuanian. They say anybody that can learn to read and write and speak our language has to have more brains than most people.

JONES   I believe it.

MARY   Take a seat, Denny.

JONES   I'll do that little thing. I have a favor to ask you, and I don't want to be standing up if you say no. And the mood you're in, you're liable to.

MARY   What is it?

JONES   You called Zimmermann? Remember I told you to be sure and call Zimmermann?

MARY   I called him and sold the stock.

JONES   Good. That's what the favor's about. I'd like to have some cash, and I know you have close to twenty thousand. Would you let me have about fifteen of it, for say two weeks?

MARY   Why not?

JONES   Why not? Because it's your money, and this would be a loan. I've just heard of something that sounds awfully good, but I have no cash to speak of. I could unload some common stocks, but I hate to do that. If you let me have the money I can almost guarantee you, well, at least a twenty-five percent profit in—say two months.

MARY   Take the whole thing, I don't consider it my money.

JONES   But it most certainly is your money. It's all in your name.

MARY   The only money I consider real money is what I have in my savings account. The stock market money— that's ghost money down in Wall Street.

JONES   Broad Street, actually.

MARY   Well, Broad Street, and that sounds like Philadelphia.

JONES   I know. I wish New York would change it. Then suppose I take fifteen thousand. I don't want you to close out your account.

MARY   But I want to close it out.

JONES   I wouldn't if I were you. Always leave something there. It's better for your credit if you don't take yourself off a firm's books.

MARY   But I want to take myself off the firm's books.

JONES   Why? It's a damn good house. I know two of the

partners and the floor man, and my firm's been doing business with—

MARY   I'm trying to tell you something, Denny. I've been trying ever since you came in.

JONES   Yes. Yes, you've had something on your mind. I could see that.

MARY   Because I was trying to tell it to you calmly.

JONES   You mean break it gently? Don't worry about me. You know what the prize fighters say: he can't take it in the bread-basket. But I can, so let me have it both barrels.

MARY   . . . We're all through, Denny.

JONES   (*Slowly*)   We? Meaning you and I are all through?

MARY   Yes.

JONES   (*Unwilling to face it*)   You mean all this? Our life together?

MARY   Yes.

JONES   (*After a three-count*)   I'm not to see you any more?

MARY   No.

    (JONES *scratches the side of his head and looks at the floor*)

JONES   (*Again after a three-count*)   What decided you? I know you're too much of a lady to give a damn about the money. And I think—it isn't that you're just tired of me, is it, Mary?

MARY   It's worse than that, Denny.

JONES   Nothing could be worse than that. But it's another man, isn't it?

MARY   Yes.

JONES   Last week. The night of the Beaux Arts Ball.

MARY   Yes.

JONES   . . . You didn't come home. You went to his place, whoever he is?

MARY   Yes.

JONES   Did he know you'd had a lot to drink?

MARY   No, but . . .

JONES   Was it just that night?

MARY   That's the only time I ever went to bed with him. But I've always been in love with him, Denny.

JONES   No. You were in love with me. You can't fake that, Mary. Some of it, the passion, that takes care of itself, doesn't it? But the rest of it, the companionship, and wanting to see each other. A man doesn't know that those three years were the best he ever had.

MARY   I love you, Denny, but with him it's my whole life. It's as if we were always making love.

JONES   And it wasn't that way with me?

MARY   It couldn't be. I've always wanted him, I always will. No matter what.

JONES   Do I know him?

MARY   No.

JONES   Does he know about you and me?

MARY   Not who you are.

JONES   And he doesn't mind?

MARY   (*With deep emotion*)   He minds. You bet he minds.

JONES   Then you're no better off than I am.

MARY   I don't know. I think I have a chance. He's always loved me too, since we were kids.

JONES   Do you think I have a chance?

MARY   You and I again? No.

JONES   As far as I'm concerned we have. I'm holding on tight, Mary. It isn't only you I'm holding on to. But I'll go, now.

MARY   Yes, do. I don't want to cry in front of you.

JONES (*With a faint smile*)   I don't want to cry in front of you, either. (*He picks up his bag and goes*)

SCENE FIVE

A Mayfair Dance in the Ritz-Carlton. Cabaret style, but with a stage as well as dance floor. This scene is all-out for the choreographer, the set and costume designer, and the composer. Its importance to the librettist is in an encounter between JOHNNY, *who is escorting and very attentive to* JEAN MC ADAMS, *and* MARY, *who is in the company of a man in his late thirties and very unmistakably not* DENISON JONES. JOHNNY *is a little tight and having a wonderful time with* JEAN, *dancing with her, when he espies* MARY, *also dancing but not very cheerful.* MARY *and* JEAN *smile at each other in friendly fashion, but* JOHNNY's *face darkens when he sees* MARY's *escort.*

JOHNNY   Is this him?

MARY   What did you say, Johnny?

JOHNNY (*Contemptuously*)   The one I said was a son of a bitch.

MARY   It's none of your business, Johnny, but no, it's not the guy.
(JEAN *is having too good a time to be very concerned about the dialog*)

JEAN   I'm staying over, Mary. I'll call you.

MARY   Swell.
(*The couples dance away in opposing directions*)

SCENE SIX

JOHNNY'S *dressing-room.* JEAN *is sitting alone and she smiles happily and rather proudly at the sounds of applause.* JOHNNY'S *dresser comes in. He is bespectacled, small, young, obviously devoted. His name is* MILTON.

MILTON   Hot damn. Five curtain calls and we've been running over a year. Of course it's Saturday night. Last Monday we only had four. Tuesday we had five. Wednesday matinee, we had *six*, but that was all women. Wednesday night . . .
(*His gabble is lost in* JOHNNY'S *entrance in white mess jacket, black trousers, wing collar, the costume he wears in the finale. He is welcomed by the open arms of* JEAN *and they embrace*)

JEAN   Five curtain calls!

JOHNNY   Yeah, they were friendly tonight. I got makeup on you. Milton, a towel for the future Mrs. Anton.

MILTON   You be careful or it'll be in Walter Winchell's column.

JOHNNY   (*To* JEAN)   Not till Monday, and by *that* time . . .

MILTON   Tomorrow?

JEAN   I want to invite Milton.

MILTON If you don't I'll quit. I swear to God, Johnny, I mean it.

JOHNNY You can come, but I won't tell you where till tomorrow. You'd have it all over town tonight.

JEAN Oh, let's tell him. It's not going to make any difference.

JOHNNY I don't want to tell anybody in the company. I don't want anybody to get their feelings hurt.

MILTON I promise.

JEAN It's going to be at my brother's apartment, East 37th Street. I'll write it down for you, and his name is Robert McAdams.

MILTON Oh, I know *Bob*. So do most of the girls in the line.

JOHNNY Will you keep your big trap shut?

JEAN (*Amiably sarcastic*) Yes, don't disillusion me about my brother.
(JOHNNY *for a second worries over the word disillusion, but when* JEAN *smiles at him he smiles back and kisses her gently*)

CURTAIN

SCENE SEVEN

MARY'S *flat. The next morning. At rise it is vacant, but* DENISON JONES *lets himself in with his key. He is untidy as to necktie, shirt collar and beard. He takes off his hat, sits down, holding his hat in his hand. He looks once toward the bedroom door, then away again, then goes to the bed-room door and knocks and says, softly, "Mary? Mary?"*

MARY'S VOICE   Who's that? You, Denny?

JONES   Yes.

MARY'S VOICE   I'll be there.
(JONES, *still holding his hat, waits for her appearance in a dressing gown*)

MARY (*Shocked by his appearance*)   What is it, Denny?

JONES   I don't know, Mary. I'm licked.

MARY   I'll make you some coffee. Or a glass of milk?

JONES   A drink. No, a drink won't do me any good. Coffee, maybe.

MARY   What's the matter?

JONES   Don't you know? I can't give you up. Not that *I* gave *you* up. I haven't been home.

MARY   Since Wednesday?

JONES   Was that the day? If that was the day. I'm not going home, Mary.

MARY   You've been on a bender since Wednesday?

JONES   Don't I look it?

MARY   . . . Yes, you do. While I'm making some coffee you can shave and take a shower.

JONES   And that will cure all my ills?

MARY   It'll make you *feel* better. And maybe you can get some sleep.

JONES (*Nodding toward sofa*)   There?

MARY   Only there. It's *over*, Denny, it's *over*. You wouldn't want me the way I feel.

JONES   I want you any way I can have you. I told you, I'm never going home, I'm—

MARY (*Anguish that has begun in previous speech*)   And I tell *you*, Denny, it's finished. *Leave* it that way. *Please.*

JONES Then I'm finished.

MARY (*After a two-count*) I'll get some coffee.
  (*She goes to kitchen and he stands still, then straight
  upright, then with a flashing suddenness he goes to the
  window and jumps out, leaving his hat tumbling on the
  floor.* MARY *comes out from the kitchen, picking up the
  hat as she goes through to the bedroom, offstage, sees
  that it and the bathroom are empty, then comes back to
  the living room and stares at the window. She crushes
  her hands to her stomach, then slowly forces herself to
  go toward the window in the midst of sounds of a
  couple of off-stage voices shouting in horror. She goes
  almost to the window, then some sense of delicacy
  mixed with horror keeps her from the unnecessary act of
  looking out and down. And in her pity she covers her
  face for a second, then falls to her knees and makes the
  sign of the cross*)

CURTAIN

SCENE EIGHT

BOB's *flat, afternoon of the same day. It is a small, Ivy
League type of group, including* BOB's *father and mother
and* JOHNNY's *mother;* MILTON, *his dresser, and a fat
Tammany magistrate. The wedding has just taken place
and the bride is being kissed, and* JOHNNY, *in short black
coat and striped trousers, is receiving congratulations. The
group is small enough so that any one person speaking can
be heard by all the other guests.*

BOB Well, good people, let's go to work on the champagne. And it's real champagne, too. Pop brought it all the way from Pennsylvania.

BOB'S FATHER   I didn't dare drive over forty. If the state police had stopped me and looked in the back of the car . . .

BOB   Oh, boy. MC ADAMS ARRESTED AS BOOTLEGGER, can you see those headlines?

BOB'S MOTHER   Yes, and I suppose I'd be mentioned as his gun moll.

BOB'S FATHER   Well, everybody got a glass? Ladies and gentlemen, the bride.

CHORUS   Hear, hear. To the bride, to the bride. (*Smashing their glasses*)

BOB'S MOTHER   And now, to the groom.

CHORUS   The groom. Johnny. To Johnny.

JOHNNY   To you, Mrs. McAdams.

CHORUS   Hear, hear. Mrs. McAdams.

BOB'S FATHER   To the mother of the groom. Mrs. Antonelli.

MRS. ANTONELLI   Much oblige, everybody. And maybe two-three weeks another wedding, wit' the priest, no?

JOHNNY   All right, Mom, sure. Maybe. We talk it over. In the old country you had two weddings.

JEAN   I'd love to be Catholic.

JOHNNY   You don't have to be if you don't want to.

MRS. ANTONELLI   Itsa not so easy, lika buya ticket to a show.

MR. MC ADAMS (*Tactfully*)   Well, it isn't easy to buy a ticket to Johnny's show, either. Ah, the cake, the cake.

OFFSTAGE VOICE   Extra! Extra! Read all about it. Read all about brbrbrbrbrbrbrb.

MR. MC ADAMS (*Humorously*)   My, they got out an extra for you, you two.

BOB   Almost every Sunday that phony comes around. Extra, extra. When I first moved to New York I used to buy them, but they're never anything.

MILTON   And they charge you twenty cents, too.

BOB   I'll close the window.
(*As he goes to the window to close it he hears what can be heard by the audience over the public address system but which is unnoticed by the principals and guests at the wedding. The newsboy is saying:* "Millionaire leaps to death . . . Model's apartment . . . Philadelphia playboy . . . Beautiful Mary Stew—" BOB, *suddenly aware, slams down the window, but no one else has heard. He rejoins the small group and eases* JOHNNY *to one side. He grips* JOHNNY's *hand*)

BOB   You love Jean, don't you, Johnny?

JOHNNY   I'll tell the world I do.

BOB   Keep telling her. She deserves some happiness. You know what I mean.

JOHNNY   What's past is past, Bob.

JEAN (*coming over; to* BOB)   Don't take him away from me.

JOHNNY   Nobody ever will, there aint nobody that could.
(*They embrace shyly but warmly and* BOB *retreats from them, with an unsuccessfully disguised look of worry on his face as he watches them and the curtain slowly descends*)